White Christmas Reunion

by

Susan Edwards

White Series
Book 12

White Christmas Reunion

Contact Information: info@thewildrosepress.com

Cover Art by *Diana Carlile*

The Wild Rose Press, Inc.
PO Box 708
Adams Basin, NY 14410-0708

Visit us at www.thewildrosepress.com

Publishing History
First Fantasy Rose Edition, 2015
Print ISBN 978-1-5092-0563-9
Digital ISBN 978-1-5092-0564-6

Published in the United States of America

She won't go home…he can't stay.

To his delight, she leaned in, wrapped her arms around his neck, her head tucked into the hollow of his throat. The night shadows wrapped them in the magic of music and night.

From somewhere in his childhood, the words to the music came back to him, and he realized the Jones brothers were playing a ballad that had been one of his mother's favorites. Their deep voices blended and added magic to the evening, and somewhere off in the distance, he heard the soft strains of a mouth organ.

Bo hummed along for a moment, setting the tune in his mind. Then he let his voice join theirs. He sang, low and soft, words of love and longing.

The magical moment brought tears to Beth Ann's eyes. The richness of his voice vibrated through every inch of her body, drawing longing to the surface with the same skill of those creating magic with a strum of their fingers over strings.

Bo's voice, his warmth, his scent wrapped her in a cloak of wonder. Her parents had danced like this for as long as she could remember and she'd danced with her father, but this was the first real dance with a man who wanted her, and she let the romance of it lead her. Tonight, she followed her feelings and gave in to the need to be held and to hold, to need and be needed.

When Bo's voice faded away, she glanced up. "You have a beautiful voice," she said, her fingers moving across his shoulders.

"Inspired by your beauty, Bethy." He lowered his head.

Dedication

This book is dedicated to my Family

In Loving Memory of Mildred Herr Swenson

Grandmother extraordinaire. You had the best toy closest in the world, a yard with lots of hiding places to fuel an active imagination and the patience of a saint! I have tons of memories of your loving and generous nature and I am grateful for the traits I inherited from you, especially my love of babies.

In Loving Memory of Allen Swenson

Uncle Al, you teased me mercilessly as a child and teen. Thank you for those good times. And my stomach does not smile.

In Loving Memory of Dean Swenson

I have faint memories of your cabin, books everywhere, and warnings to watch for Black Widows. I will always remember your sense of humor, crooked smile, and laugh. Because of you, I always check my pennies, looking for those wheats.

I am fortunate to have tons of childhood memories of family gatherings. With twelve aunts and uncles on my father's side, those gatherings were fun and a bit crazy with so many personalities and those favorite troublemakers. I am grateful to all my aunts, uncles, and cousins who make my family special.

Special Mentions

Cousin Karen: Thanks for the memories of our make believe games. Thinking back, those "fictional scenarios" we acted out were actually "stories" with plots, good guys, bad guys, and those in danger—usually us. Who knew I was a writer even back then!

Cousin Kristy: Thanks for allowing me to treat you like a walking, talking doll and doing your hair. You were a trooper!

Cousin Krissy: You won't remember the hours of me singing to you at the family gatherings and walking, rocking, and swaying with you in my arms so you could nap. You were probably my first "baby."

White Family Genealogy Chart

1st Generation
Emily & John Cartier (***White Dawn***)
 Sarah
White Cloud & Small Bird (***White Dusk***)
 Running Wolf
 Wildflower
Seeing Eyes & Hawk Eyes
 Golden Eagle
 Winona

2nd Generation
Sarah (White Wind) & Golden Eagle (***White Wind***)
 Striking Thunder
 White Wolf
 Star Dreamer
 White Dove
Winona & Clay (Sun Walker) (***White Shadows***)

3rd Generation
Striking Thunder & Emma O'Brien (White Flame)
(***White Flame***)
 Little Flame
 Red Eagle
 Mina (Eldest Daughter)
 Weeko (Pretty Girl)
 Anamosa (White Fawn)
White Wolf & Jessie Jones (***White Wolf***)
 Sara
 Sam
 Mary
 Martha

Noah
Katie
ADOPTED CHILDREN
John
Laura
Barbara Ellen
Mark
Star Dreamer & Grady O'Brien (*White Dreams*)
Emma O'Brien
Renait O'Brien
Morning Moon (Mathilda)
Running Elk (Matthew)
Daire
Kealan
Caitie
White Dove & Jeremy (Hunkuya Mato) Jones (*White Dove*)
Beth Ann Landon
Jane Landon
Spotted Owl
Teetonka (Talks too much)
Akecheta (Fighter)

4th Generation
Mattie & Reed Robertson (*White Deception*)
Danny
Lizzie
Annie
David
Renny (Weshawee) & Tyler (*White Vengeance*)
(Trowbridge Tyler Thompkins Tilly)
Grady
Margaret Mary

Beth Ann & Singing Bear (dc)
>Katarina Kimilmela
>Riker Takota
Beth Ann & Bodil Riker Quinn
>George (adopted)
>Son

Jones Family

James Jones & Eirica McCauley (**White Nights**)
>Alison
>Lara
>Ian
>Summer
>James Jr
>Allen
>Jenny
>Guy

Jordan Jones & Coralie (*Wolf/Nights*)
>Jordan Jr.
>Gary Richard
>Harvey
>Carter
>Steven
>Gordon
>Dean
>Katherine

Running Elk (Matthew) & Breena (dc) (*White Deception-subplot*)
>Red Deer

Chapter One

Nebraska, 1871

Bodil Riker Quinn rode as though the devil himself was shoving him across a sea of storm-flattened grass that stretched from horizon to horizon. A crosswind tore at his sheepskin-lined leather jacket and forced him to keep one hand on his John B to keep it from being ripped from his head and tossed clear into Iowa.

Better to ride with the devil than to be in the same room with the devil's mother. If he had to endure one more day of his stepmother's incessant complaints, false overtures of friendliness, or listen to any more sly digs, he'd strangle the conniving bitch and end up with a posse on his heels.

Overhead, the sky continued to darken, which suited his black mood. Frustration sang in his veins when a single drop of rain smacked him on the nose. "More rain, just what I need." The last two storms had dumped enough water to turn the ground into a quagmire of sticky mud. He slowed the horse to a slow gallop. "What the hell are we doing, Samson?"

He rolled his aching shoulders, unsure whether to be irritated with his neighbor or grateful to the man for pulling him away from trouble in the forms of unwanted family, not enough ranch hands, and too much work.

Last night's thunderstorm had spooked the cattle,

1

and that meant broken fences and loose cattle. At the base of a small hill, he guided the horse to one side of a large mud puddle. The gelding's hooves made muffled sucking sounds, then, with the slight rise in the path, they were once again on solid ground.

Bo sighed, tempted to turn around and return home even if it mean dealing with Jocelyn and her whinny, demanding children. But he kept riding. When Henrik Ricard Svensson crooked his finger, people obeyed. Including Bo. Not because the man was a powerful politician and the biggest landowner in this part of Nebraska.

Status and money did not impress Bo, not enough to have him neglecting his own much smaller spread. No, he jumped because Henry and his father had been best friends from childhood up to the day Bo's father died. More importantly, Henry was his godfather and all the family Bo had. He did *not* count his stepmother.

Enduring Jocelyn's presence in *his* home was worse than being trapped in a cave with a skunk. At least skunk stink wore off, whereas Jocelyn coated everything with her bad temper, demanding whines, and unpleasant personality. Forget her, he ordered himself, grateful that Henry's summons had interrupted yet another argument between them.

So what did Henry want? The tone of urgency worried him. Henry was not getting any younger. Guilt smacked him in the back of his head. He'd been so occupied with his struggling ranch the last couple of months, he hadn't given his godfather much thought.

The horse picked his way up another gentle rise in the land, around a small stand of oaks, and stopped at the top of the hill. Noting the position of the sun, Bo sighed again. He wasn't going to get back to his ranch in time to ride the perimeter before dark.

Between storm damage and sabotage that included the senseless act of gutting cattle, he worried about being gone longer than absolutely necessary, especially since firing more than half his hands for deliberately cutting fences and starting a fire that destroyed one of his barns.

Damn railroad. Fury warred with disgust. Bad enough they'd destroyed his property but to kill the livestock... The waste and wanton destruction of life infuriated him. Another glance upward had him groaning.

He yanked off his hat and slapped it against the horse's rump. "Come on, Samson. Let's go find out what's got the old man's knickers in a twist."

The horse, given free rein, flew down the hill and up a gravel-lined driveway that was a welcome relief from the sticky mud and puddles of water.

To his right, a small herd of horses ran toward him, following the curve of the fenced pasture. Samson ignored the thundering hooves and excited calls of greeting. Bo grinned with appreciation of the sheer magnificence of the animals in full gallop—tails held high, manes fluttering, heads tossing, and the strength of those stretched out bodies with their gleaming coats.

To his left lay a wide expanse of grass and farther out, outbuildings dotted the landscape. He rode toward the large, white house the size of a small mansion. He could fit three of his modest home in Henry's and still have roaming room.

The horse headed around back. He hadn't even dismounted before the kitchen door flew open and a tall, big-boned woman appeared, waving a white towel like a surrender flag.

"Bodil! Thank the good Lord you're here. He's in the study." Mildred twisted her hands in her flour-covered apron. "He's in a right state. Never seen him so worked up in all my years."

Bo studied the housekeeper for a moment, then he dismounted and handed the reins to the stable boy who came running. "Thank you," he said to the foreman's eldest son.

He should be relieved that nothing had happened to his godfather, but at the same time, his heart sank. Only one thing shook the unshakeable, unflappable Mildred Brown. He took the stairs up to the kitchen door two at a time. An old sleeping hound blocked his path. He stepped over the dog, removed his John B, and entered the housekeeper's domain. He sighed one more time as he shrugged out of his jacket and handed it to her. "Damn. Another letter?"

The housekeeper nodded. "Came this morning. He insisted I send for you at once."

He squeezed the woman's shoulders gently. So much for a quick trip and getting back before dark. "I'll talk to him."

Mildred sagged with relief.

He patted her shoulder as he left the kitchen and made his way toward the front of the house, then headed down a long, dark corridor that led to the study. When he reached the doorway, he peered in and spotted his godfather standing before open French doors, one hand resting on the wall, his shoulders hunched, a sheet of paper dangling from his other hand.

Yep, another letter.

Tapping his hat against his thigh, he took a deep breath. Get it done, he ordered himself, and strode into the dark-paneled study, his boots on the polished oak floor loud in the silence. "Henry? Your message sounded urgent."

"Bo!" Relief replaced lines of worry on the older man's face. He motioned to a group of leather chairs across the room from the wide, expansive desk of timeworn dark oak. "Thanks for coming right away."

Though anxious to get back to his own ranch and the hundreds of chores awaiting him, Bo took his customary seat on one end of the red-wine leather couch. He plopped his hat on his knee. Henry had been there for him after his father's death. He'd just turned eighteen, and Henry taught him the ropes of being a ranch owner, not just the son of a rancher. Bo owed Henry whatever time he needed.

Mildred swept in and set a tray with two mugs of coffee onto the table between the two men. The mouth-watering aroma of cinnamon and nutmeg from the generous slices of cake she'd included made his stomach rumble. He'd missed the mid-day meal.

"This'll warm you up, Bodil."

Bo grinned, picked up the mug, and warmed his hands. Steam from the rich, dark roast bathed his face, and he inhaled deeply. "I'd ride through hell and back for your coffee and that cake of yours. I should marry you."

She pulled a towel off her shoulder and swatted him with it. "Got myself one man. Don't need two." Though she laughed, the worry in her eyes remained as she closed the door behind her.

Across from him, Henry continued to pace, his

fingers raking through his full head of white hair. The old, wooden floor creaked. After a few sips to warm his insides, Bo set his mug down, leaned back, and stretched his legs out, one ankle crossed over the other. "Let's have it, Henry."

Henry sat on the edge of the matching leather chair. He leaned forward, clasping his hands, his elbows digging into his thighs. "I found them, Bo. I know where my girls are."

I knew it. "Hells bells, Henry, not again."

"Bo, it's them. I know it." Henry's eyes shone with hope.

"It's been more than twelve years since your granddaughters were captured by the Sioux. You know the odds of finding them alive. We've been through this before, Henry."

Bo hated to burst the bubble of hope that lit the man's face like a bonfire on a dark winter's night, but after all this time, the girls, who had been age six and three, were most likely dead.

But Henry was obsessed. With his money and power, he'd sent a team of men after his son-in-law to bring back his daughter and granddaughters. They'd found the wagon, and the body of Elizabeth's husband. The scouts had scoured the area and eventually, Elizabeth's dead body had been found, along with a dozen slain Crow. The arrows found at the scene belonged to the Sioux. That was the last they'd been able to confirm. The lack of bodies fueled Henry's hope. Unfortunately, this wasn't the first time the man thought he had found his girls.

He bit back a groan of frustration. He loved his godfather, as both a father and a friend and hated what the disappointment did to the man each time Henry's information proved false. Each false lead caused the proud and powerful man to sink into a pit of despair, and that lead to drinking too much. Bo had lost track of how many times he'd had to pick up the pieces of a broken man and help put him back together.

Henry stood. "It's them, Bo." He went to his desk, snatched a piece of paper, returned, and thrust it at Bo.

Bo took the short missive sent by telegraph and frowned. Henry's man had discovered two blonde girls living among the Sioux.

"The ages are right, Bo. It's them." Henry shoved his hands though his hair. "It's Beth Ann and Jane. My Lizzie's babies." Sadness, grief, and hope brought tears to his pale blue eyes, and his voice shook with emotion.

Bo remembered Elizabeth. She'd been his first love. It hadn't mattered that she was far too old for him. He had dreamed she'd wait for him to become a man. But the day came when she'd married and broken his heart.

"Dammit! Why did I leave that night? I could have stopped them?" Henry kicked the chair, sending it into a side table holding a lamp that crashed to the floor. Shards of porcelain scattered in all directions. He dug his hands into the front pockets of his jeans. "Say it, son. It's my own damn fault that Elizabeth left."

Tossing the letter onto the table, Bo fiddled with his hat. "You couldn't have stopped Stuart from taking his family, Henry." They had been through this so many times that the thought of yet another round left Bo sad and depressed. He stood and tapped his John B against his thigh. "What now?"

Henry glanced up from the letter he'd picked up.

"I'm going to find them and bring them back."

Bo slid his fingers through his reddish brown hair. "We've been through this, Henry. It's not that simple. If these girls are your granddaughters, Indians raised them. They will never be accepted back into society."

Henry waved aside Bo's concern. "My spread is the largest in all of Nebraska. Got me enough land for two girls to spend their lives. They won't want for anything. I'll hire tutors and companions." He went back to the French doors and stared out. "Hell, I'll build them those things the Indians live in."

"Tipis," Bo said.

Henry nodded and glanced over his shoulder. "I won't leave them out there, son. They belong here with me. They're the only part of Lizzie I have left." He walked out onto the terrace.

Worried that his friend was once again taking on more than he could handle, Bo joined him. Bees hummed from the wall of sickly-sweet blooms to his right. "Henry—" He shook his head. What could he say?

Twice before, the men Henry hired to find and return his granddaughters had ended in disaster. The first woman they'd found had been too old and taken from her children, she had killed herself days after being *rescued*.

The second time, not more than two years ago, his men had brought back a blonde child who had not been his granddaughter. Henry found her a home, and the last Bo heard, her transition back to society was not going well. Lives ruined with each failure not to mention the toll on Henry.

Henry leaned on the low stone wall enclosing his

own private terrace. "It's them, I feel it. You read the letter. The younger one is the spittin' image of my Lizzie."

Bo folded his arms across his chest, his gaze sweeping the wide expanse of grazing land. "They on their way?"

Turning, Henry shook his head. "My orders were to locate and hold. My man is at Fort Randall, waiting instructions." He clenched his fists and drummed them on the stone. "It's them. I know it. I've found them."

Rolling his shoulders to ease the stiffness, Bo turned his back to the chill wind that swept across the terrace. Again, he eyed the stormy sky. Damn. "What's next, Henry?"

"I bring them home," Henry said. "They belong here. This is their birthright."

"That may be, but what if they have families? Husbands and children? Beth Ann is how old?"

"Eighteen, which means Jane, is fifteen." Henry fell silent. The wind blew his snow-white hair around his head, revealing hidden yellow-blond strands. Henry paced from one end of the terrace to the other.

Both girls were of marriageable age. Another gust of wind slapped cold rain on his face. "Look, Henry. I can't tell you what to do. Take a few days to consider your options, and we'll talk again. Storm's coming. I need to get back—"

Henry waved him to silence. "No need. Made up my mind. Just hadn't thought of children. Keep thinking Beth Ann and Jane are still children themselves." He grinned, his entire face lighting up with joy. "Great grandchildren! Now that's a kick in the ass. My granddaughters and their children, if they have any, will not want for anything."

Bo swallowed his groan, but rather than point out more problems, like husbands or the girls refusing to leave the life they knew—if they were happy—Bo kept silent. Nothing would change Henry's mind. All Bo could do was be there for his friend and pick up the pieces when it went wrong. As it had so many times before this.

Henry moved with renewed energy back into the study. "We are going to get them."

Bo lifted a brow. "We?" He followed, tapping his hat against his thigh so fast it was a dark blur. "Sorry, Henry. Can't. Barely surviving, and the damn bank's threatening to take my ranch if I can't make the next payment. Then there's those damn railroad bastards hovering like vultures over a carcass. Even if I could scrape up the money, I can't hire anyone to run the ranch while I'm gone."

Not after firing his foreman and more than half of his hands. Bo gritted his teeth. How he got by with the few hands he'd kept, he didn't know. Damn, he'd been a blind fool, and by the time he figured out what was going on, the losses over the summer meant he couldn't pay the bank or hire more men.

Henry motioned for him to sit. Suppressing a sigh, Bo plopped himself into one of the chairs facing the desk.

"Got another problem, Henry. Jocelyn's back." He rubbed the tension gathering at the back of his neck. "No way in hell am I leaving them at the ranch." He didn't trust his stepmother or her son an inch out of his sight.

Henry leaned back in the desk chair that matched

the leather couch and settee, once more a man in complete control. He flicked the fingers of one hand to dismiss that problem. "Send the merry widow packing. She has no claim on your land. Your father left it to you. That's the least of your problems."

"Easy for you to say," Bo grumbled, staring at shelves filled with books behind Henry. Henry was right. He needed to kick her and her children out, but he kept putting off the much-needed confrontation. "The ranch—"

"We'll put old Charlie in charge. Those railroad bastards try anything, they'll find Charlie all horns and rattles. He'll go after them with a sharp stick."

Bo cringed. Henry's foreman could be mean as a tom turkey. The man's sharp tongue was as deadly as a whip—both could tear flesh off a body—as Bo knew from experience. After Bo's father died, Charlie had shown up on his doorstep, bags at his feet. He'd shoved his way in, declared that he was going to whip Bo into shape. And he had. Henry was right. Nobody knew what was what around a ranch like that old man. "Won't stop the bank or those railroad agents from causing problems."

Henry grinned a feral, sly smile that sent his opponents running. Whatever his godfather had devised, he, Bodil Riker Quinn, had been snared as neatly as a calf for branding in the spring.

Henry shoved a folder on the desk toward Bo. "No? I'm a rich man and a damn politician to boot. I threaten to pull my account, and that skunk-faced Winston will grovel at my feet." He chuckled. "Much as I'd love to see that, I can do better." He tapped his finger on the desk. "Help me. I help you." He sat back, as pleased as a dog making off with one of Mildred's pies.

Bo sighed. "Don't need charity, Henry." But he did need money. A lot of it. And fast. Could he do this? Go with Henry; see if these girls were his granddaughters? Wouldn't take but a couple months, if that. Quick trip up the Missouri, a few days of riding…

Resigned to helping his godfather, Bo opened the folder and read the short letter addressed to the banker. His jaw dropped at the amount Henry was willing to pay. That sum paid off his entire debt. The ranch would be his, free and clear.

He set the letter down. "Good god, Henry. I can't accept this. I might—*might*—be willing to view this as a job and take reasonable payment, enough to satisfy what I need to make this next payment, but not this." He slid the letter across the desk. "Too much."

Henry leaned back, crossed his arms across his chest. "It's done. You'll earn every penny, Bo."

Bo narrowed his eyes, not trusting his godfather, who suddenly looked like the sharp-minded politician he was. "What are you planning, Henry?"

He held his John B in both hands, running his fingers over the rim, mind still reeling. The ranch belonged to him. No more harassing visits or threats from that weasel at the bank.

"A wedding."

The hat fell, slid off his lap, and plopped onto the floor. Had Henry told him that he was going to buy an orange and purple cow, Bo wouldn't have been more shocked. "A what?"

Henry folded the note in precise thirds and pushed it back across the desk. His blue eyes gleamed with determination and pleasure. "Think of this as your wedding gift. Beth Ann will need a husband when we bring her back."

****

Wi's warmth and light speared the horizon, and like a greedy, ravenous animal upon awakening, he consumed the darkness of night. He was one of four Superior Gods, the all-powerful Great God and defender of bravery, fortitude, generosity, and fidelity, who greeted each new day by rolling ribbons of color across the sky. Birds shook out their feathers and rose into the air to greet him with their songs of joy and gratitude.

He stretched his fingers, searching, seeking, and chasing. Deep in the shadowed forest, he found a tree, long dead. He reached through the hole in the trunk, his light falling upon an owl that turned its head to the back of the hollow.

Owl!

Blinking, irritated, Owl ruffled snow-white feathers. *Why do you wake me, Old Friend?*

It is time. The woman needs you.

Wide-awake, Owl left her nest and flew to a thick branch high above the earth. Below, a young woman left a cone-shaped dwelling and stretched her arms high overhead as though reaching for the bird.

Owl's charge moved with graceful movements in her fur-lined dress the color of *Wi's* early morning light. Matching leggings warded off the chill in the air. A breath of air stirred the woman's long, pale hair that hung straight as a blade of grass past her waist. When she tipped her head back, Owl gazed into eyes as blue as the heavens on a clear, summer day.

Owl loved this child of two worlds. Many years before, she had appeared to the girl as Owl Woman to offer comfort. The years had passed without her need to appear again. It saddened her to know that the child's easy existence was about to change. *What would you have me do?*

Watch over her. And those who come for her. The time has come for her to choose between two worlds.

Owl took to the air, flying low, sweeping over the woman, the air from her powerful wings rustling the woman's silky strands of blonde hair.

****

In the early, predawn stillness, Beth Ann greeted the new day by stretching. Spotting the owl overhead, she smiled. The bird was her animal totem and had been since the age of six when Owl Woman had come to her, offering comfort.

She sent her prayer of thanks to the bird for watching over her, then rubbed her arms against the morning chill. Summer had gracefully bowed to autumn, but it felt as though winter, always impatient to rule, was trying to bully its way across the land.

Tempted to turn around and return to her warm, cozy pallet of thick furs, she stifled another yawn and joined her adoptive mother at the fire pit. Together, the two women, one of the sun, the other a warrior of the land, set about preparing the morning meal for their family.

"How are you, this day, *chunksi?*" White Dove asked of her daughter as she poured a handful of coffee beans into an old cast iron skillet.

"I am well, *Ina,* Beth Ann replied in Lakota." Satisfied that the fire, stoked from embers banked the night before, would not go out, she put the kettle of water on a grate placed over the fire pit while her mother saw to the roasting of the coffee beans.

She held out her palms to the fire and warmed her face with her hands. "Won't be long before the first snow."

"No. Winter will come early this year." Once the coffee was going, Dove handed Beth Ann a hunk of meat left from the evening meal.

Beth Ann sliced the elk, and by the time she was done, she felt less chilled. She dumped the strips of elk into an iron skillet, one of her mother's prized possessions, and set it aside.

"Ah, smells good out here" Jeremy *Hunkuya Mato* Jones slipped out of a tipi set close to Beth Ann's. Wearing pants of wool instead of leggings, an army blue shirt and a fur-lined buckskin vest, Jeremy looked both white and Indian. His long, black hair hung to his waist in gentle waves, his eyes were the green of spring grass, and his skin was tanned to a deep brown from years of living beneath the sun. He moved silently with an easy grace as he put an arm around his wife and daughter. "It's a good day when a man is greeted by the sight of the two most beautiful women in the world."

Beth Ann rolled her eyes, knowing he'd say anything for that first mug of coffee. Every morning since coming to live with Dove and Jeremy, her father insisted that a man couldn't begin to think without his morning cup. She grinned. It had taken her mother many years to learn to enjoy the bitter brew.

Dove ducked beneath his arm and punched her husband in the shoulder. "I know better than to fall for your sweet words. Say them *after* you've had your coffee, and I might believe them."

Beth Ann laughed. "He can't. If Jane or Spotted Owl hears him saying we are the most beautiful, they'll pout for days."

Jeremy winced, then grumbled, his gaze fixated on the pot like a man who'd crossed the desert and was desperate for a glass of water. He leaned over, breathing in the aroma, then turned and winked at Beth Ann. "Ah, but they are my most beautiful *girls*."

"Not so, *Ate*," a soft voice protested. "You forget. I am now a woman." Jane joined them, stifling a yawn. She had a fur wrapped around her shoulders with her waist-long blonde hair flowing like honey over the fur. Her long skirt peeked out. Jane preferred to dress as a white woman while living at her Uncle Wolf's place, to set an example to the other girls in their tribe.

"Nah," he said, pulling Jane to him. He switched from Lakota to English. "You are my little girl. You'll always be my little girl."

Beth Ann smiled at her sister, whose blonde hair was a shade darker than her own, as was her skin. Jane didn't burn or blister in the sun anymore, unlike Beth Ann who still had to take care.

"And what of me." Spotted Owl ran up to her father. The young girl had reached back a generation and mingled her grandmother's blonde hair with her parents' shades of black, giving herself hair that was a pale, golden brown in the sunlight, shining with bits of liquid light, just like her uncle Wolf's.

Dove and Beth Ann laughed. "Get out of that one, *Mihingna mici*, husband mine," Dove murmured smiling.

Loving the banter, Beth Ann enjoyed watching her

father tease his first-born. At eleven summers, Spotted Owl had Jeremy's impish, humorous and pale green eyes, along with her mother's stubbornness and determination to get her own way.

Rolling his eyes, Jeremy scooped Spotted Owl into his arms for a hug. "You are still my baby."

"Papa!" Teetonka, several years younger than Spotted Owl stood with her hands on her hips, her dark hair in two long braids and her greenish-blue eyes flashing. "Akecheta is the baby. Spotted Owl and I are nearly grown."

Beth Ann and her mother both giggled when her young brother stepped calmly out of the tipi.

"I am not a baby," he declared with his arms folded across his bare chest. He wore a tiny bow slung over his shoulder. His hair and eyes were all Lakota, revealing none of his white blood. "*Ina* is taking me hunting. Babies do not hunt," he said seriously.

Jeremy smiled. "No, I fear I have no more babies in my family. Only children growing up too fast." He accepted a tin cup filled with steaming coffee. "I am the luckiest man," he whispered in Lakota to his wife.

Dove smiled. "Yes, you are."

The noise level grew as everyone talked and laughed. Her father switched between English and Lakota as a way to teach his younger children both languages of their birthright.

Beth Ann worked flour into bread dough and plopped it into an iron pot greased with animal fat. Her mother placed it in the earthen oven. With many of her family living among the whites, they had access to things like flour, sugar, powdered milk, and actual cookware that made surviving the harsh winters much easier for everyone in her tribe but especially the elderly.

That reminded her. "Papa." She had to yell over the noise of her sisters.

"Yes, Beth?" Jeremy held a handful of small arrows in his hand and carefully examined each one.

"When do we leave?" she asked as she dusted the flour off her hands. They had arrived at her aunt and uncle's place four days ago. Wolf, her mother's brother, along with his wife, Jessie, who was her father's sister, ran a boarding school for the Lakota children during the winter months.

Jane, along with her younger siblings, would spend the winter here. All the children of her tribe were expected to attend school in the winter and learn the ways of the white man. Beth Ann was not staying. As much as she loved her aunt and uncle, she preferred to winter with her parents and the rest of the tribe on the plains.

She understood the need for their children to learn not only English but also the customs of the white man. Knowledge of both was more important now with the growing number of settlers, soldiers, and the creation of the reservation. Her family had recognized early on that it would someday become important for the Lakota to be able to survive in either world. She sighed. The changes affected the elders the most, and they spent a lot of time talking about lost ways.

Jeremy sat on the ground, crossing his legs in front of him, his cup between his big hands. "We aren't."

Beth Ann moved to stand behind her father then knelt. "We're staying? All of us? Why?" She noted the spreading pink rays across the horizon and the tiny line of yellow still beyond the trees.

She split her father's hair in half and began braiding. Jane had taken over browning the meat. Beth Ann frowned as she crossed strand over strand. The only time they stayed the winter was when Grady and Dove's sister, Star, came to visit, but they'd been murdered years before and their children hadn't made the long trip on their own.

Wolf received occasional letters from her cousins sent to Fort Randall where he picked them up when he delivered his horses. She finished one braid and tied the ends with a leather strip that had an eagle feather and blue bead tied to it. "Why are we staying?"

Jeremy turned his head, forcing her to move the braid with his movement. "It's a surprise," he said, his eyes alight with mischief.

Beth Ann finished off the braid with a plain leather thong then moved to face him. "Papa. It's Mattie and Renny! Right? Did Uncle Wolf receive a letter?" Had to be her cousins.

The rest of her father's family had moved to Oregon. Jessie and Wolf had meet and fallen in love on that trip. Jeremy had shocked everyone by deciding to return with his sister and brother-in-law.

"Yep, Mattie, Renny as well as with Star and Grady's brood. Striking Thunder and Emma will also remain here for the winter."

Beth Ann clapped her hands while Jane and Spotted Owl bumped shoulders. Everyone cheered. "I'm so excited. When are they coming?"

"Should be here any day."

After hugging her excited sisters, she asked, "What about Matthew?" She hadn't seen Mattie's brother in years. Last she'd heard, his wife had died in childbirth.

Jeremy shrugged. "I don't think so. He's pretty much a loner these days."

Beth Ann sighed. She'd always liked Matthew. He'd been a fun, energetic boy who always made her laugh. She removed the meat from the fire and glanced up in time to catch the worried look Jeremy and Dove exchanged.

Their worry confirmed in her mind that there was more going on than just a family visit. Everyone was worried about the future. Once, her tribe traveled wherever they wanted, seldom crossing paths with the white man or soldiers, but now there was something called a reservation and her tribe had to stay on that land.

And that wasn't the worst problem. The flood of outsiders brought hate and sickness with them, and fighting that ended in blood shed, which just brought more soldiers onto their land.

It always made her nervous when strangers came poking around. Not only were she and Jane white, they were also *rescued* captives. Twice soldiers had tried to *rescue* her and Jane. Her terror at being taken from Dove and Jeremy had been so great Jeremy had legally adopted them.

It didn't hurt that Colonel Grady's daughter, Emma, had married the chief or that her mother's family had been trappers who lived on this land for generations or that Dove's mother and grandmother had both been as blonde as Beth Ann.

With so many obvious ties to the white world, the soldiers left them alone. But how long would it last? Done with her part of the meal, she returned to her father's side. "It's not just a fun visit, is it? They are coming because Uncle Wolf is worried."

She kept her voice low. She'd heard her parents talking at night after the children were in bed. Though she was eighteen, they still shielded her as though she were a child.

"That is part of it, a big part," he admitted.

"Do you think he'll leave this place and move?" She couldn't imagine Wolf and Jessie moving away.

With a sigh, her father handed his empty cup to his wife. "Right now the army needs Wolf to supply horses, but there's talk that the man he's dealt with is retiring and his replacement isn't so friendly toward our people."

"So the visit is to…"

"Discuss the future."

She nodded, felt a bit let down, and then chided herself. Renny and Mattie were coming. Did it matter why? "It will be good to see my cousins," she said, wrapping her arms around her knees and hugging them to her chest. "No matter what brings them here."

Jeremy reached over and tweaked her hair as though she were ten. "You bet. Now, put the worry from your mind. I have another secret. See if you can guess." He'd switched back to English.

Beth Ann grinned. "Yes, Papa." He often told her that to worry before the need robbed oneself of the joy of living and appreciating the moment. She made a show of thinking, puzzling out her father's secret, and was ready to give in and ask what was making him look so incredibly happy. Her eyes went wide when it occurred to her that he was more than happy.

His eyes were moist, as though ready to cry tears of

happiness. There was only one thing that would make him this happy. "Someone from Oregon is coming?" Her voice ended on a squeak.

The shine of joy in his eyes grew and his pale green eyes were nearly translucent. "Yep. Jordan and James along with their wives and children are coming."

"Oh Papa." Beth Ann squealed, rising onto her knees to hug her father. "That's why Aunt Jessie's been so happy."

"Yep. Haven't seen my brothers since we left them and their families in Oregon more than what, twelve or thirteen years ago."

Dove joined them. She leaned down and stroked the side of his face. "It will be good for your father to spend time with his family."

Beth Ann loved that her parents were affectionate in front of their children and that their love remained as strong as it had been when they first married.

She glanced away, admitting to herself that love that deep and devoted also hurt, especially as she'd wanted nothing more than to have a marriage filled with love like theirs. All her life, she'd dreamed she'd have a husband who'd look at her as though she was the beauty of his every waking moment and the sweet dreams of his nights.

Beth Ann blew out a soft sigh. She'd wanted to matter to her husband, but she'd learned several painful lessons—what a person wanted wasn't always what they got and a love as deep and devoted as her parents wasn't so easy to find and achieve.

She put the impossible from her thoughts. Worry crept in and shadowed her joy like clouds blotting out the sun. The fact that the entire family was gathering meant that something was up.

Staring off into the line of trees, unaware of the bright glow of the sun struggling to rise high enough to bathe her camp in warm light, Beth Ann fretted. Bad enough her cousins were coming but knowing that their Oregon relatives were willing to make the long trip by train said things were far worse than she'd ever imagined. And she had a good imagination when it came to finding things to worry about. She pressed her fisted hand to her stomach.

"Hey, now." Her father took her chin in his hands. "Put it away. It's a time to celebrate."

"Yes Papa." She'd try not to worry, but worrying was something Beth Ann did. A lot.

"Happy thoughts, I said." He sniffed and cocked his head to one side. "Food's ready, and I hear your children waking."

She grinned. Nothing made her happier than her babies. Standing, she hurried into the tipi next to her parents and smiled at the sight of two small toddlers sitting on the pallet they shared with their mother.

"Mama."

"Mama."

She knelt beside her warm babies and gathered them close. "Good morning," she whispered.

The twins never woke in good spirits. For a while, they clung to her, their bodies limp as they nursed. She didn't provide milk anymore as they now ate with the rest of the family, but they weren't ready to give up morning cuddles. Neither was she.

Beth Ann remembered how she and her sister had cuddled with their mother on cold mornings, cozy under the thick blankets while a fire burned in the fireplace in her parents' bedroom. She sighed, unwilling to let sadness ruin a memory that gave her comfort, a memory from long ago, another lifetime, well before the Crow killed her parents.

What will be, will be.

Her father always looked for the best in all situations, but she didn't have his confidence in the future. She just hoped that whatever happened, they'd all stay together. She'd lost one family and didn't think she could survive losing another.

The aroma of bread in the air told her the morning meal was ready. "Are you hungry?" She nuzzled one dark head, then the other. Well over the year mark but not yet close to two, her son and daughter were growing so fast, though they were a bit smaller than other children of the same age.

Standing, she left the tipi with her babies in her arms.

Jeremy met her. "Let me have one."

Both lunged toward Hunkuya Mato, whose name meant Mother Bear.

Sitting beside her father, Beth Ann used her fingers to comb her son's unruly hair that was so like his father's. Her husband had been a good warrior, a good provider, but Singing Bear had been aloof and concerned with his own affairs. During her short marriage, Beth Ann had missed the warmth and love of her family.

She'd been so excited, so thrilled during their courtship, then crushed when she realized that, once married, she'd become a possession her husband could show off and someone to see to his needs. It saddened her to admit she didn't miss him, though she did regret that he had never had the chance to know his children. Maybe he would have taken more of an interest in her had he not died months before their birth.

Beth Ann hadn't spent much time grieving. How could she miss what she never had? She'd just been happy to be back with her family, and true to his name, her father had helped raise her babies.

She fed her children, grinning as they chatted non-stop.

"Beth Ann?"

"Yes?" Jane, at fifteen, was a daily reminder of their mother with her delicate features, blue eyes, and warm, golden-blonde hair.

Beth Ann fingered the locket she wore tucked between her breasts. After they had been captured, her mother had given it to her with the hope that, if rescued, it would help her children be returned to their grandfather. But after their rescue, Beth Ann kept it hidden. She'd never wanted to see her grandfather again. It was his fault her parents were dead.

A light punch to her arm brought her back from the past. "Are you going to wed Standing Horse?"

"Jane! What a thing to ask!"

"*I* think he is very handsome."

"Then you marry him."

"He's not trying to court me."

Beth Ann grimaced. "Haven't thought about taking another husband yet." She had no desire to take another husband, especially Singing Bear's brother, who considered it his duty to take over as husband. She would not become a duty-wife.

"Jane," Dove called.

Jane got to her feet and went to her mother.

Grateful to end that conversation, she eyed her father warily when he scooted closer. "You do not have to marry anyone you do not wish, *Chunksi*."

Beth Ann plucked a blade of grass from beside her. Recent rains had teased the fresh green spouts from the ground, and when the freezing snow and ice arrived, they would die until spring when they'd return and form a plush mat that covered the entire area.

"I'm expected to take another husband." She watched the twins as they tottered off to play.

Jeremy stood and held out his hand to pull her to her feet. He tipped her chin up, his expression serious. "This time, you will marry for love and not settle for less."

Beth Ann wrinkled her nose. "I thought I loved him, figured it would come when we got to know each other."

"But it didn't."

She smoothed out her skirt. "No. I expected too much. I wanted what you and *Ina* have and what Aunt Jessie and Uncle Wolf have and Aunt Emma and our chief. I thought I would have that, too." The sun peeked over the tree line and fell upon them, warming her face.

"Ah, daughter of my heart, you will, but only when you find the man who not only steals your heart but who will love and cherish you because you stole his." He pulled her close and pointed to where the twins were surrounded by a group of young girls, some in deerskin dress and others in wool or cotton prints with pinafores or aprons over them to keep them from becoming dirty so fast. "Your husband might not have been able to give you what you needed, but he did give you the greatest gift a man can give."

Beth Ann leaned against her father. "I do have beautiful children." Her husband had given her not one child, but two. For that, she would always be grateful. She stood on her toes and gave her father a kiss. "Thanks *Ate*."

From the corner of her eye, she spotted her Aunt Emma heading into the trees that led to a small stream. In her arms, she carried a new born with a head of glinting red hair like her mothers. Three older children, one redhead, two with the black hair of their father, ran ahead.

Beth Ann thought about gathering the twins and taking them down to bathe so they could play with their cousins, but first, she needed to help with the cleanup. Together, she and her mother took care of the pans while Spotted Owl and Teetonka ran down to the stream to refill the water bags. Jane had left for the classroom.

She'd just returned from scrubbing out the pans when excited shouts and cries rang out. Beth Ann glanced toward the barn and corrals and saw more than a dozen riders entering Wolf's compound. She grinned when she spotted a woman with hair that glinted like fire in the sun.

"Renny!" She wanted to run and greet her cousin. Though six years in age separated them, she, Renny, Mattie, and Mattie's younger brother had always been close. It never mattered that Renny and her family had moved to the big city of St. Louis before Beth Ann and Jane arrived. They'd come to visit every summer and when the cousins got together, it was as though they'd never been apart.

"Go."

Beth Ann reminded herself she was a woman, not a child. "I will finish."

Dove shook her head. "No. Family is more important. The rest will wait. Go. I'll bring the twins."

Chapter Two

Beth Ann did not need further urging. Shading her eyes with her hands to avoid the spear of light piercing the treetops, she hurried across the large yard in the center of buildings and tipis. Behind her and to one side, tipi's squatted in row upon row. To her right, cabins were spaced apart, allowing privacy and forming the fourth side, several long buildings made up the school and storage buildings.

Visitors, when they arrived, passed through a narrow gap in the trees that opened up to the barn, corrals, and the buildings.

Beth Ann skirted a group of boys acting out a hunt, wove around a circle of girls playing, and was nearly bowled over by two dogs running after a thrown stick.

By the time she reached the visitors who'd stopped in front of the barn, everyone was shouting and talking at once. Her gaze scanned the group. Three of the oldest children were removing saddles while the younger ones ran around her to join the rest of the children.

"Renny!" She made her way to where Renny still sat on her horse.

"Beth Ann!" Renny glanced at the man standing below her.

The man had to be Renny's husband, Tyler. He held in his arms, a small dark-haired boy. The child had his head buried in his father's shoulder and wailed each

29

time Tyler tried to set the child down onto the ground.

"Grady, I need to help your ma off the horse," Tyler reasoned but to no avail.

Beth Ann stepped forward. "Here, let me." She pulled the protesting child from his father with a mother's no-nonsense manner. "What is your name?"

Startled, the child stared at her hair. "Grady," he mumbled around two fingers. "Pretty." He pulled a length of her hair to the side and watched the shiny strands flow back like water flowing down a deep drop.

Beth Ann grabbed a strand and brushed the ends across the boy's nose, tickling him, something that always made her babies laugh. Grady giggled and looked around, suddenly aware of the other children and the fun he was missing.

"Down," he demanded.

"Please?" his father corrected as he helped Renny dismount.

"Pease." The child grinned and batted his thick, dark lashes.

"Oh, my, you are going to break hearts someday," she said as the boy slide to the ground and took off running as fast as his little legs could carry him. He ran so fast, he went sprawling. For a moment he lay there, unsure whether to get up or cry.

Two older girls ran over and made a fuss. They helped him up and dusted him off. The little boy giggled and let the girls lead him into the melee of children.

Assured that he was unhurt, Beth Ann turned to greet her cousin properly. She smiled wistfully when she noticed the infant wrapped in thick blankets in Renny's arms. She loved babies and wanted more but not bad enough to take on another husband.

"Beth Ann. It's been so long."

"It is so good to see you, Cousin." She hugged Renny, and the two women were in tears.

"Lord save us," muttered Tyler. "Gonna flood and sweep us innocents away if you two don't stop weeping."

Renny pulled back. "Watch it, Troll, or you're gonna need saving." Renny and Tyler grinned at each other.

Beth Ann sighed. Their love went so deep it almost hurt to see it. She felt a pang of regret, for she'd sought the same but failed. Her gaze fell to the infant. She held out her arms for the pink bundle. "May I?"

Renny handed her over, stretched her arms overhead, and groaned. "Feel like I've been in that saddle a month or more." She moaned.

Tyler pulled her close and rubbed his wife's shoulders. "We should have taken an extra day getting here."

"What's her name?" Beth Ann stroked the soft cheek, and the tiny bow-shaped mouth puckered.

"Margaret Mary, after my mother," Renny said softly.

"I'm glad you're here," Beth Ann said. "You'll be able to rest now." She studied the infant, pulling the shielding blanket away from the tiny face. "She takes after you." She fingered the tuff of bright red hair peeping from beneath a warm, woolen bonnet. Without conscious thought, she began swaying in that timeless manner of mothers.

"Got her mother's temper, too," Tyler said, brushing a falling pine needle off his head.

"Watch it, Troll," Renny warned. She glanced around. "I don't see Emma."

"She took her children down to the stream."

"How many? I can't wait to see her and my nieces and nephews. Seems like years since we've been here." Renny sighed beneath her husband's stronger fingers.

Laughing, Beth Ann rolled her eyes. "It has been. Your sister has four now. Anamosa, which means White Fawn, was born during the summer." The infant woke and blinked up at her, revealing blue eyes. "This little one looks like she was born while you were traveling. She is so tiny."

"She could have been," Renny said, wrinkling her nose. "I wanted us to leave earlier, but everyone insisted we wait until she made her appearance."

"Darn right," Tyler said. "Can't imagine anything worse than birthing on the road"

"Oh, you did all right." She grinned. "He had to deliver her as she came too fast to send for anyone."

"Mama!"

A tug at her skirt drew her attention. Beth Ann glanced down and saw her daughter holding her arms up in silent demand. Dove stood behind the little girl with Beth Ann's son watching the strangers from the safety of his grandmother's arms.

Smiling, she handed her newest cousin back to Renny. "Here are my babies. This is Kimilmela." She picked up the toddler, then reached over to smooth her son's dark hair. "And this is Tokota."

"Twins?" Renny's jaw dropped as she reached out to touch each child.

Beth Ann nodded. Twins were revered among her people. "Yes."

"I can't believe it's been so long since we've been back." Renny sighed. "After our parents died, it was too hard to get away, and then we all got married and then came the babies." Her features turned determined. "I promise we'll never wait this long to return. I bet your husband is proud."

Setting her squirming daughter down, Beth Ann shook her head. "He never got to see his children. He died before they were born."

"Oh, Bethy!" Renny pulled Beth Ann close for a hug. "I'm sorry, sweetie."

Uncomfortable, Beth Ann shrugged. "Don't be. I have my son and daughter."

Renny held her at arm's length, her shrewd, green eyes studying her. "He didn't love you."

Remembering how as girls they'd talked about falling in love, she felt a twinge of guilt. "No—"

Excited screams from behind cut her off. Grateful for the diversion, Beth Ann stepped out of the way as Emma, Renny's much older sister broke through the crowd. The noise level rose as both women squealed and talked at the same time.

Beth Ann continued to slide to the side as the rest of her family crowded into the area. She bumped into someone. Turning, she grinned when she saw that it was Renny's sister by marriage.

"Mattie, I'm so sorry I didn't see you. It's Beth Ann," she identified herself, remembering that Mattie was blind from an accident. She steadied her cousin, arching her brows when she noticed Mattie was huge with child. "Should you be traveling?" She touched Mattie's belly and felt the baby kick. "Very active!"

"Yes, he is," Mattie said, grinning.

"You know it's a boy?" Before Mattie answered, a handsome man put an arm around Mattie's shoulders. "You try to tell her she can't do whatever she sets her mind to doing."

"You must be Reed." Beth Ann couldn't help the flutter in her heart. Both of her cousins had married handsome men with an aura of danger about them, which was perfect for men of law. She turned back to Mattie, concerned. The woman looked exhausted. And no wonder, traveling in her advanced condition. She took Mattie's hand. "What can I get you?"

Mattie ran her fingers lightly over Beth Ann's features, skimmed her hand over her head, and fingered her long hair. "It's good to see you, Beth. I—"

Mattie's eyes went blank, her jaw slack, and her grip on Beth Ann's hair tightened.

"Mattie! What's wrong? The baby?" Her voice must have carried, because there was sudden silence.

Reed put an arm around his wife. Renny handed her daughter to her husband and took her place on her sister's other side. "Mattie?" Her voice was low.

Time seemed to freeze. No one moved or spoke, and everyone stared at Mattie. Then, a spear of light fell on the young woman's frozen features. As though emerging from a dream, Mattie shuddered, her hand falling from Beth Ann's hair.

"What's wrong? What did I do?" Beth Ann whispered, afraid she had sent her cousin into labor.

Mattie shook her head and turned to her husband. "I need to lie down." Without a word, Reed scooped her into his arms. Emma rushed over. "Use my tipi until I find out from Jessie where she's put you and your family." She led the way through the crowd.

Stunned, Beth Ann turned, calling out, "*Ina?*"

"Right here, sweetheart." Dove wrapped her daughter in her arms.

"What happened? What did I do?" Beth Ann pressed her fist into her fluttering stomach.

Dove hugged her. "You didn't do anything, Beth. Mattie had a vision. Like her mother and grandmother, she has the gift of sight."

"But—" She shook her head. She knew about Seeing Eyes and Star Dreamer. Stories of their visions were still told and retold to this day. Beth Ann had never seen or experienced anyone going into a trance like that. What had she seen in her vision? Did it mean anything that it had happened the moment the two had touched? An uneasy feeling gathered in her belly and traveled throughout her body.

"Come. Let's take the children to the water to bathe and let everyone get settled. If there is anything we need to know, Mattie will tell us when she's ready."

Beth Ann followed her mother but couldn't help but wonder about Mattie's vision. High above, a lone cloud passed in front of the new sun and dimmed the light. Some of her joy in the reunion of family faded. Her gut warned that whatever Mattie had seen—or experienced—wasn't good and that it concerned her.

****

Dusk crawled across the horizon like a transparent monster, swallowing the cool autumn light. It slid down into the forest, coating the world in a purplish-gray haze. Hard on its heels, dark chased the last of the light in that never-ending war between day and night.

Beneath the clear star-studded sky, horses in corrals called to one another, their neighs a mixture of whistles and laughter. The mooing of milk cows joined their neighbors, and as though cued by an invisible conductor's baton, crickets tuned their instruments and let their sounds provide a steady beat of chirps. High above in the treetop, an owl's hoot sounded sad and forlorn. One by one, the world of darkness came alive.

A log tossed onto a large fire sent a shower of embers into the air, quickly followed by the flare of tall, red-orange flames. Grotesque dancing and swaying shadows played over a group of old warriors gathered for an evening of warmth and storytelling.

Tucked into the forest and dotted around log cabins, cone-shaped tipis glowed brightly from fires within. Hidden in the dense forest, yellow and green eyes peered from the shadows.

Beth Ann, wearing a fur-lined cloak her father had purchased during his last trip down the Missouri, was grateful for the extra warmth. She inched closer to her small fire in front of her tipi.

Jeremy Jones had never regretted leaving his life behind when he married White Dove, but as he'd said so many times, he saw no reason why they couldn't make use of practical items from his old world. Cloaks and books, in her mind, were to be treasured. Huddled against the cold, she whole-heartedly agreed.

Holding out her mitten-covered hands to the fire, she admired the precise and even stitching on her new mittens. The colorful blend of colors matched the fur-lined cap on her head. She was amazed that Mattie made them, and her admiration for her cousin rose. She, with her sight, couldn't knit.

The memories of her mother trying to teach her how to knit made her sigh. Had her mother lived, perhaps she'd have learned. But knitting wasn't something her adopted people engaged in. Smiling, she decided to ask Mattie to teach her over the winter. It was time she mastered two needles and a ball of yarn.

In the warmth of the tipi, the twins slept. The excitement of so many newcomers had worn them out earlier than usual.

A finger of cold air snaked up beneath the fur blanket over her legs. She shifted and snugged the fur covering her lap around her legs, then let her gaze drift to the center of the schoolyard where a group of warriors in their prime joined the elders already gathered. Their voices rose and fell with the flames as they recounted stories.

Soon, her people would leave, and the children who were staying would gather around that fire pit. Beth Ann tipped her head back. A blanket of stars stretched across the sky. As a child, here at the school, the evenings beneath the stars had been bittersweet. While she'd enjoyed the stories, laughter, and good times, she'd never gotten used to being away from her parents and younger siblings. But like most of the children in her tribe, she and Jane weren't given a choice.

It hadn't mattered that they spoke English and knew their letters and numbers. Her parents insisted they learn about the world they no longer lived in and help the other children learn what they took for granted. Sitting beneath the stars, knowing her family was somewhere on the plains or hills with the same sky above them had made her feel closer to them.

She grimaced. One of the reasons she'd married at sixteen had been so she wouldn't be expected to stay and help at the school like many of the older children chose to do. No, Beth Ann preferred the safety and security of her family and her people.

A loud shout startled her, but she quickly relaxed when she saw it was just one warrior acting out his part of a hunt. Flickering light and shadows danced over the timeworn features of the elderly warrior.

The sight was both inspiring and sad, for it reminded her that every night during her marriage, her husband had chosen to spend time with the menfolk, instead of with her. He'd never returned to their tipi until she was already in bed. Then he'd come to her and stay long enough to satisfy his needs.

Not once had he stayed the night in her bed. Not once had he held her throughout the night. Not once had he murmured loving endearments. She hated to admit, even to herself, that she'd been a possession, like a hunting knife to be taken out and used when needed, then put away, knowing it would be right where he left it the next time need arose.

Jane couldn't understand why Beth Ann didn't want to marry again. How could she? She'd never shared her shameful marriage with anyone. Not even with her parents. Restless, she stood, wrapped her fur blanket around her waist, and picked up a long, thick stick to stir the embers.

Soon, she'd have to keep a fire going inside the tipi for warmth, but her warm pallet and the ample supply of furs was enough, along with the quilts Renny and Tyler presented to her after dinner. Those little touches of her old world brought comfort as well as sadness but never regret. She was content with her life.

She stifled her yawn. Though tired, she was far too

unsettled to sleep. All day and evening, she'd put aside Mattie and her vision, even pretended it hadn't happened so that nothing could mar her excitement and joy over the arrival of cousins. The vision had nothing to do with her. As her father always said, if it was there to worry about, Beth Ann was ready to do the worrying.

She told herself to let it go but how could she? All her life, she'd heard stories of the visions that Mattie's mother, Star Dreamer, had experienced. And before her, Star's mother had had the gift of sight. Beth Ann had never witnessed Star's legendary visions, and no one else in her tribe had visions. To have Mattie go into that trance as soon as the two touched was both frightening and unsettling. She'd tried to hide her fear from her parents, but they knew the experience had shaken her.

After dinner, they'd tried to talk to her, but Beth Ann had avoided them. To speak of it made it real. This way, it was just a worry, and sometimes the things she worried about faded into nothingness. She let out a long breath. Tomorrow would come soon enough.

A burst of giggles drew her attention and made her smile. She went to the tipi belonging to her parents and stuck her head inside.

"Spotted Owl. Teetonka. You answer to Papa if you wake your brother," she said to her sisters.

"Yes, Beth Ann," both responded.

As she lowered the deerskin flap, she heard another round of giggling but much lower in volume. She shook her head, remembering how she and Jane used to lie in bed and giggle, especially when they talked of the young warriors who'd caught their eye.

Too bad Jane was sleeping in the dormitories with

39

the younger children. She could use the company. Her sister needed babies of her own. Jane loved her role as teacher and was very good.

Beth Ann dug her stick into the ground and drew circles until the charred tip broke off. This, for her, was the loneliest time of the day. She didn't have anyone to share in the quiet of the evening. Even her parents were off somewhere. She smirked and didn't need but one guess as to where and what they were doing out in the forest by themselves.

She glanced past the old warriors and gave herself a self-congratulatory nod when she spotted her parents emerging hand in hand from the forest. Her father had a blanket slung over his arm. Beth Ann rolled her eyes when he patted his wife's bottom, making her jump and laugh.

She resumed her seat beside the fire and waited for them to join her, then frowned when they joined Wolf and Jessie at one of the tables where the children ate their meals. Glowing lanterns down the center of the table flickered across their faces.

She tipped her head to one side. If she had a lantern, she could read in the evenings. Whenever they came to visit her uncle, Beth Ann headed for the shelf of books in the schoolhouse. And Renny had presented her with not one book, but two.

She pulled out the locket from beneath her dress and held it tight, needing the comfort that came from remembering the mother who'd taught her to read at a young age. She decided to talk to her uncle Wolf and see if he could spare a lantern for her to use while they were here. Reading would keep the evenings from being so long and lonely.

"Beth Ann."

Turning, she smiled up at Renny. Her brother, Daire, stood at her side. Their youngest sister, Caitlin, was married and unable to join them on this trip. "Come join me. Figured you'd be asleep early." She got to her feet, grateful for the distraction from the worry that begged to be taken from the corner of her mind and pulled and pushed into its many forms. "You had a long day of travel."

"Days and days of traveling." Renny rubbed the small of her back with one hand. In her other, she cradled her infant daughter.

Beth Ann held out her arms for the infant. "She is just adorable." She brushed a hand over the infant's bright, red curls and smiled at Daire. "And you. I didn't get a chance to speak with you earlier, Daire. I can't believe you are as tall as I am." She motioned to the brother and sister. "Sit. It will be so good to catch up."

"Would love to, but we've all been ordered to join the others for the meeting," Renny said.

Beth Ann frowned, and when she glanced back to where her parents sat, she saw that the table was nearly full. "What's it about?"

"Mattie's visions," Daire volunteered.

Renny gave the back of Daire's head a hard smack. "You were told not to say anything."

He hunched his shoulders. "Sorry, Ren."

Beth Ann had deliberately put Mattie's vision from her mind. "Our aunts and uncles have been meeting each evening since we arrived. I can tell they aren't just visiting." Beth Ann sighed and let her gaze linger on her family. "I'd like to join you, and them, but I don't like to leave the little ones alone in case they wake.

41

Jane could stay with them, but she's sleeping in the dormitory with the younger girls."

Renny ruffled her brother's hair. "Daire, here, volunteered to sit and keep watch."

"Did not," he protested. "Don't see why I can't be there. I'm not a baby anymore. I'm thirteen now. That's almost a man."

"And that is why I trust you to watch your cousin's children so that she, who *is* an adult, can join the rest of the *adults*."

"Fine." He winked at Beth Ann, letting her know that, while he might not have volunteered, he wasn't the least bit resentful as he dropped down in front of the fire, pulled out a knife, and started whittling a piece of wood he'd taken from his back pocket. He whistled softly, melodically.

Renny pulled Beth Ann away. "Come on. He's good with little ones."

"He should be with all the babies and young one's in your and Mattie's family!"

Reaching the long, wooden table, Renny took her sleeping child from Beth Ann, walked around and sat beside her husband. Beth Ann slid in between her parents who'd scooted apart to make room for her. She appreciated the gesture yet, at the same time, it reminded her that she might have reason to need their love and support.

Across from her, Renny and Tyler burst out in yet another argument. Grateful for the distraction, she propped her elbows on the table. "Do you two ever stop?" She couldn't believe the good-natured bickering that flowed non-stop between them. Dinner had been very entertaining just watching and listening to them.

Tyler winked at her. "Nah, gotta fight so you can make up." He sent his wife a mock-lewd look.

Renny shifted her sleeping daughter in her arms and punched Tyler in the arm, hard enough that he winced. "Behave, Troll. Oh, wait, animals—"

Tyler wrapped one arm around his wife and child and pulled them close. He kissed her hard—and long.

Beth Ann rolled her eyes and giggled when Wolf lobbed a pinecone at Tyler, smacking him on his head. Everyone, including her, chuckled, breaking the quiet tension that hung over the gathered family like smoke in a tipi when the flaps were closed.

She felt a bit envious as everyone laughed and talked. Shifting her hands back to her lap, fingers interlaced, she let her gaze travel from person to person.

At one end of the table, Jessie cradled baby Margaret while Wolf finished adjusting the wick on the last lantern. He slid onto the bench beside his wife and rested one arm around her shoulders.

Emma arrived out of breath and took her seat beside Dove with her infant daughter in her arms. "My husband will be here shortly. The children insisted on a second story."

"Good, we're not the only late comers," Reed said as he guided Mattie to the table. She scooted onto the bench beside Renny and held out her hands. Renny smoothly transferred her daughter to Mattie.

Beth Ann studied Mattie. Her cousin looked drawn and ill. Remembering Daire's comment about Mattie's visions—*visions* not *a* vision—Beth Ann dug her fingers into the thick, soft fur of her cloak.

A loud, gruff voice boomed out. "Here we go," Rook announced as he and Sofia arrived carrying tin cups and several pots of coffee. "Gettin' a bit chilly out here. Figured you might like something to warm you from the inside out." He and his wife set cups and plates on the table. Done, he backed away.

"Sofia and I will see to the children," he said to Wolf.

"No." Wolf pointed to a spot at the end of the table beside Jeremy. "You need to be here as well." He poured a cup of coffee, then warmed his hands around it.

"This is a family meeting," Rook said. "Besides, someone has to get your brood in bed."

"You and Sofia are family," Jessie said firmly. She shifted the baby in her arms. "Sit."

"Don't have to be so bossy." Rook winked.

"I'll sit if I can hold Katie." Sofia smiled and held her arms out. "Feet killing me today."

Jessie handed her child to Wolf, who held her out to Sofia. "Left Emily and Mary in charge of bedding down our little ones. Had to bribe them. They wanted to sleep with the others in the dormitory."

Everyone smiled. Once school started, everyone over the age of five attended and that included sleeping in the dormitories. Wolf handed Jessie a cup of tea. "John and Laura are riding herd on the children, along with Jane. I think all the older children were put there?" He looked to Rook.

"Yep. Star and Grady's children are there, along with a bunch of new children from the tribe. Missing a few though," he said, spearing Dove and Emma with his narrowed eyes.

Dove rolled her eyes. "Our children will join the others tomorrow."

A young woman with black hair and black eyes walked over to Emma. "I can take the baby back to the tipi. Barbara Ellen is there with Weeko."

Handing the child over, Emma nodded. "Thank you, Ana." After Ana left, Emma thanked Wolf for lending two of his daughters to watch over her children.

Dove chuckled. "Teetonka takes after our Beth Ann and does not want to go to school. We promised one more night in our tipi, then ours will join the rest of the children."

Emma sighed. "No children in your tipi. What will you do?" She wore a wide grin.

"Means they won't have to sneak in the forest at night," Beth Ann murmured, shifting her eyes from one parent to the other.

Jeremy yanked one of her braids. "Brat."

Reed sighed. "My Danny, who is nine, should be with the other children, but he and Lizzie were quite spoiled by their grandparents. This life is totally foreign to them."

Mattie took his hand in hers. "They will adjust, and when they go to the school house, they will think it was their idea."

Reed nodded. "No doubt you are right." His shook his head in amazement at the gathering of family. "Don't think I've seen so many young'uns in one place."

Wolf nodded, and his gaze went to Dove. "Our parents would have been proud had they lived to see their legacy."

Beth Ann listened as Wolf, Jessie, and Emma talked about Golden Eagle and his wife, White Wind—her grandparents. She'd never met her grandfather.

He'd been killed right before Jeremy rescued her and Jane from the Crow and brought them into their tribe, but she had briefly known White Wind. She'd loved the blonde-haired woman with her kind blue eyes.

Across the way, the warriors left the fire and headed to their tipis. The voices of children died down, and it was as though she and her family were alone in a small, bubble of light with darkness closing in around them as, one by one, fires were banked.

Surrounded by family, Beth Ann should have felt safe, secure, and at peace, though from the looks everyone sent Mattie when they didn't think anyone noticed, she feared something was going to happen to change that.

She twisted her hands together in her lap. She didn't like change, but the growing number of settlers and soldiers flooding the area was cause for concern. Everyone hushed when Striking Thunder arrived. The chief, an imposing figure in his breechclout, leggings, and leather vest, was the only man at the table in his native dress.

Of all her uncles, Beth Ann had always been a bit overwhelmed and even a tad bit afraid of the man who ruled his tribe with a firm, wise, and fair hand. His wisdom and foresight had kept them safe. His gaze swept over each person, lingering on Mattie.

"Our sister's daughter has had many visions of late. Visions of soldiers and white men killing our warriors and destroying our land." He met and held each person's gaze for a moment before continuing. "It is not enough that they've given us boundaries and told us where we can hunt and live. Now, they try to take that from us. The time has come for us to make decisions for our future." He glanced at Wolf, then sat beside his wife. Emma leaned against him.

Wolf stood, his gaze roaming over his family. "As you all know, Jessie and I sent letters to her brothers as there are several family matters we'd like to bring up for discussion. Though not everyone is here, I think we can start the talks regarding our futures." Hearing Jessie's loud sigh, he put hand on her shoulder. "During my last trip to the fort, I spoke at length to the colonel in charge. He's always supported not just our family but our people as a whole. He now warns that those in power want more of our land. There are many in Washington who are unhappy with what they consider the *vast* amount of land we were given."

Various expressions flitted across the shadowed features of everyone gathered. In the manner of his people, Wolf took his time. "The colonel confided that soldiers are not honoring the rights of the Lakota, that they are coming onto our land, causing trouble." He shoved his hands into the pockets of his thick woolen pants. "If our warriors attack, they are hunted down and killed. We've all heard stories of our people being attacked for no reason. These soldiers tell lies to their commanders. They say that the *Sioux* attacked first."

When Wolf used the derogatory term for the Lakota people, Beth Ann knew he was angry. A glance around the table revealed both anger and fear among her family.

"Then more soldiers come and they kill." He drew in a deep breath, his pale eyes glinting silvery in the moonlight. "The white Chief, their president, and his men, are not going to honor their agreements with The People. There are just too many white folk who want to settle on our lands, and because they fear us, they are trying to get rid of us." Wolf looked to his brother. "Things will get worse, not better, my brother."

Striking Thunder crossed his arms across his chest. "We never believed the white man would honor their word. I have attended their meetings, sat in their circles, smoked pipes of peace with them. Our elders signed papers on our behalf. Many believed the white man, most did not. Those who did not realized we had no choice."

"Can't we fight them? We have guns now," Emma said, her eyes flashing with fury.

Striking Thunder smiled indulgently at his wife, but it was Tyler, who was a sheriff in the small town where he, Renny, Mattie, and Reed lived, answered. "No. If you attack the soldiers, more will come. Your people cannot win in a fight against the government and their armies."

"There must be something we can do," Beth Ann said softly. The stories of war parties attacking soldiers and settlers, then being hunted down and slaughtered often gave her nightmares, for it never mattered if there were women or children involved. On either side, they were the innocent victims. She gripped her hands beneath the table.

"We must find a way to survive and to do that, we need to go where there are no white men and soldiers." Emma's voice sounded close to tears.

"There is more." Wolf ran his hands through his graying, golden hair. "The army wants my land and the buildings. They've offered a fair price for all of it."

His news stunned the group, including Rook and Sofia. "You're not going to sell," Rook roared. "This is your land."

Wolf shook his head. "I may have no choice. Right now, they are offering a fair price. If I say no, they could just decide to take it, especially as I don't have an official deed."

He paced at his end of the table, the lantern throwing his shadow across the buildings. "The army respects my right of ownership, because of my family connection to the land, because my grandfather and his father before him were among the first trappers to call this land home."

Everyone fell silent. The loud screech of an owl high above in the trees broke the silence. To Beth Ann, it sounded as though the bird objected to Wolf's news. As did she. She might not have enjoyed all her time here, but she loved her aunt and uncle, and this was their home.

"It's not fair," she whispered. She couldn't imagine losing everything she had or had worked so hard to create.

Dove put her arm around her daughter. "Much of life is not fair."

"I know. Just as I know our family has been fortunate. Our elders are wise and guide us well, and our connections to the white world provide us with more than most of our people have, but it's still not right. If Jessie and Wolf leave, we might not ever see them again." She voiced what everyone was thinking.

Striking Thunder stared into night sky, a proud warrior torn between the past and the future. Slowly, he faced his family. "You are correct in all you've said, child, and that is why I believe the time has come for us to consider leaving this land of our birth and our ancestors."

Beth Ann's jaw dropped. Emma brushed tears from her face. Reed and Tyler were grim-faced, and Mattie... Mattie looked worn and tired and not the least bit surprised. Had she had visions of this night? Did she know what was going to happen?

Beth Ann wasn't sure how her parents felt, as she was afraid to glance up at them. Numb. That was how she felt. She couldn't imagine leaving the land she'd called home for so long.

Reed stood and leaned on the table. "Your people can live on our land. Between what Tyler has and what Mattie and I own, there's more than enough room for all of you to live as you please."

"It would be no different than living on the white man's reservation," Striking Thunder said. "We will still be confined and when people in town find out, they will fear us and that is cause enough for trouble."

"Where will we go?" Emma looked worried. "History tells us that wherever there is land, there will be people looking to move, conquer, and claim."

Beth Ann nodded. Emma had been raised in St. Louis, and with her help, they were able to teach the children here some of the history of their land, as well as land belonging to others.

Between Emma and the books that Jeremy picked up when he went into the city, she'd learned a lot about the world she saw so little of and could even appreciate the importance of using past events to determine the future.

Jeremy stood, one hand resting on the shoulders of his wife and daughter. "We will go. Wherever we need to go to provide a better life for our children."

Jessie smiled through her tears at her brother. "As will we."

Striking Thunder nodded. "There is much for us all to consider, and we have time to decide what is best."

Wolf sighed. "I say we consider our options over the winter." He smiled. "And enjoy our family being together. When our Oregon relatives arrive, they will have news. They are traveling across the country to get here. I leave in the morning to deliver the last of the horses to the fort."

He glanced at his brother. "I will take with me the furs you brought and bring back supplies and whatever news there is to be had. When do our people leave for the winter grounds?"

"In the morning," Striking Thunder announced. "I've asked some of the warriors to remain here. With so many of us staying the winter, we need them for hunting and protection." He stood and held out a hand to Emma.

Jessie stood as well and smiled bravely. "While my husband is gone, we will plan a celebration for when the others arrive."

Talk turned light, and if it sounded forced, no one commented. Beth Ann wasn't sure what to feel or think. She hated change, and it looked as though change was going to thrust itself into her life whether she wanted it or not. She squared her shoulders. As long as her family stayed together, she'd survive. With them, she could handle anything tossed her way.

About to rise and return to her children, she felt the sudden hush that swept over those still gathered at the table. Glancing around, she saw that everyone was staring at Mattie and Mattie's attention was focused on *her* with such burning intensity, it sent chills down her spine.

In the glow of the lantern, shadows danced over her cousin's face and light flickered in her wide, black eyes. Reed put his arms around his wife and leaned in close. "Mattie? What is it?"

Beth Ann held her breath. It was both eerie and scary to have Mattie staring at her in that manner, not once, but twice in one day. Beth Ann wanted to leave. Right now. She didn't want to know what Mattie was seeing, but her father put his arm around her shoulders as though aware of the turmoil inside of her.

After what seemed hours, Mattie blinked, then slumped against her husband. No one spoke. Beth Ann's heart thudded, and she tried to tell herself it had nothing to do with her. She just happened to be sitting across from her.

"Another vision, Niece?" Striking Thunder asked.

"Yes, Uncle." Mattie drew in a deep, shuddering breath. "Two men come. They bring many with them." She turned in Wolf's direction. "You will bring them back with you."

Mattie leaned forward and reached out toward Beth Ann, again as though she saw exactly where Beth Ann sat.

Beth Ann took her cousin's trembling hand. "Mattie?"

"I saw this earlier but was afraid to say anything, but now I must tell you. The two men, they come for you," she whispered.

"What?" She reared back, would have tumbled off the bench had her father not stood behind her. Panic raced through her. "What men?" Her voice rose.

"One shares the blood in your veins, the other—"

Forcing herself to sit tall and still, with her hands in her lap, clasped tight to hide their trembling, she couldn't take her eyes off Mattie. "My grandfather," she whispered, her fear that he'd find her coming to pass. She knew it, felt it in her gut. "What about the other man?" Her throat closed shut, making her voice sound low and hoarse.

Mattie sighed. "Choices, my cousin. You have many choices ahead of you this winter."

Beth Ann withdrew her hand. "I won't leave," she said, fighting the urge to get up and run back to her tipi, to her children.

Jeremy put his arm around her. "No one will take you from us."

Striking Thunder nodded. "You are one of us and have been since the first day your father brought you here to us. We will deal with these men."

Beth Ann stood and addressed her uncle, who was also her chief. "I want to leave with the others. If I am not here, they can't take me away."

Striking Thunder took her hands in his large, rough ones. "You are no coward," he said, his voice gentle. "When you first came here, you were brave and defiant. Do not give in to fear. If these men are coming, then *you* must face them, but you will not be alone. Understand?"

Beth Ann nodded, but she felt anything but brave.

"Good." He released her hands, cupped the side of her face for a moment, then turned and left with Emma at his side.

Moving as though in a daze, Beth Ann shook her head at her parents and slipped away. She didn't want to talk about Mattie's vision, not even with her father. The worry and fear that she'd always carried grew and threatened to engulf her. In the darkness, beneath the trees, she leaned against a thick pine.

"I won't leave," she whispered.

High above her came the hoot of an owl. Beth Ann glanced up but couldn't see the bird.

"You came to me once, Owl. Told me to be brave and strong. I'm not feeling brave now. I'm scared. I do not want to be taken away."

There was no answer, no appearance of the Owl Woman, no words of comfort. Turning to leave, she felt something soft brush her cheek. Reaching up, Beth Ann found a tiny fluffy feather. She held it to her heart as though it were a shield.

Knowing she couldn't remain in the darkness forever, she made her way to her tipi and her children. Daire had left, but her father stood watch in front of his tipi. She sent him a brave smile and entered.

Settled on her pallet, she pulled the twins close. Unable to sleep, she stared at the feather for a long time, then added it to a small pouch she wore around her neck. "For protection."

Chapter Three

Fort Randall bustled with activity. Soldiers in formation marched across the parade grounds while others hurried from one building to another. Mounted squads filed through the open gates, and over it all, men shouted to be heard over the din.

Bo took in the flurry of motion that never stopped. A few paces to his left, a pair of trappers older than sin sat with their backs to the wall, soaking in the bright afternoon warmth. Their stories grew more outlandish with each passing minute and swallow of rotgut.

Angry shouting hushed the trappers and drew Bo's attention. Three soldiers were marching an angry and very drunk Indian across the compound in front of him. He coughed against the rise of dust from their boots.

"Them savages can't hold their whiskey worth a damn."

Bo shifted slightly. The speaker, a rough-looking soldier other's called Yak came up beside him. "Why give it to them?" He watched as the drunk was tossed through the open and guarded gate.

The soldier smirked. "Trade is trade. Them savages bring in furs and buckskin clothing their squaws make, and we give them their firewater. Course, we water it down. That bastard's got a wife and kids camped out there. Wife'll show up soon, full of piss 'n vinegar, then we'll toss her out, too." He laughed and spat on the ground.

Before Bo could even think of an excuse to leave, the man started in again. "Seen you and your party around." He held out his hand. "Captain Raoul Martinez, though most 'round here call me Yak."

Bo reluctantly shook the officer's hand and inclined his head. He didn't like the hard, squint-eyed captain and had even less respect for the man after hearing him speak, which had not changed from his first impression of the man who seemed to latch onto anyone he could and proceed to yak their ears off. Up to now, he'd managed to avoid the man.

For the two weeks he'd been at the fort, he'd been shocked by the callous attitude many of the soldiers had regarding the Indians, especially toward the women living in pitched tipi's outside the fort. The women were no better than prostitutes, although he supposed it was no different from the brothels in the cities.

"Heard you and the old man are lookin' for a couple of girls. His granddaughters." Raoul shook his head. "Bad business. Pal of mine left the army and used to lead people out west in the fifties and sixties. Had some hair-raisin' stories of injun attacks. Gave it up after he took an arrow in the shoulder. Lucky he survived. Them Crow were vicious. Might be better if the old man didn't find them."

Though Bo was of the same opinion as the slimy officer, he asked, "Why?" He divided his attention between the activity around him and the captain.

"Them girls, if alive, will never be the same." He spat on the ground, inches from Bodil's boots.

Bo shifted his feet out of spit range. "We'll see. Might not even be them." Though from the letter Henry received, it seemed likely that his granddaughters might have at last been found.

At the sound of booted steps on the plank walkway, the captain nodded. "Best of luck," he said, taking his leave.

"Yeah." Bo figured they needed all the luck they could get. Restless, he sighed and wondered what was happening back at the ranch. The men Henry sent to take charge were good. They wouldn't be tempted by the railroad agents like the men he'd fired, but it wasn't the same as being there himself, especially with all the problems.

The railroad was playing dirty, but Bo also suspected that banker bastard was responsible for some of the mishaps at the ranch. Too bad he didn't have proof.

"Bo, wondered where you took off to."

Turning, Bo tipped his hat to Henry. "Morning Henry." The man looked rested, his color good. The trip, along with worry, had taken its toll on the older man. "Just getting some air." The chill, crisp air reminded him that winter was on its way, and that made him think of the work that needed doing on his ranch. And that he wasn't there doing it.

Henry chuckled. "Hiding from that family of leeches is more like it."

Bo shuddered and rolled his eyes. "You blame me?" He made the effort to lighten his voice and mood and shoved aside all thought of home from his mind. He was here, not there. Did no good to fret over what he couldn't control.

"Hell no, son. Got myself right out of there the minute that step-mama of yours started complainin'.

Her and them kids of hers will be the death of me."
Henry grimaced as a squad of men marched past,
followed by three men on horseback. The dust rose, and
as though waiting for that perfect moment, a swirl of
wind swooped in and sent the cloud of fine dust
twirling around them.

"Why do you think I'm out here?"

"Jocelyn could drive a sober man into drinking
himself stupid. And her children? Matt's no good, and
Margaret cares only for Margaret." Henry went into a
coughing fit. "Damn dust."

Together, they moved away from the dust cloud.
Bo removed his John B, swiped an arm across his
forehead, and stopped along the side of the long
building. "Margaret's not bad. Just not used to roughing
it. Matt's an ass." And he, Bodil Riker Quinn, was a
damn fool for allowing his stepfamily to accompany
him and Henry.

Because he didn't trust Jocelyn, not one wit. He'd
refused to allow her to stay at the ranch in his absence,
suggested she and her brood get a room in town until he
got back, or better, go home. But Jocelyn dug her heels
in.

*Why Bodil, we'll go with you and Henry. What a
great time we'll have getting to know each other again.
I do so want you and my children to be friends.*

Bo didn't believe a word of her lies. She'd hated
the ranch, hated his father, and had dismissed him as
unworthy of her time or attention. She'd done
everything possible to keep her precious children away
from Bo. He had no doubt she'd heard the railroad
wanted his land, and if he'd sold it to them, her money-
grubbing hand would have shot out faster than he could

draw his Colt on a thief.

No, Jocelyn Linberg was no better than a dirty buzzard pecking at fleshless bones. And her penchant for lies had not changed. Too bad she wasn't smart enough to realize she'd get nothing from him.

"Glad they're your problem, not mine." Henry's comment drew him from his dark thoughts.

"Thanks, Henry." Bo's voice was dry.

Henry slapped him on the back and grinned. "Anytime, dear boy, anytime."

"Oh, came out here to tell you the colonel sent word that our man arrived a couple hours ago."

Bo fiddled with the brim of his hat, then stuck it back on his head. "That's good news." He was eager to get this business over and done with and get back home.

In front of him, Henry paced back and forth, short, abrupt steps, and once more, his features were drawn with worry.

"You should have stayed back at the ranch, Henry. I could have taken care of this."

Henry stopped, his hands clasped behind his back as he stared out into the compound. "No. Had to see this through. Got a good feeling, Bo. It's them. It's Lizzie's babies."

Bo leaned against the whitewashed wall. "And if you're right, what then?"

Henry drew his brows together and folded his arms across his chest, his entire stance stiffening. "I'm bringing my girls home, Bodil."

Lifting a brow at the man's set jaw and the determination in his eyes, Bo held Henry's gaze until the man glanced away. "We had a deal, Henry. It's their choice. They come willingly, or they don't come at all."

This was the reason Bo had agreed to accompany his neighbor. Henry's money meant nothing to him. He'd rather lose his ranch than be party to destroying lives, and he'd told Henry so.

"Henry." He waited until Henry glanced back at him. "Say it," he ordered, his voice a low, firm command.

Tense seconds passed before Henry turned away. "Told you I wouldn't force them, Bo."

"I'm holding you to it," Bo said. Henry had been so sure he'd finally found his girls that he'd gone against Bo's wishes and paid the bank in full instead of the minimum needed. That meant Henry now owned Bo's ranch. When they returned, if things did not work out according to Henry's plans, Bo would be working for his godfather, and that was a hard pill to swallow.

Henry folded his arms in front of him and narrowed his eyes at his godson. "And you? Going to hold up to your end of the bargain?" Though Henry's voice bordered on belligerent, the man looked worried.

Bo didn't want a wife, didn't have the time or the money needed to keep a woman happy. "Said I'd consider it. Depends on what we find." It had been the best he could give Henry. If Beth Ann decided to go home with Henry and needed Bo's protection to return to their world, he'd marry her.

And if these girls weren't Henry's granddaughters? He stifled his sigh. Didn't matter. What was done was done. Henry, after all, was family.

"It is going to work out, Bo. I know it."

Not so confident, Bo held his silence.

"You'll marry her. For your ranch. For my Lizzie."

Henry sounded almost smug.

Before Bo could comment further, the loud, strident voice of his stepmother made both men cringe. "Bodil, there you are! You really shouldn't run off and leave us unprotected."

Biting back his groan of frustration, he turned and watched Jocelyn storm toward him, her boots slapping up dust.

"Looked like you were enjoying holding court in there, Jocelyn," Bo drawled.

Jocelyn pouted. "Bo, that's not very nice. I'm being polite. How long are we staying in this god forsaken place?"

He lifted one brow. Jocelyn was a large imposing woman with a temper hotter 'n hell, a heart the size of a gnat, and shit-brown eyes harder than the packed earth of the parade grounds. "Seems you were *very* polite to the major." Bo wouldn't be surprised to learn that she'd invited the man to her bed. He and Henry exchanged knowing glances.

Jocelyn shoved her hands onto her ample hips. "Bodil, I asked you a question."

Bo learned a long time ago that if he gave his father's wife an inch, she'd take a wide mile and then some, so he ignored her and watched the rhythm of the post. What had his father ever seen in her, he'd never know.

He waited until she opened her mouth to speak, then cut her off before she could launch into one of her tirades. "We are here until our business is finished." He held up one hand. "You didn't have to come, and if you don't like it, I'll hire someone to take you back." Not for the first time and not the last, he regretted allowing them to accompany him and Henry. With his father gone, there were no ties between them, no need to saddle himself with her.

"Mama, be nice." Margaret smiled. "I'm sorry, Bodil. She's bored. We all are. There isn't much excitement here." She blinked sweetly, begging him to understand.

"Good god, Margaret," Matt piped in. "I swear honey's oozin' out your ears. I'm with Ma. It's dusty, dirty, and boring as hell here."

Bo wasn't sure he could bear another day with his steps and was grateful that his father hadn't sired a child with Jocelyn and that she'd left in search of brighter pastures before his father died.

Henry nudged him. "Here comes the colonel."

Bo studied the man walking with the man in charge of the fort. He was tall, golden-haired with a healthy dose of graying hair, golden-skinned with bright, blue eyes. His buckskin pants were worn, and instead of a shirt, he wore a vest and seemed not to notice the chill in the air. Wolf looked like Bo's image of a trapper in his prime, except for being clean-shaven.

"That must be our man," he said to Henry. He turned to Jocelyn. "Stay." He ignored the fury in eyes and the glint of humor that lurked in Matt's as he fell into step with Henry.

"Bodil. Henry. This here's the man I was telling you about. Name is Wolf. White Wolf to his people."

Bo held out his hand. "Make it, Bo. This is Henry."

Henry's fingers shook as he handed Wolf a tintype. "We're looking for two girls—well, women now— abducted by the Crow twelve years ago. Parents were headed west when they were attacked. They were found dead, but there were no signs of the girls." He drew in a deep breath. "Girls are blonde with the prettiest blue eyes. Been searching for a long time for them. Man I hired last year sent back word that he'd found two women, one who looks like my daughter—their mother." He tapped the tintype. "Unfortunately, my man got himself killed before we arrived. Hoping you can help us."

Wolf studied the tintype, then handed it back. He crossed his arms across his chest. "Why should I help you?"

Before Henry could say or do anything they might all regret, Bo laid a hand on Henry's arm. "We aren't looking to cause trouble. We want confirmation. Henry has never given up on finding them alive."

Spearing the older man with his raised brows, Wolf asked, "And if they are your granddaughters?"

Bristling, Henry said, "I'm taking them home where they belong."

Fearing his friend, in his desperation to locate the girls, would drive away the only man who might have answers, Bo held up his hand to Henry. He met Wolf's indifferent yet sharpened gaze. "I'm here to help and support my godfather, but I'm also here to see that the women aren't taken against their will." He glanced at the man beside him. "If found, Henry promised not to force his granddaughters to leave if they were happy where they are. We expect them to be free, not captives, and able to make their own decisions."

Wolf lifted a brow at Henry. "You agreed to this?"

Henry nodded reluctantly. "Finding my Lizzie's girls is the most important thing in my life. I realize one or both might have families of their own. I give you my word that it will be their choice whether they return to Nebraska with me." He lifted his head and stood proud as a stag on a mountaintop.

Knowing how much it cost his godfather to make that promise, Bo added, "I intend to see that he keeps his word. If the girls his man located are Henry's missing granddaughters, they should know that their grandfather never stopped looking for them, and Henry deserves to know the fate of the only family he has left."

Behind Wolf, Bo saw his step family approaching, though he'd told Jocelyn to remain where she was.

Wolf shifted, his gaze scanning the new arrivals. He addressed Bo. "Your godfather can be trusted to keep his word."

Bo sighed. "Can't deny that Henry is worried and anxious or that emotion might rule his head and heart. You need to understand he's spent years searching for them and being disappointed. That's why I'm here. Right now, we want to know if his granddaughters are alive. Then we can take it from there."

The silence between the men grew and thickened. Wolf came to a decision. "My people rescued two young girls from the Crow many years ago. The Crow killed their mother."

As though someone had prodded him with a cattle stick, Henry jumped. "I want to see them," he demanded. "Are they captives?"

Wolf lifted a brow, and his voice held a hard edge when he answered. "No. They were adopted into our tribe and raised by parents who love them. Each is free to leave at any time."

"What are their names," Bo asked, putting a

restraining arm over Henry's.

"Beth Ann and Jane."

Henry sagged and grabbed Bo's arm with both hands. "It's them, Bo. I've found Lizzie's babies." Color raced into his face, then quickly fled, leaving him pale.

"Calm yourself, Henry. Didn't come all this way to have your heart go out on you before you meet your girls."

Henry drew in several deep breaths, then gave Wolf his attention, his excitement rivaling that of a child given an unexpected gift. "Tell me about them. What are their names now? Are they well?"

At Wolf's surprised look, Bo grinned. "We tried to learn all we could about the life they might be living before setting off. I asked questions of everyone we could rope into talking to us, especially here at the fort. We know they'd have been given new names."

Wolf looked surprised. "The girls each chose to keep the name their mother had given to them as a way to honor her memory and keep her alive in their hearts and minds."

Tears rolled down Henry's lined face. "I want to see them. You will take us?"

Wolf nodded. "Yes."

Relieved that this part was over and that it had gone far better than he'd anticipated, Bo asked, "When are you leaving?"

"Now."

Henry released Bo's arm. "I'll get my things." He hurried off.

Bo turned to his unwanted family "You can remain here." He looked to the colonel for permission.

The colonel looked pained but nodded. "They are welcome to stay."

Jocelyn marched forward, her skirts swishing. "No. We go where you go," she said, her voice tarter than Mildred's lemon curd or rhubarb pie.

Bo could insist on them remaining, but it didn't seem right to fob his responsibilities onto the officer. He was the one who brought them out here. He speared each of them with a hard look. "Fifteen minutes," he said "or we leave without you."

"We need more time to pack and change," Jocelyn protested, drawing herself up and crossing her arms across her more than ample breasts. "One hour."

"You heard me, Jocelyn. Fifteen minutes." He turned and walked off, ignoring the cries of protest from all three.

****

Tall cottonwoods along the river gave way to stands of pines, spruce and elms as Bo, Henry, and the rest of their group left the meandering Missouri for the gloom of the forest. Though the sun was overhead, the forest blocked both light and warmth.

Tipping his head back, Bo couldn't believe how tall the trees were. The canopy of the forest seemed to go on forever. At first, he felt closed in. Thick trunks surrounded them, most wider than a man's body.

And the darkness. He'd never have believed how dark it could be in the forest. Now, he understood why so many spooky stories were set in a forest. He shivered. Going from the warmth of the sun to deep shade felt like he'd crossed over into a new world. He wished he hadn't taken off his sheepskin-lined jacket.

He'd spent his entire life living on open ranch land

where the sea of grass, with an occasional oak, spread out as far as the eye could see. His land was exposed, open. When the sun beat down, there was no relief. If the wind decided to blast through, a person had to hold onto their hat, and if it rained, well, you got soaked through and through. But you could see in every direction for miles and miles.

But in the forest with its trees so tall one could barely see the tips, the world seemed closed in and downright secretive. No matter how far ahead he looked, giant trees the width of three large men blocked his view of what lay ahead. He glanced from side to side. It was a bit unnerving not knowing what waited in the thick brush on either side of him, not to mention behind or ahead.

The other thing that struck Bo was the cool silence. He discounted the creak of saddle or jangle of harness or the occasional animal scurrying or birdcall. For a man used to the solitude out on the range, he only now realized just how noisy his livestock could be. Out on the range, the sounds of cattle and sheep flowed across the land like honey dripping down a tree to coat everything it touched with its sweetness. And back at the house, there was the noise in the yard—banging, shouting, cursing, and laughter, or the bell at meal times, along with the constant drone of chickens, roosters, and milk cows.

Bo found this landscape both unnerving and fascinating. He rode beside Wolf, each of them leading a horse loaded with supplies. Ahead of them, two soldiers had taken point and behind him, Henry chatted with a soldier everyone called "Red Brush" due to the man's bushy red hair, bushy red beard, and bushy brows. Behind them, Jocelyn rode with her children. Two more soldiers brought up the rear, leading pack mules.

He slid a glance at the man on his right. Wolf sat tall yet relaxed on his horse, a giant black gelding. Though the man wasn't in the lead position, he looked completely at ease and in charge as he held up a hand and called out to the two soldiers. "We rest here."

Wolf dismounted and led his horse and the packhorse between two groupings of pines to a small watering hole. Bo followed. When the horses had their fill, the two men moved back to allow the others access.

"I've never been in a forest before," he began, attempting to strike up conversation with the quiet man. "Never seen one. Not sure I like it."

Wolf smiled. "There are areas in this land where there are no trees, where the land is a rolling plain that stretches as far as the eye can see. My people live on the plains, and in the past, we used to follow great herds of buffalo. But there are thick forests, up in the hills. I cannot imagine a land with no trees, though I do remember the town where I was schooled. There were large spaces where the trees had been cut to make room for buildings and homes."

"You went to school?" That bit of news surprised Bo. While he hadn't found Wolf uneducated or coarse as Red or several other soldiers traveling with them, he hadn't thought the man had had formal schooling.

Wolf grimaced. "I was schooled in the ways of the White man. My grandmother saw that I would live with one foot in each world."

Before he could ask what Wolf meant, Jocelyn limped over to join them. "I hope we are stopping for the night," she said to Wolf, adopting a haughty attitude ruined by pine needles sticking out of her mousy brown hair and a smear of dirt on one cheek.

"No. Just long enough to water and rest the horses." He turned away.

Jocelyn slapped her hands onto her ample hips. "Now wait a minute, my dear man. My children and I aren't used to riding day in and day out."

Wolf turned his head and shrugged. "Take all the time you want. Just follow the trail and catch up when you're rested." He smiled. "I wouldn't take too long. We head north in less than a mile."

Before his stepmother launched into one of her tirades, Bo held up his hand. "Get your horse, Jocelyn."

Jocelyn's belligerence melted into the smile of a loving mother. "I'm so tired, Bo. Be a sweet boy and take care of our animals. Poor Margaret isn't doing well."

Bo folded his arms across his chest and shook his head. "No. You were told at the beginning that this wasn't a pleasure ride and that you were responsible for your mounts and your share of chores. You heard Wolf. Either get moving or catch up when you feel able to continue." He watched Jocelyn's sweetness harden like an egg fried on a hot stone.

"You always were an arrogant bastard, Bodil," Jocelyn's said bitterly.

"And you, my dear stepmother, have always been a conniving bitch."

Watching her storm off gave him some measure of satisfaction. Every day was filled with her manipulations. Just like when she'd been married to his father. "What are you after, Jocelyn," he murmured. His money? The ranch she'd hated? Her black, conniving heart wanted something out of him and wanted it bad enough to be miserable on the trail instead of waiting for him to return.

He put her out of his mind and rejoined Wolf at the horses where he fished his jacket out of his bedroll and slipped his arms inside.

"Would you leave her behind?" Wolf asked softly.

"What I want to do and what I would actually do are two different things." He arched his brows. "And you?"

"I believe I echo your sentiments," he said as he watched the two women leading their horses to the spring of fresh water. "Good thing she doesn't call either of our bluffs." His lips twitched when Jocelyn's horse decided she was going too slow and yanked at the reins. Jocelyn slipped and landed on her well-rounded behind.

Bo coughed to cover his laughter.

"You do not like this woman who is your mother."

"Stepmother," he corrected. "She married my father when I was fifteen and stayed less than two years. Made my life hell. Didn't like her then, like her less now."

"Yet she is here with you." Wolf lifted a brow.

Bo grimaced. "Wasn't about to let her stay at the ranch while I was gone. Got enough problems there, and she's after something. She hated the ranch when she lived there and left after my father refused to sell. Been five years, and suddenly she's back, playing the loving mother."

He blew out a long frustrated breath then followed Wolf to take their place behind the soldiers. When all the horses had been watered and rested, and they were once again picking their way through the forest, Bo edged closer to Wolf.

"Tell me about your place." He couldn't imagine a ranch in a forest.

Wolf, wearing a buckskin shirt with long fringe that swayed with the movements of the horse, took his time answering. His voice was soft with memories. "My great-grandfather was a trapper as was my grandfather. One day my grandfather found a woman who'd been abandoned in the wilderness. Her name was Emily. They had a little girl, Sarah. After her father died, Sarah got herself into a bit of trouble. My father, a Lakota warrior, *rescued* her."

"Rescued?" Bo caught the slight emphasis on that one word.

Wolf grinned. "The family story is a bit more exciting. My father said he captured her, she said she agreed to go with him for safety." He sighed wistfully. "They are both gone now, but growing up, there was no doubt they were very much in love." He glanced at Bo. "She was given the name of White Wind by my grandmother. Her hair was as blonde as Beth Ann's."

Bo nodded and realized that from what he'd seen and heard so far, Henry's granddaughters were not being raised by wild savages. "Your family continues to raise horses?"

Wolf laughed softly. "No. Just my wife and I. We also run a boarding school for the children of my people. The rest of my family roams the land as our ancestors have since the beginning of time."

"So Beth Ann lives at your ranch?" He held out a hand to brush a low branch out of his face.

"No. She prefers to live as the Lakota. This time of the year, they travel far to the west to our winter camp."

Slightly confused, Bo realized Wolf and his family were not what he'd expected, based on everything he'd learned before setting out and the stories from the soldiers at the fort. "You said she and Jane were at your place."

Wolf nodded.

After a moment of silence, Bo sighed. "You going to make me ask?"

For the first time since setting out from the fort five days ago, Wolf chuckled. "All right. Each winter, my tribe and one other, bring their children to my…ranch is a good word. No one's called it that before. They arrived, including Beth Ann and Jane right before I left for the fort. By the time we get back, my people will have left."

His deliberate pause and sidelong look kept Bo quiet. He waited, understanding that the man spoke when and how he wanted.

"Jane always stays to help with the children and their schooling, but Beth Ann always remains with her adoptive parents. This year is different. My entire family is staying." He shrugged. "A reunion of sorts."

Wolf spurred his horse forward up a rise in the trail and around a fallen tree. The two soldiers in front had ridden on ahead to scout the trail.

Bo, following behind Wolf, still had no clear idea of where they were going or what they'd find but decided he'd just have to be patient. The man said Beth Ann and Jane were at his ranch, and that was all that mattered. He glanced back to see Henry engaged in deep conversation with one of soldiers.

Farther back, Jocelyn's strident voice broke the peaceful atmosphere as she picked at Matt and he snipped back. As soon as the trail widened, the soldiers paired back up, and a few minutes later, Margaret rode up beside Bo.

"Ma is fit to be tied, and Matt isn't making things easier. You don't mind if I ride with you, do you, Bodil?" She adjusted the bonnet on her head

Bo shrugged. He felt sorry for her. She was the brown mouse trying not to be noticed yet eager for any crumb of attention. She also tried to be the peacekeeper between mother and son.

"Suit yourself, Margaret." He waited a few moments. "Why is she here, and don't feed me that bull that she just wants to get to know me or for us all to be one happy family."

"Bodil!" Margaret protested his crude language. Under his hard stare, she shrugged. "You know her well, Bo. I'm sorry for the way she treated you and kept us apart when we lived at the ranch. We could have been friends when our parents were married."

Reaching over, Bo grabbed her reins and led her horse up a rise in the landscape. Dried pine needles formed a thick blanket, and the horses had to scramble up to firmer ground. He handed the reins back as he thought back to those two, miserable years when he'd welcomed siblings in his life. The hurt that followed when Jocelyn made it clear she wasn't going to let his "rough ways and crude manners" rub off on her perfect little society offspring had driven him away. He'd spent each day, all day, out on the ranch, and at night, he'd kept to his room.

"Bodil?"

Bo didn't respond. What could he say? That part of their lives was done and over. He wanted to know what she wanted of him now.

Margaret sighed so soft, he barely caught it. "I think she'd like us to get to know each other, Bodil."

"Why?"

Margaret drew in a deep breath. "She wants *you* to get to know *me*." She fiddled with the ribbons of her bonnet. "I'm supposed to make you want me." She attempted to laugh, but it came out a pitiful mix of shame and sob.

Bo, caught by surprise, nearly fell off his horse when he whipped around to stare at Margaret to see if she was serious. Of all the schemes his stepmother could hatch, he'd never have suspected she'd toss her darling at his feet. "You're joking."

He winced when Margaret stared down at her hands. "Don't have to be mean, Bo. After all, we're not related."

Keeping his own gaze focused on the trees, the nonexistent trail Wolf led them on, he shook his head. "Don't wish to hurt you, Margaret. You were always sweet and nice. You deserve someone who will love you and coddle you in luxury."

Hearing a sniff, he swallowed his groan. High above his head, the cry of an eagle sounded shrill. He wished he could fly away from the situation he had no one but himself to blame for. He finally glanced at Margaret, and for the first time during the entire trip, she met his gaze with an adoring look.

"I've always wanted you, Bodil. But Ma made it clear she had better plans for me." She sighed. "I don't want to marry some old man who has lots of money.

That's what she wants. I want to marry someone who knows what he wants and goes after it. I've always admired and looked up to you, Bodil, and when Mama said I should try to make you love me, well, it wasn't hard to agree."

Bo narrowed his eyes and swatted at a fly. "What does she get out of it? You marry me, she returns to the ranch, and then what? Money?"

Margaret looked humiliated. "I told her it wouldn't work, but it sounded so romantic, like a fairy tale."

"She was told a long time ago she wouldn't get the ranch. My pa was smart."

"Bodil," Margaret said reproachfully. "She just wants security. Life has been hard on her since she left your father. I think she regrets leaving him."

That was utter bullshit, but Bo kept his opinion to himself. Behind them, Jocelyn and Matt continued to argue. Margaret sighed again. "Don't hold this against me, Bo. Sometimes I think I'd do just about anything to get away from those two." She turned her soft, baby blue eyes to him, silently begging him to understand and not hate her. "I guess I best go back. Think about it—us—Bodil. I'd make a good wife for you." Her voice broke as she pulled off to the side and waited for her brother and mother to catch up.

He urged his horse forward. Wolf dropped back. Though the man's attention was on the jungle of trees and shrubs in front of them, Bo knew he'd heard every word.

"She's a pretty woman," Wolf said, slanting him an amused look.

"Yeah. Always was sweet and quiet" Bo pulled his hat off and swiped his arm across his forehead, then set the John B back in place. "She'll please some man." He glanced back and noticed Jocelyn had turned her bad temper onto Margaret. "Poor kid. Feel sorry for her but not enough to make my stepmother my mother-in-law. My life would be hell."

Wolf chuckled. "Gotta agree with you, there." He pointed. "Just about home."

He led the way between two thick-trunked trees. As though opening a doorway, the landscape changed. The forest gave way to mostly cleared land to make room for large, fenced pastures with stands of trees to offer shade and relief from rain and snow.

Instead of cutting down everything, Wolf had carved his ranch out of the forest. Trees wider than his mount's girth lined the pastures and smaller corrals. The smaller enclosures on his left were empty, but on his right, one fenced pasture held a dozen or more mares, along with a handful of youngsters, ranging from those born that season to half a dozen one and two-year olds.

Drawing in a deep breath, the smell of barnyards, animals, and wood smoke made Bo homesick for his own spread. The only difference between his and Wolf's was the pungent aroma of pine trees and rotting vegetation. He tipped his head slightly. In the distance, he heard the sounds of children.

"The two year olds will be moved and broken over the winter," Wolf commented as the young horses ran alongside the newcomers, following the curve of the split-log railings.

They passed another corral farther down that held several geldings, their tails lazily swishing flies off their backs. Beyond them, a small barn housed two stallions, each with its own pen on either side of the enclosure. Bo wouldn't have minded if they'd stopped so he could admire the magnificent animals, one black with a white star, the other a brown and white paint.

After riding past several small outbuildings and a large barn, the line of trees on either side of him and Wolf thickened, standing trunk-to-trunk, reminding him of sentries about to block their passage. Above his head, spreading branches formed a tunnel overhead. As soon as they rode beneath, it was as though a gate had opened onto a magical world. Sounds and color assaulted his senses.

Another shrill cry echoed overhead. Now that they were out of the forest, he saw two dark birds soaring high in an incredibly deep, blue sky that seemed darker and richer than the sky above his own ranch.

His gaze drifted down to a large grassy meadow spread out before him. It was surrounded on two sides by log cabins. One was the length of the large barn and just as tall. Several cone-shaped tipis formed a third side. Tall trees behind the buildings and tipis stood guard, hovering over the homes of man like a mother hovering over her child.

And children. Bo had to stop to take it all in, for he'd never seen so many children of all ages in one place. Some sat in groups on the grass, others at long, wooden tables, and still others were running every which way.

Each child was dressed as any ranch or town child dressed, all but one boy leaning against one of the log cabins with his arms crossed in front of him. He wore what Bo figured was his native dress, which was not enough to be considered dressed in his mind

"Not what I expected," he said finally. "This could be a Sunday Social, except that I don't see many adults."

"While here, the children are expected to adopt the ways of the white man in dress and schooling." Wolf held Bo's gaze. "These children might look like children raised in your culture, but they are Lakota in their hearts and minds. The boys hunt and train as warriors, but they also learn to shoot rifles, break and train horses, and even take part in plowing our gardens."

"And the girls?" Bo was more than impressed. He was amazed.

"As is normal among our women, they tan the hides and use the skins to make clothing, but they also learn to sew what they wear here as well as the clothing the boys wear. They are also taught to cook and bake in the way of the white man and can food for the winter."

Bo lifted a brow. "Why? I mean, knowledge is a good thing, but I've never heard of this."

"Long ago, my grandmother saw in her visions that our ways would die out with the arrival of the white man. She said it would fall to me to teach our children to live in both worlds. Each year, I was sent away to boarding school." He grimaced. "I hated every moment of those nine months away from my family. I was not allowed to speak my tongue, dress in the way of my people, or worship the Great Spirit or Father Sky or Mother Earth. Any time I disobeyed the rules, I was beaten."

Bo studied Wolf, remembered the smacks of the ruler applied to his own hand in school, and couldn't imagine how a boy from such a different world survived. "So you decided to provide better."

Wolf nodded. "Here, we encourage. We do not demand or punish." He indicated the lone boy. "George Runs Fast will eventually give in. Each year, there are one or two who do not want to be here. The unspoken pressure of the others will bring him in line. And yes, each child has an American name as well. If any of our children need to live among the cities and towns closing in on the Lakota, they will be able to do so. Whether they are accepted?" He shrugged. "That is another matter."

A loud cry drew Bo's attention. A trim, black-and-gray-haired woman ran toward them. He lifted his brows. She wore men's breeches and a plaid shirt.

"You're back." She stopped short when she saw soldiers and strangers and sent Wolf a questioning glance.

"Papa!"

Following the excited cry, a horde of children were suddenly there, jumping up and down. His horse sidestepped but calmed with a touch from Bo. He dismounted and held the reins firmly.

Wolf dismounted, then hugged and greeted each child. He hoisted the two youngest into his arms. "We have guests," he needlessly announced to the woman.

"I have eyes, Husband." She came forward as everyone dismounted. "I'm Jessie Cartier, Wolf's wife. These are our children, or most of them." Her voice, while not unfriendly, seemed reserved, and her eyes held a wealth of distrust.

She pointed as her children fell in line, eldest to youngest. "Sarah. Her twin brother, Sam, is out with the other older boys, hunting. This is Anabelle, Emily,

Mary, and Martha. Noah and the baby are asleep. John, Laura, and Barbara Ellen, our adopted children are in the schoolhouse, preparing lessons." She frowned and glanced around. "I have no idea where Mark is. Since losing his parents, he's become a bit of a loner."

Bo tipped his hat and smiled. He didn't want to start out with any hostility. "Nice to meet you, Ma'am, and your children, though I don't think I'll remember all those names." He winked at the children, and they giggled. He motioned to Henry who'd come up beside him. "This is Henrik Ricard Svensson."

. "Nice to meet you, Ma'am." Henry tipped his hat, revealing his white hair with faint traces of pale yellow running throughout.

Bo caught the knowing look that passed between husband and wife and decided it best to get the reason for their visit out into the open. "Henry is here to see Beth Ann and Jane. He is their grandfather."

Henry smiled a bit uncertainly when Jessie only nodded. He reached into his pocket, drew out a small cloth bag, and looked to Jessie. "Can I offer them a sweet?"

Jessie narrowed her deep, green eyes and raised her brow. "Only if you have enough for *all* the children."

Henry nodded. "Yes, Ma'am. I have more than enough."

Jessie wrinkled her nose. "Make it Jessie."

Wolf put his arm around his wife and nodded to Henry. "The children will swarm on you like flies on dung."

Jessie jabbed her elbow into Wolf's ribs. "What a thing to say. Bees to honey is much nicer sounding."

Shifting away from his wife, Wolf lifted a brow.

"Nicer perhaps, but mine's more accurate."

Jessie just shook her head and motioned her children to come forward to get their sweet.

Bo watched as each child reached into the bag for a treat, then thanked Henry. As Wolf warned, the moment their children made it known there were sweets to be had, the rest of the children swarmed, and Bo had to admit, Wolf's description was far more accurate. Even George Runs Fast had come over, though he held back.

Jessie made sure each child waited their turn and thanked Henry.

Bo took his time surveying Wolf and Jessie's ranch. He wasn't sure *ranch* was a term to fit what was here, but it worked in his mind. Out by two of the cabins, he spotted several adults sitting on long, wooden benches, watching. He scanned each one, then shifted his gaze to the line of tipis, searching for Henry's—

Holy shit! He just about tripped over a small child in his shock. There they were. Beth Ann and Jane. Though he knew they were here, that he'd see them, it felt as though he were seeing ghosts from the past as he stared at two blonde women standing in front of a tipi, one combing her fingers through her long, blonde hair.

Even though Henry's man had said one of the girls resembled Elizabeth, Bo hadn't believed it, figured the man was simply stringing Henry on. That had been his deciding factor in agreeing to leave his ranch during this difficult time. He wanted to protect his godfather.

Had Henry's man been lying, had he cooked up a scheme with Wolf to get money from Henry, the two would have faced Bodil's fury—dead or not. But the dead man hadn't exaggerated, and Wolf hadn't lied. Henry finally found his girls.

Elizabeth's girls were alive. Time fell away. It didn't matter that they had been three and six the last time he'd seen them, and him a gangly sixteen year old. One glance at the two women, and he knew who was who. Jane, as a young child, had been small and petite, like her mother, while Beth Ann had been taller than most girls her age.

He'd bet his ranch that the short, doll-like woman was Jane, for she reminded him of Elizabeth—perfect pale features, soft blue eyes, and perfect manners in a perfectly frail and delicate body. Henry's man had said Jane was the spittin' image of her ma. He hadn't lied or exaggerated.

The other woman also shared her mother's good looks, but there wasn't anything frail or delicate about her. She paced, spoke to her sister, and stared across the grassy meadow at the group of strangers. No doubt, he and the rest of his party were the topic of conversation between the sisters.

The taller one, Beth Ann, wound strands of hair around her fingers, a nervous habit he remembered when she'd been six and upset over the fighting between her parents and grandfather. Her hair flowed over her shoulders and down her back like molten rays of moonlight.

A bit poetic, he thought, like the books of poetry that belonged to his mother.

Bo couldn't have looked away had his life depended on it. Everything around him muffled and dimmed. He only had eyes for Beth Ann. Even from this distance, she was more than he could have ever imagined. Gone was the gangly girl who'd been all spindly arms and legs like the fillies in the pen, who'd hounded his every move when she and her family visited.

He knew he was staring but couldn't have taken his eyes off her had someone put a gun to his head. When folks talked about a woman having a willowy figure or the graceful neck of a swan, he'd always rolled his eyes. Now he understood.

Beth Ann, tall and slender in shape, reminded him of a gorgeous, graceful swan floating through a pond turned golden at sunset. Her dress of softened deerskin fit like a glove and flowed around her calves. Her arms and legs were pale, not white and not the golden honey-brown of her sister's skin. All he could think as he stared at her was that she looked like an angel who'd returned to earth.

Jane drew his attention as she pulled on her sister's arm. Jane wore her honey-blonde hair in two long braids, and her complexion was a shade deeper than her hair. Both women glowed with health.

Women.

Not children.

So much for a wild-child who needed protection.

"I want a bath and clean clothes." Jocelyn's demands shattered the hold the women had on him, but he couldn't tear his eyes from Beth Ann.

He held up his hand, palm out when he noticed a tall, imposing man emerging from one of the tipis. He looked Indian from his leather breeches, leather shirt, and moccasins to his black-as-night hair that hung in two long braids nearly to his waist. Feathers dangled from above one ear and fluttered to his shoulders.

"Bodil!"

"Quiet! You'll just have to wait," he said, his attention on the man who radiated power.

Wolf clapped his hands. "Off with all of you." He shooed the children. He turned to Bo and Henry. "This is my brother, Chief Striking Thunder. My brother, Mr. Henrick Ricard Svensson, grandfather to Beth Ann and Jane."

"Just Henry," the man said, holding out his hand. "Don't stand on much ceremony."

Striking Thunder shook hands. "We expected your arrival."

Bo frowned. How could the man have known they were coming? Before he could ask, the chief turned his nearly black gaze on him. Bo shot out a hand. "Bodil Riker Quinn. Henry's neighbor and friend."

The chief's eyebrows shot up, and he slid a questioning glance at his brother. Wolf shrugged. Bo wondered if he'd done something wrong, but Striking Thunder took his hand and shook. Bo hadn't encountered true power often, but he knew it when he saw it and felt it. The chief was a powerful man.

"We come in peace." he said, then winced, as it sounded trite yet being in the presence of this man made him want to be sure the man understood.

Striking Thunder's lips twitched. "I know why you are here." He inclined his head. "You're welcome." He looked to the others.

There it was again. The man knew. What did he know and how? Now wasn't the time. Bo indicated his stepmother. "Jocelyn Linberg. She was once married to my father, and over there, are her children, Matt and Margaret. My stepmother insisted on accompanying us."

Striking Thunder lifted one brow. "They knew Beth Ann and Jane?"

"No. They showed up before we heard that Henry's girls had been found." Bo tried to keep his voice neutral yet he wasn't about to pretend any family affection or closeness.

Jocelyn sashayed over to Bo and smiled sweetly at the chief. "I wanted my children to spend some time with their big brother. I wasn't married long to his father, but I still consider Bodil my son." She slipped her arm into Bodil's.

Bo tried to pull away, but she tightened her grip on his arm like rattler squeezing its prey "Jocelyn—"

"I wasn't a very good mother." She pouted. "I'm trying to make up for the past." Sighing, she turned to Striking Thunder, her gaze sweeping over the man and obviously liking all she saw. "It's been such a long trip. I would love a bath and a place to rest. My daughter requires the same. We are not used to traveling for days on a horse."

Bo yanked his arm free, then gripped her arm hard. "You've waited this long. You can wait a bit longer. Go back to your children and wait for instructions." He held her furious glare until she pulled away and swished her way between horses. He turned back to the chief, returning control of the meeting.

Striking Thunder's lips twitched. "Your mother—"

"Stepmother," he corrected. "She was never a mother."

The chief acknowledged the correction with a nod of his head. "You are welcome." He glanced at the group of soldiers. "Major, thank you for seeing to the

85

safe arrival of our visitors. You may take your horses to the barn, then see Rook for a meal."

The major smiled. "Thanks, Chief. Move it, men." He led his men into the barn.

Glancing at Henry, Bo saw that his friend had spotted Beth Ann and Jane. Wolf and Striking Thunder noticed as well

Striking Thunder spoke to Henry. "I will take you and this man to see your granddaughters." He shifted his gaze to the others. "You will wait here."

Bo hid a smile. Jocelyn was furious, but even she knew enough to simply nod. Then he followed Wolf, Striking Thunder, and Henry across the grass toward the row of tipis—and Beth Ann.

Chapter Four

Beth Ann, sitting outside her tipi, heard the thundering hooves of the horses in the pastures. She lifted her head and listened. The horses only got this excited when visitors passed their corrals. Judging from the sounds of horses calling to one another, Wolf had returned, and she didn't think he'd returned alone.

According to Mattie's vision, her grandfather was with Wolf. Her throat closed up, and her heart thumped in her chest. She pulled out her locket and fisted her hand around it. She pressed her other fist to her stomach to quell the growing queasiness. "Ma, I wish you were here."

Overhead, the shrill cry of an eagle sounded liked a trumpet announcing visitors. The flock of ravens that took to the air had her standing, her sewing falling to the ground.

"*Ina!*"

Dove stepped out of the tipi, took one look at Beth Ann, and hurried over.

"Uncle Wolf has returned," Beth Ann said. "Do you think my grandfather will be with him?"

"Mattie said he would return with Wolf. If my brother is back, then your grandfather is here."

"What do I do?" Instinct made her want to pick up her babies, run into the forest, and hide until they left.

As though she knew exactly how her daughter felt,

Dove took Beth Ann's hands in her own. "You will stand tall and proud and hide your fear. You are my daughter, my little warrior."

Beth Ann drew herself up and couldn't help but smile. From day one, she'd followed Dove everywhere and had been called *little warrior*. Like Dove, she hunted, could fight with knife or without, and she faced her fears and did not run and hide. Chin up, head back, back straight, and hands at her side. *You are Dove's daughter. Remember that.*

"Good," Dove said, nodding her head in approval.

Together, mother and daughter watched as Wolf, soldiers, and a large group of strangers left the tree line. Studying the group, Beth Ann dismissed the soldiers. Her gaze roamed the rest of the strangers, searching for—

She sucked in a breath when she spotted her grandfather. Even after all this time and the fact that he now had snow-white hair instead of blonde like hers, she recognized him—his stance, his profile, and his aura of power.

"It's him," she whispered.

"Wait here," Dove said. "I'll find Jane."

Beth Ann rubbed the chill from her arms as the group dismounted. *Be brave, daughter, be brave.* Her mother's words echoed in her head.

Her sister ran up to her. "Is it him?"

Beth Ann nodded. "Yes. It's our grandfather."

Jane hugged her arm. "He's going to take us away."

"No. We do not have to go." Though she spoke firmly, her stomach fluttered. She glanced away, looking everywhere else but at the hated figure of her grandfather. Too bad she couldn't just cover her face with her hands and adopt the if-I-can't-see-you-you-can't-see-me game the twins loved and often used when greeting strangers for the first time.

"He's looking at you, Beth," Jane whispered.

She shrugged. Feeling someone watching her wasn't new. All her life, her pale hair and skin drew attention, even from those she'd lived among. She was used to it.

"Oh, there's another man. A very handsome man," her sister said.

Beth Ann panned her gaze back over the group. Wolf shifted, revealing a much younger man standing with arms crossed across his chest. She had to admit, Jane was right. He was very handsome.

Then he shifted his head, and their gazes connected. Beth Ann nearly stumbled back. His eyes were as silver as the blade of a knife, and when a spear of light shifted over his face, they sparked.

Staring at him, she realized that *he* was looking at *her* just as intently.

And it hit her like a thunderbolt. "Bo," she whispered, shocked. Her body pricked and tingled from the top of her head to her toes. She'd never thought to see the boy next door again.

Bo who used to tease her mercilessly. Bo, trapped between boy and man who'd listened to her fears and dried her tears when the fighting between her parents and grandfather had become too much. Bo who had made her laugh or made her so mad she wanted to scream.

He removed his hat and dipped his head at her. Sunlight glinted off his head, bathing him in a reddish-gold light, as his hair was neither brown, nor red. Not even the pale golden shade of her sister's hair. His hair reminded her of the hide of a deer or beaver—many colors that formed its own unique shade.

Unconsciously, she reached up and threaded her fingers through her own hair. Of everyone in that group of strangers, it was the old man who should hold her attention, for he was the threat to the life she lived. Instead, Bo held her gaze with his.

A memory of a family gathering flitted across her mind. The two families had been gathered outside, a holiday celebration. She'd been a bit peeved at Bo for ditching her, and during the meal, she'd announced to all that when she was grown, she was going marry Bo.

Everyone had laughed and thought she'd been cute, except Bo who'd excused himself. Of course, she'd gone after him.

A sigh escaped. Her memories and childhood love of the boy next door had helped her survive captivity with the crow as she dreamed that he'd come find her. Later, during the long, lonely nights of her miserable marriage, she'd thought of Bo and wondered what kind of man he'd become.

Her body hummed with awareness—and need. For the first time since losing her husband, she felt desire…and desired? Yes, definitely desired. His gaze roamed over her body. There was no doubt in her woman's mind he was not only stunned by the sight of her, but that he liked what he saw.

Mattie's vision. Two men. Choices.

A shiver snaked down her spine, and she felt cold—even with the sunlight falling on her—and heat spreading awareness inside her. She scanned the rest of the strangers, her gaze sweeping over the two women. Was the younger one his wife? The older one married to her grandfather?

Her stomach clenched, and the air left her lungs as though a fist had been driven into her gut. *Please don't let him be spoken for.* She didn't think she could bear losing the dreams that centered on the one person who'd gotten her through so many unhappy times.

Choices.

What were her choices? Stay with her people or return to life with her grandfather? She dropped her arms back to her sides. There was no decision. This was her place, her life. She closed her eyes and willed her wildly beating heart to calm.

"Here they come," Jane squeaked as she grabbed her sister's arm.

A quick glance over her shoulder confirmed their mother had returned to her tipi, and Beth Ann's young brother and sisters were sitting quietly. Dove, with one hand on her young son's shoulders, nodded encouragingly. It was all Beth Ann needed.

"Calm yourself, Jane, and stand tall and proud. We are Lakota, and we will make our mother—both our mothers—proud." Her gaze followed the progress of her uncles, her grandfather, and the silver-eyed Bo as they headed toward her and Jane.

Beth Ann studied her grandfather, watched him skirt her son, his grandson. Not only did she recognize him, but images from her early childhood flooded her mind. Her grandfather shouting at her father, her mother leaving his study in tears, then the huge fight when her father announced they were heading west.

Her stomach felt hollow, and for a moment, she

was a child, hearing those ugly words hurled from one adult to another. She'd been afraid, remembered something crashing to the floor. After the fight, her grandfather had slammed out of the house, but the fighting between her parents continued.

She didn't remember a lot after that. Just that her father had bundled them all into a wagon and they'd left the ranch for good before her grandfather returned. The pain and anger that came from remembering stiffened her resolve. If not for the man coming toward her, perhaps her parents would still be alive. Anger and resentment crowded out her fear.

Striking Thunder's dark eyes swept over her, and as though pleased with what he saw, he gave a small nod. "Child." He held out his hand.

The affection in his voice eased the tightness in her chest and allowed her to breathe. At eighteen, with two babes, her uncle was letting her know she was still under his care and protection.

She stepped forward. "I know why they are here, Uncle," she said, staring bravely at her grandfather.

"Do you recognize these men?"

Beth Ann took her time. "It's been a long time…"

Her grandfather took one small step forward. "Beth Ann." His voice low and gruff. "You have your mother's eyes." Tears rolled into her grandfather's white beard, and he had to clear his throat twice before he could speak. "My man was right. Jane is the spittin' image of my dear, sweet Lizzie, and you have her eyes."

Her grandfather's voice triggered more memories, painful memories of the time she'd been held captive by the Crow, and the day her mother sacrificed herself to allow Jeremy and Striking Thunder and the other warriors time to get her and Jane to safety.

"Child?" Striking Thunder prompted her gently.

Glancing at her uncle, she nodded. "He is my grandfather." Tears and anger threatened, but she refused to show weakness. To give herself time to soothe her aching heart, she slowly turned her gaze to Bo. His eyes were a violet-gray, like the edges of a storm cloud that had yet to swallow the sun. She scanned the rest of his features. He was achingly familiar, and at the same time, very different. The boy-man of her memory was now all man. He'd filled out, grown taller, and his face had lost the softness of boyhood.

But his eyes had not changed, and they regarded her with an intense, yet unreadable expression. He removed his hat. "Hello, Bethy. Remember me?"

"Boo." The childhood nickname slipped out. Her earliest memories were of him jumping out and scaring her to make her laugh and giggle, but as she got older, he'd tried scaring her to make her mad so she'd stop dogging his heels whenever their families got together. He'd tolerated her, tormented her, and teased her, but he'd also made her laugh.

Bo grinned. "Forgot you used to call me that." He rocked back on his heels, speaking to everyone. "When she first began to talk, that's what she called me. Boo instead of Bo. Last time I saw you was in our barn, rolling in the hay with a new litter of puppies." He paused. "I was sixteen, and you'd just turned six."

Her eyes went wide as the happy memory returned, the first happy memory she'd recalled of her old life. "You said I could pick any puppy I wanted for my birthday." She glared at her grandfather. "I never got my puppy," she said, her voice hard. "We left before they were ready to leave their mother. We left because of you." She tipped her chin, daring him to deny her accusation.

Henry met Beth Ann's accusing gaze. "I've regretted that day every day of my life. When I came home and found you all gone, I set out for St. Joe to bring you all back, but you were gone." He stared between Jane and Beth Ann, his eyes unfocused as though he were back in the past. "When I learned your parents had been killed by Indians, I looked for you. I never stopped. Believe me, I've paid—"

"Crow," Beth Ann interrupted, gripping her fingers tightly. "We were taken by the Crow. They killed my father, and later, my mother." She didn't want to hear his excuses. She just wanted him gone. "What do you want? Why are you here?"

Henry drew himself up. "I came to take you home."

Though she knew why he'd come, dread the size of a fist lodged in her throat. "No." She cleared her throat. Her voice sounded worse than a barking deer.

"Beth Ann. You're family. You and Jane are all I have. I—"

She held out one hand, palm out. "I have a family. My life is here, and you cannot force me to leave."

Before Henry could reply, Bo cleared his throat. "No one is going to force you to do anything you don't want to do."

Without taking her eyes off her grandfather, Beth Ann drew herself up. "Good, because I refuse to go anywhere with him." She glared at her grandfather.

"Our parents are dead because of you. As you can see, I'm alive, I'm happy, and I'm staying. Go home."

"Beth Ann."

She sighed at the quiet rebuke from her mother. "I'm sorry, but I want nothing to do with him."

Bo, aware of Henry shrinking into himself, had had enough. His hat beat against his thigh. "Beth, your grandfather, whatever his faults, and yes, he has many, loves you and your sister. He never gave up hope that you were alive, even when everyone told him you were dead, or worse, that you'd be unfit to return to his world." He jammed the Stetson back onto his head. "I watched him come alive each time news that blonde children were spotted by trappers, soldiers, or those heading west, and when those reports proved false, a part of him died. He is my friend. He is generous, always willing to help those in need and often puts the needs of others ahead of his own. The least you can do is spend some time with him before you judge him." Softening his voice, he added, "Your grandfather is not the same man he was when you were six, and at that age, you weren't old enough to fully understand the problems between your parents and grandfather."

Beth Ann put her hands on her hips and glared at both men. "I understood enough. My grandfather was angry and shouting all the time, and he made my mother cry." She'd been old enough to know her mother had been deeply unhappy living with her father.

Sighing, Bo shook his head. "You got it wrong, Bethy."

Henry put his hand on Bo's arm. "Leave it, Bo—"

"No. I won't have her blaming you. Let her hear the truth, then she can make her mind up based on the facts." Bo glanced from Beth to Jane, then back to Beth. "Truth is, your father was an arrogant bastard who couldn't keep his pecker pocketed. He went from one woman to another and made your mother's life hell."

Beth Ann gasped. "You're lying," she said, fighting the urge to cover her ears. "You're making this up to protect *him*." She jutted her chin toward her grandfather.

Spreading his legs and crossing his arms across his chest, Bo regarded her for a long, tense moment. "I never lied to you, Beth Ann, and I have no reason to do so now. I adored your mother, grew up with her, much the way we grew up together. We were friends and stayed friends. Even though she was ten years my senior, we talked. She confided that she wanted to leave your father, but he threatened to take you girls if she did."

"Bo." Henry raised his voice.

"Nope. I'm not gonna sit here and let her blame you for something you had no control over. You can tell her or I will."

"That's not true," Beth Ann whispered.

"I'm sorry, Beth. I don't agree with Bo, but maybe his way is the best. We don't have a lot of time." Henry ran his hands through his hair, creating deep furrows. "I *was* angry back then, but never at you or Jane or your mother. I hated what your father was doing to all of you. I kicked him out once when he struck Lizzie. You were two and your mother with child, carrying Jane." He rubbed the back of his neck, looked up at the sky as though seeking strength then back to Beth. "Your father came back during the night and took you from your bed. Took us three days before we found him holed up with one of his whor—women. He refused to let your mother have you unless I agreed to let him return and to do as he pleased."

His hand touched the gun he wore. "Should've shot the bastard—I'll not apologize for my language—but I agreed, as long as he never struck my girls or took them from the ranch."

Beth Ann wiped the tears from her face. Could he be telling the truth? She just didn't know. "You fought that last night." White Dove's arms wrapped around her shoulders.

Henry sighed. "Your father stole ranch money to buy a wagon and supplies to head west. Told him to go, told him I'd give him enough money to start new, but he wouldn't leave my girls." He closed his eyes. "I left. Rode into town to get the sheriff, planned to have your father arrested and charged for stealing. But when we got back, you were all gone."

Jeremy, who'd arrived with the twins in his arms, handed one to Dove, then stood on the other side of Beth Ann, with Jane between them. He nodded to the two men, then glanced down at his daughter by choice. "You were a child and would not have understood everything going on."

Beth Ann's head and heart felt both bruised and confused. She was overwhelmed, her mind trying to take in all that she'd learned from both men. Of the two, she believed Bo. He'd never lied to her, had never been mean, and most of the time, he'd indulged her in whatever she wanted. But could she believe the man he'd become?

"Mama." Her daughter reached for her, and Beth

Ann took her into her arms.

Henry eyed the babies with wide, watery eyes. "Are—are these your children?"

She nodded. "This is Katarina Kimilmela. She is very shy."

Tears in his eyes, Henry stared at the little girl. "You named her after your mother?"

Beth Ann thought of her mother, of Elizabeth Katarina Landon. "We don't speak the name of the dead aloud, but I wanted her to carry my mother's name. We call her Little Kat or Kimi. Her Lakota name means Butterfly."

"That is beautiful, and I couldn't be more pleased or honored." Glancing at the other child, Henry lifted a brow. "And your son?"

Beth Ann shifted uncomfortably, horribly embarrassed. "His Lakota name is Tokota, which means Friend With Everyone." She rubbed noses with her daughter, refusing to look at the others.

"Does he have an English name as well?"

"Yes," Beth Ann mumbled.

Henry frowned. "If you named him after your father, there is no reason to be ashamed or worried that I'd be angry."

Sighing, seeing no way out of telling the two men what she'd named her son, she lifted her head. "I didn't name him after my father. Part of me wanted to do so, but something inside me refused. Nor did I name him after his own father for he went to the Spirit World before their birth."

She glanced at Bo and stared into those silvery-violet eyes. "His English name is Riker."

Bo's eyes went wide, his jaw dropped, and he

stared at her as though she'd grown a second head. "You named your son after me?" His voice sounded clogged with shock and emotion.

Silence fell, broken by the babble of the twins. Beth Ann wanted to run into the forest and hide. When she'd chosen to name her son after Bo, she'd never thought to see him again. Those childhood memories with him had been her only happy ones, aside of those with her mother and Jane.

"I am honored, Beth. His voice was thick with emotion, and he tapped his Stetson against his thigh.

She sighed. "I never imagined I'd ever see you again. Whenever I remembered my mother, I also remembered you, the boy next door who was kind. I wanted to honor those good memories."

If she was lying—and oh boy, was she—she was only lying to herself. Her memories of Bo and the hero-status she'd elevated him to over the years were her own, and she didn't plan to share them.

At that moment, Kimi reached over and poked her brother in the arm. "Boo." She giggled.

Riker giggled back, covered his eyes, and copied his sister. Together, the toddlers burst into laughter.

Her checks heated. Could this get any worse?

Bo's eyes twinkled in that old, familiar way he had when he was about to tease her, but he just shook his head. "Words fail me."

"I got enough for the both of us," Henry said. "I was afraid you wouldn't remember me, Beth Ann."

Beth Ann might have been confused about many things at the moment, but she knew one absolute truth. She was not leaving her family. Her real family. She kept her eyes on her grandfather. "None of this changes anything. I will not leave."

Henry glanced from her, to Jane, to his great grandchildren. "I can't lose you again." He looked miserable, determined, and as stubborn as a mule. "I won't."

"Henry—"

Henry rounded on Bo. "Damn it, I know what I promised, Bo. And I'll keep that promise, but I can't just turn around and leave. Not now."

Jeremy held his hand out to stop Beth Ann from speaking. "Perhaps it is time to get to know your grandfather as an adult, Daughter."

"He won't be here long enough for me to get to know him, and I will not leave. I am happy where I am."

Striking Thunder lifted a brow. "I am not sure that is true, child."

Beth Ann opened her mouth to protest. Of course, she was happy, but her uncle held up a hand.

"I fear that because of what happened to you, Jane, and your mother, you are afraid to step out into the world and find your place. You seek safety and security, yet there are times when we have to take risks to become the person we are meant to be."

Holding her daughter tightly, Beth Ann fought tears. "You would send me away?" Her blood pounded in her ears and chest, and her throat burned and tightened. If her chief ordered her to go, she'd have no choice but to leave.

"That is not what he said, Daughter," Jeremy's gaze held his brother-in-law's, his expression letting him know that no one was forcing Beth Ann or Jane to leave.

"I would never send her away. She is family and a member of our tribe." Striking Thunder met and held Beth Ann's gaze. "Consider who we are and what is important to us. And to you."

As Beth Ann stared into her uncle's intense black eyes, she knew he was right. He was a wise man, even if she didn't like it at times. Like now. Knowing he expected a response, though he'd asked no question, she sighed. "Family is important to us, to me."

"We cannot choose wisely if we deny ourselves knowledge. How can you decide your future without knowing your past?" He turned his attention to the two white men. "Are you willing to remain and give your granddaughters time to get to know you?"

Henry didn't hesitate. "Yes."

Bo frowned. "How long?"

The chief considered. "Two months."

"Two months?" Beth Ann's gaze shot to Bo's. How could she bear to be around him for that long, knowing he'd ride back out of her life?

To her relief, Bo shook his head. "Too long. Have to get back to my ranch—"

Henry slapped Bo on the back and grinned like a man given a new lease on life. "Your ranch is in good hands, Bo." He addressed the chief, but his eyes, moist with unshed tears, held Beth Ann's. "We will stay."

"At the end of the two months, you will accept the decisions made by Beth Ann and Jane?" Jeremy's voice held doubt.

Beth Ann had her own doubts. No matter what Bo said, her grandfather was a stubborn man.

Bo looked at Beth Ann. "Yes, we will abide by your daughter's decisions." His gaze shifted to Jane, then back to Beth Ann. He elbowed Henry.

Staring at his granddaughters, Henry didn't hesitate. "Agreed."

Striking Thunder lifted a brow. "And you, child? You will give your grandfather a fair chance?"

Beth Ann didn't want to agree, didn't want to get to know this man, and didn't want to risk changing her very comfortable and secure world. Jane slid beside her sister and reached for her hand. She didn't speak, just smiled wistfully, her pale blue eyes speaking her heart.

And that was that. She could hold out against each man gathered around her, but she could not—and would not—deny Jane the opportunity to get to know their grandfather.

"What you ask is fair, Uncle," she finally said. "We agree."

Everyone drew in a collective breath of relief. Her mother nodded approvingly, and Jane leaned against her sister.

Striking Thunder smiled, also showing his approval. "It is settled. Jane and your grandfather will share your tipi. You will live as a family while he is here."

He glanced at Wolf. "This is your place, Wolf. I leave the rest to you." He turned and walked off.

Beth Ann swallowed her groan. It was bad enough knowing her grandfather was staying, but now she had to share her tipi with him?

Wolf glanced at Henry and Bo, then to Beth Ann. "We will take care of the horses and the rest of our guests. Then your grandfather will return here. Jane, gather your belongings. You will spend your days teaching as normal, but evenings, your place is here with your family."

Grinning, Jane took off running for the two-storied school building.

Watching everyone leave, Beth Ann clung to her daughter, afraid that change had swept in, swept her off her feet, and would sweep her down a path she did not wish to take.

****

Two months. The rest of autumn and into winter before they returned home. It didn't matter that his ranch was in good hands. It wasn't in *his* hands and wouldn't be until nearly spring by the time they finished here and made the long trip home.

Wolf stopped when a young man approached with a question. Bo's boots sank into the grass, damp from a recent rain. He shifted to firmer ground. A quick glance up into the sky showed scatterings of clouds. That would soon change as the air held the promise of more rain, and the chill in the air warned that winter was well on its way.

He glanced around while the two men conversed. White Wolf's wife was standing in the doorway of what he assumed was her cabin. Another couple emerged from the cabin beside hers and made their way to a third building where smoke rose from a short chimney.

Seeing the neatness and feeling a sense of orderliness, he frowned. He was stuck here, so what the hell was he going to do for two months while Henry got reacquainted with his granddaughters?

He didn't blame his godfather for jumping at the chance to spend time with Jane and Beth Ann. No, she'd always been Beth to him, in part in his mind as a reminder of her mother whom he'd adored, and because, as a little girl, it had irritated her. He shook his head as little memories floated back. Then shoved them aside. The girls were the only family Henry had, and after so many years and disappointments, Bo was happy for Henry. But two months?

Two months that you'll have to get to know Beth as a woman.

That thought left him strangely energized. Over the years, he hadn't thought much about her. In his mind, she'd remained the young girl who both idolized and tormented him, and he, the young man who'd endured her pesky, inquisitive nature. He nearly chuckled aloud when he remembered how he'd dodged her, hidden from her, and yes, jumped out to make her scream when she'd found him.

Boo.

Yeah, he'd earned the nickname. What had started out as a game between a toddler and child had become a game between child and teen. Back then, he'd been flattered and annoyed by the six-year-old and, at the same time, oddly protective of her. But she wasn't that cute child who held the promise of grace and beauty. Little Beth Ann had grown up, and damn it, she was a woman he was attracted to. He wanted to get to know her as an adult woman.

She was beautiful with her long blonde hair, blue eyes, and tall, slim figure, but her nature drew him. He'd never gone for the simpering, submissive girls he'd endured at dances and socials. He wanted a wife who'd be a partner, not someone like Margaret who'd agree with whatever he wanted because her biggest aim was to please her husband. No. When he married, it would be to a woman who'd stand her ground, give as good as she got, and love him with passion and fire. Like his mother had loved his father.

And even thinking of Beth in that role had to be the most foolish notion he'd ever had. What good would it do? Her life was here, and his was back on his ranch. He shoved his hands in his pockets and sighed.

"I'm sorry, Bo. This wasn't part of the bargain, but I have to do it. You understand, don't you, son?"

One glance at Henry was all it took for Bo to settle his mind. His godfather looked years younger and happier than he could ever recall. Though Bo worried about what was happening at home, he figured fretting and stewing wouldn't change a thing.

"Yeah, Henry, reckon I can't blame you." He was here and committed to staying for two months. He'd make the best of it. Only a cold-hearted man would deny his godfather the chance to get to know his granddaughters. He just hoped Beth gave Henry the chance he deserved.

Impatient, Henry spoke. "If you don't mind, I'm going to go get my things." He hurried off.

Waiting for Wolf to finish his conversation, thoughts of Beth kept intruding. One thing hadn't changed. Beth still had fire in her eyes when riled, and he'd bet his last nickel, she was stubborn to boot. So much for finding a wild-child who needed protection and shielding.

Her English was as good as, if not better than, his. He had no doubt that should she return with her grandfather, she could hold her own against a growing town of nosy folk with nothing better to do than butt into other people's business.

In the short time he'd seen her, he reckoned that

Beth knew her own mind. Henry would have to win her love and earn her trust. He grimaced. He'd bet the ranch that, in his mind, now belonged to Henry instead of the bank, nothing would induce her to return to a world long forgotten and full of unhappy memories.

Even if she grew to accept or hopefully love Henry, he suspected it all boiled down to one undeniably fact. She was happy. She had family who loved her, children, and a life that obviously agreed with her.

And those children had grandparents.

No, Beth didn't need a husband to protect her, though with two young 'uns, she could still benefit from having a husband who would love and support her.

Bo frowned, realizing he wasn't opposed to courting her, even if his chances at winning her heart were slim to none. But he wouldn't do it for Henry. Or to get his ranch free and clear. Beth had the right to choose the life she wanted, and if he couldn't fulfill his obligations to Henry, he'd just have to work out a plan to pay Henry back for the ranch. But he had no regrets. Henry had at last found his girls, and knowing his godfather would now rest easy was a gift to them all.

Threading his way around children and teens, Bo eyed the sturdy fences and buildings. There was pride in the layout, the neat borders that kept forest from taking over and in the gleaming coats of the horses in the large fenced pastures.

A bell rang from one large cabin. Immediately, the children stopped what they were doing and ran for the tables. He liked the happy chatter, the loud booming voice of the man bringing out a large platter of food. He recalled his own school days and remembered that he hadn't been all that fond of learning and had ditched school in favor of tossing a line in the creek.

Hearing sounds of a stream off to his left, he grinned. How long had it been since he'd allowed himself the luxury of a day in the shade of a tree, the river flowing and a fishing pole in his hands? Looked like he'd have more than enough time and opportunity so he just might indulge himself.

But not every day. He addressed Wolf as soon as he was free. "I'm not one to sit on my backside when there's work to be done. Hope you can use some help around here."

Wolf turned his head, his eyes glinting. "To earn your keep?"

"One can only spend so much time with a rod and line." He shrugged. "I have a ranch of my own. I'm used to working sunup to sundown."

"Ever broken a horse?" They were now back with the others.

Bo grinned. "Ain't no one better. Broke my first one the day I turned sixteen. Present from my pa. Had to train him from the get-go. He busted my arm and twisted my ankle something bad, but we came to an agreement. Been my companion since." He patted Samson affectionately on the rump.

After giving Bodil's mount a once-over, Wolf nodded. "Got some two-year olds in the pasture. Could use help breaking them over the winter. Even have a couple wild-caught mustangs. No one else here dumb enough to get near them."

Before Bo could let Wolf know that he was more than up to the challenge, Jocelyn marched over,

Margaret and Matt right behind her. She planted her hands on hips, her face streaked with anger. "It's about time you remembered us." She glared at Bo. "And what this about breaking horses over the winter?"

Bo grinned. Ah, sweet revenge. He might still be stuck with Jocelyn, but she was not going to like what he had to say. What a shame. "Got some good news, Jocelyn. Henry's found his granddaughters. After all these years, Beth Ann and Jane are not only alive, but are happy and well."

Jocelyn widened her eyes and pasted on a false smile. "How wonderful for them. Henry has his little family." Her smile dimmed, her eyes narrowed, and her voice hardened. "Now, we can return home. Tomorrow."

Bo pulled his hat off and tapped it against his thigh. "Well, that was the good news, but I'm afraid that there's bad news as well. We're staying a bit longer so Henry and his granddaughters can get to know one another."

"What?" Jocelyn stomped her foot, causing the horse behind her to shift nervously. "How long?"

"Oh, I reckon we'll be here two months." He set his Stetson back onto his head, then crossed his arms across his chest and waited for the explosions that didn't disappoint him.

"Two months?" Jocelyn's voice rose to a shriek.

"What? Mama," Margaret added her voice to her mother's protest.

Matt's jaw dropped. "Why the hell do we all have to stay?"

Three voices rose in protest, twisting, and twinning around him and Wolf.

Bo held up a hand. "Enough."

Jocelyn stepped forward until she was toe to toe with him. "This will not do. Not at all." Her voice a near shriek. She sucked in a deep breath and leaned forward. "The old man wants to stay, fine. But there is no reason for the rest of us to remain. You will take us home." She drew herself up, her buxom bosom heaving and sticking out. Her chin, not quite doubled, quivered with fury.

Bo felt small and petty for enjoying the moment, but the woman had made his life hell for two years and she'd been a right nasty thorn in his side since showing up at the ranch out of the blue. Served her right for forcing herself and her children on him.

He waited until she met his stare. "I warned you, Jocelyn. Told you I didn't know how long we'd be gone, but you insisted on coming, said it was a free country and I couldn't stop you." He jerked his chin in the directions of the soldiers who were erecting their tents behind the barn. "You are free to go. I'm sure the soldiers will take you back to the fort. Might be that the colonel will even provide you with escort until you find a boat headed downriver."

Hell, he'd pay the man handsomely to do so. "Your choice. I'm staying." Bo turned his back on her and started unloading his horse.

"I'm not leaving without you, Bodil."

Bo turned his head. "Then you stay. Fresh air might even sweeten that disposition of yours."

Wolf coughed, but whether it was to hide his laughter or gain attention, Bo didn't know. He swore he caught amusement in the man's gaze.

"Everyone earns their keep." Wolf smiled at Henry

when the man joined them, wearing a heavy pack. He had two additional bags that he set down. His gaze took in Henry and Matt. "You boys hunt?"

Henry's grin was wide as the Missouri. "Been hunting longer than you've been alive, son. Even had me a trip to Africa and a go at some mighty big game. Horse is unsaddled. Just need to know where to put her."

"I'll take care of her," Bo said.

"Thank you, son." Henry hurried off, loaded down by his belongings.

As soon as Henry rushed off, Wolf lifted a brow at Matt.

Matt spat on the ground. "Barbaric." He brushed dust off his once-polished and stylish boots. "Won't catch me out with those wild animals."

"Then I guess you're assigned with the rest of the boys to feed and clean up after the animals. You'll start by taking care of Henry's horse and your own." Wolf turned his attention to the two women. "You two will help Rook and Sofia with the cooking, cleaning, laundry, and whatever else they need a hand with." He hefted his saddle off his horse.

"Now, wait a minute, young man." Jocelyn glared at Wolf, her hands waving wildly. "Not my idea to be stuck out in this godforsaken land for two months, so you listen up and you listen up good. I do not cook. I do not clean. And I do not take orders from anyone."

"Then mount up and leave." Wolf brushed past her and set his saddle onto the fence rails.

Jocelyn tapped her foot on the ground, then let out a low, throaty sound of disgust when bits of mud sprayed outward, getting the hem of her dress. "I'm not leaving without my stepson." She glared at Bo. "I see no purpose in our being here."

Wolf's eyes were hard and flat. "I agree. There isn't anything here for you." He indicated the soldiers. "You can leave at first light with them, or you follow my rules like everyone else. I warn you now, woman. You earn your keep or you don't eat. If you do not contribute, you won't get housing." He pointed out into the forest. "Plenty of space to sleep and lots of game to catch. You won't starve. Your choice."

He eyed Matt and Margaret. "Same goes. Saddle up or take care of your horses. Work or go." Wolf glanced at Bo who had his gear slung over his shoulders.

"You can use this corral. It's big enough for your horses. Follow me, and I'll show you the tack room and where we keep food and supplies. As of tomorrow, the boys will take over the grooming and feeding, but if you'd see to your parties mounts tonight, Bo? Not sure I'd trust the care of such magnificent animals to their care." He jerked his head toward Jocelyn and her children.

Before Jocelyn could launch into another angry tirade, he speared her with another hard stare. "I expect each of you to unsaddle and bring your equipment to the barn yourselves or you don't eat." He made sure each person heard and understood.

Bo nodded and coughed to cover his chuckle as he followed Wolf. Mean of him? Hell, yes, but the woman was still making his life hell. He glanced over his shoulder when he heard the snap of twigs. Jocelyn and Matt were arguing viciously. He met Wolf's amused expression. Yep, this time from home might prove to be very interesting.

****

Jocelyn fumed as Bo and Wolf walked away as though she didn't exist. She stomped her foot, then kicked a pile of pine needles and dirt into the air. A hidden rock struck Matt's shin. She ignored his yelp.

"How dare that man treat me like hired help!" She was no one's servant. Spotting a scantily clad boy heading their way, she beckoned, "You, boy. Take care of these animals."

Pleased when the near naked boy obeyed, she tapped her foot impatiently. Could he walk any slower? When he drew level with her, his sullen gaze held hers. Then he gave her the once over, made a face, and said something she couldn't understand. Then turned sharply away and continued on to the barn. His devious smirk told her that whatever he'd said, she wouldn't have liked.

"Well, I never. Damn savages." She slapped her hands onto her hips, ready to explode, yet what good would it do her and her children. "Damn that boy if he says anything to that bastard Wolf." She really didn't want to rile the man up. There was no doubt in her mind he'd meant every word he said.

Frustrated, tired, hungry, and spittin' mad, she swung back to her horse and struggled with the saddle straps. How was she going to convince Bo to take them back to the ranch? Pulling a little too hard, the horse shied away. "Hold still, you damn beast."

The horse flipped its tail and pawed the ground when Jocelyn yanked on the reins. As soon as she reached up for the saddle, the horse sidestepped toward her. She shoved. The mare shook her head, forcing

Jocelyn back until she was neatly pinned against the rail of the corral.

Shoving at loose wisps of hair, she glared at the animal. "Matt! Get over here."

"Got my own horse to see to," Matt shot back, clearly as unhappy as his mother.

"Mathew Claude, I'll toss you out to the wolves if you sass me."

Muttering curses, Matt dropped his saddle onto the ground. He shoved Jocelyn's horse away, then quickly removed the saddle.

Jocelyn grabbed his arm, her fingers digging into the soft flesh. "You mind your mouth, or I'll cut you off and let you fend for yourself."

Matt's lips curled. "You don't have money to threaten me with, remember?" He dropped her saddle.

Jocelyn jumped back to avoid having her toes smashed, then reached across and gave one of Matt's ears a vicious yank. "You watch it, Matt. Soon, we will have money, lots of it, and you'll get your share. *If* you do as you're told."

"Yes, Ma," he said, his voice too sweet.

She waved him away. "Deal with the saddles. Margaret and I cannot be expected to carry them all the way to the barn. Just not done."

Watching her son heft her saddle and head for the barn, she fumed. She wanted that ranch—rather, she wanted the money she'd get after she sold it to the railroad. Dammit, she'd earned every penny of what the ranch would bring her. Living with that lowborn, crude rancher had been the worst two years of her life, but now she regretted leaving.

"Should have stuck it out," she muttered to herself.

How could she have known the old bastard would die less than a year after she'd divorced him to take up with the rich as sin man she'd earmarked husband number four. Too bad his heart had given out before he could marry her and make her a wealthy woman.

She kicked a stone, watched it bounce off a tree and roll to a stop. Hells bells, nothing was going as planned. She marched over to Margaret. "You aren't doing your part, girl."

Margaret cringed against her mother's fury. "You said Matt was going to take care of the saddles."

"You stupid, stupid girl. I'm talking about Bo."

Margaret hung her head in shame. "I can't make him love me, Mama."

Disgusted with her weak, wallflower daughter, Jocelyn poked her hard enough to make Margaret wince. "You can and you will. By the time we get back to the fort, you'd better have him wrapped around your little finger and ready to marry you."

The sounds of yelling and happy shouts distracted Jocelyn. The mid-day meal was over, and everywhere she looked, children were running and playing. "Dirty, disgusting urchins." She leaned close to Margaret. "You rode with him today. Did you do what I said?"

"Yes, Mama." Margaret's blue eyes were wide and moist. "I confessed how I felt. Just like you said I should." Margaret looked hurt. "I think he felt sorry for me, but I could tell he wasn't interested." She stared at her linked fingers.

Jocelyn wanted to scream. How it was that she had a child this dense, this stupid? "Then start using what the good Lord gave you." She moved in and unbuttoned the top three buttons on her daughter's blouse, then spread the top open, revealing pale curves from neck to the generous swell of bosom.

"Mama!" Margaret covered herself with her hands.

Rolling her eyes, Jocelyn slapped Margaret's hands away. "You got it. Use it" She leaned close, nearly nose to nose. "You get him to take you to his bed, and you make sure he gets you with child. Two months. That's all the time we have. By the time we leave here, he'll marry you."

"What if this doesn't work, Mama? I think he really sees me as his sister."

"Then you sneak into his bed after he's asleep. He's a man, and men can't resist temptation when it falls into their lap." She smirked. "Better yet, my girl. Get yourself naked before you slip into his bed and touch and stroke him awake. I promise, he won't say no."

"Mama," Margaret wailed.

"Don't mama me. You heard me. You do it until you're with child, then you can play the fragile mother-to-be."

Her face red, eyes horrified, Margaret sobbed and ran into the trees. Jocelyn fought the urge to go after her twit of a daughter. Instead, she glared at Matt when she heard him laughing.

"God, Mama, you're a bitch."

"Bitch Mama, and don't you forget it." She narrowed her eyes. "When the time comes, you'll do your part or get nothing."

"Yes, Mama."

Jocelyn scowled. "Two months in this hellish, godforsaken place. We're going to earn every damn penny from the sale of that ranch."

Chapter Five

Beth Ann waited for her grandfather to return. She was alone, except for her daughter who rested her head against her breast. "What are we going to do with that man?" she asked softly as she rubbed her daughter's back in small, soothing circles.

She remembered the large bedroom she'd shared with Jane and wondered what her grandfather would think of her tipi home. It was much smaller than a single room in his house, she was sure.

Then there were the things in his house. She had tried to explain to the other children in her tribe what it was like to live in a wooden building with so many rooms and each of those rooms filled with furniture and objects. And stairs leading to more floors of rooms and furniture and pictures and trinkets decorating each room and hallway.

That life seemed foreign to her now. In her mind's eye, she could still see her mother's sitting room, filled with furniture, fine lacework covering the backs of the chairs and settee. Mostly, she remembered all the beautiful bits and pieces set on cloth-covered tables that she wasn't allowed to touch.

Beth Ann peered into her tipi and grimaced. How was her grandfather going to adapt to this? She didn't even have what he'd consider a decent bed let alone candles. Her gaze slid up, and she grinned. She did have a lantern. Her smile dimmed. Her old life was quickly coming back to her, and the more she recalled, the more agitated she became.

She hated change, but more, she shied away from confrontations and angry words. And that, she just now realized, was why she'd been so unhappy in her marriage. Hidden away deep in her mind, she'd never forgotten the angry fighting between her parents and grandfather. She'd just locked it away.

And because of it, she'd not once tried to talk to her husband or even berate or shame him for the way he treated her. She'd allowed him to treat her like a possession without ever protesting. Peace between her and her husband had been more important than her happiness. She'd traded happiness for having her own family.

Staring down at her daughter, Beth Ann had no regrets. Though the next time she took a husband, she'd make sure he loved and cherished her above all else. Which was fine and good, but it didn't help with the problem at hand—what to do with her grandfather who was heading toward her loaded down by three heavy looking packs.

"Kimi," she breathed her daughter's name. "What do we do now?" She didn't want to live with anger, yet she was done living in miserable silence.

Henry stopped before her. Grandfather and granddaughter stared at one another, both uncomfortable and feeling awkward. "Beth Ann, if you truly do not want me in your tipi, I can sleep in the barn."

"No. You are family, but before I take you inside, there are some things you need to understand."

She indicated the tipi beside hers. "My family live there." She pointed to a tipi set a short distance on the other side of hers. "Our chief, his wife, Emma White Flame, and their children share that tipi. If you wish to speak to a person inside their tipi, you are to announce yourself by calling out, *hau* or hello, then wait for their response."

Henry nodded. "Much the same as we do when we call upon friends or neighbors."

She inclined her head. "Our openings face east, to the rising sun. When a man enters, he goes to the left, women to the right. This is the way it is always, unless you are told differently. You will learn much by observing."

Again, Henry nodded. Beth entered, stepping to the right. Her grandfather followed, stepping to the left. "Jane and I will sleep on this side. We'll gather pine needles and make your pallet."

"I have a bedroll," Henry said. "I don't wish to be any trouble."

"You are here." She left unspoken that his very presence was trouble enough. She indicated an area behind the fire pit. "That is our altar. We do not step over it. You go around."

"But I stay to this side of the tipi?"

"Once inside, you may go where needed."

"So long as I go in this direction?" He made a clockwise circle with his finger.

Beth Ann couldn't help the twitch of her lip and gave him credit for trying to grasp their ways. "Here, in our tipi, it does not matter so much. Within a family, we often do not follow the rules. But if you are invited to the home of another, like our chief, or to a meeting held in a tipi, then rules are followed."

"Got it." Henry glanced around the neat interior of the tipi, his expression curious.

She figured he'd never been inside the cone-shaped tents and was amazed at how much room there actually was. As a young child, used to a large, rambling ranch house, it had taken her a long time to get used to the different lifestyle. Now she couldn't imagine living any other way.

Piles of furs lay in neat stacks around the edge, along with several quilts, a small stack of books, pouches bulging with what he suspected were food or other household supplies. Some hung from poles. Others were gathered in groups on the hide-covered floor.

The inside was light, airy, a bit on the cool side but not cold.

He set his packs down and turned, looking ill at ease. "I have more. Bo said he'd bring the rest." He fidgeted, his hat in his hands, then he blurted out, "I brought gifts."

A faint memory of her grandfather with candy in his pockets flitted through her memory. And dolls. The room she'd shared with Jane had been filled with beautiful dolls in fancy gowns. As though a wall were being torn down, other memories flooded her mind. Tea with her mother wearing a pale gown, a very tiny Jane who looked more like a doll, and a pink and white room with lots of frills, ribbons, and roses. Her bedroom. She gasped against the pain of the vision.

"Beth Ann?" Henry took a step but stopped.

"No. I don't want to remember that time." She needed her anger to keep tears from falling.

Henry looked sad. "We had a lot of good times in that house. It wasn't all sadness and fighting." Silence stretched between them. Beth Ann didn't want to upset her daughter, who stared at her great grandfather, or to shame her family with angry outbursts. She was a grown woman and was expected to deal with the situation in a way that brought honor to family and tribe. Yet she could no longer live in silence or fear of speaking her mind.

"I have happy memories of my *Lakota* family. Why did you have to come? Why are you staying? I won't change my mind."

Henry's arms dropped to his sides. "Maybe I need good memories to replace the bad memories. I have all those good memories, but all I see or think about is the day I came home and found my girls gone."

Reaching out, Henry fingered a strand of her silky-soft blonde hair. "Can you give me some good memories? Help ease the years of guilt and hate I've felt? Be my granddaughter? No matter what happens, I love you, and I can't believe I've found you after all these years," he said, tears in his eyes. He dropped his hand to his side and stood there, a proud man.

Despite herself, Beth Ann couldn't stop the flow of tears. What if she lost her babies and had no idea where they were? Hugging her child so tight the little girl protested, Beth Ann watched the emotions chase across her grandfather's face. She felt for him, and maybe, deep inside, something she'd thought long dead stirred.

"This is my home," she said softly. "I will not give you false hope."

"But you will give me a chance? A fair chance?"

"Yes." And she would. Perhaps, like him, she

needed good memories to chase away the bad.

He lifted a hand. "I have a great granddaughter. Will she come to me?"

Speaking *Lakota*, she pointed to Henry. "This is your grandfather. Will you greet him? The little girl giggled and buried her head in her mother's neck.

Henry sighed sadly. "Maybe in time."

Beth Ann jiggled her daughter. "Go to your grandfather," she said and held the little girl out.

The utter joy in her grandfather's face as he gently held Kimi hurt.

"She looks like you," Henry said.

Before she could answer, Jane gracefully entered the tipi.

"Hi, Grandfather." Her soft, blue eyes were uncertain.

Tears rolled down Henry's face. "You look so much like my Lizzie."

Jane nodded. "This is so. Beth Ann has a picture of our mother."

Henry's jaw dropped. "You have Lizzie's locket? The one I gave her the day she married?"

Beth Ann pulled it from around her neck. "She gave it to me the day we were captured."

Henry flinched as though Beth Ann had struck him.

"Beth." Jane glared at her.

"I didn't say it to cause pain. She wanted me to have it in case we were rescued or managed to escape. She wanted me to use it to return home." She stared at the floor. "I never told anyone about it. I didn't want to go home."

Henry nodded. "It hurts, but I understand."

With the locket fisted in her hand, Beth Ann found

herself asking, "Would you like it back?"

Henry looked shocked, then pleased. "It pleases me more than anything that you would offer it to me. That is the gift I will take from you, but the locket belonged to your mother and it is right that it went to her eldest daughter." He jiggled the child in his arms. "Someday, this little beauty will wear it, and she'll have something of her grandmother's."

Glancing past her sister, Beth Ann saw Bo standing at the entrance. "You may enter."

Bo glanced at Henry, his grin wide when he saw his friend holding his great-granddaughter. "Brought the rest of your things, Henry."

Lifting her brows at the pile Bo was handing to her grandfather, she smiled. "Gifts?"

Henry grinned like a little boy who'd been given a sweet. "Not just for the two of you. I brought enough for everyone. Will you help me sort everything and decide what to give to each person?"

Jane nodded, eyeing the packs. "Oh, I love gifts."

Laughing despite herself, Beth Ann tweaked her sister's braid. "Tonight. How about you show our grandfather around."

Grinning, Jane nodded. "Would you like me to show you around?"

Henry smiled. "I'd be honored." He turned to go, and then stopped. He reached into his pocket and withdrew his pouch of sweets. "I remembered how much the two of you liked these." He held it out. "Peppermints."

Beth Ann couldn't resist. Neither could Jane. "Your pocket. You used to carry them in your pocket for us." She popped the treat into her mouth and savored the explosion of sweet. Perhaps getting to know her grandfather again after all these years wouldn't be so bad.

****

Bo left the stream and returned to the barn where he stowed his towel and soap. Between travel, grooming horses, and moving tables and benches from the schoolroom to the center area where meals were served, he'd decided a quick bath wasn't just needed but mandatory if he was expected to be around others.

Sniffing, he figured he was cutting it close. His stomach rumbled and urged him to move before whatever smelled good was gone. The level of noise grew louder, and when he reached the first building, he stopped. The sight that met his eyes was more than he could have imagined.

Two words came to mind.

Utter chaos.

Bo couldn't even begin to guess at the number of children spaced between the adults. At his best guess, there were close to thirty adults, and they were outnumbered by at least five children for every adult. The only thing that out-shadowed the sight of so many people gathered in one area was the noise that ranged from the low hum of many conversations, to good-natured shouts and laughter. More tables had been added, and each and every available seat seemed taken.

"You look a bit dazed, Bo." Wolf joined him.

He grinned sheepishly. "I'm an only child, and Henry's my only family. My pa wasn't much for church socials or picnic days. We had our own cookouts put on for the ranch hands and their families."

Wolf chuckled. "You'll get used to it. You and

Henry will take your morning meals with Dove and Jeremy while you are here. The mid-day meal is served here but informally. But dinner, or supper as I imagine you call it, we come together like one big family. Once the weather turns for good, we'll eat in the school building."

Bo nodded, spotting Henry. His granddaughters sat across from him, along with their parents and more children. "There are so many children," he said, noticing that they seemed to be divided among the groups of family.

"This year, each child was encouraged to adopt a family for the winter. They'll still sleep in the school house and take their morning and mid-day meals together, but for the evening meal, they eat with their chosen family." He surveyed the large gathering, his sharp gaze roaming from one table to the next.

"You do this every year?" Bo wasn't just amazed. He was impressed.

Wolf shook his head. "Normally, my family is not here for the winter. This year is special as we are having a reunion." He eyed Bo. "There are others who have not arrived yet."

Before Bo could comment, he heard a loud shout. Wolf laughed when two boys jumped down from their bench and drew imaginary guns. "My nieces, or rather, their husbands were most popular among the boys."

Recalling the two men he'd been introduced to were lawmen, Bo nodded. "I can see why."

"You and Henry are also popular." Wolf jerked his head, indicating a large number of boys who were talking to Henry. "There are your children. They're waiting for you to join them."

Bo's jaw dropped. "You mean *we've* been adopted? Why?" What did he know about children? He fiddled with his Stetson, not sure what to do with it. None of the other men wore hats, including Henry.

Chuckling, Wolf indicated the gun Bo wore. "You look like a man of law yourself. You're also a rancher. Most will be eager to learn about your life, and you'll be expected to teach them what they want to know." There was an edge of challenge to Wolf's voice.

Bo tapped his hat against his thigh. He believed in taking what life tossed at him by the horns and either hanging on or wrestling the beast to the ground. He flexed his mental muscles.

"Could be I might just enjoy being part of a large, crazy family for the next couple months." He headed toward the table, jamming his hat on. The two lawmen sat at one end of the table, Henry and his family at the other end. Bo slid onto the bench beside Henry. The boys fell silent and stood there, uncertain, dark eyes waiting.

Bo lifted a brow. "You boys going to join us?" Immediately, the boys broke out into wide grins, took their seats, and shot question after question at him and Henry.

Sitting next to Bo, Henry wore an expression of sheer joy as he bounced his grandson on his knee and told the boys and those across the table about his ranch.

A bit bemused himself when he found the girls staring at him with stars in their eyes as though he was an important man like a president or a popular politician like his godfather, he shifted his own gaze to the one woman who fascinated him—Beth.

She sat in the midst of the girls. Her daughter,

named after her mother, sat on her lap. Beth a mother. And of twins. Watching her, he admitted she wore the role like a well-fitted gown.

He tried to listen in on her conversation, but it was too noisy. So he watched—the strand of loose hair that fell across her cheek and begged to be gently tucked behind her ear, the twinkle in her eyes as she whispered something to one of the girls, the wide grin that brightened her face when she said something that made the girls giggle.

A loud roar startled him. He whirled around on the bench.

"Get the food on them tables before we have a riot!" The shout came from an old, bearded geezer wearing a tattered hat of undetermined material and age. The man stood between two log cabins with hands braced on his hips, feet planted apart.

Bo knew one building was the school's kitchens and that the other belonged to the couple in charge of meals. As he watched, a line of boys and girls rushed from the kitchen with bowls and platters of food. An older woman left the second cabin, carrying two jugs.

"That's Rook and Sofia. They run this place with a firm hand and a bellow or two," Dove said from across the table.

Bo leaned forward. "Looks like he belongs on a ship, not in a school."

From the end of the table, Tyler chuckled. "The man runs this place with the efficiency of a ship's captain. When he hollers, everyone jumps."

The moment the platters of food hit the table, Bo expected a mass mob scene, but to his surprise, everyone waited until all adults were seated and grace given before calmly and, with manners, dishing up the food and passing the platters down the table. His ranch hands could do with learning some manners. No tossing rolls from one end of the table to the other.

As he ate, he watched and listened. But his gaze always came back to Beth's wide, blue eyes. The woman drew him like a bear to honey, and she looked just as sweet. A lingering ray of sunlight found its way through the trees and hit her hair from behind, giving her the glow of an angel. She glanced up from her plate and her eyes, a pale blue, met his, then quickly shifted to her grandfather who was talking ranching with Jeremy.

He bit back a sigh. Dammit, he could lose himself in her heavenly blues. He wanted to strike up a conversation with her just so she'd look at him. He tried to speak, but had no idea what to say or even to ask. With shock, he realized he felt like a tongue-tied schoolboy, not a grown man.

Forcing himself to relax, Bo told himself he had lots of time get to know her, to court her. He froze, fork halfway to his mouth. Court Beth? Bethy? Swallowing, uncaring what he ate, he considered the idea of courting this woman.

He'd come prepared to court her, to become her husband and protector, out of a sense of duty. But at that moment, what he felt toward Beth had nothing to do with marrying her to save his ranch. Beth intrigued him. She wasn't anything like he'd expected, and he found he wanted to get to know her.

The sound of a throat clearing interrupted his thoughts. He shifted on the bench and saw Wolf and George Runs Fast standing there, clearly needing something. Bo had spent a fair amount of time with the boy in the barn caring for their mounts. In that entire time, the boy hadn't spoken one word.

"Yes?" It was clear, with Wolf standing behind the boy with one hand on George's shoulder, the boy had something to say, whether he wanted to say it or not.

The boy stood tall, shoulders back, his gaze looking over Bo's head. "I adopt you." There was a hint of challenge in the boy's voice.

Bo lifted a brow. "Are you speaking to me or to Jeremy across the table?"

Dark, glittering eyes shot to Bo's. George wore sullen better than a sheriff wore his badge. "It is you I speak with."

Catching the tug of amusement to Wolf's lips, Bo nodded seriously. "Then I will consider it an honor to count you as family while I am here." He scooted closer to Henry, making room for the boy who reluctantly sat.

Wolf nodded then left.

Picking up a hot biscuit, Bo broke it in half. "Why me?"

The boy shrugged. "I like hat."

"I can live with that," Bo said, careful not to laugh.

"You promised to teach me to tie fancy knots," he added.

"That I did." He took off his hat and set it on the boy's head. "I'll share my hat."

George looked shocked, then downright pleased as the rest of the boys started talking. Bo nudged Henry. "Don't suppose you brought any hats for gifts did you?"

Before Henry replied, the arrival of Jocelyn and her children drew his attention. Most everyone was nearly done eating, yet those three were walking toward the tables at a deliberate saunter.

Rook marched over to her. "Woman, you don't get here on time, you don't get food. Plates and forks are over there. Find a place before food's gone."

"We'll take our food back to our tent," Jocelyn sniffed. She'd declined the use of a tipi, preferring the canvas tent she and her children had shared on their journey.

Bo settled back, a grin on his face, when Rook stabbed a finger at her. "Now looksee here, woman. Rules be rules. You want to eat on your own, that's fine. Families sometimes choose to do that, but they fix their own food. You want to eat what I fix, then you get yourselves here. On time or you don't eat."

Face flaming red, Jocelyn swept past him, grabbed a plate, found a seat at a table where Rook, Sofia, and the servers were eating. She and her children sat at the end, away from everyone else.

Henry nudged Bo. "She's going to have a right time of it here." He chuckled.

Jeremy smiled across at Bo. "No one goes against Rook or Sofia. Your family will either do what they're told or go hungry."

Grimacing, Bo shuddered. "Not my family," he said, wishing he'd left them behind.

"A thorn in his backside is more like it," Henry agreed.

"That they are," he agreed, his gaze once more falling on Beth who was watching and listening.

"I don't recall her. Or her children." Beth Ann looked at Bo.

"Whenever your family came over, Jocelyn found

an excuse to stay in town. She never liked Henry and hated being a part of our cookouts.

"That must have been hard on you. I can't imagine not wanting to be with my family." Realizing what she'd said, she turned to her grandfather. "I'm sorry—I didn't mean—"

Henry waved her embarrassment aside then winked. "I think my old friend planned his cookouts as a way to get rid of her for a day or two. When she left for good, not a single person was sad to see her go. Even Bo's pa. Swore he'd never fall for a woman's wiles again."

"Still," Beth Ann said, looking from Bo to her grandfather. "It's sad."

Bo studied Beth. Family was important to her, and for that reason, he couldn't court her or try to win her heart. In that one comment, the look in her eyes told him just how much family meant to her. She'd never be happy if taken away, and he wasn't going to repeat his pa's mistake in taking a wife who'd end up not just hating ranch life but him as well.

With a heavy heart, he finished his meal as a second group of children began clearing the tables. He stood with the others and was about to follow Henry and Jeremy when a tall, muscled warrior approached. He had a blanket slung over his arm and stopped in front of Beth. He spoke to her, and the two walked off.

"Who is that?"

Jane grinned. "Standing Horse, brother to her husband who died. He's courting my sister."

"Courting her?" Even though he'd just decided it wouldn't be right to court Beth, he didn't like the idea of another man doing so.

Jane grimaced. "He tried to claim her, as a brother often does when a woman is left alone with children, but my sister turned him down. So now he's trying to change her mind."

Everyone walked off to enjoy what was left of the daylight but Bo. He stared as the couple strolled in a circle, staying to the edges of the grassy center between tipis and buildings. He didn't like the fact that the man had tried to *claim* her but also realized that Beth had children and would naturally seek a father for her babies.

Why it bothered him to see that others were attracted to her, he didn't know. He just knew no matter how much he might like to get to know her—hell, court her like that strutting peacock—he wouldn't. He might be able to form a family with her, but he couldn't take her away from what she seemed to value the most—her family.

****

Beth Ann strolled around the schoolyard with Standing Horse, their steps small and unhurried.

"The children of my brother grow strong."

She nodded. "Yes. They are healthy."

Standing Horse kept his eyes trained ahead. "Soon, my nephew will need a father to teach him the ways of a warrior."

"There are many men in my family." Beth Ann wanted to groan. How many times would she have to tell her husband's brother she would not accept him as her mate?

"I carry the blood of their father. It is my right to assume this role."

"You are always welcome to see your nephew and

niece. My son will enjoy spending time with his uncle."
She kept her gaze fixed in front of her as they passed
the line of tipis. Jane grinned as they passed. Beth Ann
used all her will power to keep from grimacing.

"I have not changed my mind, Brother To My
Husband." Why hadn't she refused his request to walk?
This was his way of courting her. She sighed. She'd
agreed because she didn't want to hurt his feelings. He
was family, just not in the way he wished.

"You have no other warrior courting you?"

"No." As they passed the large army tent, she heard
sharp words coming from inside and shuddered. Poor
Bo. The shouting between her grandfather and parents
had been bad enough. She couldn't imagine having a
mother who treated her children the way that woman
treated hers.

Ahead, she spotted Bo leaning against one of the
corrals. When they neared, he turned. Once again, Beth
Ann was struck by how handsome he had become. Her
memories of him as a child—or rather, a young man—
were a bit hazy, but she remembered his smile, his
laugh, and most of all, his eyes.

For as long as she could remember, she'd been
fascinated by the way they changed color. Right now,
in the twilight, they were like dark clouds just
beginning to darken in the center yet the edges still a
bright silver. There wasn't enough light to reveal the
reds and golds of his hair or to make the strands shine
and spark.

Unlike most of the men in her tribe, he wore his
hair short, just so it brushed his collar and framed his
lean face and strong jaw. Though fully dressed in a
plain blue shirt, dark pants, and boots, she had no

trouble imagining the hidden whipcord strength. An unbidden question came to mind. Was his body as brown as his face and hands?

She was used to looking at a man's body and not really thinking much about it. Like the man walking beside her who wore only his breechclout and leggings. Seeing Bo completely covered made her curious to see his body. Too bad he wasn't the one strolling beside her.

Realizing where her thoughts were headed, her cheeks burned. Here she was being courted by one man, yet she was thinking about what another man looked like without his clothes.

Bo's gaze met and held hers, then he tipped his hat as she and Standing Horse passed. Part of her wanted to turn her head to see if he was still watching but she didn't.

"You knew that man when you were a child?"

Beth Ann nodded. "Yes. He was our neighbor."

"Do you plan to take my niece and nephew and return to the white world?"

Standing Horse didn't sound happy at the thought and she couldn't fault him for that. "No. I will remain here, with my family."

"That is good. My brother's children do not belong in the white man's world. They belong here." For the first time, he turned his head and stared down at her, his gaze hard. He stopped in front of a small log building that served as a kitchen. "You need the protection of a husband. It is the way of our people for you to become my wife."

Keeping her emotions tightly in check, Beth Ann saw that once again Standing Horse was staring over the top of her head whereas Bo had boldly and so easily met and held her gaze.

"I do not love you, Standing Horse. I cannot become your wife."

Standing Horse held his hands behind his back. "That is of no importance."

"It is for me." Beth Ann wanted to shout at the man that she'd had one loveless marriage already and was not entering into another. "Do you love me?" She knew the answer.

Standing Horse took his time answering, and when he did, he still did not glance at her. "Duty is more important. Feeling come later."

"No, they don't," she said sadly as she resumed walking. She remembered the many times she'd told herself that very same thing while married—Singing Bear would learn to love her if she was a good wife, her husband would love her after she had their baby—babies. Love would grow. She'd believed that and so many more lies she'd told herself.

And the truth was, love hadn't grown, and she didn't believe it ever would have. Had her husband lived, she'd still be in a loveless marriage where the only respect she earned came from being a good wife—cooking, cleaning, providing clothing, and easing his body's needs. But no respect for her as a person, no thought to what she needed or wanted.

Deciding enough was enough, Beth Ann held up a hand when she reached her tipi. "Thank you for the honor of walking with you, Standing Horse. I know you want to take care of me. You feel it is your duty, but it is a duty I refuse. When I take another husband, it will be a man I love and respect, and my husband will love and respect me in return. Do not ask again."

Standing Horse fisted his hands in front of him. His nostrils flared and his lips tightened. "Come spring, if you still deny me, I will return to my family's tribe. If you do not have a husband and father for the twins, then I will take the children to my family to be raised. As is my right."

Furious, Beth Ann glared at the arrogant warrior who was every bit as cold as her husband had been. "My children will remain with me. They are well taken care of by *my* family and *me*. And *that* is my right. Know also that my chief will not allow you to take my children from me. Do not ever speak of this again."

"I will do what I see is right." Standing Horse stalked off.

Beth Ann watched him go, fury turning to worry. She would not lose her children, and she would not marry for anything less than love. Hearing sounds from inside her tipi, she entered to find Spotted Owl trying to settle the twins. Her grandfather and Jane hadn't returned. Beth Ann was grateful. She needed some time alone. Just her and her babies. "Thank you, my sister, for watching my children."

Spotted Owl turned at the doorway. Her eyes were wide. "You won't let him take them, will you?"

"No. Now, off to bed with you."

Chapter Six

Bo watched Standing Horse storm past where he stood in the shadows of one of the buildings. The man walked as though he had a stick up his ass. Somewhere deep inside, Bo was relieved. The sight of Beth strolling casually with the man hadn't set well with him.

For weeks, ever since Henry talked him into making this trip, he'd held in his mind an image of the Beth he'd last seen, older, of course, given the passage of time but still young and innocent. He'd known one or both of the girls might have been married, but the reality of finding Beth with a randy stud sniffing after her bothered him more than her having children. A lot.

Leaning his head back against the rough log wall, he told himself he should go back to the barn. He planned to be up with the sun to get the lay of the land. If he was stuck here, he'd earn his keep. To his right, Jocelyn marched across the compound to the cookhouse.

Rook, for a price, had decided to allow the "tenderfoots" to bathe there twice a week. He and Henry had declined, and Jocelyn, instead of being grateful, had complained bitterly that a lady bathed daily and she most definitely needed more than five minutes to do her business.

Rook left the cookhouse and sat at one of the

tables. He took out a knife and a chunk of wood. Maybe he'd give whittling a try. Normally, his evenings were spent pouring over his ledgers or sitting in front of a fire with a book. His father and mother had loved to read, and he had a decent library. Out here, he had a feeling he was going to have lots of free time.

Movement in the shadows drew his attention. Bo frowned when he spotted George Runs Fast. The boy looked as though he wanted to approach but wasn't sure of his welcome.

Still shocked and surprised that the boy had adopted him, Bo motioned him over. "What's up, George?"

George shuffled his feet, his toes digging into the dirt. He held out Bo's hat. "This is yours."

"Keep it." Inside, he winced. He loved that hat, but remembering how the boy's face had lit up, he figured George needed it more than he did.

"No." George stood firm. "When you teach me, I will wear it."

Bo nodded. "Tomorrow you will wear it again. After school and chores, I'll show you those knots."

"And you will show me how to shoot your gun," George added, pointing to the revolver Bo wore on his hip.

"This beaut is not just a gun, boy. It's a Smith and Wesson revolver." He stroked his palm over the grip.

George nodded seriously. "I will learn to shoot your revolver." He turned and walked away.

"Bo!" Henry rushed toward him.

"What's wrong?" He scanned the area but didn't see anything amiss, but Henry's face was red and every step a pounding stomp.

"That bastard is threatening to take my grandchildren." Henry was breathing hard, and his voice was tight with fury.

"Start over. Who's going to take Beth's children?"

"The bastard courting her. He's the children's uncle, and if my granddaughter refuses to marry him, he's told her he would take the children to be raised by his family." Henry punched his fist into his palm. "No one is going to take my great-grandchildren from me."

"You mean no one is going to take them from Beth."

"Same meaning."

Bo didn't argue. He'd already made his feelings clear. "I agree. We won't let the bastard take her children."

Henry dug his hands deep into his pockets. "You going to keep to your end of the bargain?"

Removing his hat, Bo tapped it against his thigh. "She's not in need of a husband, Henry. If she returns, she'll have no trouble fitting in."

Henry folded his arms across his chest. "Boy, she needs a man, and it's high time you took a wife. You saying you don't want her?"

Bo sighed. "Didn't say that. She just might want that bastard with the stick up his ass for her next husband."

"Bullshit. Heard her tell him no. That was when he threatened her." He paused. "You owe me, son."

Lifting a brow, Bo leaned back, his arms crossed, his hat in his hand. "You are correct. I owe you. If Beth chooses not to return, I'll pay you back for the ranch, but I won't force or coerce her. Her choice, Henry. Said what I meant, meant what I said."

"Dammit, boy, you got your father's scruples." Henry paced in front of Bo.

A loud bellow drew both men's attention. Rook was at the door, pounding.

"Yer five minutes is up, woman. You get out here, or I'm coming in."

"Looks like Jocelyn's causing trouble."

"Yeah, it's what she does best." Bo spotted Margaret standing a short distance away, awaiting her turn. Rook yelled again, then to Bo's surprise, the man shoved the door open and stormed into the cookhouse.

A loud shriek split the evening air. At the sound of loud arguing, everyone turned to see what was going on. Moments later, Jocelyn ran screaming out the door, clutching her clothing to her.

"When I say five minutes, I mean five minutes, not ten," Rook shouted after her.

Bo burst out laughing, as did Henry. Jocelyn's chemise was soaked, leaving little to the imagination as she ran past them and ducked into her tent.

"That's not a pretty sight, boy," Henry said, gulping air, and the tension between the two men was broken.

Bo struggled to compose himself. "Look, Henry, we have two months. Let's see what happens. We just got here." He liked the idea of courting Beth Ann, but he wasn't going to court her for Henry.

"All right. But she'd make you a fine wife." Henry walked off.

Bo headed toward the barn and figured Henry was right. Beth would make a fine wife. Question was, did he want a wife? The soft hoo-hoo of an owl in the tree drew his attention. The night bird took wing, soaring into the loft of the barn.

He wasn't a religious man, but he did believe in fate. The fact that he was here and Beth Ann was no longer a married woman might just be fate. She obviously wasn't interested in that other warrior, which made his steps lighter.

Up in the loft, he rolled out his pallet and thought of Beth Ann. Courting her for himself, not for Henry held a lot of appeal. A lot. But he foresaw one major problem. Her family. Could he ask her to leave everything and everyone here to make a new life with him? Was that fair to her? And would she even consider it? Memories of the past slid through his mind. He dwelled on the woman she'd become and knew that, yes, he wanted Beth Ann. Henry was right. She'd make him a fine wife.

Slipping between the covers, he pillowed his head on his hands and stared out the opening in the side of the loft that the owl had used to enter. Stars in the crystalline sky winked magically and one star shot across the sky.

Like the boy who'd once wished upon the stars, Bo made a wish.

****

Pale gray clouds hid the light of the new day like a greedy child stashed sweets. Darker clouds on the horizon warned of an approaching storm while the cold breath of air said winter was nearly upon the land. Overnight, puddles of water froze, and plants and grass out in the open withered and died.

Returning from the river from her morning bath, Beth Ann paused when Bo stepped out from behind a tree. His hair was wet, testimony that he too had been down to the river to bathe. "Morning, Bo."

He smiled, and her heart beat just a bit faster. His handsome looks literally stole her breath.

"Morning, cupcake." He halted in front of her, reached out, and fingered a long strand of water darkened blonde hair. He wound it around his finger and brought it to his nose, drawing her ever closer.

"Water and sunshine," he murmured.

She rolled her eyes. "No sun yet." She found his poetic words moving and romantic but refused to let him know how he affected her. Every time they were together, he drew her like honey drew cubs. Unlike the furry critters, she didn't have a thick hide to protect from being stung.

"Going to save me a spot during breakfast?" He tucked the stray strand behind her ear, his knuckles brushing her cheek.

Mouth dry, she nodded shyly, unable to tear her gaze from his. She loved his eyes, those silvery-violet eyes with long dark lashes, not to mention his full lips that could curve into wide, amused smile. "I always save you a spot."

In fact, her family had noticed the two of them sat together for the morning and evening meals, with Henry and a handful of schoolboys surrounding them, including George who'd taken possession of Bo and always sat on Bo's other side.

It surprised her how both Bo and her grandfather had fit right in as though part of the family. His stepmother? Not so much. "I've got to get back before the twins wake."

"See you soon." He tipped his hat.

Smiling as she continued, she hesitated and

listened before stepping into her tipi. She'd slipped out, leaving her grandfather and her children sleeping. Henry, an early riser like Bo, was talking to the twins. She heard Kimi giggling. Since his arrival nearly two weeks ago, the twins had taken to waking when he did. They adored their grandfather. Her lips twitched. It didn't hurt that he carried his sweets with him and was generous in sharing those treats, not just with his great-grandchildren but with all the children.

At her mother's tipi, her parents were going through their morning ritual of roasting coffee beans and bantering back and forth. A glance around the yard revealed smoke rising from the chimneys of the cabins, and out in the pastures, horses called out greetings. Behind Rook and Sofia's cabin, a rooster announced the beginning of another new day.

She watched her world come alive for a few moments longer before stepping into her tipi. As she'd suspected, her grandfather sat holding the twins in his arms.

"Good morning, Beth Ann. I stumbled getting up and woke the twins."

She bent down and kissed her grandfather. "They would have woken in any case. They enjoy their morning time with you."

"I'll take them outside. I hear your parents outside. They have coffee."

Jane, who'd been sitting beside Henry, jumped to her feet and waited until they were alone. "What's taken you so long? I want to give Grandfather my gift now."

Beth Ann sighed and rolled her eyes. "You didn't need to wait for me."

Jane stepped back, shoved her hands on her hips, and glared at her sister. "Beth Ann!"

Beth Ann made a face. "All right, I'll get mine." She picked up a large bundle.

"Do you think he'll like these, Beth Ann?

Seeing the anxiousness in her sister's eyes, Beth Ann nodded. "Yes. He will like our gifts. Let's go." Jane had insisted they give their grandfather something in return for the presents he'd given them. She took hold of her sister's arms and pulled her to the door. "Let's get this over with."

Jane rejoined her grandfather who now had a mug of coffee warming his hands. "Grandfather, we have something for you."

Henry glanced up in surprise. He still had the twins on his lap. Kimi was playing with a tiny cloth doll he'd brought in his bag of gifts while Riker spun the wheels on a wooden wagon. Henry eyed their packages. "You don't need to give me anything, children."

"We wanted to do something for you," Jane said, her gaze shooting up to her sister.

Another sigh and eye roll, and Beth Ann took her seat. "You were very generous. Please accept these." She handed him her bundle and took her daughter while her mother, seeing what they were doing, came over to claim her grandson. Jane placed hers on top of Beth's gift.

Henry picked up the smaller package wrapped in a large square of softened deer hide. He untied the length of sinew and peeled away the hide.

"Jane," he said, awe in his voice as he lifted up a finely crafted pair of moccasins. "Thank you," he added, tears in his eyes. "I'm putting them on right away."

Seeing the happiness glowing from Jane's face, Beth Ann was glad her sister's relationship with their grandfather wasn't marred by the past. She wished for that same innocent acceptance. Even though she'd accepted his explanation for the past, part of her still didn't trust him completely. When the time came for him to leave, she worried he'd find a way to force her to return.

A thread of nervousness ran through her when he unfolded her gift. Would he like it? Like Jane, she wanted the man, who was also part of her family, to like what she'd made him.

"Beth Ann, you made this?" Henry held up a long-sleeved buckskin shirt. A line of fringe swung from the yoke and the hem. His fingers stroked the soft material.

"I lined it with rabbit fur," she said. "It will keep you warm during your stay. I am sewing pants as well. They will also have a fur lining."

"Thank you, Beth Ann." He stood. "I'm going change." He ducked into the tipi and closed the flap.

"He liked them," Jane whispered, hugging her sister.

"You were right. I should have thought to do this."

"You said you'd give him a chance, Beth Ann." Jane took her sister's hands in her own. She looked worried.

Beth Ann sighed and gripped Jane's hands. "I will. I promise." She vowed to keep her word. In truth, it hadn't taken him long to slide past her initial mistrust. She liked her grandfather, the man he was here and today. She just hoped he'd accept her decision to stay and not do anything to destroy their newly found peace.

Jane nodded and studied her grandfather when he left the tipi. "Do they fit?"

Henry hugged Jane. "Like gloves," he said, beaming. "Hey, Bo. Come see."

Beth Ann watched Bo approach. He wore a blue shirt with a form-fitting leather vest that revealed a wide chest and narrow waist. The bright red scarf around his tanned throat drew her attention to his hair and the way it curled softly over the scarf. Tight, dark pants encased his long legs and thick thighs. The man's every step showed strength and power. And made her wish she could claim him as hers.

Out of the corner of her eye, she spotted Standing Horse walking toward Bo. The warrior wore a vest and leggings, revealing lots of lean flesh. He'd walked past the tipi half-a-dozen times already that morning, drawing her attention to him. She swallowed a sigh. He was her problem. She didn't want to worry her sister or grandfather, although she suspected she'd have to talk to her father about him.

The warrior cut across Bo's path, forcing Bo to step to the side. Seeing the two men, each dressed so differently, Beth Ann wondered what Bo would look like wearing just a vest and leggings. She had no doubt he was all lean muscle beneath his clothing.

She shook herself mentally when Bo reached them. She told herself it didn't matter. She wasn't seeking a mate, especially one who wouldn't be staying.

"Looking good, Henry," Bo said.

"Gifts from my girls." Henry held out his arms to show off the fringe along the length of the sleeve.

"Fine work. Looks warm."

"I could make a pair of moccasins for you as well,"

Jane offered, elbowing her sister.

Beth Ann glared at her sister who innocently widened her eyes. Then she looked at Bo, in his blue shirt and cow-skin vest. She liked very much what he wore but had no trouble envisioning him in a soft, supple buckskin shirt. He'd look a bit wild. Her fingers itched to make him a shirt, see him in clothing made by her hand. "I will make you a warm shirt."

Bo looked uncomfortable. "Don't have to do that."

"True," she said, eyeing his frame. He was close in size to her dead husband, a bit taller, arms longer, and maybe just wider at the chest. She narrowed her eyes. "You will have to talk to my Aunt Emma. I don't have a hide ready but she does. You'll trade something you value for it." She nodded. In her mind, the matter was settled. She also decided to add more fringe to his shirt so it'd swing and flow with his every movement.

"I can do that," Bo said, looking both surprised and pleased.

A loud shout followed by a woman's cry startled everyone. As one, they whirled around. Bo's hand went to the butt of his revolver. Beth Ann grinned, reached out, and rested her fingers on his tensed arm. "More arrivals," she said excitedly, watching her father and her Aunt Jessie running for the barn.

"Family?"

She nodded and smiled, her eyes roaming the newcomers. "Our Oregon relatives. Aunt Jessie and my father have two brothers. I've never met them, but my father gets letters from them. Twice a year he goes down the Missouri with Wolf for supplies and news. Guess this means the morning meal will be late. Come on, let's go see."

Bo and Henry hung back.

"Don't want to intrude," Henry said.

Jane grabbed him by the arm. "You are family." She led her grandfather toward the swelling group spilling into the schoolyard.

Beth lifted a brow at Bo.

Bo shrugged. "Looks like they'll need help with unloading and caring for their mounts."

Laughter, tears, and voices raised to be heard greeted Bo as he ventured forward. The reunion of Beth's family was overwhelming for a man with no family, yet at the same time, he found the energy and emotion of so many family members gathered invigorating. It didn't matter that he and Henry were strangers. They were pulled into the family circle and included, as though they belonged.

He tried to count the number of newcomers, kept losing track, and finally gave up. Discounting the soldiers who'd accompanied the family, he figured there were four adults and at least three times that many children. Some looked to be young men and women on the brink of adulthood while a few were barely tall enough to come to the knee of a horse.

Seeing a small boy about to walk beneath a horse, he grabbed the child. "Whoa there, son. You're going to get stomped on." The little boy with bright green eyes and dark hair laid his head on Bo's shoulder, stuck his thumb in his mouth, and closed his eyes.

Stunned, Bo glanced around. He had no idea who the child's parents were. Beth, with a child on each hip, joined him. "He looks good in your arms, Bo. You should have a dozen of your own. Want me to take him?" She moved close.

Bo had never held a child this small and wasn't sure what to do with the boy but found he liked the feel of the small body relaxed in sleep. The child's trust in him, a stranger, pleased him more than he could express. He shook his head.

He swayed in a rocking motion, allowing his body to brush hers. "You've got your hands full." With little Kat and Riker. Bo still couldn't believe Beth had named her son after him. He grinned down at Beth. "Besides, this one's sleeping." He enjoyed each and every little conversation with her, and sharing this moment, him with a sleeping child in his arms and her with the twins in hers, he could almost imagine what it would be like if the boy in his arms was his. His and Beth's.

That thought should have shocked him or even scared him a bit, but it didn't. Instead, it felt right, and in that moment, he wished it were true.

"I bet that's his father," Beth Ann said as a dark-haired man moved through the crowd. When he reached them, he held out his hand. "James Jones," the man said. "I see you've met Guy."

"Bodil Quinn."

James eyed Beth. "You'd be Beth Ann or Jane."

"Beth Ann, and this is Tokota and Kimilmela."

James smiled. "Must keep you both busy," he said, turning his attention back to Bo. "Can't imagine having two at once."

Bo, realizing the man thought he and Beth Ann were married, shook his head. "I'm not family. Just visiting with my godfather, who is Beth's grandfather. Growing up, Beth and I were neighbors." He winked at Beth. "Guess she never forgot me as she named her son after me. *Riker* Tokota." That ridiculous male pride in having a boy named after him made him grin and wish he could call his namesake *son*.

Beth Ann stubbed the toe of her moccasin in the dirt and flushed bright red. "Never thought I'd see you again." Her voice was a low mumble.

Bo enjoyed her embarrassment and the fact that she'd never forgotten him. He was truly smitten, and he knew he'd court her and try to win her over, not for Henry but for himself. He wanted nothing more than to be part of her little family. He mentally shook his head. Father to her children, husband to her. He wanted it all.

James put an arm around Beth and Bo. "Interesting. Come meet the rest of the family. I have a brood of eight, and Jordan, my brother, has seven."

Several hours later, sitting around the table, Bo leaned close to Beth Ann, letting his shoulder rub against hers. Her scent during dinner, one of sunshine and fresh water as it burbled down a rocky stream had distracted him during the evening meal. He made it a point every evening to sit as close to her as he could manage. It was the only time guaranteed that he could talk to her, get to know her, and allow her the same. Daytime, the women were busy with their chores, and later, she was always surrounded by her family. "Is this it? Has everyone arrived?"

Smiling, perfectly content, Beth Ann nodded. "I think so. All but Mattie's brother, Matthew. I don't think he's coming. He just lost his wife. She died giving birth."

"Up!" Kimi squeezed between Bo and her mother. Instead of crawling into her mother's lap, she plopped herself onto Bo's and leaned back against him.

Bo wrapped his arm around the child to keep her

from falling. Why, all of a sudden, did the little ones want to be held by him of all people? He didn't care and was once again surprised by the depth of emotion coursing through him. The little girl felt right in his arms, as though she belonged there. Belonged to him and to Beth. Once again, an image of forming a family with Beth intruded, and it wasn't an unwelcome thought. But there were many obstacles to overcome. In order to form a family with her, she'd have to leave hers, and he wasn't sure she would or that he had the right to ask that of her.

He studied the noisy, rowdy group. Growing up, he'd never been lonely, but there had been times when he wished for siblings. Mostly he'd accepted that after his mother died, it was just him and his father, except the short time with Jocelyn.

No, he'd never lacked anything. And when Henry brought his family over, he'd had Beth Ann. She'd been like a young annoying sister and he the big brother who didn't want to be bothered, yet he'd also been pleased to be the center of her attention. Not that he'd ever shown her that.

He stared at her now, watching the play of emotions chase across her features. Her eyes, a dark, mesmerizing blue reminded him of warm summer days. His gaze dipped and lingered on her parted lips and traveled down her throat. The tugs of attraction—okay, outright lust—said there was nothing brotherly about his feelings for her.

"It's quite a family you've got, Cupcake. Makes me wish I wasn't an only child." He tucked a stray strand of blonde hair behind her ears and traced his finger along her jaw.

Her gaze searched his. "Then you understand why I won't leave."

A light inside him dim as he read both happiness and sadness in her eyes. He didn't like what she said, but he understood. He also knew that when he left, a part of him would remain, because he had to return to his ranch, to his way of life. The thought of never seeing her again sat like a hard lump of coal in his belly.

****

Bo regretted turning down Rook's offer bathing in the kitchen in a tub of warm water as he eyed the swelling river. Sighing, he sucked in a deep breath, took three steps back, then with a yell that would have made any warrior proud, he ran and took the plunge.

Literally.

By jumping buck-naked into the frigid water.

The shock of icy water closing over him shut down his lungs, which was good. Otherwise, he'd have gasped the water into his lungs. "Hell and damnation," he shouted as soon as his head broke the surface and he could speak. "You people are crazy fools." He paddled to the shallow waters where a group of men was laughing good-naturedly.

On the bank a few feet above him, one of the soldiers flew over his head with a battle cry. Bo waded a short ways downriver to make room for the other foolish bastards stripping their clothing. He scooped a handful of sandy soil then scrubbed his body.

"Damn, can't feel a thing," he swore, his teeth chattering. "Should have stuck with a bucket of cold water." But he wasn't about to endure George's taunts another day. The boy's disdain rankled. If the kid could handle the cold, shocking water treatment, then dammit, so could he.

Striking Thunder joined him. He shoved his wet hair out of his face. "You get used to it."

Wolf swam over, then stood. "Gotta agree with Bo here. A nice, warm bath is the way to go."

"You, my brother, are soft," Striking Thunder taunted. "Think I don't know you bathe in that tub you brought back for your wife and children?"

Smirking, Wolf smacked the flat of his hand on the surface of the water and splashed his brother. "You have ice for blood. We all know that." He glanced up at the bank, narrowed his eyes, then grinned. "You boys gonna just stand there?" He jabbed Bo with his elbow.

"If this Yankee can manage, so can the two of you. Unless you want me to tell my wife her brothers are afraid of a bit of cold?"

Bo would have laughed at the reactions of James and Jordan. Both men rolled their eyes, then stripped and jumped, splashing everyone as they hit the deep middle of the river.

As soon as they reached the shallows, they stood and deliberately splashed Wolf. Bo, suddenly caught between another water battle, held up his hands, his fingers blue with cold. "Enough. I'm done."

He climbed out and scrambled up the bank. Tomorrow, he'd go back to a wet rag and a head dunk in a bowl of soapy water. Spotting George, he tried to grimace, but his teeth were chattering so hard, he had to grit his teeth together to keep them from shattering.

George nodded, gave what might almost pass for a grin, and leaned against a tree. Damn kid, knew he'd show up here in the morning with the rest of the fools.

At this rate, he might never get home. He'd surely catch his death first.

Using a stingy square of toweling, he dried himself quickly. About to step into his pants, he heard his name. Glancing at the bank, he spotted a blue-lipped, teeth chattering Matt.

"Give me a hand out of here, will ya. I can't feel my damn feet."

Laughing, Bo stuck out his hand and hauled the younger man out of the water.

Matt practically danced on his toes as he ran to his pile of clothing and a cloth to dry himself. He glanced down. "Shit, I think my John Henry froze and fell off." He winced. "Sorry, Henry," he muttered to the man who joined them.

Henry let out a string of colorful curses. "Don't think mine's any happier, boy." He sent a baleful glare toward Wolf and Striking Thunder who were already dressed. And laughing. "You boys got ice in your veins if you do this every day."

Wolf shook his head. "As my brother said 'you get used to it.'"

"Not in this lifetime," Bo said as Wolf and the chief walked away, still laughing at the tenderfoots.

James and Jordan joined Bo. "What say we drown those two? Don't care what anyone thinks. I want my bath water warm." Jordan dressed quickly.

"You'd care what Jess thinks. I'm not giving her the chance to give me a bad time. She hasn't changed that much."

Bo eyed Matt, surprised the man had taken part in the painful ritual called bathing. "Speaking of warm baths, you lose your tub privileges?"

Matt shrugged. "Nah. By the time Ma and Margaret are done, the water's cold and dirty beside." He grimaced. "And it's three days till the next bath. After wading in mud from the rains and mucking out the stables, I stink worse than a pissed off skunk. Figure if the rest of you can do this, so can I." Even while shivering, he looked at Bo with defiance, as though daring the older man to belittle him.

Bo stepped into his pants. "How old are you now?"

"Almost twenty. Why?"

Shrugging into his warm, winter coat, Bo pursed his lips. "Seems like you're finally growing up." Working from sunup to sundown, so to speak, had kicked much of the immature defiance out of Matt.

"Still don't like this place," he grumbled as he hurried into his clothing.

Bo hid his smile. There was no heat or anger or even resentment in the boy's tone. "Might be the best thing to happen to you and your sister." Margaret, as always, obeyed meekly, but Matt? Matt had surprised him. In a mere two weeks, he'd taken to the routine put before him and seemed to be thriving. For the first time since Jocelyn came into his life with her children, he felt a connection. Maybe in time, he'd actually come to view them as family.

"Can't believe what my sister and her man have done here," James said between tightly clenched teeth.

Bo turned his attention to James and Jordan chatting with Henry. He'd liked both men on the spot. They were as down to earth as he and Henry. Coming from Oregon, he'd expected the lot of them to be a bit nose-in-air and too good for his sort. But James and Jordan each owned farms. Put the two of them with him

154

and Henry, and the four of them could talk ranches and farms all day long and far into the night. Not that anyone allowed that.

"You boys gonna yak all day or join us?"

At first, Bo thought Wolf's shout was for their group but noticed that everyone was suddenly rushing to get dressed.

"Hells, bells, shake a leg, Matt," Bo called out to the younger man who seemed to be struggling to dress. "We'd better get moving."

Matt slid his feet into boots that had started out shiny and new and were now looking well broke. "Don't know anything about hunting." He shrugged into his coat, which looked good on him but lacked the warmth of Bo's.

Bo hid his grin. He heard the wistfulness in Matt's voice. Slapping the boy on the back, he led the way up the embankment. "Seems like now's a good time to learn."

James fell into step and rubbed his hands together. "Glad we arrived in time. Would have hated missing out on a hunting trip."

"Bo!"

Turning, Bo saw George running toward him. He stopped and waited. The boy held the Stetson in his hands. Bo took the hat. George had worn it all of yesterday and kept it overnight.

"I said you could keep it." This had become part of their routine. Bo giving the hat to the boy and George handing it back.

"I will earn it."

Bo set the hat on his head and sighed. "You coming?"

George shook his head, the sulk returning to his eyes. "School," he said, the word derisive.

"Hey, you remember what I said. Learning is good."

"Don't need to know the white man's world," the boy scoffed. He eyed Bo. "I'm a better hunter than you with my bow and arrows than you with your fire-stick."

"No doubt," Bo said. "But only because I don't know how to use a bow and arrow." He wanted to make a point that all learning was good, whether a person used that knowledge or not. In just his short time here, he'd heard enough talk to know what Beth Ann's family was afraid of, and he applauded their decisions to educate the next generation.

George drew himself up. "I could teach you. I could be your *waunspekhiye*."

Bo grinned. "I don't have a bow or any arrows. Think maybe we can arrange a trade?"

Eyes bright, George nodded. "Trade and barter." He eyed the coveted hat. "Bow and arrows for hat. And *I* will teach you to shoot." He frowned. "You will also learn to make arrows."

Bo watched the boy walk away, his shoulders thrust back proudly, his step filled with purpose.

"You are good with him," Wolf said from behind as he left the trees.

"I admit, he's a bit of a challenge. Why is he so different from the rest of the children?" The other four boys who'd adopted him and Henry were eager to learn and constantly begged for more stories. But not George. Though he took his place with his adopted family each evening, he remained standoffish.

"He lives with an uncle who is old and lame.

Mother died when the boy was young, and father decided he'd rather drink rotgut than raise a son. Father left one day to go get more whiskey. Didn't return. His tribe sent George to his father's brother who belongs to our tribe. The uncle tries his best but fears the boy, who was not raised as our children were raised, will follow his father's steps. George resents being here."

"Said his place was with his ill uncle," Bo said. "He might have a point."

Wolf, hands on his hips, sighed. "If I truly believed the boy cared, I wouldn't have taken him. He's only been with my tribe this summer, and this is too new to a child his age, but staying with an old, sick relative will only give George the opportunity to get into trouble."

He rolled his shoulders, then looked Bo square in the eyes. "That is the main reason he is here. Since his arrival, he's been trouble, and his uncle is too sick to take him in hand. Doubt he lives through the winter."

When Wolf indicated they should walk, Bo fell in step. "What's going to happen to George come spring?"

"He'll stay here, if he doesn't run off."

"Orphanage *and* school," Bo said, his admiration for the man growing day by day. He knew half of Wolf and Jessie's children were adopted. He hoped George stayed and decided he'd do what he could for the boy.

Wolf visibly shook off his worry. "Enough worry. Today we hunt. Gotta feed all them children."

Bo grinned. "After you, boss."

Rolling his eyes, Wolf laughed. "Told you enough times I'm not your boss. You are a guest here, even if you more than carry your weight."

"Boss, host, what's in a name?" Out of the corner of his eye, he caught sight of George standing in the shadows of the trees. After brief eye contact, the boy whirled around and walked back toward the school buildings.

Bo's heart went out to the troubled boy. He couldn't imagine being unwanted or unloved. After resolving to spend more time with George, he focused on getting ready for the hunt. He planned to present Beth with whatever he hunted in order to prove he could provide for her and her children.

He grimaced. Back home, he could buy whatever she needed but not out here. He kicked a stone. He'd hunt and be successful, not that he figured it would make any difference. They came from two very different backgrounds, yet he had to try to win her over. Something inside him demanded it.

Not only was he going hunting, he was going courting.

****

Inside her tent, Jocelyn kicked bedding and clothes out of her path. Matt and Margaret's pallets were tidy, their clothing folded neatly. Her bed was torn apart due to her inability to get comfortable and fall sleep, and her clothes were strewn all over the tent. Everything she'd tried to put on that morning smelled moldy and damp.

She let loose with a low growl of frustration and anger that startled Margaret. "I hate this place," she said between clenched teeth. She wished she'd gone back to the fort with the soldiers. At least she'd have been treated with respect and courtesy and not been forced to work like the hired help.

Working and doing mundane chores offended her sensibilities. Work. Did they think she was some poor lower class sop? She'd always had enough money to pay for whatever she needed done, but thanks to that damn interfering Henry who'd talked Bo into this trip, she was nearly broke. The old bastard had made her pay her way.

Jocelyn picked up one of her favorite dresses that had a torn hem from gathering firewood. She shrieked and tossed it across the room. "Ruined. Everything I have is going to be ruined." Her plans to set herself up for life had been ruined as well, and she didn't have the money to buy her way out of this mess, not that money would do any good with that old goat or his horse-faced wife. That rat bastard Rook got perverse pleasure in her comeuppance.

She disliked being forced to do menial labor, but she hated Rook and Sofia with every fiber of her being. There had to be a way to get Bodil to leave. Stomping to the opening of her tent, she flung the flap out and glared at the world outside.

The sky hung heavy with another storm, puddles dotted the ground, and several muddy paths marred the school grounds. She grimaced. The inside of the tent smelled musty from the last rains. A blast of wind slapped against her, making her shiver and wish she had a warmer coat.

A group of children ran past, ignoring her as though she didn't exist. God, she hated them. Noisy brats up at sunrise. No respect for those trying to sleep.

Loud, boisterous voices drew her attention. Groups of men and boys with wet hair emerged from the forest. The younger boys ran off to play while all the men headed for one of the tipis with smoke rising from the center hole.

Her gaze fell on the two newest men who'd arrived two days ago. More family, she sneered to herself. Each man had black hair shot with gray, a wife, and a horde of brats. Didn't these people do anything besides breed? Birthing two had been more than enough for her.

She glared at the fire pit in front of her tent. She had yet to master keeping the embers going throughout the night. It was stone cold and wet from the moist morning air. She shivered and looked for Matt. She'd have him get the fire going again. Spotting him with Bo and Henry, she frowned. Matt's hair was wet and his lips blue. Had he really bathed in the frigid water with the rest?

She didn't understand how these people could do so. She'd talk to him later and order him to stop. He'd catch his death, and she hadn't gone through two days of the worst pain in her life to lose her son. Especially when she needed him just to survive her time here. "Matt!"

He turned, said something to the others, and hurried over. That pleased her. At least someone listened to her.

"What?"

She arched a brow. "Don't speak to your mother in that tone." She pointed to the cold fire pit. "I'm cold. Get a fire going. You can warm up as well. I can't believe you were foolish enough to bathe in that river. You're not one of them."

Matt rocked back on his heels. "I'm a bit old to be told where and when to bathe, Ma."

"You'll catch your death. Your lips are blue and so are your fingers. Now start that fire."

Shaking his head, Matt glanced over his shoulder,

then back to her. "No time. Got to get to the meeting Wolf called. We're going hunting in the morning."

"You do as told, and you sure as hell are not going hunting." She glared at her torn fingernails and shoved her hands on her hips. "You remember who you are and what we're doing here."

Matt squared his shoulders. "Sorry, Ma. You'll have to make your own fire." He turned to go.

"Don't you walk away from me," Jocelyn screeched, but to her utter shock, her son took off running and rejoined Bodil and Henry, who'd waited for him. Together, the three men entered the tipi.

Furious, she spun around and let loose a scream of frustration.

"Now what's wrong?" Margaret asked wearily.

"Your brother. Refused to light us a fire." She kicked Matt's bedding, bent down, and tossed his pack across the tent. It hit the side and slid to the cold, damp, musty, floor where the cold, damp, stinking bedding lay, which hid rocks that poked during the night.

"I hate this place." She rounded on Margaret. "Go find someone to deal with our fire."

Margaret got to her feet, went to the doorway, and wrung her hands. "There isn't anyone, Ma. The children are in school, and all the women went to Jessie's place. There's no one out there."

"Go find Rook, then," Jocelyn ordered.

"I'm not going to bother him," Margaret said, her eyes wide, her voice pitched so high, she squeaked. She started picking up the clothing Jocelyn had kicked from one end of the tent to the other.

Although she couldn't blame her daughter, Margaret's refusal, coming on top of Matt's defiance pushed her over the edge. She grabbed her daughter's arm and swung her around. "You do what you are told."

She held on and waited until Margaret's head dropped, and she muttered, "Yes, Ma."

Jocelyn let her go but stopped her before she left the tent. "Tonight, you'll take care of our other problem."

Margaret looked like she'd swallowed an entire lemon. "It's not going to work, Ma. He's not the least bit interested in me."

"It doesn't matter. He's a man. You bare yourself and shove those pitiful breasts at him, and he'll be grunting like a rutting pig."

"Ma!"

Jocelyn ignored her daughter's wail. "Don't argue. Tonight."

A blast of wind slapped at the tent, filling the inside with cold air that bit through clothing and stung her skin. The canvas shook, and one corner came loose from outside. Both women ran out.

Margaret stuck the long wooden stake back in the ground, but it came back out. Another blast of wind nearly uprooted the tent. "Ma, help me."

Swearing, seeing no one around, she grabbed the rope and pulled while Margaret tried to secure the line. The wind died back. Jocelyn glanced at the sky and frowned. Another storm.

Back inside, she glared at her filthy dress, groaned at the number of leaves, twigs, and pine needles stuck to the hem. She pulled her skirt up and began pulling off bits of nature.

A sharp burr poked her finger, making her swear again. She narrowed her eyes. Maybe there was a way for her to get Bo to take them home. She glared at her daughter who was lying on her bed, face buried in her arms. Her daughter would do her part, as would her son, but they needed to leave this place. The sooner the better.

Another blast of air shook the tent and that same corner came loose. She ran out, yelling for Margaret.

Chapter Seven

Beth Ann braced herself against the wind as she made her way to Jessie's cabin. She held her son against her, inside her coat. "Winter's coming, *Ina*."

Dove, with Kimi wrapped in a fur cloak caught up. "Early this year," she huffed out. "I'm glad we are staying here. Won't be so harsh."

Nodding, Beth Ann reached out and pulled the door to the cabin open. The aggressive wind nearly wrenched it from her fingers. She stumbled inside as though an invisible hand shoved her from behind. "Wow."

Immediately, waves of warm, scented air washed over her. She sniffed. The tantalizing aroma of spice and sweet, along with the yeasty smell of rising dough had her belly growling.

"Smells good," she called out as she set her son down then removed her coat. Dove wrestled the door behind her.

"I swear, that door is going to fly off," Jessie called out from the stove.

"Nearly did." Beth Ann chuckled.

"Tea or coffee, Beth?" Sofia asked.

Having had her morning coffee, Beth Ann smiled. "Tea. It will go wonderful with those sticky buns I smell."

"Grab a seat then."

She hung her coat on one of many hooks on the wall and glanced around. "Morning, Emma. Mattie." Mattie was stuffed into a padded chair, and Emma sat in a rocking chair, nursing her daughter. Her twins joined the children too young for school playing in front of the large fireplace.

She went to the fire and held out her hands to warm them, her gaze roaming over the young ones. Weeko, Emma's daughter was playing with Annie, Mattie's two year old and the twins while Grady and Guy sat back to back, each occupied with a pile of blocks.

Heading for the table, she stepped over another child. "Coralie, what's his name?" There were so many new children.

"That's Dean," his mother called out. "He's three, and his sister Katherine is crawling under the table."

Beth Ann loved her aunt's large, open and airy cabin with its many added on rooms and lofts for her growing family, which included five homeless children whose parents had taken ill.

Soon it would be wall-to-wall with women, babies, and toddlers. Beth Ann moved to the right where the family ate at a long wooden table. She'd leave the comfortable chairs for her elders. Sofia set a pot of tea in front of her just as the door burst open.

"Going to be raining buckets by dark," Renny announced.

"Wind's stripping the needles from the trees as well." Winona, who'd just arrived, pulled pine needles from her hair.

Beth Ann hurried over to help the elderly woman out of her cloak. The two hugged. "I can't believe you and my great-uncle came." They lived with the

Cheyenne tribe.

Winona held out her arms to Renny and took the fussy baby. "Wouldn't miss a family gathering and neither would Sun Walker. Getting too old to make this trip, though having a nice soft, warm bed makes it worth it." She nodded at Sofia who'd insisted she and Sun Walker stay with them.

"Rook and I love having you. Now, everyone find a seat. Food is nearly ready.

Beth Ann sat on the bench and pulled her sewing out of her pouch. Across from her, Jessie's sisters-in-law had their sewing in their laps as well. Eirica Jones concentrated on making tiny stitches on a boy's shirt while Coralie attached lace to the dress she was making.

Beth Ann glanced out the window and smiled at the sight of the two additional tipis squatting beneath the trees to one side of the canvas tent. Her smile faded when she saw Jocelyn and Margaret heading to the schoolhouse. She mentally shook her head. A more unpleasant person she'd yet to meet.

Turning back to the women from Oregon, she asked, "Do you have everything you need for your stay? Are you warm enough?"

Eirica brushed a stray strand of red hair from her face. "We are quite comfortable. Between what you've all provided and the provisions we purchased before heading upriver, we are well set."

She leaned forward. "I love the tipi, and so does James. It's so different from a house. And the children... This is all they've been talking about for months. They are having lots of fun so far." She bit off her thread and stuck the needle safely in a pincushion.

Coralie chuckled. "Your kids were telling everyone they were going to go see their Indian relatives, even though that's not strictly true. Raised a lot of eyebrows at the store."

"True enough," Beth Ann said. "Family is family."

Smiling, Eirica turned to speak to Jessie in the kitchen. "James has missed you and Jeremy."

"Jordan, too," Coralie added.

Jessie came out with a platter of sweet rolls, her green eyes alight with pleasure. "I can't believe we're all together again. This is wonderful. And sad, because we'll have to part again."

"But not until spring," Eirica said, grabbing Jessie by the arm and squeezing. Tears moistened her eyes.

Coralie lifted a brow. "And me? You're glad to see me as well?"

"Of course, Cora." Leaning down, Jessie hugged her old nemesis. "Wouldn't be the same without you." Both women grinned.

Beth Ann snickered. Last night, after dinner, around a roaring fire, Jessie had regaled everyone with tales of her and Coralie's childhood feud.

"I can't believe some of the things you did, Aunt Jessie." Her aunt had always had more spunk than sense, according to Jeremy, but Beth Ann admired Jessie. The woman took no guff from anyone.

Jessie laughed. "I was rotten, I suppose." Her eyes glinted with mischief. "Didn't tell you some of the best stories."

"And I think you will leave it at that, Jessica Naomi," Coralie said, her own eyes narrowed.

"You say that because I trounced you but good."

Beth Ann let the laughter and conversation wash

over her. Rolls of sausage and bread were passed around and eggs for those who wanted them. Talk turned to men and babies. Of all the gathered women, she was the only one unmarried.

"You must be pleased to have two men courting you, Beth."

Beth Ann glanced up from her sewing. "Just one, and I've told him no."

"Standing Horse is the brother of her departed husband and has threatened to take her children if she refuses to marry him," her mother announced. She and Winona had joined them at the table to eat.

Immediately, everyone stopped their handwork and conversation and started protesting.

Beth Ann grimaced. "You know?" She narrowed her eyes. "Spotted Owl tattled."

"As you should have told us," Dove said, angrily. "He will *not* take our babies and you will *not* marry him."

Beth Ann nodded. "No. I won't." She glanced around the table. She knew the stories of each woman present and how each had met and fallen in love with their mates. Beth Ann vowed she would never again settle for less.

"What of the other man?" This came from Winona who stood beside the sink, helping Sofia with the dirty plates.

"There isn't any other man." Beth Ann didn't want to talk about Bo. She knew he was courting her, or at least paying her a lot of attention, especially during the evening meal. It would be easy for her to avoid him, after all, she had a lot of family she could sit with, but she found she looked forward to their shared time. He was intelligent, engaging, and just plain handsome and compelling. But it didn't do any good to allow him to court her as her place was here and his in some far off land. Still, she enjoyed the man's company, and she was woman enough to enjoy being courted. And he *was* courting her, not just being friendly. So what was she going to do about it? She had no idea.

Renny rolled her eyes. "Come on, Bethy. We all know that the good looking rancher is sniffing after you."

"Bodil?" Eirica sighed. "He reminds me of James and how he courted me on the Oregon Trail. Wouldn't give up or take no for an answer. I bet your Bodil is the same."

"He's not *my* anything." Well, maybe he was a fantasy of what could be but no more than that, no matter what her secret yearnings wanted.

Coralie looked at Beth with pity in her eyes. "The man watches you every chance he gets."

Beth ducked her head to hide her grin. Yeah, every time she glanced around, there he was, watching her. When their gazes met, he'd tip his hat to her—if George didn't have it. If Bo had no hat, he gave her a salute, and her heart pattered and a warmth stole through her.

And each night, sitting beside one another, he'd touch her, small gestures—an arm pressed against hers or a thigh, tucking her hair behind her ear, or if they were in a playful mood, a finger stroking down her nose. And the look in his eyes all spoke of a man courting a woman.

And it wasn't just him making the moves. She found little ways to touch him as well—reaching across him, tickling her daughter when he held her, just to breath in his masculine scent, a mixture of woods, smoke, and horse. When he wasn't looking at her, she watched him, studying his every movement. The way he held himself, the way he walked or just stood, surveying his surroundings.

One of the things she loved was the way he interacted with the children who constantly sought him out to learn about his world. Then there was George and Bo's obvious interest in the boy and the way the boy idolized Bo. But she kept those thoughts to herself and allowed the other women to think she had no idea and no interest. But, oh, she was interested, even if it came to naught.

Winona sighed. "Oh, to be so young again and in love."

Comments and stories of love went on until Beth Ann held her hand up. "Bo is my grandfather's neighbor. I haven't seen him since I was a child."

When he was Boo. And I was Cupcake. She couldn't help smiling. Since accepting her grandfather and Bo's explanation of how things had been between her parents and grandfather, her memories of that time were returning. Including her antics with a boy named Boo.

"And he'd like to get to know the woman you've become," Renny tossed out.

"No, he's just being nice, hoping to convince me to return with my grandfather." Just yesterday, he'd presented her with two rabbits and a squirrel. Two days before that, a deer. Almost no day went by that he didn't present a gift of some sort to her. A feather, a pretty stone, and her favorite, a carved horse, the detail so lifelike. The meat was shared, and she was in the process of tanning the hides. Her growing children needed new winter garments, and she wanted to make her young cousins gifts to take back with them when everyone left. And she planned to make him a pair of moccasins from the aged and smoked hide she'd traded Emma for.

"You are not blind, daughter."

Beth pushed her plate away and gave in. "All right, he watches me and talks to me each evening." *Courting her*. The words thrilled her, even as they made her nervous. She admitted she looked forward to the evening meals, made sure she sat where he could join her. Part of her enjoyed hearing about his ranch, even though she'd never see it. Still, the time they spent talking and getting to know one another was one she'd treasure when he left.

She spared Renny a glare. "But Bo will leave, so there is no point in letting him court me because my family is here." She ignored the pang of regret that sat in her belly like food gone bad.

She held back a sigh of regret. She really did enjoy being with Bo and did find herself constantly looking for him, watching and admiring him. Part of her wished there was a chance he might remain, but that was wishful thinking. Seeing both Bo and her grandfather leave was going to be hard. She was surprised by how much she enjoyed her grandfather, how much closer to her mother she felt when he told her and Jane stories of her mother's childhood, and even stories of their own childhood. She'd miss both her grandfather and Bo and would always wonder what it would have been like to have Bo for her husband. But her life was here, and he belonged elsewhere.

She glanced out the window, ignoring the fact that she hoped to catch a glimpse of the man who occupied so much of her mind of late and instead saw the tent flapping. "Oh no, that woman is going to lose her shelter."

Everyone turned. Sofia clucked her tongue against her teeth. "Stubborn woman. Serves her right if it rips loose and blows away. Tried to convince her that the tipi is better for the winter." She glanced up from her knitting with an evil grin. "Tent's wet inside. Woman reeks of mold."

Jessie frowned. "We have to do something. Might not like her, but she is a guest here."

"An unwanted guest," Sofia said. "Like weevils in the flour."

Emma wrinkled her nose. "Jessie's right. What can we do? She refused our help."

Standing, Jessie rested her hands on her hips.

Coralie shuddered. "I know that look, Jessica. What are you planning?"

Everyone turned to Jessie. Jessie eyed each woman. "What do we do with stubborn children who won't listen to reason?"

Chuckling, Coralie put her sewing away. "We step in and do what needs doing."

Sofia nodded. "We should have done this to begin with. I'll go to the schoolhouse and make sure that woman is kept busy inside for a while. Then we'll get to work."

Jessie glanced around, her gaze on the half-dozen babies and toddlers.

Winona waved her away. "Go. I will watch over

the young. When Sofia is done, she can come back and help out me here."

Mattie held out her hands. "Let me have your little girl, Renny, and Winona can have Emma's daughter."

Emma chuckled. "Pass the babes." She handed her sleeping baby to Winona. "Let's go. We don't need but fifteen minutes to do this." She slipped her arms into her fur cloak. "While we're at it, we might as well put the big tipi up. With the weather turning, might be nice to have a shelter large enough for all."

"Anyone up for a challenge?" Jessie eyed each woman as they shrugged into coats or pulled warm shawls over their shoulders.

"You bet," Dove said. "I'm still faster than you."

Beth Ann rolled her eyes. For as long as she could remember, the women took great pride in seeing who could erect their tipi the fastest. Before she could blink, Dove and Jessie had split the group in two. Eirika and Coralie, who'd never seen a tipi set up protested being included, but Jessie simply assigned each to a team.

Laughter and good-natured jeers accompanied the women as they spilled out into the blustering wind.

****

Inside Striking Thunder's tipi, the men had finished their plans for their hunt. The approaching storm forced a delay and was a bit of a disappointment. Between the crowded bodies and the embers burning brightly in the center, Bo found the air stifling, making him itch to get out into the fresh air.

Outside, the wind howled, sounding like the maniacal laughter of a drunk swaggering down the road. Seeing those closest to the door glancing out and their wide grins that followed, he realized something was going on.

"Looks like we have a competition going among our women," Wolf announced. He sat on one side of the opening.

Henry stuck his head out. "Why are they putting up more tipis? Thought everyone was here."

"Think the women have decided to teach the outsiders a lesson." Wolf chuckled. "Don't know about you boys, but I'm not missing this."

As one, the men rose and ducked out of the warm tipi and out into the frigid air. Bo and Henry followed.

"Nice to see one of these set up," Henry commented.

"Yep." Bo and Henry had left to go hunting right after the Jones family arrived. When they got back, the tipis had been erected.

"Ought to be interesting." He fell into line with the rest of the men, then frowned when he saw the army tent had already been emptied and taken down. A handful of women were setting long poles in place. Matt squeezed in beside Bo.

"Looks like your ma's getting a new shelter." Bo folded his arms across his chest.

Matt groaned. "Shit. She's gonna be fit to be tied."

The women were split into two groups. One erecting a tipi where the tent had been, the other group putting one up in the center of the huge, grassy yard.

"Why two?" Bo asked.

Wolf pointed. "That one is larger. It's used for council meetings and for large groups of guests. We'll eat and gather there when it rains" He leaned forward and eyed his brother. "Want to wager? I say Jessie's group finishes first."

Striking Thunder folded his arms across his chest and rocked back on his heels. "She may have more women, but Emma is with Dove, and she's the fastest. You bet, you lose."

Wolf considered a moment then grinned. "I win, you make me a new bow."

"I win, you hand over that new knife you got at the fort."

Jeremy slapped his thighs. "You might as well give him that knife, Wolf. I'm with the Chief. Dove, Emma, and Beth Ann will beat the rest of them."

Tyler joined in. "Renny has a tipi she sets up for the children to play in. She's good. How about we all join in. Losers haul hot water for baths for the fastest team. That way the winners truly win."

Henry slapped his hands on his thighs. "Bo and I are on Beth Ann's team." He wore a proud look on his face as he watched, fascinated by the process.

Bo frowned. "I figured the men put up the tipis." His gaze followed Beth's every movement, his gaze lingering on her womanly figure and shapely legs. She had to be cold, but her laughter sounded warm and slid into his heart, binding them together even though his chance of succeeding was slim to none.

Wolf, Striking Thunder, and even Jeremy looked horrified. "If we tried to step in and help, we'd be skinned alive."

In the wind, the hides flapped and fought the hands struggling to hold them in place, but in the end, the women prevailed.

Cheers went up when both sides finished, Jessie's team a split second behind Dove's.

Amid the laughter and praise, the men decided all

the women deserved a hot bath, although Wolf sighed deeply as he passed his new knife to his brother.

When Beth ran over to join her grandfather, Bo couldn't help but admire how the cold turned her cheeks rosy and brightened her blue eyes. He resisted the temptation to warm her chilled face with his hands and his breath.

"We did it," she said proudly. "No one beats my mother." There wasn't any awkwardness when she referred to Dove as her mother. Everyone knew and understood that Elizabeth was gone. Henry was downright grateful his granddaughters had had a loving woman who'd raised them well.

The doors to the school opened, and children spilled out. "I'm going to go see Jane," Henry said, with a wink at Bo.

Bo sighed. Henry desperately wanted him to marry Beth. In part, to convince her to return with them, but the man had also decided that Bo and Beth belonged together. Beth was looking everywhere but at him. She knew what Henry was doing, what he wanted.

"I should go check on the twins," she began.

Bo didn't want her to go, didn't want to wait until the evening meal to talk to her. *If* he managed to get a spot near her with all these people here. Most nights he managed it, and he wanted to believe she actually saved him a spot beside her, but it wasn't enough. He grabbed her hand and pulled her between tipis. "Got a better idea. Walk with me for a bit."

Beth Ann protested. "Bo, we can't. We have to stay in view of the others. That's how our people court, and we aren't courting."

Bo didn't want to be reminded that she had

someone courting her. Nor did he like knowing if he asked whether *he* could court her, she'd tell him no. Bo shrugged. "As you said, we aren't courting, so what's the harm." His grin turned mischievous. "We're old friends just trying to catch up," he said, following a narrow trail through the forest that led to the stream.

"Unmarried women don't go off alone into the forest with any man who is not a relative."

His smile turned wicked as he led her to a fallen tree near the edge of the river. "I bet those rules don't apply to you. You were married. In my culture, rules are different for young, innocent women and those who've been married."

Beth Ann sat. Had she been wearing a gown, he'd have said she'd flounced, but he kept that to himself, knowing she wouldn't appreciate being put in the same category of women like Margaret and Jocelyn. She wrinkled her nose, and he instantly recognized the young girl he'd tormented in their youth. She sat straight and tall, all very prim and proper with her hands resting in her lap. "Are you saying I have no reputation?"

Sitting beside her, he stretched his legs out. "Well, now, I didn't say that. Just those rules aren't as strict."

"And how would you know?" She glanced at him, nose in the air, lips pursed, tempting him to lean forward and kiss her.

His gaze focused on that sweet mouth. "Henry asked around. Wanted to be sure he understood your way of life. Talked to every trapper and soldier we came across."

Her lips parted, and desire struck Bo in the gut. He needed more than conversation at meal times or those stolen touches that seemed so innocent but were his way of letting everyone know of his interest in this woman. Now, he wanted to kiss Beth and feel those plump, ripe lips moving beneath his. His gaze slid back up to her eyes, and he grinned when he saw the rise of color flooding her face. She'd known exactly where his thoughts had gone, and if he wasn't mistaken, there was an answering need in her eyes.

Then she glanced away. "We should return." She started to rise.

He grabbed the sleeve of her coat. "Afraid?"

"Why would I be afraid?"

"Because I want to kiss you, Beth."

Her color deepened, her eyes shifted, looking everywhere but at him. "As you said, I was a married woman. Your words don't shock me."

"Then maybe you won't mind this." He lowered his head and moved his mouth over hers. She swayed, and he slid an arm behind her and pulled her close.

"Put your arms around me," he whispered,

"Why," she asked, her breath caressing his lips.

Beth Ann wasn't sure she could even move her arms. For nights, she'd dreamed of this, wanted this, needed to know how it would feel to be held by Bo. Each evening, with him sitting so close, she had to resist the urge to lean into him and feel his hard strength, or better yet, feel his arms around her, holding her, cherishing her. As a young girl, she'd idolized him. Had she and her family not left, would things have changed as she grew up? She'd never know.

But he was here now. She was no longer married, and they were adults. As he'd so sneakily pointed out, she wasn't held to the same strict rules as her sister Jane or the other young women. Slowly, she lifted her arms and slid them over his shoulders, her fingers threading through the richness of his hair. He pulled back, just enough so she could see into his eyes and he into hers.

She should have been embarrassed. It was daytime, they were out in the open, and in his silvery-violet gaze, there was no doubt that he wanted her as a man wanted a woman. He lowered his head. Her lips parted, and once again, he kissed her, his mouth moving over hers, sucking at her lips, his tongue stroking.

"You can kiss me back." He nibbled at the corner of her mouth, easing her head back, his fingers trailing up her back to offer support.

"I don't know how." Her eyes went wide when she realized she'd spoken aloud.

When Bo pulled back, she wanted to die a slow, agonizing death. "You were married. You have babies to prove you've been with a man."

She pulled her hands away and stared at them resting on her lap. "My husband never kissed me."

"Then he was a fool," Bo whispered, taking her hands in his and guiding them back around his neck. He held her face between his large, calloused palms. "Do you want me to kiss you? Do you want to kiss me?"

Shy, she nodded. "Yes, but—"

He rested a finger on her lips. "No buts. Just you. Me. And this." Bo lowered his head, captured her lips with his, and kissed her.

"Do what I do," he instructed, his voice a low murmur. "Do what feels good. Kiss me back, Bethy."

Beth Ann didn't need to be told twice. Giddy with excitement, she mimicked his every move. When his tongue flicked out to lick the corner of her lips, hers did the same. She gasped when their tongues touched.

"Open for me," he urged.

Beth sighed, welcoming him inside. She shivered as need coursed through her. She knew about need, but this was different. It was more. Desire surged through her, zipping through her blood to heat her from the inside out. She struggled with her coat, afraid she'd burst into flames.

"Your turn." He yanked her coat off her arms then wrapping his arms around her. He opened his mouth, his tongue dancing, luring, so that she followed. Then it was his turn to moan and groan.

Beth Ann felt powerful, in control. Never before had she been in control. There was no doubt in her mind Bo was feeling the same wild urgings. His breathing turned harsh as her lips captured his tongue. Her fingers slid into his hair, one of his hands gripped the back of her head.

When his hand slid down her throat, over her shoulder, she shuddered, and knew there was more. Much, much more this man could teach her.

"I want you, Bethy." He pulled her onto his lap.

His hard male member throbbed against her. That part of men she understood. "I—"

He stopped her with his lips. "Not now. Not here. Maybe not at all." He drew in a deep, shuddering breath. "Don't say it. Don't say anything. Just sit here with me in this quiet spot."

In truth, Beth Ann had no idea what she had been about to say. For the first time in her life, she understood what it was like to long for a man, to feel that driving need that consumed all thought and reason. Living as they did, there were no secrets about what went on between a man and a woman. She'd certainly come upon her share of couples in the woods who thought themselves alone or heard the often loud sounds of mating coming from tipis.

But she'd never felt the urge to be so vocal. She sighed. She'd felt something grow inside her, something that lifted her, taunted her but always seemed out of reach. And before she could discover what it was, her husband was done and off her, leaving that something to wither and die, leaving behind an aching need.

After a while, she stirred, sensing Bo had calmed himself. She eased back so she could see into those strange and beautiful eyes that reminded her of the sky just going dark, not blue, not black, but somewhere between. "Bo?"

"Yeah?" He glanced down at her.

"Thank you."

"Better not thank me, Cupcake. I want a lot more from you than a kiss or two."

"I think you need to go back to school and learn to count," she teased, then sobered. "I liked it. A lot."

But. The unspoken word floated between them.

"No promises," Bo said, feeling torn. "I can't promise I won't kiss you again."

Bo wanted her, knew this was exactly what Henry wanted as well, and though she clearly wanted him, had enjoyed her first kiss—and how the hell could she have not ever been kissed—there was the unspoken reminder that this was her home. He was playing a dangerous game but couldn't resist taking anything she might be willing to give him, however long it lasted.

"I might like that." She trailed her hand up to cup

the side of his face. "I might like it a lot."

He kissed her fingers, hugged her tight, then stood, lowering her gently but keeping her close. "I might like a lot more than a kiss." He saw her answer in her eyes and sighed. "How about we take it one day at a time."

She nodded and allowed him to help her into her coat. With his hand on her arm, he headed back to where her family waited.

Chapter Eight

Beth Ann left Bo at the edge of the forest and hurried across the yard. Her heart still raced, and she still felt his lips on hers. She smiled, hoping he'd kiss her again. She had the feeling that things had changed between them. Seeing him at meals wasn't going to be enough. Not nearly. She entered Jessie's cabin, found everyone sewing, knitting, or talking quietly. She sighed with relief. Maybe no one had noticed her absence. After hanging her coat, she greeted her children.

Kimi led her to the floor in front of the fire. "Sit, *Ina.*"

She sat. Her daughter handed her a small, carved wooden horse. The floor was littered with toys, each made by relatives. Noah babbled and held out a bear while Mattie's young daughter tumbled into her lap.

Kimi wrinkled her face, dropped her toy, and eyed the girl on her mother's lap. Beth Ann put her arm around daughter. "Would you like to sit with us?"

Renny, nursing her baby, eyed Beth Ann with a mischievous grin. "Where did you go off to?" Renny's son, Grady, leaned against her knees.

"Walked down to the river." And what a walk. She still felt Bo's lips on hers. She had no doubt he wanted her as a man wanted a woman and that thrilled her as much as scared her.

Renny tipped her head to the side and lifted one brow. "Well?"

Recognizing the look, Beth Ann busied herself with the youngsters. "Well, what?"

Renny kicked Beth Ann lightly. "Don't play dumb—or innocent—with me, Beth Ann. I know better." She shifted her infant and leaned close. "Did the wind put that color in your cheeks or did you kiss Bo? You were gone long enough."

"Renny!" Beth Ann glanced around, grateful the older women were still bantering back and forth over the outcome of the tipi contest, offering advice to the newcomers, and talking about the hot water baths that they were all getting. Last thing she wanted was for her female relatives to know she'd kissed Bo and that she didn't think it would be their only kiss.

"Don't make me raise my voice," Renny teased.

Beth Ann glanced around and noticed her aunt Winona, seated at the end of the long table closest to them, watched her intently.

"Don't have to. Some of us might be older, but we aren't deaf." Winona shifted on the bench to face both Beth Ann and Renny.

"What's going on?" This from both Emma and Coralie at the other end of the table, who both craned their necks to see Beth Ann and Renny.

"Renny asked Beth Ann if Bo kissed her." Winona raised her voice so everyone heard.

Immediately, women were nudging each other with elbows.

"I say they kissed. Look at the girl. Red as a newborn," Sofia said from her position at the counter where she was pounding bread dough.

Heads nodded.

Mattie waddled out of the small room she and Reed were using. She moved with confidence to a chair she obviously knew was left unused just for her, though she did check the seat to be sure no child had climbed onto it. Then she glanced toward Beth Ann with a wicked smile. "They kissed."

"Mattie!" Beth Ann wanted to fall through the floor in horrified embarrassment, yet she couldn't stop her wide, happy grin as she met the knowing looks of her female relatives. They were waiting for her to say something.

Instead, she passed her son another toy when his walked off in the hands of one of his cousins. She didn't want to share that special moment with anyone. The memory was hers and hers alone. Plus, she wanted time to absorb the kiss, the feel of Bo holding her, actually holding and cuddling her. Heat rose in her cheeks when she remembered how he'd touched her with his lips and tongue and hands, how he'd explored her as though she were some rare and special treasure. And he'd encouraged her to do the same.

Bo desired her.

And she wanted him.

The longing he'd awoken inside her still hummed through her body.

"Not nice to leave us hanging, cousin," Renny said, sitting back.

Beth Ann stood when her daughter rubbed her eyes. She grinned. "All right. We kissed," she confirmed. "And that is all I'll say." She scooped up Kimi. "Time for rest." Her son yelled when one of the toddlers pulled on his long hair. "Yep, for both of you."

Her mother rose, but she shook her head. "I've got it, *Ina*. You stay and visit."

Renny leaned forward. "You won't avoid me tonight, cousin."

Laughing, Beth Ann shook her finger at her. "Behave, Renny. You're a married woman now." She made her escape but sucked in her breath at the chill in the air and the smattering of rain falling.

Back in her tipi, once the twins were asleep, she stood in the doorway looking for Bo. She touched her lips. Her first kiss. And it had been better than anything she'd ever imagined. She wanted to kiss him again, and he'd said he wanted to kiss her again.

And more.

And that got her thinking about the rest of the mating act. If kissing Bo was enough to have her acting like a dreamy girl, what would the rest be like with him?

She wanted to know. Ever since his arrival, she'd been drawn to him. At first, she'd simply looked forward to talking to him in the evenings and getting to know him again. But now, she wanted him as a woman wanted a man.

Spotting movement out by the barn, she smiled. Her arms crossed comfortably across her breasts as she watched him enter a corral with saddle and bridle. One of Wolf's dogs followed. The stallion that previously allowed only Wolf and the dog—half wolf—near, stood still for Bo. And as soon as the object of her thoughts mounted, the horse rose onto its hind legs and the dog barked.

Beth Ann wasn't worried. This seemed to be part of the ritual between this man and horse and dog. Sure enough, the stallion settled, and then shot out of the enclosure with the dog shooting out after them like a bullet fired from a gun. The sight of that strong yet gentle man atop a wild and magnificent horse made her sigh with longing.

Yes, she wanted more kisses and maybe, just maybe, *more*.

Before she could turn away, Standing Horse stepped out of the shadows of the forest beside Jocelyn's newly erected tipi. He glared at her for a long moment, then stalked toward the barn.

Sighing, she felt sorry for the warrior. He was a good man trying to follow his sense of duty. But he'd have to accept that, although she'd spent more time in this world, she was of two worlds.

Choices, Mattie had said. Beth Ann understood it wasn't just a matter of choosing between two men or two worlds. Now she had to choose between her life here and life with Bo.

She'd already rejected Standing Horse, and by kissing Bo, she'd clearly chosen him, but she'd also made her decision to stay with her family. So where did that leave her and Bo?

"You look like you've lost your best friend, daughter."

So lost in her own thoughts, she nearly squealed at her mother's silent approach. "*Ina!*"

Dove grinned, grabbed her daughter by the arm. "Come. I brought us lunch. You left rather suddenly."

"The twins—"

"Will be fine."

Beth Ann went, knowing there was no way she was going to get out of a mother-daughter talk. She decided to head her mother off. "I can't fall in love with Bo," she said, entering her mother's tipi. "I can't be in love with him. He hasn't been here that long."

Dove lifted a brow as she sat. "My daughter, we do not choose to fall in love or not. It happens or it does not. Time makes no difference."

Beth Ann took a bite of the warm stew and enjoyed the way it chased away the chill. "It isn't wise," she finally said. "I won't leave."

Dove chuckled. "Wise or not, you do like him, do you not?"

Beth Ann nodded. "He talks to me. Asks my opinion and shares his stories with me." She sighed. "He makes me laugh."

"In ways your husband did not," Dove said.

Beth bit her lip and considered what to say. "I belonged to my husband, but he never belonged to me. He never shared himself with me. With Bo, it's different." She hesitated then burst out, "He kissed me and he wanted me to kiss him back." Heat rose in her face again, and she bent her head to her stew.

"I see. And did you?"

Beth Ann couldn't help grinning at the memory. "Yes. I did."

"And?"

"It was wonderful. I've never been kissed before."

Dove looked shocked. "Never."

Beth wrinkled her nose. She hadn't realized how much she needed to tell her mother the full truth of her marriage. "My husband performed his duty, and it was my duty to allow him."

Dove set her food down. "Oh, child, there is duty, but between a husband and wife, it should be a shared pleasure."

Licking her lips, she couldn't meet her mother's gaze. "Bo held me. He wanted to just hold me."

Dove reached over and not so gently, tipped Beth Ann's chin up. Her eyes were dark orbs that glittered with the emotion a mother feels when she learns her child has been ill-treated. "He never held you?" She saw her answer in the sadness Beth Ann knew had to be in her eyes. Dove got to her feet.

Appetite gone, Beth Ann set her stew down and drew her knees to her chest. "Never. I always thought a husband held his wife all night, as Papa holds you. But Singing Bear mated with me, then went to his own bed." For the first time since her husband's death, she used his name aloud, even though they never spoke the name of the dead. She was angry he'd denied her so much and left her feeling as though it was her fault, that she had been lacking.

Dove paced. "You deserve much more than what you've had, daughter. I knew you weren't happy, but I had no idea."

"How could you? I was too ashamed to say anything. There was nothing I could do. I was his wife." She leaned back on her arms, feeling the weight lift from her shoulders. "I belonged to him. It was that simple. He didn't treat me bad, and he provided everything I needed. How could I complain that I was lonely?" And empty and lacking. But she kept that to herself. She'd existed, knowing there was more, but hadn't any idea of how much more. Today, in the space of two heartbeats, Bo had shown her just what she'd missed.

"Past is past," she murmured. "I have my babies,

and for that, I have no regrets."

"What of Bo? And your grandfather?"

Beth Ann folded her legs to the side and plucked at her belt. "I'd like to see my grandfather again. I hope we can find ways to visit. But I don't know about Bo. He'll leave when the time is up."

"Do you love, Bo?"

She shrugged helplessly. "I want him and I like spending time with him, but I do not know if that is love." Her heart and mind called her a liar, but if she admitted to loving him, then she'd have to make more choices, and she wasn't ready to do that.

"Then you need to find out." Dove dug into one of her hide pouches trimmed with beads and feathers. She pulled out a small square of cloth.

"There's no point." Beth Ann frowned as her mother rooted inside a pouch filled with feathers and beads. "I won't leave."

"You can. Whether you will is another matter. Love changes everything, daughter."

"Then I don't want to fall in love with him."

Dove chuckled. "You are young yet. You'll learn that when it comes to your heart, it rules. Now, how about sharing this? We both deserve a treat."

Beth Ann gasped at the chocolate her mother held. "Where did you get that?"

"Wolf brings me treats. No telling your brother or sisters. Or your father. He'd devour my stash in one night if he knew I had sweets."

Beth Ann took a dainty nibble and moaned. "I think I like this as much as Bo's kiss." She glanced at her mother. "Maybe better."

The two women giggled and ate their sweet.

****

"What the hell were you thinking," Bo asked himself. He sat on the split-log railing surrounding the largest fenced pasture. The stormy weather mirrored his thoughts. Spotting Samson standing beneath a stand of pines on the other end, he whistled. Samson immediately galloped toward him, and Bo fed him the carrot he'd snatched from the kitchen. He grinned. Both Sofia and Rook knew he sneaked food out for the horses, but no one said anything.

"I'm a fool," he said to his horse. "Got no business sniffing after that filly, and I'm even more a fool to kiss her."

"Only a fool if you don't take the time to win her love."

Bo nearly fell off the railing when Wolf spoke behind him. "Damn, can't you make any noise when you walk?"

Wolf hoisted himself up, swung his leg over, and straddled the rail. "And miss out on listening to you beating yourself up? Nope, much more fun this way."

"You're an evil man, Wolf." He braced his feet around the railing when a strong gust of wind nearly knocked him off the railing.

"And you look like a lovesick fool. Heard you kissed my niece."

Bo narrowed his eyes. "From who?"

Wolf chuckled. "Son, we all saw you go off with her, and none of us are blind. Falling for her, aren't you?"

Bo shrugged.

Wolf slapped him on the back. "What's the problem? Aside from her refusing to leave her family."

"That's not enough?" Bo sighed glumly. He wanted nothing more than to openly and actively court Beth Ann. At first, the idea had appealed because she was attractive and sweet and he'd been drawn to her. They had a past to build on, a foundation and a friendship. But sharing that kiss changed everything. And nothing. He wanted Beth Ann to marry him, to be his wife. But that wasn't going to happen. "It's complicated."

"Love always is. It winds us up like a spinning top."

Bo thought of the top his father had carved for him as a child. He still had it, in a small trunk back in his closet at home.

"Yeah, I do feel like I'm spinning out of control. But that's the easy part. I can handle that." He grimaced. "It's Henry I worry about."

Wolf stretched his arms overhead, sending the fringe on his buckskin shirt swinging. "He doesn't approve?" He looked skeptical.

Bo leaned over and swatted Samson on the rump when the horse almost bumped him off the railing in his quest for more treats. The horse took off with tail held high. "Hell, if I married Bethy, he'd be as thrilled as a boy getting his first real fishing pole." Bo took a deep breath. He wanted no secrets between him and Beth's family.

"I promised Henry I would marry Beth Ann." Seeing Wolf's brows life, he hastily added, "This was when he was afraid she'd be a wild captive or otherwise unacceptable socially and in need of rescuing or saving. As my wife and the granddaughter of a powerful politician, Beth Ann would have the best of everything she needed."

"So what's the problem?"

Bo went to pull his hat off his head but it wasn't there. He dropped his hand and tapped his fingers against his thigh. "Beth Ann doesn't need marriage to return to society."

"Henry wants you to marry her." It was a statement of fact.

Staring at Wolf, Bo nodded. "Suggested I court her and win her love."

"So she'll return."

"Yeah. He means well. Losing his family almost destroyed him."

"Still don't see the problem. You want to court her, or you wouldn't be kissing her." His expression hardened. "At least you'd best have honorable intentions, son."

Bo, in that moment, knew that if he played fast and loose with Beth Ann, he'd have a lot of angry male relatives to contend with. "Told Henry I wouldn't do that to her or to any of you. Trouble is—"

"You are falling in love with her."

Bo watched the wind tear through the trees, tossing leaves and sending branches swaying. "Henry bought my ranch. Beth was part of the deal. Well, in Henry's mind. He said he'd give the ranch back as a wedding gift." Once again, Bo straightened and met the man's gaze. "From the beginning, I said she had to be willing. Trouble is, if she finds out, she won't trust me, and I'm not foolish enough to think she won't find out."

"Couldn't agree more. A smart man does what is right. Takes his chances."

"My place isn't here. I have a home. A life. What

point is there in me courting her? I won't use my feelings to make her leave."

Wolf hopped down and waited for Bo. He pointed to Samson. "Was the pain of being thrown while breaking him worth it?"

Bo grinned. "Worth even the broken arm he gave me. Best horse I've ever had." Without Wolf saying anything more, Bo understood. Risk and reward.

A loud *halllloooowwww* echoed through the trees.

"Who the hell is that?" Bo asked.

Wolf let out a piercing whistle that sounded more like the wind shrieking through the treetops.

Bo peered down the trail in deep shadow. He spotted movement. "More company?" He fell into step with Wolf.

"Couple of trappers who sometimes spend the winter. Haven't seen them in a few years though."

"More people."

Wolf just smiled. "We like visitors."

The men, when they came into view, were everything Bo imagined a trapper to be. Both men were huge mountains of men, standing a good head taller than him and Wolf. Both were barrel-chested, wearing coats with thick fur cloaks that made the men look almost cone-shaped. Deep auburn hair shot with gray clouded around their heads, and facial hair hid their faces. Glinting pale eyes and bulbous beaky noses were all Bo could see of the men's features. Each wore a pack that looked to weigh close to a hundred pounds.

"Bo, meet Duckman and his brother, Stinky."

Smiling politely, Bo wasn't sure whether to offer his hand or not. Both men were a bit on the ripe side, and the one called Stinky did have a strange odor coming from him. He frowned when something inside the man's coat moved. He lifted a brow and wouldn't have been surprised had a snake poked out.

To his utter surprise, a black and white striped head popped out. He stepped back.

Wolf chuckled. "Still got Blackie."

"Nah. This here's 'er little girl. Lost Blackie a while back. Kept one of 'er babies. Call 'er Blackie. Easier to 'member

The men headed back toward the school and cabins. Bo kept a wary eye on the skunk. As long as that tail remained in the trapper's coat, he figured he was safe.

Rook came out to meet his old cronies, greeting them warmly. "Was wonderin' if you ol' coots would show this year. I was gettin' worried."

Talk turned to the storm, the delayed hunt, and the best place to find game. But Bo had only one thing— one woman—on his mind. Beth. His Bethy. And the more he thought of her, the more he realized he had to come clean with his deal with her grandfather.

****

Jocelyn tossed the rag she'd been using to wipe down tables and benches into her bucket of ice-cold water. "Filthy children," she muttered, swiping her arm across her forehead. Standing, she pressed a hand to her lower back. All morning, that bastard Rook had her cleaning in the schoolroom. She glanced around, tempted to sneak out but knowing she didn't dare. John would tattle to Wolf, and Wolf would tell Rook.

Across the large, open room, John and Laura were reading to the younger children while Jane worked with the older students.

Margaret slipped over to her. "I'm done." She set her bucket of water down. She'd been scrubbing the wooden floor. She stared at her hands. "Look at my hands, Ma. They've turned into red prunes." Her voice was a soft wail. "And my dress is ruined."

"Enough of this," Jocelyn said. "I'm going back to the tent." She marched to the door, daring anyone to stop her. The wind slapped her when she stepped outside. Margaret followed. After dumping the water and stowing the buckets and rags in the small storage closet, she stalked across the yard. She was going to stretch out on her bed, and Rook could go hang himself if he didn't like it.

She was so tired; it took her a moment to realize her tent wasn't there. She turned, thinking maybe she'd gotten herself turned around. Or had the wind blown it away? No, she and Margaret had put all their bedding and clothing in the corners and on the edges to hold it until Matt could fix the lines.

Frowning, she stared at the tipi standing like a sentry where her tent had been. "They moved our tent," she said, anger growing. Each day it seemed as though another tipi went up as more family arrived. She heard a door slam behind her and turned to see Jessie, Sofia, and an older woman walking toward her. She had no idea the woman's name and didn't care to learn. Several other women peered out the window of the cabin.

"Hi Jocelyn. Margaret." Jessie smiled.

"Where did you put our tent? How dare you touch our belongings?"

Jessie's smile remained. "Your tent was in danger of blowing away. And it was damp inside, along with everything in it. There's a storm coming, and we were concerned that you and your children would get wet so we took it down and gave you a tipi." She pointed. "It won't blow away, and we'll show you how to close the flaps. Plus, you can have a fire inside so you'll be warmer."

Jocelyn glared at the three women and felt their amusement at her expense. "I told you I didn't want one of those. I want my tent back. Now!"

"You are under our hospitality and care, Jocelyn. I won't allow you to make decisions that will be harmful to your health or to your children's. There are no doctors out here." She wrinkled her nose. "Besides, your clothing and bedding already stink. Everything needed to be washed to get rid of the moldy smell. You'll find your belongings drying on the lines behind my home."

"You have no right to paw through my things." She swore at the women.

Sofia planted her hands on her ample hips. "You unpleasant, ungrateful woman. We could have sat back and let you get wet and watched your tent fly away. Then you'd have nowhere to sleep. Which is what you deserve." She shook her finger at Jocelyn who slapped it away.

"Look here, you old sow. I've had as much as I can take from you and that old man."

"This old sow and that old man are the ones who feed you, you ungrateful woman."

Jessie and Winona moved closer in case they needed to intervene.

"Put it back," Jocelyn screamed. "I'm not sleeping in one of those."

"What the hell is going on?" Bo stared at Jocelyn.

"They took my tent down."

Bo glanced over. "I know. Watched them do it."

"And you didn't stop them?" Jocelyn would never admit she hated the tent, was afraid it wouldn't keep them dry, and her clothes would rot, but she refused to accept charity from these heathens.

Wolf sighed. "The tipi is waterproof and warmer, and it won't blow away." He held up his hand, catching the drops of rain starting to fall.

"Jocelyn, say thank you. You might not like it, but the women are just trying to help." Bo's patience was quickly running out.

"Never," she said bitterly. "I hate this place."

Wearily, Bo started to say something, but Winona stepped forward, a calm smile on her face. She took the furious woman by the arm and steered her toward the tipi. "Come. We have a nice fire inside. You're wet and cold." She glanced back at Jessie. "Jessie and Sofia will bring your clothing and bedding. Should be dry, and we'll get you settled."

Shocked by the woman's boldness, Jocelyn protested, but there was no escaping Winona's firm hand. Margaret trailed dejectedly behind.

Chapter Nine

The winter storm lashed out at the earth below. Spidery fingers of light flew from cloud to ground. Trees toppled and buckets of rain poured from the sky and ran in rivers, making it difficult to walk without slipping. The river rose but not high enough to escape its confines.

For two days, the stormy weather kept everyone in their shelters. Days began late, ended early. Men gathered in the large tipi and concentrated on making new weapons or repairing old ones. Women with young children were in the cabins or their tipis and the school ran as usual.

The third day greeted the world with weak rays of light breaking through the gray cloud cover that slowly scattered. The school and buildings were situated higher than the river. Most of the puddles of water had run downhill, though the ground was saturated and muddy.

In her parents' tipi, Beth Ann watched her father wind strips of sinew around the shaft of an arrow he was making, tying the carefully chosen feathers in place. He whistled as he worked. Behind her, the twins quarreled. Two days confined left them cranky. Dove stood. "I'll take the children to Jessie's to play. It'll be warm there as well."

"Thank you, *Ina*. I'll be there soon. I want to finish this little dress."

Dove looked at the beadwork and fringe across the tiny yoke she was sewing. "You have a fine hand, Beth. You are much better than I."

"That's because you're always off hunting, instead of cooking and sewing," Jeremy said, winking at Beth Ann.

Dove smacked him. "Watch it, husband. I sew well enough." She grinned. "Just not as fancy as what Beth Ann manages." She hefted both children into her arms and left the tipi.

"You know she's leaving, so she doesn't have to sit here and do women's work with you." Jeremy wore a wicked look in his eyes.

Beth Ann giggled. "She's as cooped up as the twins." She tipped her head to one side and studied her father. "You look happy, Papa."

Jeremy glanced up from the arrow he was making. "I am very happy, Beth Ann. We're going to bring back enough meat for the feast of all feasts." He held up his arrow and grinned. "I'm going to show those brothers of mine that our arrows will bring down more deer or elk than their rifles."

Seeing his boyish smile and hearing the joy in his voice, Beth Ann frowned. "You've missed them."

"Yes, more than I realized." He stuck his new arrow in his quiver, stood, and pulled on a buckskin coat that he'd picked up during his last trip down river with Wolf.

"But they are going to be leaving again and you won't see them for a long time." How could her father not also be sad, knowing that his happiness wouldn't last?

Jeremy slung his quiver across his shoulder. "That

is why I will enjoy every moment I have." He cocked his head. He knelt in front of her. "If I worry about their leaving and how that is going to make me feel, then I've robbed myself of the time we do have."

She set down the gift she was making Renny's baby. "But how can you stand knowing you might never see them again?"

Jeremy reached out put his arm around her shoulders and drew her in for a hug. "Because I have my life here. I have my wife and my children. My brothers have their own lives."

Beth Ann frowned. "I cannot imagine not being with my family."

Sitting, Jeremy took Beth Ann's hands into his and gripped them firmly. "Sweetheart, I understand you. More than anyone else I suspect." He heaved out a sigh. "There comes a time in our lives when we have to choose between what we know and are comfortable with and something new, exciting, and maybe scary. I could have stayed in Oregon with my brothers, but had I not returned here with Wolf and Jessie, then I wouldn't have Dove, or you, or any of my children."

"You at least had your sister," she said.

"Yes, I had Jessie, but when I decided to win your mother's love, I had to leave her and Wolf behind. I left everything I knew behind to adopt your mother's way of life." He reached out and tipped her chin. "I have never regretted my decision."

Beth Ann knew he spoke the truth. "I don't think I can do that." Her feelings for Bo were growing, twisting her from the inside out, but her need for her family was so strong, she knew she wouldn't survive without them. Bo's love would not be enough.

Jeremy sighed. "There is something you need to consider, Beth Ann." He waited until he had her complete attention.

"There will come a time when your mother and I will not be here." He held up a hand. "Let me say it, because it's true. And though you have your sisters and brother, they may at some time choose to move away to live their lives as they choose. When my brothers and I decided to head west, we planned to be together, but Wolf refused to allow single women in his wagon train. We were going to send for Jessie after we were settled."

He chuckled. "My sister was a lot like you. Family was important, and she wouldn't let us go without her."

Beth Ann loved hearing the story of Wolf and Jessie and how her aunt had bested Wolf. "She pretended she was a boy so she could go."

"Yeah. Really upset James, but my point is, family was just as important to her. Yet when she fell in love with Wolf, there was only one decision for her. She belonged with him. And if you ask her, she'll admit, as I did, that she's missed her brothers, but she'll also tell you she has no regrets. Neither do I."

Beth Ann understood what her father was saying. She just didn't think she was strong enough to give up everything, and she didn't want to admit to being weak.

Jeremy broke the silence. "You have feelings for Bo."

She nodded. "It's almost like I never left. We were friends, even with him being so much older. And we are friends again."

"Maybe more than friends?" Jeremy narrowed his eyes and lifted a brow.

She flushed, thinking about the kiss and how she

wanted more kisses and…just more. "Perhaps. But I still can't leave." She didn't understand why. Just the thought of leaving made her heart race and her blood pound painfully in her head.

As though he understood, Jeremy drew her to her feet and hugged her tight. "Nothing has to be decided now, sweetheart. You have time. Get to know the man. Follow your heart."

Miserable, Beth Ann sighed. "But what is the point? The more I feel, the more it will hurt when he leaves."

A bell rang from the kitchen. "That daughter, is what life is about. Experience and what we learn from those experiences. Better to have memories of something wonderful, even if painful, than to live a life living in the past, full of regrets. Come on. I'm hungry." He held out his hand.

Though not the least bit interested in eating, Beth Ann took a plate from Rook. Bowls and platters of food lined two tables. Everyone had cooked something to add to the shared meal. The noise level rose. She glanced up, saw that the clouds were lighter in color with a bit of blue overhead. Darker clouds on the horizon warned that another storm was on its way.

She filled her plate then glanced around for a place to sit. The tables were full. She could go into the large tipi or to the schoolhouse to eat but didn't want to be closed in with so many others. She turned to head back to her tipi.

"Beth. Over here." Bo came trotting up to her. "Come on, before our seats are taken."

"What seats? There's none left." She followed him, her heart beating a bit faster. She was far too happy he'd sought her out. How would she manage once he was gone? But right then, she didn't care. She wanted to be with him as much as possible.

He led her around the large tipi. "Over there." He pointed to where several fallen logs had been dragged out of the forest. They'd been neatly arranged in a semi-circle with a brightly burning fire in the center. Jane, Matt, John, and Joy sat on the closest one to her and Bo. Sam, Sarah, Alison, Lara, Ian, and Summer took up the second log.

Behind them, Laura called out, "I talked Margaret into joining us."

Beth Ann shifted to allow the two young women to enter the circle. Laura was pulling the other woman, making it clear to all that no one, including Margaret, had a choice.

Beth Ann and Bo looked at each other, shocked.

"Bo, Beth Ann, get over here," Daire shouted, waving off a group of younger children. "Can't hold these spots forever." Daire sat on the log that formed the other end of the partial circle. Beside him, nine-year-old Allen whittled a hunk of wood. He was Daire's shadow.

James Jr. and Jordan Jr. ran over with Gary Richard, Harvey, Steven, and Carter. The boys plopped onto another log. Everyone started talking.

"Who did all this?" She sat between Bo and Daire, and if she sat a tad closer to Bo than what was deemed proper, well, too bad

Daire grinned. "We all helped, but it was Bo's and Matt's idea."

"Yeah, we wanted someplace to sit away from all the youngsters." Jordan Jr. glared at his younger brothers.

"And adults," Ian added.

"And gooey-eyed married folk." This from Daire who gave Bo and Beth Ann a narrowed-eyed warning.

Beth Ann wrinkled her nose at her cousins. "Where does that leave me?" She wasn't married, but she wasn't an older unmarried woman either. At least she wasn't the oldest in the group. Not counting Bo, Allison, James, and Eirica's eldest were older, and Lara was the same age as Beth Ann.

"Leaves you with me," Bo said, wagging his eyes at her before stabbing his fork into his hunk of meat then eating it.

A flow of warmth slid through her at his words. Yes, it left her with Bo but only until he and her grandfather left to return to their own lives. She thought of what her father said about her aunt Jessie and how she'd given up her family to create a new family with Wolf.

She watched Bo as he ate and interacted with her cousins. He fit right in, had become one of the family. He turned his head and held her gaze with his.

Leaning forward, he grinned. "Like what you see, Bethy?"

Instead of being horrified, he'd caught her staring, she smiled, her gaze dipping to his mouth. "I like what I see very much."

Bo tugged her braid. "Maybe later we can take another walk and do more than look."

"Maybe." Her heart sped up at the thought of another kiss. Or two. She licked her lower lip, deliberately teasing him.

Gagging noises drew her attention to Daire who

was glaring at her.

"You guys get mushy, you're outta here," he said.

"Yeah, no kissy-kissy." This came from one of the boys across from her and Bo.

Bo lobbed a small, hard roll at the boys who all started making kissing noises. "Be mindful of your elders," he said, a smile in his eyes.

"Yeah, you're an old man. This spot is for us young adults," Daire shot back.

"Well, if there is room around the fire, us old people will even the numbers," Renny said. "Squish together, you youngsters."

Tyler, beside her, grinned. "Yeah, you all might need some adult supervision," he added, staring hard at Daire who suddenly busied himself eating.

Groans followed, but everyone shifted to allow Renny and Tyler to join them, which, to Beth Ann's pleasure, gave her an excuse to sit even closer to Bo. Thigh to thigh and shoulder to shoulder, she was practically leaning into him, and she didn't mind, not one bit.

Surrounded by her cousins, Beth Ann felt a warm glow. Family. Hers was large, noisy, boisterous, and so loving. And totally accepting of their Oregon relatives. Even Matt and Margaret were being included in the conversations.

Which was more than she could say of their mother. Beth Ann glanced back where all the older adults were seated. She didn't see Jocelyn and figured the woman was eating in her tipi. She noticed Standing Horse watching her. As soon as their gazes met, he strode off into the woods. She decided to ignore him. Since that last evening together, he hadn't tried to talk to her and seemed like he'd given up on courting her, which was a relief.

Bo took her empty plate and set it on the ground with his. "Some family you got here, Cupcake."

"Yeah. It is."

Nonchalantly, Bo shifted slightly to give them more room and casually rested his arm across her shoulders. Conversation flowed around them and no one seemed to notice. Glad for the deepening shadows as night fell, Beth Ann leaned into him and gave herself over to just being close to him and sharing the magic of her family with him. When the time came for him to return to his ranch, she hoped he'd better understand why she couldn't leave. These people, from the eldest adult to the tiniest baby, were so very important to her.

****

Watching from the shadows, Standing Horse clenched and unclenched his fists. He palmed his knife and eyed his enemy. He had a clear shot to the man's back. One throw of his blade would take care of the white man, but he didn't dare. His eyes roamed over his brother's wife. Her hair, the color of the sun, spilled down her back and seemed magical to him.

She tipped her head back to speak to the white man, then leaned into him. Standing Horse kept his breathing deep and even. The woman was his. He'd just have to be patient.

Patience was something he excelled at. He'd watched and waited for her to grow up, determined to make her his. While gone one summer, he'd returned to find she'd married his brother. He'd been furious. Singing Bear had known he wanted to court the white girl.

But he'd bided his time, kept his true feelings hidden, though knowing his brother shared her bed had nearly driven him mad. But the sight of his brother's babies growing in her had been more than he could stand, for it was the ultimate proof that the woman belonged to another.

He watched the woman. He'd courted her, and even threatened to take her babies, but she'd still refused him. Flipping the knife hand to hand, he narrowed his eyes. He'd killed one man to get what he wanted. He could, without a shred of guilt, do so again. Once he had her, he'd plant his own seeds inside her, and once she mothered his children, he'd find a way to get rid of the evidence of his brother's treachery.

****

Bo sat squeezed between Jeremy and Henry in the large tipi. Tyler sat in front of him beside Reed. In the center, well behind the softly glowing fire, Sofia sat on a wooden stool, fiddle in hand, as she played some old ballads. James and Jordan sat on either side of her, softly strumming their guitars, lending their voices to the musical instruments.

On the far side of the tipi, Eirika and Coralie were teaching some of the girls how to dance. Giggles accompanied the music. Jessie sat cradled in front of Wolf, who was singing, along with his older sons. The rich baritones and alto singing about lost love brought a pang to his heart.

Glancing up through the smoke hole, he saw a clear, dark sky with a dusting of stars winking around a smattering of clouds. Shadows from the fire and the lanterns Wolf had hung danced along the walls.

He wondered what Beth was doing. He'd seen her

leave with Kimi crying in her arms. Part of him wanted to go to her. Not smart. Despite his conversation with Wolf, he knew he should forget about her.

He couldn't.

He wouldn't.

Especially after sitting with her and her openly showing her affection toward him. Better or worse, he was falling in love and destined for the heartbreak the men were singing about. Flickering shadows drew his gaze to where a large moth was trying to get closer to the lantern. He felt for the poor insect, for he was doing the same with Beth. She was his light, and he was going to flutter around her until he got burned.

Beside him, Henry tapped his fingers on his thigh in time to the fast tempo. His godfather was so damn happy that he worried about what would happen when it came time to leave. He didn't have the heart to bring up the matter.

When Sofia finished, everyone clapped. Then she stood and went immediately into a jig. James and Jordan matched her quick tempo.

Everyone, including Bo, clapped in time to the music. Glancing around, he saw that many had left. Those remaining were mostly the older children and younger couples. Bo enjoyed being included in the festivities.

Henry leaned close. "Gotta admit, Bo, I am enjoying our stay."

Bo nodded. He had a feeling they were both destined to leave with unhappy hearts.

"*Ina!*"

Bo glanced around and spotted Riker standing alone. Jeremy and Dove were sitting beside Wolf and

Jessie in deep conversation.

"*Ina!*" The child began wailing.

Henry, in deep conversation with Reed started to get up. Bo put a hand on the man's shoulder. "Stay here. I'll take him to his mother." Bo ignored Henry's knowing wink. Yep, he was walking down that slippery and dangerous slope of heartbreak hell.

"Come on, little man." He scooped the tired boy into his arms. Outside, the air was fresh. It carried the scent of wood smoke and coffee, something Rook and Sofia kept well supplied to anyone who wanted it.

Reaching Beth's tipi, he called out, "Beth?"

Her soft voice answered. "Come in, Bo."

Bo entered. "Got someone who was looking for yo—"

He broke off when he saw her nursing Kimi.

"Hell," he turned. "Didn't know—" He set the child down and side stepped to the door. "I'll go."

"Bo." Her gentle voice stopped him.

He hesitated.

"There is nothing to be ashamed of."

"Um, no, but women never do this in mixed company. Not where I'm from."

She giggled. "I know. My grandfather told me. But I told him the same thing I told you." She pointed to a pile of furs. "Now sit." She put her daughter down on her bed.

Bo turned slowly and watched the little boy run to his mother and insist on his cuddles. He told himself to keep his eyes fixed above her head, but he was a weak man slipping down that slippery slope and couldn't look away from her creamy flesh, the puckered and hardened pink tips the color of a rosy dawn morning, had his life depended on it.

Watching Riker, his namesake latch on, sent arrows of lust straight to *his* John Henry, and he shifted uncomfortably. He'd never thought he'd ever be jealous of a toddler, but watching the boy suckle made him crazy with need. He tore his gaze from her full breast. "Aren't they too old for this? I've seen them eating at mealtimes."

He reached across and patted the little girl on her back when she stirred and fussed. He smiled, amazed at how quickly he'd taken to her children. Actually to all the youngsters but especially Bethy's. Just holding and interacting with the twins made him feel closer to their mother.

Beth smiled wistfully. "I no longer provide any nourishment. They find it comforting. Some nights they forget, but with so many people here, they are a bit overwhelmed."

A slow grin split his face. "I wouldn't mind some comfort?"

Beth Ann's eyes widened, then she blushed from the tip of her ears all the way down her chest. "You'd want—" She cleared her throat. "You can't want—"

Bo's eyes traveled boldly back over her exposed breast. "Oh, I can, Bethy. You look as sweet and good tasting as all those cupcakes you used to make me sneak out of the kitchen."

She sighed and sent him a helpless look. She obviously didn't believe he was serious.

Quickly realizing her fool of a husband hadn't explored *all* this woman had to offer, Bo was pleased. "Cupcake, you keep looking at me like that, and I'm gonna come over there and prove how much I want to kiss and explore your breasts with my mouth, tongue, and hands, but I won't. Because when I touch you, I won't be able to stop." Hell, the throbbing between his legs warned that he might not be able to move at all without revealing to all just how much he wanted this woman.

The softness in her eyes said that maybe she wouldn't mind, but she got up and tucked her children into bed. The light from the lantern bathed her in gentle light. He crossed his ankles, drew his knees up, and wrapped his arms loosely around them, letting his hands dangle. In just a few weeks, his entire life had changed. He shook his head, glad Henry had talked— no, bullied—him into accompanying him to find his granddaughters.

Though he still worried about his ranch from time to time, he'd mostly put it from his mind.

What will be, will be.

His father's favorite saying flitted through his mind. Didn't mean a man didn't work his ass off toward the outcome he wanted, but his old man hadn't been one to fret over what he couldn't control.

Control.

Right now, he was in control. Mostly. He and Beth were friends, like days gone by, but if she learned what he'd promised Henry, she might not understand. He frowned. Would she be angry? Would the truth destroy the easy friendship and growing attraction that was blooming into something much more?

Control.

How would she react? He sighed.

"Bo, what's wrong?" She scooted close, sitting in front of him, her knees touching his.

He sighed again. "We need to talk, Beth. I have something I need to say."

She tilted her head to one side. "I'm listening."

"I made a promise to your grandfather, back before we knew for sure that he'd found you and Jane." He ran his hands through his hair, then picked up his John B and fiddled with it. "Henry was worried about you, how you'd be accepted back in our world. We had no idea if you were still captives or what your life had been like for those twelve years." He told her of the two women who had been found and how one had killed herself, and the other, a rescued captive who hadn't adjusted well to the new way of life. "He wanted to protect you and was willing to give you whatever you needed."

Beth Ann nodded. "I can understand."

"There's more. My ranch was in trouble. We made a deal." He held her gaze.

Her eyes narrowed.

"He paid the bank, and in return, I agreed to marry you. The ranch would then be our wedding gift."

Bo waited for her to speak, but she stared out into the night until the silence grew and thickened. He tossed his hat down, reached out, and took one of her hands in his. "Beth, he wanted to be sure you were taken care of."

"And you wanted your ranch."

"Yes, no. Hell, it was more than the ranch. He needed me to go with him, and I couldn't leave the ranch. Henry made it so that I could. But the one stipulation I had, from the very beginning, was that you had to be willing."

Her gaze shot back to his.

"Bethy, you had to be willing to come back, and

you had to be willing to marry me. I was firm about that."

"And now? Was that why you kissed me earlier? To get me to marry you so you can get your ranch back?" She pulled her hand free.

Bo shook his head. "No. I accept that you belong here, with your family. I'd already decided that I'd just have to pay Henry what I owe him."

"Why are you telling me this?" She tipped her head to one side.

"Because I have feelings for you." He scooted closer, reached out, and skimmed the back of his fingers against the smooth softness of her face. "Because I want you, for however long I have, and I wanted you to know the truth. From me. I don't want anything between us."

"Bo—"

"I know you won't change your mind. And if I'm honest with myself, I understand. I've never had family like you have and have little to offer you when I'm out on the ranch all day. I know this. But there is something between us. I want what you're willing to give and won't press for more."

"You won't ask me to marry you and leave my family."

Bo tucked a strand of hair behind her ear. "I might ask, because there is always hope, but I will accept your answer, and I won't use your feelings for me against you. I promise you that."

The music from the large tipi changed from loud and boisterous back to slow, love songs. He stood and held out a hand. "Dance with me, Bethy."

Beth Ann looked ill at ease. "I can't leave the

children."

"We'll be right outside." He bent down and stared deeply into her eyes. "I want to hold you and feel you against me." He gripped her elbows and pulled her up, slipping his arm around her waist. He wanted so much more, but he didn't say so.

She stared at him helplessly. "This is foolish, and besides, I don't know how to dance the way you do."

"Yeah, it's foolish." He grinned. Falling in love with her had to be the stupidest thing he'd ever done. He wasn't just walking down the slippery slope now, he was rolling head over heels like a rock. He just hoped the landing wouldn't be too painful. "It is what it is." He led her out.

Behind the large tipi, the grass was wet, but he didn't care. He drew her close, wrapped one arm around her waist, and held her hand. She leaned into him and let him lead her in a slow, twirling dance beneath the stars and the crescent-shaped moon.

Bo stared down at Beth, captivated by how the moonlight turned her blue eyes into a silvery sheen and her blonde hair nearly white. He let his gaze roam over each delicate feature, as though committing them to memory. She sighed, her lips parting. Mesmerized, he leaned forward, but instead of kissing her, he drew her close, slipping both hands around her narrow waist and rested his chin on the top of her head.

To his delight, she leaned in, wrapped her arms around his neck, her head tucked into the hollow of his throat. The night shadows wrapped them in the magic of music and night. From somewhere in his childhood, the words to the music came back to him, and he realized the Jones brothers were playing a ballad that had been one of his mother's favorites. Their deep voices blended and added magic to the evening, and somewhere off in the distance, he heard the soft strains of a mouth organ.

Bo hummed along for a moment, setting the tune in his mind. Then he let his voice join theirs. He sang, low and soft, words of love and longing.

The magical moment brought tears to Beth Ann's eyes. The richness of his voice vibrated through every inch of her body, drawing longing to the surface with the same skill of those creating magic with a strum of their fingers over strings.

Bo's voice, his warmth, his scent wrapped her in a cloak of wonder. Her parents had danced like this for as long as she could remember and she'd danced with her father, but this was the first real dance with a man who wanted her, and she let the romance of it lead her. Tonight, she followed her feelings and gave in to the need to be held and to hold, to need and be needed.

When Bo's voice faded away, she glanced up. "You have a beautiful voice," she said, her fingers moving across his shoulders.

"Inspired by your beauty, Bethy." He lowered his head.

Beth Ann rose onto her toes and pulled his head to her, meeting him. With no shyness, she kissed Bo. There was no dancing, no teasing, just hot, burning need. He pulled her closer, one leg pushing between her legs, one hand at the small of her back, the other behind her neck.

Need pulsed within her. She moved restlessly, burrowing closer. His knee brushed her center as she sank into him, seeking everything she knew he could and would give to her. She moaned when his hand slid down to cup her buttocks. Then he pressed her harder against his thigh. He swallowed her cry when her center flared with need. Never had she felt this crawling hunger that demanded satisfaction. Both of his hands cupped her from behind and guided her, rocking her against him.

Music filled the air; voices from the tent lifted in song as Bo guided them deeper into the shadows. The magic of the night, of Bo, had her panting and making soft little cries that Bo swallowed. He finally lifted his head, allowing them both to draw in a deep breath, but he kept her pressed hard to him.

She felt her own moisture and heat, along with that same tenseness deep inside that never went away and left her feeling unsatisfied. "Bo."

Desperate, she rocked harder, a movement encouraged by his hands, his fingers digging into her flesh. He kissed her again, and this time, he slid one hand beneath her skirts and feathered his finger through her soft curls with his calloused hands. Then he lifted his leg, pressing his thigh to her center where the fire he'd ignited threatened to burst into full flame.

"Easy, Cupcake. Go easy."

She shook her head. "No. Can't." Her head fell back, and her hips followed the primitive urge to move faster, to circle and grind and thrust. Bo, with his hands, guided her, set the pace even when she felt as though she'd burst apart and lose control.

Then it came together, all those feelings, needs, aches. Her back arched, and like a falling star glowing brightly during that last ride across the sky, Beth Ann shattered into thousands of pieces.

Bo leaned forward and drank in her cry of release. He shook and trembled, his own need so close to the surface, he wasn't sure he was going to be able to control himself. Wrapping his arms around her, he pulled her close, buried his head beneath her jaw and stayed where he was until her heartbeat calmed and her breathing evened out.

He lifted his head and stared into her glazed eyes. "God, Bethy, I need you."

"Bo, that was amazing. I've never felt—never—"

Bo swallowed the lump in his throat. Never been kissed, never experienced the wonders of an orgasm. Her husband had been a selfish fool, and Bo was honored to be her first, at least in some areas. Watching her experience the joy of making love, being a part of showing her just what it was like between a man and woman made his own eyes water. She was so innocent, so beautiful, and he wanted to make her his and show her there was still so much more to making love.

"Bo," she whispered.

"I want you. All of you." He held her face in his hands. "Come to me. Tonight."

She looked torn, uncertain. "I don't know—"

"No pressure, Bethy. I won't use my feelings for you against you."

"I don't want to hurt you," she said.

He knew the risks, accepted that he'd end up leaving with a broken heart, but it didn't matter. He'd been slipping down that slippery slope all night had slammed into that rocky bottom. What would be, would be. Right now, he wanted whatever she was willing to give. "Too late for that. Give me this, Cupcake. Let me have you, all of you, for whatever time we have."

Beth Ann stared into his eyes. In the starlight, he saw her indecision, her hesitation in her shadowed, blue eyes, and to his relief, her surrender.

"I'll come," she promised, then turned and hurried back to her tipi and her children.

****

Beth Ann stared up at the bit of night sky revealed through the smoke hole. Stars winked among the poles. What was Bo doing? Was he waiting for her? Staring up into the same sky? She was torn between doing what was right and what she wanted. Her body ached with need she knew he could and would fulfill completely.

She turned over, careful not to disturb the twins. She shouldn't go to him, couldn't give him what he wanted and what he deserved. So what was the point?

She remembered his hand cupping her so intimately and the myriad of feeling he'd aroused in her. He could give her what she needed. He'd given her so much pleasure. Her body had exploded with satisfaction. She bit back a moan as heat washed through her.

Oh, yes, he'd take care of her and all her needs, and she had no doubt he had the patience to teach her to please him. But to what end? In six weeks, he'd return to his ranch, and she'd be left here, alone.

She flipped onto her stomach. No, not alone. She had her family, her children, and her sister. Suddenly, it didn't seem enough. Could she let him walk away from her? Perhaps if she asked him to stay, he would. She grimaced. Could she ask him to give up his ranch to stay with her?

No. She flipped back over and rested her arm over her eyes. It wasn't fair to ask him to give up what was important to him when she couldn't do the same. She sighed.

Where did that leave them?

Come to me, Bethy, tonight.

Raw need, mingled with something she didn't want to name, haunted her mind and made her body ache. She wanted to go. But she was afraid. Their futures were already so complicated.

With closed eyes, she saw the pain of raw need in his eyes, along with love. She smiled when she remembered how he'd watched, hungrily, as she nursed her son and his desire to do the same. Her nipples hardened just thinking of cradling Bo's head between her breasts, and the center of her womanhood throbbed with need. He was willing to take the chance. Could she do less? She flipped to her side.

"Damn it, girl. Just go to him."

Beth Ann bolted up in bed. "Grandfather!" She glanced at Jane who was snoring lightly.

"A blind man can see you have an itch that boy can scratch," he grumbled. "Go. This old man needs to sleep. Gotta keep up with all them younger hunters tomorrow, and I won't be doing that if I'm falling asleep in the saddle."

Without giving herself a chance to change her mind, Beth Ann jumped up and practically ran out of the tipi.

Chapter Ten

Clouds rolled across the sky, swallowing stars like a greedy child who refused to share with others. Embers from fire pits offered glowing spots of light. Staring out into the darkness, Bo sighed.

Would she come? Had he pushed her too far? Frightened her off? He took two steps out of the barn, ready to go get her but stopped and returned to the darkened barn. He glanced toward the loft where a lantern gave off enough light to chase the shadows. He'd fashioned a soft bed, using his bedroll and a quilt Jessie had lent him.

He paced, both body and mind taut as the strings on Sofia's fiddle. His mind said it was smarter for both of them if she didn't come, but his heart yearned for her. He needed Beth Ann.

He let out his breath. If she didn't come, he was in for a long, lonely, and painful night.

He eyed the sky, but without the moon, he had no way to judge the time. But he knew it was late. She wasn't coming. Maybe the twins were having a rough night. He groaned. More likely, she'd changed her mind.

And maybe he was a fool.

Knowing he had to be up before first light, he turned and made his way to the stairs that led to the loft. He'd douse the light, grab his bedroll and sleep in the tack room. He couldn't bear to sleep in a bed he'd made to be shared.

His feet dragged and felt far too heavy to climb the ladder. He had one foot on the lower rung when he heard his name.

"Bo?"

The weight flew off his shoulders, and he spun around, hurrying to the entrance. "Bethy."

She was a dark shadow with a faint halo of light above her head. Even the blackest night couldn't hide the paleness of her hair.

He reached her, his arms snaking around her to pull her close. He buried his nose in her hair and inhaled her sweet scent. "I was afraid you'd changed your mind."

She sighed against him, her fingers running through his hair. "I did. A dozen times." Her fingers glided down, found his jaw, and stroked. "There are so many reasons why this is not a good idea."

"And just as many that say this is meant to be." He nibbled on her finger.

"You're going to leave."

"And you're going to stay."

She stared into his eyes. "Henry wants this. I'm glad you told me about the ranch and the deal you made with him."

"I want complete honesty between us, Bethy. We at least know where the other stands."

He pulled back, ran his hands up the sides of her neck until he had her face framed in his hands. It didn't matter that he couldn't see her clearly or she him. At that moment, they saw each other with their hearts. "No regrets, Bethy."

"No regrets, Bo."

He smiled, hoping when it came time to leave, he'd be able to ride away without any of those regrets. His heart had been well and truly snared and tied to hers. Maybe this intense connection started with their bond as children. He didn't know, didn't care, only knew he had to have whatever she was willing to give.

He drew her inside the barn, shoved the doors shut behind him, then scooped her into his arms. He kissed her, long, hard, and with the promise of so much more to come as he carried her to the ladder. "Don't want to set you down to climb the ladder."

Her finger trailed over his lips, stroking, probing, caressing. "You'll have to. Don't think you can carry me up without us both falling."

Bo bit her finger not so gently. "Oh?" In one quick shifting movement, he slung her over his shoulder, his arm forming a band around the back of her knees.

Her startled shriek turned quickly to laughter. "You crazy fool. I can climb up on my own."

"Nope. Not letting you go. Besides, this is more fun." He trailed his hand up her thigh and nearly wept with need when he found her bare bottom exposed.

Her giggle turned to a gasp, then a small cry when his fingertips brushed her center.

Focusing on getting them up into the loft, Bo climbed. As soon as he was able to stand, only slightly hunched, he let her slide down the front of him, inch, by slow, agonizing inch.

Before her feet touched the ground, Beth Ann wrapped her legs around Bo's waist and kissed him, thrusting her tongue inside when his jaw dropped at her boldness. She explored his mouth and engaged his tongue to dance with hers.

It didn't take Bo long to get over his surprise. He kissed her with a hunger of a man starved of love, and that fit. Aside from Henry, he hadn't had anyone special in his life for too many years to count. He'd had women, not so many that he couldn't remember each one, but at this moment, he couldn't have named names or described what they looked like.

There was no one for him but the woman clinging to him with a desperation that echoed inside him. He palmed her bare buttocks, squeezed the firm flesh, and eased his fingers toward her center. He found her moist and ready.

"Bethy, I want you. Right now." He left her mouth and trailed his lips along her jaw then down her throat. She held on, arching her back, letting her head fall back to give him complete access.

He slid her up and down his hard length, still painfully confined. He rocked his hips against her sweet, wet center, feeling her heat and the shudders as her need built.

He swallowed her moan with a groan of his own. One hand trailed up her back while his lips kept hers busy. He wanted this woman so much he ached with a need that threatened to spill before either of them undressed. He groaned when her legs tightened around him, when she rocked and circled her hips as she'd done earlier against his thigh. Small cries escaped from her lips.

With one hand, he tugged at her dress, wanting to see her, touch her, feel her, and damn it, suckle those rosy-tipped breasts. She pulled away and slipped her arms from her dress, revealing herself.

In the faint light, her white breasts gleamed like

twin moons. Her nipples were hard, thrusting nubs, begging to be laved. The ache between his legs leapt into raging need. He moved toward the bed, passed under the hanging lantern, and sucked in his breath.

Her misty-blue eyes were filled with intense longing, her well-kissed mouth red, full and parted, begging for more and waiting with pouty tips, her breasts rising for his tender touch.

He slid her down, so slowly; they both gasped. He reached between them to undo the belt at her waist. Her deerskin dress fell in a pool at her feet, and Beth stood proudly before him, all gloriously naked woman.

She wasn't shy with her body. Like nursing her children in front of him, standing before him without clothing was as natural as breathing, as it should be, Bo thought. His gaze traveled over her breasts and skimmed her slightly rounded belly, then feasted on her nest of pale hair.

"You are beautiful," he said, cupping her palm-sized breasts. He rolled her nipples between his fingers.

Beth Ann, her body already on fire, nearly fell to her knees. She grabbed his shoulders and arched her back, telling him with her body that she liked what he was doing.

He moved closer and eased one leg between hers as he pulled her close. One arm snaked around her waist while the other cupped and explored her firm breasts. He kissed her long and deep, then trailed his mouth along her chin, her jaw, planting tiny kisses along her throat, lingering in the hollow. She gave herself over to the joy of so many feelings and sensations attacking her body.

Her fingers threaded through his hair. His mouth

and tongue left a trail of fire where they touched and kissed. She sucked in her breath when his lips closed over one aching tip. Her breasts swelled and ached as he mouthed her and scraped his teeth over her. "Bo!"

He released her and used his tongue to paint ever-smaller circles around her hardened nipple until he touched tongue to tip. For a moment, he teased her, flicking his tongue over her until Beth Ann thought she'd scream with need. Then he took her back into his mouth, and this time, he suckled hard and the pull to her center sent her hips into a frenzy of jerks. She moaned, needing more.

"Easy, Cupcake. We have all night."

"Bo," she cried, gasping for air, holding on to him to keep from falling as she bucked her hips. Hard. Desperate. Up and down, demanding circles. He eased away slightly, but before she could protest, his hand was there, stroking through her blonde curls, his long fingers opening her, the heel of his hand pressing hard.

She jerked, and when two thick fingers slipped into her and matched the rhythm of his hand, she came apart.

For the second time that day, she flew high into a world of rainbows and shooting stars. Her core throbbed and pulsed long after Bo removed his hand. She wrapped her arms around him. "I didn't know it could be this way. So *Wakan*. So mysterious. So wonderful."

Bo backed her up to the inviting bed and eased her onto the quilt. The light above them reflected the wonder in her eyes as he lay stretched out on top of her. Her legs opened for him, accepted him. He held her face and kissed her gently, tenderly. This time, he'd show her how it was supposed to be between a man and a woman. He'd go slow, be everything the bastard she'd called husband had not been.

"It gets better, Cupcake," he murmured in her ear. He kissed her again, small, light, touches of his lips to hers, then made his way across her face to her nose, to each eye, nuzzled her ear, and traced the line of her jaw back to her eager mouth.

He held himself back, kept it light and tender. Each time she tried to capture his lips, he darted away.

"You're teasing me, Bo," she finally moaned as she tried to pull his head back to hers.

"Yep." He laced his fingers between hers and held her hands beside her head. "God, you're perfect." He got up on his knees and rocked back so he could tease her breasts back to perfect, hard nubs. When he took her full breast into his mouth, she shifted, moaned, and begged. Freeing his hands, he palmed both wondrous globes of flesh and buried his head between them. "Perfect," he breathed, squeezing gently, rolling her twin peaks between his thumbs and forefinger.

Her fingers dug into the quilt beneath her, and she bucked when he blew across the wet tip of each nipple. She whimpered.

"I want to kiss you, everywhere, Bethy. I want to know every inch of your body."

"Touch me again, Bo." She clamped her fingers around his wrists and tried to push his hand to her throbbing center. She felt like a water pouch filled so full it was in danger of bursting. And she wanted to fly apart and soar upon that wondrous and magical feeling.

Bo trailed kisses over her belly. Her muscles contracted, and she sucked in her breath. His finger spread her, and opened her. Seeing him staring at her should have embarrassed her, but the desire glazing his eyes said he was more than pleased with what he saw.

Her thighs fell farther open under his gentle pressure. When he lowered his head, she had no idea of what he intended. But as soon as his mouth closed over her, her hips bucked and she nearly screamed. She covered her mouth with her hand.

"Bo," she said, her voice muffled. "Bo!" Over and over, she gasped as need built and built and built. Her hips writhed, and his tongue… She'd never known a tongue could create such mind-numbing pleasure. He dipped inside her and out, stroked her sensitive flesh, and when he discovered her hidden heart, he flicked his tongue back and forth.

Her body sored, climbing that ultimate climb until pleasure once again overwhelmed her.

Bo slid up her body. "Too much, Bethy?" He whispered against her mouth.

Spent, overcome, and incredibly satisfied, she shook her head. "No. Never."

"Good." He eased off her.

Afraid that he was done, that he was leaving her, she sat. "Bo?"

"I'm not going anywhere, Cupcake." He sent her a wicked grin. "I'm not done and neither are you."

Relieved, Beth Ann watched him unbutton his shirt. She got to her feet, her fingers closing over his.

"Let me." She held her breath, half-afraid he'd say no. He dropped his hands.

Empowered, she undid each button slowly, her fingers skimming his chest. When she touched his belly, his muscles contracted.

Smiling, she parted his shirt, repeated the process with his undergarment, and trailed her palms up his abdomen, up his chest, slipping the clothing off. His wide chest was brown, hard, and dusted with black curls. She ran her fingers through the thick mat and over his hardened nipples. He jerked, surprising her.

She lowered her head, ran her tongue across his firm, brown disks, pleased when his breathing grew ragged. She glided her hands over his warm flesh from chest to waist, unhooked his belt, and undid the first button on his pants, then the second. Her knuckles brushed along the hard length, feeling his pulsing with need.

She stroked one finger up and down until he stopped her. "God, Bethy, I'll be done before you free me at this rate."

She giggled, feeling for the first time in her life like a desirable woman. Desired. He desired her as she him. "Then you'll just have to do it again," she said, dispensing with the next button.

"I created a monster."

Serious, she stared into his luminous gaze and shook her head. "No, you gave me the gift of knowing what it's like to be a woman in all ways."

He slid his fingers into her hair. "Not all ways. Hurry up."

Getting on her knees, she shoved his beeches down, watched with delight as he sprang free and bounced inches from her face. Reaching for him, she touched him, felt his hard length and the wondrous softness of his tip where a bead of moisture leaked. She wiped it away with her thumb.

"Bethy!"

"Do you like it when I touch you?" She closed her hand over him, pleased when he shuddered.

"Hell, yes," he said, the air hissing through his teeth. His fingers twisted in her hair.

She frowned. He'd kissed her in her most secret place. Did he want to be kissed in the same manner? His hands in her hair felt as though they wanted to move her closer, yet he was pushing her back.

She decided that tonight was for them. Not just her, not just him. But them. Shyly, she touched him with her lips, and the low growl he let out told her he liked being kissed in his most private place. Boldly, she ran her tongue around his hard length to where his hair curled tight and black.

He trembled, he gasped, and he groaned. Her tongue touched his very tip, and he sank to his knees.

"Enough," he said, pulling her to him. The kiss ignited the sparks between them. By the time they fell onto the quilt, fire consumed them.

"I wanted to go slow, Bethy. I wanted it to be perfect between us." He rose up on his hands and knees. He was poised at her entrance. She was wet and so ready for him.

"Don't want slow. I want..." Beth Ann pulled him to her, waiting, eager to feel him inside her. She didn't care if this part wasn't as good as all the rest. He'd given her the most wonderful gift—the gift of discovering herself—that she was more than willing to give him this. She'd give herself to him.

"Wrap your legs around me, sweetheart, and hold on."

She did, felt him seeking entrance. She closed her eyes, but his voice stopped her.

"Watch me, Bethy." He held her gaze as he inched slowly into her then stopped.

She moaned. He felt so good inside her. She wanted to move, to make him move, but this was for him so she tried to keep perfectly still. When he eased almost all the way out, she protested, then bit her lip.

"Tell me you want me."

"I do. I want you, Bo."

He moved. In. Out. Watching her. He stopped. "Are you okay, Beth?"

She gasped and shook her head. "Don't stop."

"Why aren't you moving?"

"This is for you," she whispered. "My gift to you."

Bo let out a shaky laugh and rested his forehead on hers. "Cupcake, I forget that you're a woman with no concept of how it is supposed to be between a man and a woman." He pulled out inch-by-inch and when her hips involuntary followed, he nodded, and thrust back in.

"Move with me, Bethy. Share this with me. What we did before were gifts we gave each other. We gave and received. But this…" Again, he stroked. In. Out. In. "This is our gift to each other." He set the pace.

Beth Ann matched his rhythm, and once again, that wondrous need built. She felt him growing inside her. He trembled and sweat gathered on his skin as they climbed that high mountain together.

"Now, Bethy. Fly with me."

"Yes," she cried, letting herself go.

Together, they flew to the moon and shattered into millions of sparks of light.

****

Beth Ann woke to something crawling along her

jaw. She swatted at it. It went away. Moments later, it was back, tickling her nose. She groaned and tried to turn away, but something heavy lay across her.

She opened her eyes and found Bo grinning down at her. "We gotta get you back to your bed."

"Don't want to get up." She tried to turn over, but Bo chuckled. "Someone is grumpy in the morning. Bet I can fix that."

He wrapped himself behind her, his hands cupping her breasts. "Unless you've had enough? Maybe I wore you out?"

Beth Ann flipped over so fast she lay on top of him. "You're the one who fell asleep, not me." She giggled, wiggled, and found him hard and pulsing between her legs. She lifted her brows. "I think you want me. Again."

Bo grinned. "What are you going to do about it?"

She tried to move off him, but he stopped her. "Ride me, Bethy." He lifted her up, plunged inside her, and palmed her breasts, his hands warm, his fingers squeezing enough to make her gasp with pleasure.

Beth Ann's pleased smile turned to a low groan of ecstasy as she rode him into the predawn.

Later, much later, Beth finished dressing. "Too late for me to sneak back into my tipi. I won't get any more sleep this night."

She glanced at Bo as he dressed and sighed. She was so happy it scared her. As many times as they'd pleasured themselves, Beth Ann knew it wasn't enough.

She'd ridden him, then he'd ridden her. And if her legs weren't so tired and sore, she'd have begged another round. She stifled a yawn. It was going to be a long day.

"How about a bath. That should wake the pair of us and cool our lust."

Beth Ann rolled her eyes but nodded. Together, they cleared all signs of their activity and left the barn for the river. No one else was up. The land was still dark.

Finding a secluded spot, they undressed and, hand in hand, waded into the water.

"Damn, how do you do this? My, um, do-dads are going to shrivel up and fall off."

She studied him and his "do-dads" with a grin. "They don't seem to like the cold, do they?" She winked. "Maybe I can warm them for you."

"Oh, no, you don't." Bo stepped out of her reach. "We are here to bathe." He splashed her.

She gasped as the cold water hit her breasts. She didn't think her nipples could tighten any more but they had.

"Maybe you're the one in need of warming?"

She sent a spray of water at him. "I think chill water and air are what we both need."

After bathing, he helped her out, pulled her into his arms, and just held her, their bodies cold, wet, and shivering. "I love you, Beth Ann."

She stiffened and pulled back.

He held firm. "No guilt. No pressure. Just a simple I love you with no expectations. Open and honest between us. Remember."

Incredibly moved, Beth Ann stared into his eyes and thought, in that moment, she just might love him. Unable to speak, she nodded.

He released her, and they dried and dressed. Back in the schoolyard, Bo started a fire in the fire pit in the center of the log seating area he and Matt had built. She watched and she studied, and tried not to think of love. But it was nearly impossible.

I love you.

His declaration of love rang in her ears, and she knew it would be hard to watch him leave. The thought of never seeing him again sent panic coursing through her.

Was that love? Her body responded to his in a way she'd never felt toward her husband. But was that because Singing Bear had never wanted her, all of her. He cared only about satisfying his own needs and hadn't ever cared enough to see to hers.

Bo was different. He'd made sure she'd been satisfied, well satisfied, before seeking his own release, and instead of taking what he offered, Beth Ann had wanted to give to him in the same way.

Wasn't that love? That need to put the other person's needs first? She sighed, wanting to give Bo the words. She treasured the gifts he'd given her, including his love. But part of her was afraid of saying aloud what could tear her in two.

To confess her love would hurt him more when it came time to say good-bye.

"Bethy, I don't expect you to say it. I meant what I said. I want whatever you are willing to give." He drew her into his arms. "Give me what you can. It will have to be enough."

They sat in front of the roaring fire, watching the sun streak the sky pink and blue. It wasn't long before the rest of the tribe stirred.

"Say, can anyone come enjoy the fire?"

Beth Ann glanced over her shoulder at her

grandfather. Her cheeks bloomed with heat. "Of course, Grandfather."

To his credit, Henry didn't say a word. He and Bo talked about the upcoming hunt.

Jane wandered over. "Twins slept all night," she said, a wicked, teasing glint in her eyes.

Okay, now she was embarrassed. Bad enough her grandfather knew but her younger sister? "Your day will come, sister."

"Oh, I hope so," Jane said, her eyes going soft and dreamy. "I hope so."

Before Beth Ann could ask which male had her eye, her parents joined them. "Did the two of you get any sleep last night?" Jeremy narrowed his eyes as he studied both Bo and Beth Ann.

Dove coughed to hide her laugh.

"Papa! We do not need to announce this to all." She didn't know how he knew but wasn't surprised that he did. Growing up, none of them had been able to hide anything from their father.

Letting everyone else talk, Beth Ann silently sighed with happiness. This was her family, and she loved the easy acceptance they gave Bo. With his arm around her, she knew this was what a family was supposed to be like.

"What's this?" Rook stood, a wooden spoon in hand.

"Just getting warm." Bo tried to look innocent.

"Harrumph. Not blind, lad. Seems yer blood's plenty hot these days." He speared the men in the circle with a sharp eye. "Food's ready. Get eating. Long day ahead of you." He turned, nearly bumped into Wolf. "Got food packed for the day."

"Good." Wolf's gaze scanned the group, then he grinned but didn't say a word as he turned away.

Bo stood, as did Jeremy and Henry. Immediately, Beth Ann felt chilled. And lonely. Even with her mother and sister and the other women who came over to enjoy the large fire, the contentment of a few minutes ago was gone.

In that moment, she knew that if Bo left, and she had no reason to think he'd give up his life or his ranch for her and stay, she'd be lost and lonely. Even surrounded by her family.

It wasn't long before the fire died down and everyone got up. She headed back to her tipi, using the twins as her excuse, but she wanted to be alone and hide her tears when they fell.

Chapter Eleven

The sun had risen completely by the time the men were mounted and ready to ride out. Beth Ann stood with the rest of the women, waiting to see their men off. Beside her, Dove framed her mouth with her hands and let loose a loud yell that had all the men whipping around as though afraid of an attack from the rear.

She innocently waved to her husband while everyone laughed.

Beth Ann's ears were ringing. "*Ina!*"

Dove folded her arms in front of her, her eyes narrowed. "I should be going," she grumbled. For most of their marriage, she went with the warriors, and he stayed behind with the youngsters.

"Let the men have their fun, Dove," Winona said, her own gaze on Clay.

Jessie laughed. "Let's send them off right, ladies." She let loose with a long, loud whistle that sent crows flying out of the trees. The rest of the women followed, each yelling or shouting to their man.

Beth Ann joined in, feeling such kinship with these women that it confirmed in her heart and mind that this was where she belonged. Striking Thunder's horse pranced then rose up on hind legs. The chief thrust his rifle into the air, and his war cry drowned out the voices of the women. Immediately, the men followed suit, then rode off, yelling, whooping, and whistling.

Shaking her head at their almost childish joy of the greatly anticipated hunt, Beth Ann kept her gaze on Bo's broad back until he crossed the tree line and the shadows swallowed him and his horse.

Falling into step with the others, she tried to ignore the ache in her stomach. She missed Bo already. She frowned. *He will be back long before dark. Today is no different than any other day. You have your chores and routine, and if he were here, he'd have his.*

Sighing, she admitted that it *was* different because he wasn't here where she could watch him or just know he was close if she needed him. And the whole conversation she was having with herself was pointless because in one month, Bo would ride away for good.

The thought of him leaving left her with a hollow feeling gut. How was she going to bear it and survive? In a short time, Bo Riker Quinn had become an important part of her life, even before they'd become lovers.

Each morning, he and Henry joined her family for the meal before heading out to take care of their assigned chores. And evenings, they again gathered as a family. She enjoyed hearing about his day and felt special when he asked about hers.

Best of all, he loved her children. And he loved her. Her stomach fluttered when she thought of his declaration of love. Knowing he loved her ignited a glow deep inside her, but at the same time, it made her want to cry because she didn't think she could bear losing the man she loved.

She stopped, turned, and stared off in the direction the men—Bo—had taken.

She loved Bo.

There, she'd admitted it to herself. She loved Bo, so how could she let him walk away from her? She sighed. His life wasn't here. It was far away, too far for her to be able to see her family more than once a year, if that. Especially if her people moved.

"You are so in love, Beth Ann. Now what are you going to do about it?" Renny watched her with narrowed eyes. The rest of the women moved toward the cabins, gabbing, and laughing.

Beth Ann tried to smile but fought tears instead. "I love him, Renny. I really love him."

"Then do what it takes to stay with him."

"How? I can't leave my family. I want my children to know their grandparents and their aunts and uncles."

Renny wiped the tears from Beth Ann's face. "Love demands sacrifices, Beth."

"He could stay," Beth Ann said softly. She'd never ask that of him, but deep in her heart, she hoped he would do so.

"You know he won't."

"No. He'll go. Besides me, there's nothing here for him. Which makes what I'm doing foolish." She sniffed, wiped her tears, and smiled bravely. "Guess we'd better join the others."

"Yeah, Rook called a meeting, and he doesn't like it when we're late."

Beth Ann and Renny entered Jessie's cabin and found everyone gathered. They took their seats at the table. She held out her arms for Renny's baby, seeking comfort in holding the infant. As she stared at the infant with her glinting red hair and sweet blue eyes, Beth Ann wished it were her and Bo's baby in her arms. Maybe he'd gift her with a child before he returned to his own life.

Letting her gaze roam over each person, she just couldn't imagine leaving and not seeing these women again. Across the table from her, her mother and Emma chatted while Emma nursed her daughter. Sofia and Winona sat at the end of the table, across from each other, like two aged bookends, while at the other end, Eirica oohed and ahhed over the tiny dress Coralie had just finished.

"Here, Renny, for little Margaret Mary." She handed it over the table.

Renny held it up and stroked it tenderly. "I love it, Coralie. Thank you."

Beth Ann added her own ah's of appreciation. She loved the fussy dress. A long-lost memory slipped across her mind of the last Sunday best dress her mother had made her. It had had lots of lace and ruffles, and she'd felt like a princess wearing it. Maybe she'd ask one of the women to make Kimi a dress with yards of ruffles. Her daughter wouldn't be able to wear it except here. Out on the plains, garments like that wouldn't hold up, but here, the children dressed like children in the white world. She handed the infant over to be nursed.

Craning her neck, she checked on the twins who were playing in the large living room. Riker sat on Mattie's lap in the overstuffed chair with her feet stretched out, resting on a small stool. "Mattie, do you want me to take him?"

Mattie rubbed her belly and looked miserably uncomfortable. "He's fine, Beth Ann."

Beth Ann recalled how large she'd been, how her back and feet had ached during those last few weeks.

She felt for the woman. Staring around the room, she couldn't help wondering if this large, loving family would ever be together again.

It had taken time, money, and sacrifice for each family to come. And if they were to repeat this reunion, where would it be? It wouldn't be here. Not if Wolf and Jessie sold their land to the army. And the Oregon branch of the family might not be able to return, certainly not all the children for many of them were of marriageable ages and would be busy with families of their own.

Rook and Sofia entered, and Rook's booming voice broke the thoughts circling her mind.

"Enough chatter, all you women. We got plans to make." He stood like a general waiting to address his army. When he had everyone's attention, he continued. "Not often this family gets together so we're gonna have us a fancy dinner with everyone wearing their Sunday best. I want a fancy feast with a fancy table. And I want nice decorations."

"Decorations," Beth Ann blurted, her eyes wide.

Rook pointed the wooden spoon he seemed to carry with him at all times at her. "Don't go getting smart with me, Missy," he said, using his schoolroom-no-nonsense glare. "You heard me. This is a special occasion. A reunion. And it's going to be special. The best night of everyone's stay. I want those tables prettied up as though the president himself was coming to dinner."

Renny, sitting beside Beth Ann, tapped her on the foot, then grinned when Beth Ann glanced over. Primly, as though once again in the schoolhouse, she raised her hand and waited until Rook glanced at her.

"What happens if it rains? The tipi we set up isn't large enough to hold this lot."

"Rain or no, we'll be eating in the school house. We'll have a nice fire, and maybe even some entertainment."

Beth Ann lifted her hand. "What about the children? We all adopted the children of our tribe. Doesn't seem fair to not include them."

Rook waved aside her concern. "We'll make room. Got it all planned out."

Beth Ann tapped Jane's foot. She'd been ordered to attend Rook's meeting.

Jane, catching on to what her sister and Renny were doing, shot her hand straight up. "What kind of entertainment?"

About to launch into his plans, Rook frowned and swiveled his head back to the table. "What tha—"

Seeing the ill-concealed amusement of the women, Rook realized they were playing with him. He put his platter-sized hands on his wide hips. "What are the three of you playing at now?"

"Just making sure we understand." Renny was all wide-eyed innocence.

Rook's lips twitched even as he glared at Renny, Beth Ann, and Jane. "Then put on your listenin' cap and sit on them hands."

Around them, the older women chuckled.

"This sounds wonderful, Rook," Emma offered. She sent a good-natured glare at her sister. "The children, and those who act like children, can eat in here."

"Got it figured out. We'll all fit in the schoolroom. Just got to move all the tables from outside inside." He speared the young women with his narrowed gaze. "Seein' how you three are so concerned and all, you're in charge of the decorating."

Renny groaned. "Oh, no—"

Beth Ann punched her cousin and laughed. "This will be so much fun."

Rook shook his head, then pointed at Coralie. "You're a fancy miss. You're in charge. Rope in the rest if you need. I want a grand celebration." He folded his arms across his massive chest in case there were protests, but everyone began talking about ideas for table decorations, what the children could make to put on the walls and even dangle from the ceiling.

Happily engrossed, the wail of a child startled Beth Ann. Her head snapped up, and she glanced over by the fireplace where the twins were playing with Annie. Her son had knocked the girl down. Kimi reached over to pat Annie on the head to comfort her.

Immediately, the girl's wail cut off as though the child's throat had been paralyzed. She went stiff as a tree trunk, her face turned red, and when she got her breath back, her screams filled the room. Startled, the other children began crying and screaming.

Mattie tried to get up to go to her child but was stuck in the chair. Beth Ann scrambled off the bench, rushed over to pick up the little girl, and turned to hand her to Mattie. She froze. Mattie's eyes were glazed and unseeing, her jaw slack. "Renny!"

Renny knelt beside her sister and held her hands.

In Beth Ann's arms, Annie was kicking and flailing her tiny fists. Beth Ann tried everything to calm the child, but nothing worked. Alarmed at how red the child's face had become, Beth Ann was ready to ask someone for some cold water to try to shock the girl out of her fit. As sudden as it began, Annie went limp.

"That's it, Mattie. Come back to us. Come on."

Seeing that Mattie had snapped out of her vision, Beth Ann felt the prickle of hairs on her arms and neck. "Renny? What happened?" She looked from mother to child. "Does Annie have the gift of sight?"

Renny sighed. "I think this means she does."

Mattie had had two visions that Beth Ann knew of since arriving and both had involved her. Chilled, inside and out, she hugged the limp child closer. "What does this mean, Renny?"

Everyone else in the cabin sat in stunned silence. She was aware, barely, that several women had moved into the room to pick up and console the crying toddlers.

Shaking her head helplessly, Renny turned back to Mattie who was sipping tea from a cup Sofia held. Her sister's hands were shaking uncontrollably. "Mattie?" She spoke softly and gently as she sat on the edge of the stool. "Annie is okay. She's right here."

In Beth Ann's arms, the little girl lunged for her mother, and Mattie gathered her close and drew in a deep, shuddering breath. "I know how my mother felt when she realized I inherited her gift. And her mother must have felt the same."

Tears tracked down her cheeks. "I never wanted any of my children to suffer with this gift."

"What is wrong? What did you see?" Beth Ann's heart raced, and a chill ran down her spine.

Mattie fixed Beth Ann with her dark, troubled, unseeing gaze. "I've never had a vision like this," she murmured. "As soon as Annie began screaming, everything went black and red, like smoke from a fire hiding the sun in the sky."

Mattie's visions so far had been about her, Bo, and Henry. Was something wrong even now? Her gaze fell to the little girl in Mattie's arms who'd fallen into a fitful sleep. What could the child have seen to make her scream the way she had? Beth Ann's stomach clenched.

Mattie reached out. Beth Ann took her hand. "What is it, Mattie?"

"I don't know what the vision was about or why I had it, except that it was connected to my daughter's. I wish—" Mattie suddenly closed her eyes and grimaced as though in pain.

Beth Ann held her breath. *Please, not another vision.* "Mattie?"

Mattie clutched her belly and smiled weakly. "I think the baby is coming."

Emma got up and gathered her children. "We'll get out of the way."

"Why don't we move to the large tipi so we can work on planning this celebration?" Coralie tossed out the suggestion while gathering her stuff and scooping up Beth Ann's daughter.

Beth Ann forced her fear aside and told herself that the child's vision had nothing to do with her. "I'll take Annie." At Mattie's nod, she reached down and gently scooped the sleeping child into her arms while Dove gathered Riker.

She followed her mother out of the cabin and couldn't help but look toward the barn and remember her incredible night in Bo's arms. Shivering, she prayed Mattie's vision had nothing to do with Bo or Henry, but was very much afraid it did. What would she do if anything happened to either of them?

Her grandfather was family, and she'd miss him terribly when he left. It shocked her to realize that in so short a time, he'd become just as important as her family here, maybe in some way, more so as he was her only connection to her mother.

And Bo. Bo was everything she wanted in a man. He was her heart. If anything happened to him, her heart would shrivel and die. He loved her. Something deep inside shifted and rose to the surface, something she hadn't wanted to free because it meant choices.

She loved Bo, had already admitted loving him to herself, but she hadn't told him. If anything happened to him, she'd never be able to gift him with the words she longed to shout.

"Come, daughter."

Beth Ann stared at her mother and realized she'd returned to the fire circle where she sat with Bo that morning. "I love him, *Ina*."

Dove sat and wrapped her arm around Beth Ann's shoulders. "I know."

"I love my grandfather as well." She felt guilty for saying it aloud. She didn't want to hurt the two most important people in her life.

"As you should." Dove smiled gently. "There is no shame, nor do you hurt or betray your father and me. Your heart is large enough to love us all."

"What should I do? I belong here, but they will both leave."

Dove hugged her tight. "Follow your heart, daughter of mine. Follow your heart."

Beth Ann let her mother led her to her tipi where her children were playing. With Annie cradled in her arms, she sat and leaned against her backboard.

Follow her heart.

Trouble was, her heart was torn between family—her family here and Henry there. How could she choose one over the other? And if that wasn't bad enough, there was Bo. He held her heart and he'd given her his.

Silent tears rolled down her cheeks. No matter what her decision, her heart would never be whole again.

****

Bo, downwind of the large herd of deer in the meadow, surveyed the animals from his hidden position near the edge of the forest. His rifle rested on his thighs. Henry and Matt were close by. A short distance away, James and Jordan were concealed by low growing shrubs.

Wolf, his sons, along with Jeremy, and the warriors he'd brought with him were circling the herd on foot. The plan was for them to attack with arrows. The herd, when it scattered toward Bo and the others, would then be targets for their rifles.

Matt moved closer. "Bo, I need to talk to you."

Bo glanced at the younger man. He couldn't believe the change in Matt. Gone was the sullen, taunting young man with nothing better to do in life than be at the beck and call of his mother. He'd grown up on this trip. For the first time, someone had made the boy work, and that had given him purpose. "Okay. After we get back?"

Matt nodded and moved away.

Bo kept his grin to himself. Matt was sweet on Jane. He'd seen the way Matt stared at her, and with his own heart bursting with love, he recognized Matt's feelings.

Thinking of his night with Beth made him shift uncomfortably in the saddle. God, she was everything he'd ever wanted in a woman but had never come close to finding. He glanced at Henry. He owed the man. Had Henry not roped him into this trip, he'd never have had the time and leisure to fall in love with Beth Ann. And God help him. He loved her.

Remembering how it felt to wake with her in his arms, to see her sleepy smile and hold her warm body close made him realize he wanted forever. Not days or weeks. But years.

He'd promised he wouldn't use his feelings against her and he wouldn't, but how the hell was he going to walk away when the time came? He couldn't bear the thought of returning home alone, but how could he stay? There was nothing here for him.

Sighing, he wished Wolf and the others would hurry. He didn't want to sit and brood. He needed action.

"Boy, I'm sorry."

Bo didn't have the mental energy to pretend he didn't know what Henry was talking about. He took off his hat, fiddled with the brim, and shrugged. "It is what it is."

"I wanted you to love her."

Bo glanced at his friend. "Got your wish, Henry, 'cause, God help me, I love her."

Henry looked sad. "She's not going to come home with us, is she?"

"No."

"She loves you, Bo. Anyone can see that."

"Love isn't enough for her. My love isn't enough.

She needs her family." He smiled sadly. "Can't say I blame her. She's got one hell of a family." He pulled himself out of his cloud of misery. Henry didn't look any happier.

"She loves you, too, Henry."

Henry sighed. "I know. But not enough to come home with me." He stared at the rifle laying across his lap. "There's talk of them moving further west."

Bo's heart clenched. "Yeah, heard that." He felt for the old man. If Beth and her family remained here, Henry could arrange visits, but once they moved, he and Henry might never hear from them again.

"You sorry you came?"

Thinking a moment, Bo finally shook his head. "No, but don't ask me that once we're back."

A loud whoop startled the two men. The thundering of the herd drew them both back to the task at hand. Wolf and the warriors were chasing the elk toward the men while firing off arrows. Several went down.

"Spread out," he ordered, moving into position, rifle held ready. He heard Matt's rifle, then Henry's. Then he fired, saw his target fall. Before he could reload and fire again, the herd split, leaping into the woods on either side of the meadow. One huge buck leapt high, twisting in mid jump to avoid Henry.

A shriek above his head startled Bo. He glanced up and saw an owl swooping right at him. He ducked, nearly falling off his horse. His hat flew off his head, followed by a stinging pain. He put his hand to his head and felt something warm and sticky. In disbelief, blood coated his finger.

"God damn owl!" He glanced around then froze

when he spotted his hat stuck to the trunk of a tree with an arrow clean through. He rode over, yanked it free, then whirled his horse around.

On the other side of the fallen animals, Standing Horse was looking at him—no, glaring—hate in his eyes. He gave a mock salute then rode off.

Furious, Bo went after the warrior.

The man had already dismounted and was approaching the buck he'd killed. Bo dove off his horse, took the warrior down, and smashed his fist into the man's face. Immediately, the warrior flipped him off, gained his feet and drew his knife.

Bo drew his as well, and the two men circled each other. "You bastard. You tried to kill me."

"The girl is mine. It is my right to claim her and my brother's children." He lunged.

Bo, no stranger to fighting, maneuvered out of the man's reach. "Beth isn't a horse to be claimed. She's a woman, and she has chosen." This time when Standing Horse charged, Bo stuck his foot out.

The other man went flying but rolled and came up with a roar of fury. "I'll kill you." With the knife held high, ready to charge, the sound of a shotgun stopped him.

"What the hell is going on?" Wolf dismounted and strode into the middle of the two men.

Bo swiped at the blood seeping into his eyes with the back of one arm. He picked up his hat with the arrow stuck in it and waved it. "Bastard tried to kill me"

Wolf lifted a brow at Standing Horse who didn't look even remotely apologetic. "The white man got in my way," he said with a shrug.

"You lying bastard. I was in the trees and not

moving when you fired that arrow. That buck was a good ten feet to my right when he ran between me and Henry and into the forest. If that owl hadn't dive-bombed me, I'd be dead!"

The rest of the group rode up. Henry eased his horse forward. "Bo's right. That animal just about knocked me off my horse. It wasn't anywhere close to Bo."

Wolf remained silent a long time. Then he pointed to Standing Horse. "You leave today. I won't have you on my land."

Striking Thunder moved to stand beside his brother. "Your actions bring shame to our people, to our tribe. To the memory of your brother, who was a brother to all warriors in my tribe. You are banished from our tribe."

The warrior stood stoic, shoulders back, head held proudly as though he had no fear of the half-dozen rifles pointed at him. "My brother's children go with me to be raised by my family."

Jeremy grabbed Bo's rifle and pointed it at Standing Horse. "Come after my daughter or her children, and I'll hunt you down and kill you myself. As will my wife and every man in *my* family."

Wolf pointed to John, his eldest adopted son and two other warriors. "Take him back, and see that he leaves. With only his possessions."

With a look of fury at the four men, Standing Horse stalked off to reclaim his mount with John and the other two warriors following.

"Beth," he whispered as he watched the warriors mount up. He longed to ride back with them. He wanted to be there and make sure Standing Horse didn't try anything, but that was out of the question. No way would Wolf trust him and Standing Horse in such close proximity after the warrior had deliberately tried to kill him. He wasn't sure he could trust himself with the man, even with others close by.

Jeremy eyed Bo. "I'm going with them, and if you don't mind, I'll hang onto this." He held up Bo's rifle.

Nodding, Bo handed Jeremy his pouch of ammo. "He tries to go near Beth or the twins, you shoot."

"That's the plan." Jeremy stalked off, his bow and his quiver of arrows slung across his back.

"You all right?" Wolf asked.

"Grazed by the arrow." He glared at the hat. "Damn, my favorite hat, too."

Wolf slapped him on the back. "Better the hat than an arrow between the eyes," he said, trying to lighten the mood. "Good thing his shot was off."

Bo grimaced. "It wasn't. I ducked to avoid the owl." He didn't want to think how close to dying he'd just come. "Come on. Let's load up these animals and get back."

To Beth and her babies.

****

The air of celebration had dimmed, the laughter forced as the men, working together, loaded their horses with their kills. The larger bucks were gutted and dressed, the smaller females slung over the backs of the horses. Bo worked silently. He was worried about Beth. It didn't matter that she had her family with her. *He* wasn't with her.

"Wish I'd gotten one," Matt said as he watched Bo expertly gut a young buck. Together, they slung the carcass over the back of Bo's horse. Samson had his ears back. None of the horses liked the scent of death.

"Give it time and practice." Seeing that Matt truly looked disappointed, he slapped an arm around the boy's shoulders. "Tell you what, from now on, you'll go hunting with me. Only way to learn is to do it."

Matt beamed. "If that's all right with Rook." He grimaced. "Better than chopping wood and peeling them potatoes we eat by the buckets.

"I'll talk to him."

"Hey, you two. Some help if you don't mind."

Bo and Matt led their horses to Henry who stood over his deer.

"You young muscles can load this beaut." He hauled himself into his saddle.

The two men slung the animal over the rump of Henry's horse. The horse immediately screamed, bucked, and kicked up its rear legs, barely missing Bo who dove out of the way. The animal rose up onto its back legs and pawed the air. Matt tried to grab the bridle when the horse came down hard on all fours before kicking its hind legs high into the air.

Henry, caught by surprise, went flying over Matt's head. Matt reached out and snagged the older man by the shirtfront. Both men went tumbling back.

Bo grabbed the bucking horse and quickly calmed it just as Wolf rode up and took the reins from Bo.

"Henry!" Bo ran to his godfather who lay sprawled over Matt. "Can you sit?"

Henry moaned and with Bo's help, sat cradling his left arm to his chest. "Think I broke it, Bo."

Bo's heart sank.

Wolf strode over. "Everyone all right?"

"Think we have a broken arm." He glanced at Matt

253

who was gasping for air and struggling to sit. "Lost my breath," he wheezed, "when Henry fell on me."

Henry glanced over, his eyes glazed with pain. "Saved my life, boy. Broke my fall."

Matt smiled weakly and tried to stand. His foot gave out. "Damn, think it's broke," he moaned, falling back down. "Guess you aren't taking me hunting, Bo."

Wolf knelt, removed Matt's boot from his swelling foot. Matt's face went pale as Wolf probed.

"Not broken. Twisted. Rook and Sofia will fix you up." He repeated his examination on Henry's arm. "Yep, broken."

Henry gave a weak, pain-filled grin. "Good thing this happened after the hunt. Would hate to return to all them women without anything to show but a damn broken arm."

The men laughed.

"At least you have something besides a broken arm," Matt said. "All I got is a foot the size of a fat hog."

"Guess you won't forget your first hunting trip," Bo said.

"What got into that horse? Acted like it had a bee up its ass." Henry stood with help and grimaced in the direction of his now peacefully grazing horse.

Striking Thunder examined the placid animal. He turned and held out a hand. He didn't say a word.

Bo stared at three nasty thorns. "Where did those come from?"

"Under the saddle blanket."

"How'd I pick up those," Henry asked. "Didn't ride through any underbrush, and I checked that blanket before I saddled."

Wolf, who'd joined his brother, was also examining the padding. "Looks like they were inside. There's a couple cut marks. Took them while to work loose." His voice was deadly calm.

Stunned, Bo stared at the neat slices in the blanket. "Someone did this on purpose? Who would want to harm Henry?"

Matt had gone white, his eyes fixed on the burrs in the chief's hand. "She wouldn't."

Everyone turned to Matt.

"Speak up," Striking Thunder ordered, his tone brooking no argument.

Matt squirmed. "Can't say for sure," he began, looking miserably from one to the other.

"Say what you can," Bo said.

"Might have been my ma," he said, his voice low with shame.

"Why would she go after Henry?"

Matt sighed. "Bo, you know she hates it here. She needs to get you back home."

"Needs to?"

"Help me up. Got something to say, Bo, and I'm not saying it sitting on my ass." When he was standing, holding onto his horse for support, he returned his gaze to Bo's, man to man. "Don't think badly of me, but I can't go along with her and her stupid plans. Not anymore." He looked from Henry, to Wolf, to the Chief, then back to Bo. "Remember that I told you I wanted to talk to you after the hunt? I was going to tell you everything. You remember that?"

Remembering how serious and uncomfortable Matt had been when he'd asked to talk to him, and how he'd assumed Matt had wanted to talk about Jane, Bo narrowed his eyes but nodded. "Hunts over. Spit it out."

"Ma wants the ranch to sell to the railroad, and we're supposed to help her get it."

Bo shrugged, completely unsurprised by his confession. "Figured that much out on my own, especially with your sister throwing herself at me. I assume your mother wants me to marry your sister."

He nodded, keeping his gaze on Bo's. "Margaret doesn't want to do it, but you know Ma."

Struggling to keep the anger from his voice, Bo asked quietly, "And you? What are you supposed to do?"

Matt hunched his shoulders. "Make sure you don't live once you and Margaret are married."

Longing for a rock to kick or throw or, better yet, wishing Jocelyn were there so he could kick her all the way to hell and back, Bo sighed. He should have known. He stared thoughtfully at Matt. The boy's confession was a surprise. A pleasant one. He also recalled that Margaret had been open with him. Seemed Jocelyn's children had minds of their own after all. "I should have figured something like this was behind her sudden interest in me and her determination to accompany us."

"Thing is, Bo, I'd decided a long time ago not to take part. Don't like traps. Not sporting-like. Didn't tell her that, though. She'd make my life hell." He lowered his gaze to his swollen foot. "I like you just fine, Bo, and don't want what's yours."

Bo wasn't sure what to say. What could he say?

Taking a deep breath, Matt lifted his gaze. "That's what I was going to tell you so you could watch your back. Didn't worry about you here. Not even with

Margaret, who is supposed to seduce you and get with child, because a blind man could see you are smitten with Beth Ann."

"Ah." Bo drew the single word out.

Matt sighed with disgust. "She wasn't going to do it, Bo, but you know Ma." His gaze swept over Wolf's, then away. "I was going to ask if I could stay." He plucked at his horse's mane. "I wasn't very nice to you or to anyone when I first got here. Didn't realize how unhappy I was. Never had a purpose other than whatever my ma demanded of me." He looked ashamed.

"And now," Wolf asked.

Matt squared his shoulders. "Like what I'm doing just fine, and for the first time in my life, I got respect, though I suppose that's now gone."

Bo put aside his fury toward Jocelyn. She'd be dealt with later. "Don't reckon you've done anything to lose what you've earned, Matt." He glanced from man to man. "It's what we do that counts, not what we might have done."

Striking Thunder nodded. "Agreed. It is up to my brother whether you stay."

All eyes turned to Wolf who folded his arms across his chest. "Reckon we could use another hand around the place. John and Laura said you're good with the children."

"You mean that?" Matt's eyes shone with tears and hope.

Wolf nodded. "Never say what I don't mean. Remember that."

Matt nodded vigorously. "I won't forget. I promise. And I'll work hard."

"Then it's settled," Striking Thunder said.

Matt frowned. "Why did she try to harm Henry? It's you, Bo, that she hates."

Henry spoke up. "Reckon it's because I'm the reason Bo left the ranch. As long as I'm here, so is he and the rest of you."

"So what do we do?" Matt looked apprehensive. "She was wrong to do this and everything else, and I know she needs to be punished." He shrugged, then let out a long, low sigh. "But she is my mother."

Wolf looked to Bo.

Bo understood. Jocelyn was his problem. "We have no proof. I say we treat this like an accident and watch her."

"Maybe we should leave," Henry offered, his eyes clouded with pain not just from his arm. "Get her out of here."

Wolf shook his head. "You are not in any shape to travel."

"She's my problem," Bo sighed. "I'll take her to the fort and leave her there to arrange to go wherever she wants."

"Not about to trust that woman alone with you," Wolf said. "My niece would never forgive me if that woman managed to do you in."

"Send her with the soldiers," Striking Thunder suggested.

Wolf nodded. "I'll speak to them."

Relieved but feeling guilty for selfishly not wanting to leave, Bo helped Henry back onto his now calm and docile horse.

Wolf mounted his horse and glanced at Matt. "You'll move into our cabin. A bit crowded, but you can share the loft with John, once you're able to climb the ladder. Meanwhile, we'll find you a spot."

Bo mounted, keeping his horse close to Henry's while they waited for everyone else. Reaching up with one hand, he felt the dried and caked blood in his hair and his thoughts returned to Beth and the danger Standing Horse posed to all of them.

"Let's go," Wolf ordered.

Glancing at Wolf, Bo lifted a brow.

"You and I will ride back ahead of the others. There are enough of us to split the group."

Bo wanted nothing more than to do as Wolf suggested, but he also knew his duty. "I'll stay with Henry."

"Go," Henry said. "You go and make sure our girls are safe."

Bo didn't need further urging. He and Wolf rode hell for leather with two warriors trailing behind them.

Chapter Twelve

School lessons were done, and the children were outside, enjoying the brisk afternoon air. Beth Ann threaded her way through a group tossing balls, past others with hoops, and to the log circle. Her sisters sat with James and Eirica's girls. The older girls had books. Alison was reading her book aloud to the younger girls playing with dolls.

Daire led a pack of boys on a run through the trees. They shimmied up the thick trunks and into the branches, whooping and yelling. Beth Ann stepped out of the way of another charge of children. She loved the noise, the confusion, and the sheer joy of children having fun.

Children, so innocent, they had no idea something bad might be happening. They took each moment as it came. She wished she could put her worry aside. There was so much to do, she didn't have time to fret and stew. Yet she continued to pace.

Tipi to tipi, tipi to barn, barn to corral, across the yard then back. Over and over. Back and forth. Reaching the barn, she stopped. Hours before, she and Bo had made love up in the loft. She turned and eyed the log circle where he'd told her he loved her then pressed a fist into her stomach.

She loved him and hadn't told him. What if something happened and she'd never get the chance to tell him how she felt?

"Where are they?" It didn't matter that it was early yet. She needed to know he was all right. She drew in several slow, deep breaths and tried to convince herself she was overreacting, but Annie's terrified screams echoed in her ears and she couldn't get them or Mattie's vision out of her mind.

"Bo's a good hunter. Why are you worried?"

Turning, Beth Ann spotted George leaning just inside the barn. "Hard to explain," she said to the boy who worshiped Bo. Looking into his dark eyes, she realized that she wasn't the only one worried.

The boy stood stiff, his head high, eyes searching hers, a far cry from the sullen child who wouldn't look anyone in the eye. "Heard about the woman who sees things."

"Mattie. Yes, she has visions."

"Visions about Bo?"

Beth Ann sighed. "I don't know, George."

"You believe he's in danger. That is why you keep coming back here. You are waiting for him."

Deciding to be open and honest with the child, she nodded. "Yes. I can't explain it. Ever since they arrived, Mattie has been having visions. She knew he and my grandfather were coming. I'm afraid today's vision means something bad. I just want him to return."

Silent, he seemed to absorb what she said. The change in him was amazing. He had become a miniature of Bo. He wore a blue shirt, his pants were brown, and he'd found a pair of boots from the school wardrobe. He even wore a leather vest. All he needed was a hat and a leather belt.

George stepped back. "Reckon I will watch for

him." He turned and headed up the path leading away from the barn.

His use of one of Bo's favorite words made her smile. Behind her, a door shut. She turned and spotted her mother leaving Jessie's cabin. She ran to her. "How's Mattie?"

Dove smiled and put her arm around Beth Ann. "She's fine. Has a beautiful baby boy. Named him David."

"That's good." She didn't want to take away from the happy moment but needed to know. "Did she—"

Dove shook her head. "Nothing more. Reed said he'd let us know if she has anymore visions or if Annie goes into a fit."

Nodding, knowing there wasn't anything else to do, Beth Ann smiled weakly. "Kimi and Riker are in the schoolhouse. Jessie's girls are watching them."

"Good. You and I will help Sofia prepare dinner." She steered her daughter to the cookhouse where Rook had commandeered the outside tables. He passed out cooking assignments like a teacher giving out homework.

Beth Ann could have protested and no one would have pressed, but she figured if she was busy, the time might pass faster than if she were watching for Bo's return.

Rook handed her a peeler. "Potatoes," he said gruffly, pointing her toward the table where several others were busy peeling.

She'd barely started her fifth potato when she heard the sound of riders. "They're back," she said, standing. She breathed a sigh of relief when she saw her father in the lead. Then came John. Standing Horse and two warriors brought up the rear.

"Where is everyone else?" Her heart sped up when no one dismounted. They were waiting. For what? Dove joined her. "Something's wrong."

Standing Horse rode behind the barn where several smaller tipis were set for the unmarried warriors. The warriors followed him. Jeremy remained on his horse right behind them, his rifle in hand.

She took a step forward, but Dove held her back. "We wait. Your father will come to us."

John ran into one of the storerooms, came out with a canvas sack, then hurried past the silent women and into the kitchen. Moments later, he was running back toward her father. Why did John need food?

After what seemed like hours, the warriors returned with Standing Horse.

"He's leaving," Beth Ann said, staring at the bedroll tied to the back of the horse. The sack of food was quickly added.

In silence, everyone watched as the warriors escorted her brother-in-law back down the trail. Jeremy followed but wasn't gone long. When he returned and dismounted, Beth Ann ran to him. Her mother was right behind her.

"Papa? Where's Bo?" There was no sign of anyone else returning.

Jeremy held her at arm's length. "He's fine. Just a scratch."

Her knees went weak. "A scratch?"

"What did Standing Horse do?" It was clear the warrior had been sent back, and that meant he'd done something serious enough to be banished.

Jeremy glanced around. He had an audience bigger

than a man of god standing before his pulpit on Sundays. Everyone was silent, waiting. He lifted his voice so all could hear. "Standing Horse tried to kill Bo." Beth Ann gasped, and he held up a hand. "Bo is fine. Just got a scratch. But it was clear the warrior meant to kill him and make it look like a hunting accident."

She launched herself into her father's arms. "You are sure he's okay?"

"Yes, daughter—" Both turned at the sound of riders. "There, you can see for yourself."

Beth Ann didn't care how it looked. She ran to Bo and stopped to wait for him to dismount. Her eyes cut to his face, and she cried out at the sight of dried blood on his face. "You're hurt! What did he do?"

Bo swung down from his horse and caught her up into his arms. "Just a scratch, Bethy. I'm fine."

As soon as Bo set her down, she framed his face in her hands and searched for the wound, needing to be sure. "Where?"

He tipped his head down. She parted his hair, searching for the source of the dried blood, then sucked in her breath at the sight of the long, angry-looking groove down the center of his head. When Bo lifted his head, she stared into his eyes, his wonderful, silvery eyes that were dark with emotion. "What happened?"

Bo snagged his hat from behind his saddle and held it out to her.

"Bo!" Her chest tightened at the sight of the arrow stuck right through his hat. Only now did she fully realize that the grooves on Bo's head had been made by an arrow. "If that arrow had been lower, it would have gone straight into your head." Her stomach rolled with nausea.

Strong hands forced her to meet his eyes. "But it didn't, Bethy, and that is what counts." He glanced around. "Where is he?"

Bo didn't mention that he'd pushed his horse hard to get back to her, to be sure she and her children were safe.

"He's gone. Left just before you arrived," she said, then threw her arms around his neck and held him tight.

Wrapping his arms around her, Bo breathed a sigh of relief. After a few minutes, he pulled back. "I need to see to Samson—"

"Got it, Bo," George called out.

Bo nodded, saw the boy's emotionless features, and knew he was upset and angry. He didn't want to embarrass the boy by reassuring him. Instead, he tossed the hat to him. "Reckon we both lost a hat. Not much good now."

George pulled the arrow out, broke it over his knee, and stuffed the pieces in his pocket. He studied the hat, then grinned. "Reckon I can mend *my* hat." He slid the hat onto his head and walked toward the barn, leading Samson.

"That was nice, Bo. He's been worried. We've all been worried." She looked at him. "Mattie had another vision. I'll tell you about it later, and you can tell me what happened as well." She threaded her arm through his. "We need to take care of that wound."

Bo planned to go down to the stream and bathe, but he let Beth lead him to her tipi and tend to his wound. Then he pulled her onto his lap, not caring who might see. He needed to hold her. She was safe. She was his. How could he bear to let her go? How was he going to ride away in a few short weeks? His heart, so full of love, wept.

****

Jocelyn beckoned for Margaret to join her outside. "Bo's hurt. Go to him, see if he needs you."

Margaret glanced around. "Where is he? What happened?"

"The warrior mooning over that woman shot him."

Margaret stepped outside and returned to her mother. "Beth Ann is taking care of him."

"I don't care. You go over there and help and make sure he knows you're worried."

Margaret shook her head. "No."

Her gaze strayed to one of the heathens untying a dead deer from Bo's horse.

"What do you mean, no!" Jocelyn's tone turned ugly.

"You heard me. I need to get back to the children," Margaret said, backing away.

Jocelyn grabbed her arm. "You listen to me."

"Problem?"

Margaret shook her head at Wolf then turned and ran into the schoolroom.

Jocelyn glared at Wolf and started after her daughter.

Wolf snagged her by the arm. "You got chores."

Hating the man, Jocelyn flounced off. In the washing shed, she tossed dirty clothes across the room. The man had turned her own children against her. First Matt and now Margaret. She was still fuming over her daughter's clear defection when the rest of the hunting party returned. She glanced out the open door. Two men supported her son as he hopped on one foot to one of the tables.

"Matt!" She picked up her skirts and ran. "What happened?" She shoved through the thong of people gathered. Rook knelt in front of her son, probing his ankle with his big, beefy fingers.

"I'm fine, Ma."

Spotting his swollen foot, she yelled, "He needs a doctor."

"Ma! Just twisted. Not broke." He didn't look at her.

"You are not a doctor, Matt." She turned to Bo who was helping Henry sit beside Matt.

Careful to keep her features twisted with worry, Jocelyn rejoiced inside. Her plan worked. "What happened?" She glanced from one man to the other.

Henry, lips white around the edges, sent her a look of loathing. "Got bucked off my horse. Haven't lost my seat in too many years to count." He patted Matt's arm. "Good thing this young man broke my fall. Might've been worse than a broken arm."

Jocelyn's jaw dropped. "You broke his fall?"

Matt wouldn't meet her eyes. She struggled to keep from losing her temper and calling her son a fool. Having Henry injure himself had been her intention. Her quick mind latched onto the double bonus of her son's injury. She sat and hugged Matt, ignoring the fact that he was trying to pull away.

"My brave boy," she gushed. She glanced around, tears in her eyes. "We need to take both of these men back to the fort. They surely have a doctor there." Finally, a way to get them out of this forsaken wilderness.

Bo shook his head. "Henry can't travel."

Jocelyn stood, hands on hips. "They can rest tonight. We leave tomorrow."

"No need for that, Mrs. Linberg. They'll be fine here. Don't need no army quacks." Sofia pushed through the crowd.

Deciding she'd have to get Bo alone and guilt him into doing what she wanted, she turned back to her son.

"If someone would help me get him to our tent so I can tend to him?" She glanced at Wolf and Jeremy.

"Matt will be staying at the cabin," Wolf said.

The two old trappers framed him like antique bookends that hadn't seen the best of care.

Jocelyn's jaw dropped. "Now see here. He's my son and you cannot tell him—"

"Already been decided, Ma."

"Now Matt—"

"Forget it," Matt said angrily. "They know what you did. Can't prove it, but *I* know you did it."

Shocked, Jocelyn narrowed her eyes at Matt and saw something between pity and hate in his eyes. Around her, everyone watched silently. "Matt, you're in pain."

Bo stepped forward. Enough was enough. They'd planned not to say anything until her return trip to the fort was arranged, but he wanted it out in the open. "Matt told us your plans for me, Jocelyn."

"My what?" Her voice rose to a shriek. Seeing the truth on her son's face, she flew at him. "You traitor. How dare you?" She lifted her hand to slap him, but Bo caught it.

"Forget it, Jocelyn. Your children have grown up and taken charge of their own lives."

Yanking her arm free, she glared at Bo. "I'm

leaving tomorrow, and I'm taking Matt and Margaret with me."

Wolf nodded. "You know, that might be best." He ignored Matt's cry of protest and Bo's frown.

Wolf leaned forward and murmured, "Trust me," in Bo's ear.

Bo nodded and crossed his arms across his chest. "Wolf's right."

Jocelyn drew herself up. "Then we're leaving." She said it as though it were settled.

"Yes, you've outstayed your welcome," Bo said. "And these good people are trying to celebrate family, something you have no concept of."

She glared at Bo. "Good. I want to leave at noon. No more up before the sun for me."

"You leave in two days." Bo turned to Wolf who nodded to both Matt and Margaret.

"Your children are more than welcome to remain here as long as they choose."

Jocelyn narrowed her eyes and fisted her hands at her hips. "My children will, of course, return to the fort with me. I'm their *mother*."

"No, Ma. I'm staying," Matt said.

Furious, she turned. "You will do as you are told. We are leaving, and that is final."

Margaret sat beside her brother, putting her arm around his shoulders. She glanced at Wolf and Jessie. "You mean that? I can stay?"

This time, Jessie answered. "Yes. You're wonderful with the children. But are you sure?"

"Now wait just a minute—"

Bo stopped the angry outburst before Jocelyn got wound up. "Margaret?"

The girl grinned. "I'm sure. I'm staying." She hugged her brother. "We're staying."

"Then it's settled," Bo said. "You leave in two days. Stinky and Duckman will take you."

Rook folded his arms across his chest and nodded. "It's about damn time. Now out of my way, woman, so I can see to the wounded."

"I am not going with those—those—disgusting creatures."

"Yeah, you are, Jocelyn. You're going. How is up to you. Push me, and I'll tie you to your horse."

"You'll be watched for the remainder of your stay." Wolf motioned to one warrior.

"You wouldn't!"

Bo put his arm around Beth and walked away.

He heard Rook clap his hands. "That's settled. Now get out of here, all of you. Got injuries to tend to."

"I'm his mother. I'm staying."

Bo turned back and motioned to Wolf. The two men picked Jocelyn up by the arms and carried her, screeching all the way, back to her tipi.

****

If a herd of cattle had stampeded him into the ground, Bo didn't think he'd have felt worse. Had it only been this morning that he'd kissed Bethy good-bye, eager to take part in the celebration hunt? He sighed, finished scrubbing his hair, and winced at the sharp sting. Damn bastard's arrow tip had gouged his scalp raw, leaving a long, narrow wound.

On the ride back, he'd replayed that scene. That owl had saved his life. Too bad Wolf had stopped the fight between him and Standing Horse. He'd have liked to beat the crap out of the chicken-shit warrior.

Forcing himself out of the stream, he stood, rolling his shoulders, wishing he'd taken Rook up on that nice hot tub of water. He had bruises, scrapes, and a couple of pulled muscles. But he'd insisted that Henry use the hot water.

Dressing quickly, he wanted nothing more than to fall flat on his face and sleep. It wasn't the day of hard riding that left him so exhausted. At the ranch, he normally spent most of his day in the saddle, sometimes, days at a time riding and checking his herd.

No, it was worry that made him feel so fatigued. Worry about Henry, fear for Beth and her children, and to make things worse, there was Jocelyn and her never-ending theatrics and tears.

Least you can do, Bo, is take me back.

You brought me out here.

It's your duty to take me back.

And her pledges and false promises to behave if he'd let her stay until he was ready to return. When he refused to back down, she'd tried tears, threats, and tantrums.

Dressed, Bo entered the village. Wolf and Jessie's place, with their buildings, homes, and people was large enough to call a small town.

Dinner was long over, but he hadn't been hungry and even if he had been, by the time he'd left Jocelyn's tipi, mealtime was over so he'd gone down to the water to bathe.

Scanning the village center, he saw Wolf setting out lanterns. Though it was cold, Beth's family had gathered at the tables. He didn't see Beth. Shifting his attention to the log circle, she wasn't there either. He shoved his hands on his hips and searched. All he wanted was to hold the woman he loved and have her hold him back. He needed Beth. He jumped when someone touched him from behind.

"Just me, Boo." Beth Ann's voice was soft, warm.

Her use of a childhood nickname eased the tension in his body and mind. Turning, he gathered her into his arms.

"Bratty Bethy," he replied, nuzzling his cheek against the top of her head. "I'm so glad to see you. Seems like it's been a week since this morning."

"Come with me, Bo. You're exhausted." Beth Ann led him to her tipi.

Bo wanted nothing more than to follow her inside. He wanted to hold her. Just hold her and ease the ache in his heart and, yes, the guilt he felt for sending Jocelyn away with strangers.

He needed to know Beth was safe from the man threatening to take her children, the man who'd come close to killing him that day.

He just needed Beth.

To himself.

He sighed. "Can't. Need to check on Henry."

"He's fine. Rook says he's sleeping. While you were gone, I checked. Matt's okay as well."

She grinned. "Rook asked Margaret if she'd like to look after Henry, said she'd have to sleep there. She jumped at the chance."

"So Jocelyn's alone."

Beth rested her head against his chest. "It's sad, Bo. So sad that she's driven her children away from her. I can't imagine having a mother like that."

He stroked Beth's silky blonde hair. "Some women aren't meant to be mothers," he said sadly. He followed

Beth inside her tipi. A lantern hung from the center, casting a soft glow of light.

"Come sit. I brought you some food."

Bruised and battered, he gave in and let Beth fuss over him. After he ate, Beth Ann checked his wound, applying more smelly salve. He glanced outside. Night had fallen. Shadows moved as everyone drifted to their tipis.

Next to Beth's tipi, he heard laughing and giggling followed by the deeper voice of Beth Ann's father.

Family. It all came down to family for Beth. Sighing, he got to his feet. "I should go, Beth. Your sister and children will be here soon."

Smiling at him, Beth Ann moved to the doorway and pulled the flap closed. Then she turned. "Jane is back in the dorm with the children—where she wants to be—and Henry is at Rook and Sofia's cabin."

She took two steps toward him. "My babies are asleep with my parents."

Bo lifted a brow. "Planned this, did you?"

Her lips curved sweetly as she took one last step and stood before him. "You look so tired, and you didn't eat." She lifted a hand to cup one side of his face. "And you've had a bad time with that woman. You don't need to be alone."

Stroking his hands up her arms to her shoulders, Bo pulled her a bit closer. "And you're worried Standing Horse might return?"

She nodded. "I confess I am also being selfish."

He lifted a brow. "How could the woman who tended to my wound, fed me, and offered to share her home with me be selfish?"

Beth Ann flushed. Bo tipped her chin up with one

finger and waited.

"I want you with me," she whispered.

"Then how can I deny a pretty woman her wish."

She lowered her eyes. "I know you're tired, and I-I won't mind if you want to sleep where Jane or my grandfather slept."

Bo wanted to yank her so close she'd never have doubts as to how much he wanted her beside him. Always. Instead, he swept her up into his arms. "Be a cold day in hell when we sleep apart." He carried her to her pallet and let her slide down, inch by excruciating inch. Fatigue warred with need.

Staring into her eyes, he frowned. Normally, they were a warm, soft blue, like the sky on a gentle summer day. But right now, they were dull and the flesh around them bruised looking. For the first time since he'd returned, he realized she looked as exhausted as he felt.

Bo kicked himself mentally for not noticing that something was wrong, something more than what had happened to him. He rested his forehead against hers. "I'm a selfish bastard to not see you're upset."

"Oh, Bo." Beth Ann held up one hand. She didn't want to worry him. "It can wait until morning. You look ready to fall."

Shaking his head, he fingered a strand of her hair. "You took care of me, Cupcake. My turn."

Stepping back, Beth Ann nodded. "In Bed." She pulled down the lantern and blew out the flame. The fire in the center had burned low and provided a bit of light and warmth against the chill creeping in. She tossed a couple more small twigs onto it, then turned back to Bo.

He sat and removed his shoes, socks, and shirt. His

hand stopped at the waistband of his pants. "Uh, Beth, I know I said we were going to sleep. Would you be more comfortable if I kept my clothes on?"

Beth Ann shook her head. "No. When we sleep, I want to feel you beside me." She pulled the hem of her dress up and over her head and, not the least bit embarrassed, walked over and slid beneath her blankets.

Bo made quick work of removing the last of his clothing and joined her. He pulled her into his arms, pressing her head down onto his chest, and sighed deeply, content as he'd never felt before. He put the future from his mind, vowing to treasure every moment with her.

She remained silent. Her breathing told him she wasn't asleep, as did the nervous play of her fingers across his chest. He didn't press or ask. He'd learned the Lakota took their time before speaking. Breathing in her scent, he rubbed his cheek on her soft hair and committed the feel of her to his memory.

Beth Ann snuggled close to Bo and took her time getting her thoughts in order. She loved Bo, and the thought of him leaving hurt worse than any wound. His heart beat strong and steady beneath her ear. He was alive and he was here, with her.

She'd waited all her life to fall in love. This was what she'd believed she'd have with Singing Bear. She'd believed love would grow between them, but it hadn't.

Now she understood the difference. What she felt for Bo had sprung into being the moment their gazes met across the yard. Before Bo, she'd thought love was like the rainbow in the sky after a rain, like the fairy tales her mother had read to her when she was a child. No one told her pain and despair were a part of loving.

Beth Ann forced the fear and pain away, unwilling to tarnish this time with Bo. She had love, and she had Bo. Rainbows and that happy-ever-after were not to be hers. "You know Mattie had visions before you and my grandfather arrived?"

He nuzzled his cheek against her head. "Visions that warned of our coming."

She nodded as she absently threaded her fingers through the thick mat of hair on his chest. "She said I had choices." She squeezed her eyes closed to stop the tears. How could she choose between Bo and her family? She loved all of them, needed them all.

"Once you and grandfather arrived, her visions went away. But today—" She broke off, her fear returning.

"They returned?" Bo drew her closer.

"Yes." Her voice trembled as she told him about Annie. "It was awful, Bo. Something terrified her." She lifted herself up and propped herself on one elbow. She needed to see him. "I was so worried. All the other visions were about you."

"And Henry?" Bo copied her move so they faced each other. Firelight played across his features.

"Mostly you, I think," Beth Ann whispered. "Mattie said I had choices."

He ran his hand behind her neck and rubbed the tense muscles. "No choices, Cupcake. I made you a promise, and I intend to keep it."

"It's not that easy, Bo." She trailed her fingertips over his shadowed jaw, feeling the rasp of hair. Each morning, he shaved, and by nightfall, his jaw was dark once more.

Taking her fingers in his, he kissed each one, then the pulse at her wrist. "I don't think love is supposed to be easy, Bethy. Then it wouldn't be special."

For a long moment, they just stared at one another. Shadows swayed on the walls of hide, a slow and gentle dance.

"What else?" Bo prompted.

"As soon as I gave Annie to her mother, Mattie went into one of her trances. It was scary. Mother and daughter both had visions at the same time. But this time, Mattie said it was different. Everything was dark." She frowned. "Mattie said everything went black and red, like smoke from a fire hiding the sun in the sky."

Beth Ann took his hand in hers. "It scared me, Bo. Mattie got so upset that she went into labor."

Reaching out, he pulled her back into his arms. "Maybe the vision was about what Standing Horse did. He shot that damn arrow at me." He frowned. "Or it could have been about Henry's fall."

"But Bo, everyone is still worried. My aunts and uncles can't hide it from me. They think there is more, but Mattie doesn't know anything else. I'm afraid he'll come back and kill you."

He nodded. "That explains why there are more guards tonight. Not just the warriors. Heard Reed and Tyler say they'd take first watch with two of the warriors. I volunteered, but Wolf said he had it covered."

She was glad he wasn't out there, making himself a target. "They are afraid for you."

Bo shook his head. "It's you they are protecting,

Bethy. He threatened to take your children." He kissed her gently. "I can take care of myself."

"Promise not to go off by yourself."

"I'm not a coward, Beth."

"I know. But I am. I am afraid for both of us."

He rubbed his cheek against her forehead. "Nice try, Cupcake. Don't worry about me. Besides, I plan to stay close, to protect you and the twins."

They fell silent for a long while. She couldn't sleep without one last thing. "Are you asleep, Bo?"

"No." His warm breath fanned her face.

"I want to tell you something." She slid her hand to caress the side of his face.

"I'm listening, Cupcake."

Beth Ann smiled. She loved the endearment that had started so long ago as a way to tease her and now spoke of love. "I love you, Bo."

Chapter Thirteen

God, how she hated this place—the land, the people and most of all, her damn stepson and that neighbor of his. Never liked Henry when she was married to Bo's father. Interfering old fool had caught her in town when she'd gone to meet her lover. Bastard couldn't wait to inform her husband.

Weak, stupid man loved that ranch more than her. When she'd met him, she'd known he was rich, figured she'd live in style and her children would have the life she wanted for them—private schooling, parties where they'd meet rich ranchers and make good marriages.

What a fool she'd been! The man had been a stingy old fart. She'd had to pry every single cent out of that bastard's tight fist. Every penny earned went back into the ranch. No fancy clothes, no parties, and no private schools. Her poor babies had to endure the same one room school with the rest of the brats from town.

All her dreams had been ground into dust. Venting her frustration, she kicked a pile of pine needles and nearly screamed when her toe connected with a hidden stone held so tight to the earth it didn't budge. She blamed Bo. Like father, like son. He had ruined everything, and he'd turned her own children against her.

She'd never forgive him for that. Just as she'd never forgiven Bo's father for giving her son a "paddling long in coming" after the boy refused to shovel out the stalls.

Her poor boy, forced to work like a lowborn ranch hand's child. That's what he paid all those hired men for. And poor, delicate Margaret, forced to work in the kitchen or in the gardens. It still infuriated her the way he'd treated her children.

"Everyone earns their keep," he'd said when she'd protested. "Children will appreciate what they have when they have to work to get it."

Hah! Easy for that old fool to say. His son didn't have to shovel shit, clean the coops, or any of the other dirty chores. He got to ride the ranch like some high and mighty lord-of-all-he-surveyed.

Jocelyn returned to the fallen log and sat, crossing her arms in front of her. What was she going to do? "I am not leaving with those heathens." But in the hours she'd sat out here, not a single plan had come to her.

She glared at the warrior standing a short distance away. It rankled that she was under guard like a common criminal. What was she going to do? The burr she planted in Henry's horse blanket had worked, but she'd never figured on Henry staying or her own son getting hurt.

Jocelyn jumped up, grabbed a branch, and tossed it. This was Bo's fault. Too bad that warrior hadn't killed him. She'd have found a way to get the ranch.

She took off walking and glanced over her shoulder to see the warrior right behind her. "Go away. I don't need you invading my privacy." When the warrior just stared at her, she brushed past him. She'd return to that damn tipi and plot.

****

It was still dark when Bo woke with Beth in his arms, half on him as though she couldn't bear to be apart from him even in sleep. He snugged her close and made sure she was covered. The fire had gone out, and the chill in the air turned his breath into steam.

I love you.

He'd fallen asleep with those words ringing in his head.

Beth loved him.

Her declaration made him incredibly happy.

And sad.

He'd known, without the words, that she loved him, but he hadn't allowed himself to hope to hear her say it. Dare he allow himself a thread of hope for more?

Choices.

He dreamed she'd choose him over her family. Life at the ranch would not be same without her, and he couldn't make this life his.

He fingered a strand of her hair, rubbing the silky softness. What if she chose him? He'd be happy to the point of bursting, yet at the same time, he didn't want her to make that choice.

What if, like Jocelyn, she hated ranch life? What if she became unhappy and unsatisfied with him and his life? What if their love turned to resentment then hate? Wouldn't it be kinder to both of them to walk away as he'd planned? Either way, they'd both be hurt.

There was no immediate answer so he tucked away his worry and fear and stared up through the smoke hole, judging it to be well before dawn. Better to enjoy what he had, for as long as he could. The pain of heartache would come soon enough.

Shifting, he stared at her tousled hair and smiled.

Slowly, he stroked a hand up and down her back, following the line of her spine from neck to the soft curve of her buttocks. He kissed the top of her head, and when she stirred, he feathered tiny kisses across her forehead.

Her head fell back, settled on his shoulder. He continued to trail kisses down her nose, across her cheeks, along her jaw, in the tiny dent in her chin, and down the long line of her exposed throat.

He shifted until he was cradling her on her back, leaning half over her. While he kissed her, his free hand stroked her cheek, glided down her throat, then closed over one small, perfect breast.

With the flat of his hand, he teased her nipple until it stretched into a tight peak. His fingers trailed over to her other breast, found her already hard. His lips took over.

She moaned as he took her fully into his mouth. Her fingers tangled in his hair and held him to her.

Hard and throbbing with need, Bo eased over her, rested his weight on his arms as he stared down into her sleepy gaze. "Morning, Cupcake."

"Morning, Boo." She pulled his head down and opened her mouth for a soul-deep kiss.

He slipped between her legs and stroked himself against her belly. Beth held him to her with her legs wrapped around his hips.

Staring into her eyes, he framed her face in his hands and shifted his hips until he found her center. "I love you, Beth." He slid into her warm, velvety sheath, joining them completely and utterly.

"I love you, Bo." She arched, taking him in a bit further.

He groaned. "You feel so damn good."

Holding her gaze, he moved slowly. Out an inch at a time, then in, using firm but slow and easy strokes. Her eyes closed, her lips parted, and her head dropped back, revealing her vulnerable throat.

Dipping his head, he kissed and suckled the soft flesh, paying special mind to the soft fluttering pulse.

Beth Ann wanted more. Lots more. When he pulled nearly out, she tightened her legs around his waist and took him back in, held him tighter, and rocked her hips, feeling her desire building, building.

No matter how hard she tried to get him to move faster, he kept his pace to an easy tease until she wanted to scream.

"Slow, Cupcake. We have time."

Time was their enemy. Beth Ann knew this. Accepted this. But she didn't say anything. She pulled his head to hers and lost herself in his kiss, his torturous caresses, and his heady scent.

Her hands trailed down his back. When he groaned and shuddered, she repeated her long, sure strokes along his spine, then dug her fingers into his twin, hard cheeks, feeling them tighten, release, tighten. She squeezed, keeping rhythm to his movements.

The pleasure inside her grew with each stroke, each withdrawal. "Bo…"

He lifted his head. "Look at me, Beth."

She stared up into his eyes, a silvery-violet, like dusk settling across the sky.

He shifted, threading his fingers with hers and holding them beside her head. "I want to watch you."

Biting her lip when he stroked harder but not faster, she bucked beneath him, feeling that glorious momentum growing, drawing near yet just out of reach. She wanted it, wanted him to fill her with it, then fly apart with her.

No matter how much she tried to make him give in, he kept it slow, steady, and hard. She whimpered.

"That's it. Feel me, Bethy. Feel me. Look at me. Let me see your beautiful eyes."

He stroked harder, deeper. "I love you, Beth."

Everything inside her burst apart with his words. She flew, one with the stars. She gasped. She hadn't believed this completion to the mating act could get better, but the explosions deep inside her didn't end. They kept coming.

When she lay limp and exhausted, she throbbed, inside and out. "Bo." She nearly wept his name.

He rose to his knees, pulling her hips closer, driving deeper, with as he held her legs on either side of him. "Watch, Beth. Watch."

Once again, she locked her gaze on him as he resumed his pace. Raw inside with feeling, she was afraid he'd send her off the edge with one stroke, but her body settled back into his rhythm. Her hands stretched out to her sides, digging into the furs. She wanted to touch him but couldn't reach. She tried to move her hips, but he held her firmly.

So she watched him, saw the pleasure-pain etched along the corners of his mouth and his eyes darkened. His breathing grew ragged, as did hers.

He pulled almost out, then plunged, faster, harder.

"Beth," he cried out, pumping his hips hard and fast, driving them both to the peak.

"Bo!" She fought to keep her eyes open as he stroked her ever higher. She saw in him the same pain, the same desperate need. One squeeze of her thighs would send her over, but she waited until he threw his head back, his body arching into hers before she joined him in that glorious flight across the heavens.

Bo collapsed on top of Beth then rolled onto his back, draping her over him. Something wet dripped down the side of his neck.

He lifted her so he could see her face. She was crying. "Did I hurt you?" He wiped the tears with his thumbs.

She shook her head. "No. It was wonderful, the most beautiful thing I've ever known. I know that sounds silly."

Grinning, he shook his head and encouraged her pale hair to fall and curtain them. "Not silly. It was better than wonderful. It was heavenly." He sobered. "How am I going to live without you, Beth?"

With a cry, she fell onto him. "I don't know if I can bear to let you go."

He turned them onto their sides, and for a long moment, they stared at one another. "I won't ask you to leave your family, Bethy."

"What if you don't have to?"

Hope rose inside him but was just as quickly dashed when he remembered his fear of something so wonderful turning into something very ugly. "You won't be happy without your family."

"But I'd have you and my children. And we'd have children. We'd make our own family."

"But will it be enough." He saw the doubt in her eyes. "I can't let you do that. As much as I want it, as much as I need you, your happiness is everything."

"I won't be happy when you leave."

Bo sighed and ran his thumbs across her cheeks, wiping her tears. There was no satisfying solution so he just drew her close and held her, their hearts beating as one.

****

It was still dark when Beth Ann and Bo dressed, gathered their things for a bath and left her tipi. Hand in hand, they slipped through the trees silently, not wanting to wake those still sleeping.

He stopped, his hand resting on the butt of his revolver when two figures stepped out of the shadows. "You should not be out here," one of them said.

"We're going to the river," Bo said. "To bathe."

The warriors parted, letting them pass.

Bo took two steps then turned. The two warriors were behind them. "We don't need guards. I can protect her." He patted his weapon.

She held up her hand. "And who will protect you." She addressed the warriors. "We would be pleased if you'd follow and stand guard." She took Bo's arm, and together they moved to a part of the river lined with thick shrubs. She parted the brush and led him to the water.

Without hesitation, she removed her dress. Bo sighed. "Those two had better be guarding, not staring," he said, moving behind her as though to shield her.

Grinning, Beth Ann pulled him into the river with her. "They will be respectful."

"Damn, it's cold."

She glanced over her shoulder. "Good for you. Gets your blood moving." She giggled. "That's what *Ina* used to tell me and Jane when we first came."

Bo moved close and wrapped his arms around her

waist. "Cupcake, all I have to do is look at you and my blood moves just fine." His hands trailed up to capture her peaked breasts. "Perfect," he breathed, dipping his head down to nuzzle her neck.

"Bo! We can't. Not here. Not now." For all her words that the warriors would be respectful, this was different. She tried to look behind, but he blocked her view.

"Yeah, we can."

And they did. Afterward, they quickly washed, dressed, and headed back. She didn't see the warriors but knew they were there.

The aroma of freshly roasted and brewed coffee greeted them when they returned. Beth went immediately to help her mother, but Dove waved her off. "Nearly done, daughter. Go sit with your father and Bo."

Beth Ann dropped down beside Bo. The twins ran over to greet her with a kiss, then ran to play with their cousins.

"You have wonderful children, Bethy." Bo pulled her close and kept his arm around her shoulders.

Content, she nodded. "They are. A bit of a handful with two of them, but they are good babies."

Dove brought over two cups of hot coffee and a smile. "You look rested, both of you."

Bo, noticing that Jeremy was working on an arrow, reached over. His hand hovered a moment. "May I?"

Jeremy nodded, and Bo picked up the arrow and admired the smooth shaft and the feathered vane. He tested the tip with his finger and nodded. "Sharp."

The groove on top of his head ached at the sight of the arrow.

"Want to learn to make one?"

Bo scooted closer so he could see what Jeremy was doing.

Glancing around, seeing that the four adults were alone, Beth Ann set her cup down. "*Ina?*"

Dove settled beside her husband. "Yes?"

"Has Mattie said anything else?"

Her mother sighed, shook her head, and took a sip of coffee. "Jessie said last night there weren't any more visions."

Beth Ann wanted to be relieved. "Do you think what happened yesterday was the cause of their visions?" In her gut, she knew it wasn't. Mattie's vision had seemed so dark and scary, especially as both Bo's and Henry's injuries were minor in comparison.

"There is no way to tell. It could be over." She reached down and took a feather in hand, studied it, then held it out to her husband. "Use this one. It will match the other better."

Jeremy held up the feather he'd chosen, compared the two, then sighed. "Right as usual, love."

"Always right, husband."

Catching the look exchanged by her parents that had nothing to do with arrows and feathers, Beth Ann drew her knees to her chest and wrapped her arms around them. "But you don't think so," she said, catching the quick look between her parents. "I don't either."

Bo glanced up from his study of the arrow in his hand. "I don't understand. She sees the future?"

Dove shook her head. "It's hard to explain. My grandmother and my sister both had the gift of sight. What they see isn't totally the future as future can be changed."

"Warnings then?" Bo asked, setting the arrow down.

Dove nodded. "That's closer. Sometimes, they know exactly what is going to happen, other times, like yesterday, there is only a sense of darkness."

"Danger." Bo tightened his arm around Beth.

Dove shrugged helplessly.

Jeremy cleared his throat. "Until we're sure that Standing Horse is not returning, the two of you need to stay close and not go off alone." He speared Bo a look. "And you keep your gun on you." He set down the arrow he was working on and stood. He went into the tipi and came out with Bo's packs and bedroll. "Don't even want you going off to the barn." Bo's belongings were set beside Beth's tipi.

Bo nodded. "Thank you." Unspoken was Jeremy's acceptance of him in Beth's life.

The sharp, clear clang of bell drew their attention. "After we eat, Rook says you and the others need to plan your decorations." Amusement sparkled in Bo's eyes.

Groaning, Beth Ann would have liked to beg off, but she wasn't about to risk Rook's displeasure. At the same time, she didn't want Bo out of her sight.

She nudged Bo. "Want to help?"

He looked like he'd rather scoop poop than make decorations. "Sure. Love to."

"Liar," she chided as they headed for the cookhouse and got into line.

****

After the morning meal, Bo left Beth with her family and hurried to Rook's cabin to check on Henry.

289

He found his friend and neighbor shifting restlessly in the chair he'd obviously slept in. "Hey, Henry, how are you doing?"

"Arm hurts like a bitch." He tried to change positions. "Damn that woman to hell and back. Never been tempted to hit a woman before."

Bo harbored the same sentiment. His stepmother had caused more than enough trouble.

"She's leaving and won't cause any more trouble." Of course, they had no proof, but that was bullshit. He didn't need proof. Her behavior upon their return said it all. But she'd gotten hers.

"Damn!" Another wave of pain struck Henry. "Good thing there's no young ears here."

"You wouldn't hurt so bad if you'd take the laudanum." Bo wished there was more he could do for the older man.

"Bah! Not taking drugs."

"Stubborn man." Sofia joined them and stood with her hands on her hips.

"You talking about me," Rook boomed out. "That horde called Family is fed, and the children are dealing with clean up."

"Might well be. You're no better. Know you didn't sleep much last night with that knee paining you."

Rook entered the room, limping slightly. "Better to feel pain than be dead 'n feeling nothing." He glanced at Henry. "You were lucky."

Henry sighed. "Should never have come," he said sadly.

Rook frowned, cocked his head at his wife. When Sofia backed out, he sat, stretched his leg out and rubbed. "Busted arm not worth finding your kin?"

Staring in the man's fierce glare, Henry waved at him. "Hell, finding my girls is worth breaking every bone in my body." He narrowed his eyes. "But don't even think about it. One is enough," he said wryly.

"Then what's the problem?"

Henry sent Bo a long look but only said, "Beth."

Rook settled back. "Ah. Young love."

Bo sighed. "I'm right here you old coots."

"Then wise up. You and my granddaughter are in love but—"

"It's complicated. You know that."

"Is it? Love is all the pair of you need." Henry winced when he banged his good fist on the chair, the movement jarring the rest of his body.

Bo stretched his feet out and folded his arms across his chest. "I won't take Beth from her family, and I can't start anew out here. Heard enough talk since I've been here to know you all are planning a move. What happens if Beth returns with us and then can't find her family again?"

Sighing, Rook fingered his chin. "Love is messy business," he muttered.

"But worth all the fuss and worry, old man, and don't you forget it." Sofia came in with two plates of food on a tray. "Eat. And don't go meddlin'. Let them two young 'uns work it out between themselves."

A knock on the door was followed by two trappers entering. "Hiya, Sof. Rok." They nodded to Henry.

"Bad luck," one muttered.

Henry held out his right hand. "Henry."

"Stinky and Duckman."

When the small head of the skunk popped out of Stinky's coat, Bo's eyes went wide. Sofia reached out and gave the animal's head a rub.

"Go ahead and let her down. Didn't see you with the others. You eat?"

"Had some jerky," Duckman said.

Sighing, Sofia motioned them to a couple chairs. "That's not a morning meal. I'll get two more plates." She turned back to eye the animal sitting in the center of the room. "You best not go waving that tail in here."

Stinky took a chair that creaked under his weight. "Now Sof, it was jest a'cause you scared the poor mite's ma last time. She didn't mean it."

"Ruined my favorite chair."

"Got you a better one." Stinky smiled sweetly beneath his gruff and rough exterior.

"Humph." Sofia left.

Bo watched Henry eat and saw the man eyeing the skunk with an eagle's eye as he chewed on his biscuit, dipping it into the gravy. The men talked. Bo kept an eye on Henry's plate, balanced on his lap in case he needed to grab it to keep it from spilling. He also kept his eye on the animal as it moved toward Henry's chair and start climbing.

The appearance of the skunk head over the edge of the chair startled Henry who nearly tossed the plate. "Uh, Stinky, what's she doing?"

"Oh, looking for some food."

Henry eyed the creature. "I don't feed my dogs at the table. Not going to feed you."

The skunk made a sound much like a cat's meow. "Figure the only way to get rid of her is to feed her." He gave her a small piece of his biscuit. The small animal snatched it and dropped back to the floor.

Bo smothered a chuckle. He couldn't count the

number of times the older man had *dropped* food at the table for the dog waiting beside Henry's chair. The two trappers across from him were chowing down on their breakfast. The skunk put her paws back up on the chair and looked at Henry.

"Outta luck," he told her. Henry's jaw dropped when she climbed up and looked at him. "Shit, get her off, will you? Don't need to stink *and* have a broke arm."

"Won't hurt you, Henry." The two men continued their conversation with Rook.

"Go back to him," Henry told the beady-eyed animal.

Instead of listening, the skunk climbed onto his lap, made soft, mewling sounds then curled up on the blanket, wrapped her tail around her body and rested her head upon it.

Stunned, Henry glanced at Bo who just shrugged, then watched as Henry, the old softie, reached out tentatively and touched the skunk's fur. She actually butted her head against his hand.

Bo wanted to burst out laughing as the two stared at each other until Henry's eyes closed and he fell asleep with the skunk on his lap.

Assured that his neighbor was as comfortable as was possible under the circumstances, he said his farewells to the trappers, thanked Sofia and Rook for caring for Henry, and headed outside. Grinning, he knew Beth would appreciate the story of Henry and his newly found friend. God only knew, they could all do with something lighthearted.

Chapter Fourteen

Beth Ann met up with Bo coming out of Rook's cabin when Wolf called Bo's name. She turned. Her uncle didn't look happy.

"Now what has Jocelyn done?" Bo sighed with resignation.

"Go. I want to check on my grandfather."

Bo strode off. Beth Ann knocked softly on Rook and Sofia's door.

Sofia answered. "Come inside, child. No need to knock."

She stepped inside the warm, cozy cabin. "How is he?" She peered into the room. He was sleeping in a chair positioned in front of the fireplace.

"In pain, but he won't take anything."

Beth Ann chewed on her lower lip. "I don't want to wake him. I can come back later."

Sofia pulled Beth inside. "Nonsense. Sit down and warm up. You eat?" She hung the towel she'd used to dry the dishes on a peg on the wall.

"Yes." Beth Ann took one of the chairs around a small table near a wood stove.

"Where's that man of yours? Figured he'd come back in with you."

Beth Ann couldn't help the blush that heated her face or her wide pleased grin at having Bo called her man, for he was hers as much as she was his. "He'll be here. Wolf needed him."

"That woman, no doubt." Sofia sniffed her displeasure.

Turning in her chair, Beth Ann studied her grandfather. He slept in a chair with his feet propped on a flat-topped trunk. She giggled when she spotted a skunk sleeping on his lap. "Does he know about that?" She pointed to the ball of fur.

Sofia chuckled. "Shocked the hell out of him—"

A loud screech from outside made both women wince.

"Poor Bo." Beth Ann felt sorry for him but wasn't about to go see what the problem was.

"Go on in with your grandfather. Henry goes in and out. I've got washing to bring in. I don't want to leave him alone."

Nodding, Beth Ann got up and took the seat across from her grandfather, grateful for the warmth. Her grandfather's face was pale, and even in sleep, lined with pain. Slumped in the chair, he looked old and frail.

She grimaced. In all her inner turmoil of having to choose between Bo and her family, she hadn't considered that this man was her family as well. Though she hadn't seen him since her father had taken him away, had misjudged his role in what happened to her parents, she loved him every bit as much as her parents and siblings.

That meant her choices were really between two families—her birth family and adoptive family.

And Bo. The man who held her heart.

Beth Ann plucked at the fabric of her dress. She was wearing a blue dress Jessie had made her years ago. Everything was changing. Less than a month ago, she'd been content with her life. She had her children and her family. The only shadow had been the uncertainty of the future, but she'd known that as long as she and her family were together, she could handle any changes to their lives.

Then came Bo. Well, Bo and her grandfather. The two men from her past had changed everything. Her grandfather shifted in his sleep and moaned. She leaned forward in case he called out, but he settled back into a fitful sleep.

Choices. Staring at the man who was her mother's father, she sighed. He was her last link to her beloved mother who'd died a terrible death trying to save her girls.

Family and sacrifices.

Choices and her future.

Love.

Her thoughts were fragmented as she watched her grandfather stir restlessly. Rubbing her hair between her fingers, she wove a strand over and under her fingers as she considered her choices.

Did she have a choice? She dropped her hand back into her lap.

No. She'd been lying to herself when she believed she'd ever had a choice, because deep in her heart, the moment this man showed up, her future had been sealed.

The door opened behind her. She turned and smiled at Bo.

He leaned over and kissed her lightly, then pulled her up out of her chair, sat, and gathered her on his lap. "How is he?"

"Bo!" She looked nervously at her grandfather.

"Everyone knows we're lovers."

Recalling how her grandfather had told her to go to Bo that first night she'd given herself to him, her face burned. "I know but—"

"If I can help with girl work, you can let me hold you." He wagged his brows. "You can reward me later," he whispered.

Beth swatted him. "Behave, Bo, or—"

"If the two of you are going to act like a pair of lovesick fools, I'm kicking you out." Henry opened his eyes.

Standing, Beth Ann walked over to her grandfather. She leaned down and kissed his cheek. "What can I do for you, Grandfather?"

He lifted his good arm and patted her hand. "Just being here is enough, child."

Bo joined her, then grimaced when the skunk lifted her head, yawned, and stretched out her front paws. He stepped back. "Careful, Henry. That skunk's still on you."

Henry lifted a bushy brow. "Nice to see you haven't lost your eyesight, boy." He grimaced. "I *know* there's a damn skunk on me. Can't for the life of me figure out why."

Chuckling, Beth Ann reached out and stroked the small creature. "She's sweet."

"Cupcake, she's a skunk."

She rolled her eyes and returned her attention to her grandfather. "I could read to you after lunch. Bo and I are supposed to work on decorations until then."

Henry looked pleased. "I'd like that. Now, how about you two finding that damn trapper and telling him to come get his little pet."

"Have to wait for Sofia to return. Promised her I'd stay."

"Not helpless, child."

Beth Ann widened her eyes. "I believe you, but when Sofia tells you to do something, you do it. No one disobeys her or Rook."

Bo wrapped his arms around her. "You got a point there." He recounted how he and Henry had witnessed Jocelyn's bathing disaster.

Her grandfather laughed and added to the story.

Beth Ann leaned into Bo and listened as the two men talked. The pain etched around her grandfather's mouth lessened. How could she have ever thought this man to be a monster?

Smiling, she knew what she had to do. She waited for a lull in the conversation. "Grandfather, I have something I want to tell—"

The door flew open. "Lands sake, thought the old man was gonna talk my ears off." Sofia burst into the cabin in a flurry, her arms loaded with clean laundry. "Ah, he's awake." She pointed to Beth Ann. "You two best get yourselves over to the school. Rook's hounding your cousins and asking where the pair of you are."

Groaning, disappointed that she couldn't tell both Bo and her grandfather her decision, Beth Ann kissed her grandfather's cheek. "I'll be back." No one kept Rook waiting.

Bo held the door open for her. "I'll go find the owner of that creature, then come join you."

Beth Ann slipped outside. After lunch, she'd tell both men she was returning with them. A bit of her happiness dimmed. Telling them also meant telling her parents.

****

Storm clouds darkened the sky and the wind whistled through the trees. But inside the school, a fire burned brightly in the hearth and the chatter of girls and women lent the large room a warm glow.

Beth Ann sat at a table with Renny, Jane and Coralie. They'd spent most of the morning deciding what to do, then assigning tasks to everyone after lunch. Henry had been sleeping when she went to see him, so she decided she'd read to him before dinner. Sofia promised to let her know when he woke.

Giggles from another table drew her attention. The older schoolgirls were making centerpieces using pine boughs and the cones of fruit. Eirica's girls, Alison, Lara, and Summer were popular among the girls from her tribe.

Shrieks of laughter sounded from the corner of the room. Beth Ann elbowed Renny. "Look." She indicated Bo who was on his back with knees bent. Grady was leaning against his legs. Bo grabbed the boy's hands, then drew his knees toward his chin.

Grady, on his belly, laughed. "Me fly!"

Bo lifted his legs up and down then back and forth. Grady shrieked and laughed.

As soon as Bo set him down, Riker was treated to the same ride. One by one, each young child took a turn, until Bo groaned and sat. "Uncle Bo's tired." He grabbed a pile of blocks. Immediately, the toddlers began building.

Bo stood and returned to sit across from Beth Ann.

She grinned at him, happy that he liked not just her children, but all the children. She ducked her head and hoped she'd soon be carrying his child.

"Wish you could have gone with Wolf?" Wolf and Tyler had accompanied Eirika, Jessie, Winona, and Jessie's girls on a mission to find moss, leaves, branches, pinecones, and berries for the decorations and feast.

"And miss this?" He eyed the strips of leather he was trying to braid with a dubious eye.

Giggling, Beth Ann took it from him, undid it, then braided it so it lay flat.

Margaret came over. "Can I help?"

Everyone smiled.

"Of course." Beth Ann pointed to a spot beside her sister and let Jane explain what they were doing. Margaret grabbed a needle and thread and set to work.

Beth Ann let the warm laughter and chatter surround and fill her. She glanced at each person with love. Especially Jane. Of everyone here, she'd miss her sister the most when she left. Across from her, Margaret was patiently showing Bo how to string berries.

Beth Ann grinned. Yes, she'd miss her family, all of them, but as long as she had Bo and her children, she'd never be lost, lonely, or without family.

For the first time since her grandfather's arrival, she admitted that her uncle was a wise man. Striking Thunder had been right when he'd said she was afraid, that she'd needed security because of her past. That had been the reason she'd never wanted to attend school. She'd been afraid that over the winter, something would happen to her parents. Now she realized that, whether she was with them or not, she couldn't control what happened and that kind of worry took away from the pleasure of the moment.

With her new revelation in mind, she vowed to enjoy each and every day with her family. With every single man, woman and child.

"Sh—Ouch!"

Beth Ann hid her grin when Bo blushed. "Sorry, ladies." He glared at his finger and the drop of blood where he'd stuck himself with the needle.

"Maybe Rook needs help," she suggested.

"Not letting you out of my sight."

A loud wail came from the corner. All the adults turned. Bo hurried over to stop Kimi from clobbering Riker with a block. Bo scooped them up, one under each arm.

Beth Ann sighed and set her strand of berries down. "That's it for me." She took her daughter from Bo, and together, they headed for her tipi.

She and Bo settled the babies, then left the tipi. Beth Ann closed the flap to keep the cold wind out, then they joined her mother in front of Emma's tipi. The women were slicing hunks of elk for the evening meal. Across the yard, racks held strips of drying meat.

Bo took up a knife. "Now this is something I can handle."

Beth Ann enjoyed the lazy afternoon of chores and chatter. She and Bo stayed close to her tipi so she could hear the twins when they woke. When Sofia headed their way, she glanced at Bo. "I need to go read to my grandfather."

Bo nodded. "I'll stay and listen for the twins."

She fell in step with Sofia. "How is he?"

"Slept pretty good. Happy that Stinky came and got the sku—"

A piercing scream had Beth Ann and Sofia

whirling around. Emma and Dove ran to where a group of older girls combed and braided the hair of the young children, a favorite pastime. Beth Ann ran, nearly crashing into Mattie who'd flown out Jessie's cabin.

"Annie!"

Reaching out, Beth Ann caught Mattie by the arm. "I'll take you to her." Her heart jumped to her throat. The screams from the little girl sent chills up her spine. Was Annie having another vision?

Mattie gasped. Her eyes rolled back in her head, and she went limp.

"Oh, no." Beth Ann struggled to keep her cousin from falling. Breathing hard, she lowered Mattie to the ground then knelt beside her. "Mattie!"

She glanced around for help. She'd been so hopeful the visions were gone. She'd made her choice, and both Bo and her grandfather were okay.

Bo and Reed hurried over. Reed cradled his wife in his arms, speaking softly and calmly.

Was Bo or her grandfather still in danger? She watched Mattie anxiously. Somehow, she'd protect the man who'd claimed her heart and given her his.

Jessie joined them, holding Annie who continued to scream, her small body rigid.

Mattie moaned. "Beth Ann?" Her hands lifted as though searching.

Beth Ann bent down and took one of Mattie's hands in her own. Her cousin's eyes were still unfocused. "What is it? Is it Bo?"

"I hear crying. Screaming. It's so dark and cold. They are so scared." Her eyes bore into Beth Ann's. "Find them."

Chilled to the bone, Beth Ann leaned forward.

"Who, Mattie?"

"Babies. Your babies. Trapped. Danger." She closed her eyes and slumped against Reed.

Reed scooped her up and sent Beth Ann and Bo a worried look. "I'm taking her back inside. If she says anything more, I'll find you."

Beth Ann stood. "My babies." A cold shiver skated down her spine. She ran to her tipi, flipped the flap open, and stared at her pallet where she'd left the twins sleeping on top of the quilt Renny had given her. Her heart slammed into her throat. It was gone along with her babies. Denial numbed her mind. She blinked rapidly and told herself to move but her legs wouldn't obey and her mind went blank.

Bo caught her as she whirled around. "Beth?"

Her heart pounded, and she swallowed past the lump in her throat. "They're gone." Her voice came out a harsh rasp. "My babies are gone." This time her voice rose to a shriek.

He peered into the tipi, then whipped around to search the yard. All the children were sitting quiet and scared. "Maybe they woke up and left the tipi."

Beth Ann shook her head. "I'd know. Kimi always needs a cuddle when she wakes. She'd have come found me. And we were right here." Her breathing grew ragged. Each breath became a struggle, as though someone was holding her head beneath the water. She reached up and fisted her hands in his shirt. "Bo, he has them." Her voice rose to a hysterical pitch.

"How?" He entered the tipi, keeping his arm around Beth. A strong gust of wind hit the backside of the tipi. A long slice had been cut in the back wall.

"Damn." He crossed the space and pulled the slit

open to the forest beyond. The man had slipped in, wrapped the twins in the quilt, and lit out of there.

Beth Ann fell to her knees. Her world darkened and narrowed to the pain slicing through her. She covered her mouth with her fingers to still her trembling. "He has them. Bo, he has my babies."

Striking Thunder ran inside. "What's wrong?"

"That bastard kidnapped the twins." Bo pointed to the slit.

"Where were they sleeping?"

Beth pointed to the pallet. "There."

Striking Thunder knelt and felt the pallet. "Cold. He's been gone a while." He strode out and let loose a shrill whistle that brought warriors on the run. Speaking Lakota, he ordered them to spread out and find the trail.

Wolf, who'd joined them, shouted out orders for horses to be saddled. "Reed, you and Tyler stay here, protect the women and children. You, too, Rook."

Dove returned from her tipi with her weapons. "I'm going."

Wolf and Striking Thunder nodded. She was as good as, if not a better than, any of the warriors in her tracking and shooting skills.

"What's going on?" Henry, white-faced and cradling his arm, joined them.

Beth Ann, with tears streaming down her face, stumbled to her grandfather and gripped his good arm. "Standing Horse took my babies."

Bo met Henry's furious gaze. "I'll find them, Bethy. I'll bring them back to you."

A shout from behind the tipi drew everyone to the wall of the forest where two warriors were dragging an injured man. Bo pulled Beth to him when he saw the shaft of an arrow in the man's chest.

Rook joined them. "Still alive. Missed the heart. Move it, fools. Get him to my cabin." He glanced at Wolf. "Gonna need them to help get that arrow out."

"Ya need a couple trappers! We'll find tha' trail." Old Stinky pulled his skunk from his jacket and handed her to Henry. "Take care o' her, old man." He and his brother headed into the forest.

Henry sputtered, but the skunk simply climbed onto his shoulder and watched the humans racing around.

Good god, was all Bo could think. Drama and mayhem, and then a tiny spark of comedy that broke the paralyzing fear and spurred everyone into action. Women gathered children into the schoolhouse, Jessie's cabin, and the large tipi, while men calmly saddled horses and mounted up.

Bo started to pull his arm from around Beth Ann so he could go saddle Samson, but she grabbed him. "No! You can't go." Tears tracked down her face, and her lips trembled. She shook in his arms. "I can't lose you, Bo. He hates you, and this might be a trap to get you."

Bo wanted to be the one to find the bastard. He'd never killed a man, but he'd put a bullet in Standing Horse's black heart and feel not a morsel of regret. "I love you, Beth, and I love your children. I'll get them back for you." And he would. Whatever it took.

"No," that's what he wants. He'll kill you, Bo. He could hide in the woods and shoot you with an arrow, and you'd be dead. I can't lose you and my babies."

One look at the devastation in Beth Ann's eyes and the pain and stark fear in his godfather's, he knew he had to stay with them. He couldn't leave either of them alone with their fear. He held Beth Ann close and stood beside Henry. "I'll stay."

Wolf rode into the yard. He held the reins of two horses. When the trappers came out of the forest carrying a quilt, Bo and Beth ran to meet them.

"Bastard didn't even try to hide his trail. Heading north."

Beth Ann hugged herself. "If he's taking my babies back to his people, he should be riding west."

Wolf handed each trapper the reins to a horse. "Saddle up you two. My guess he's heading toward that outcropping of rock just north of here. Knows he can't outrun us with two babies. Even with a head start, we'd catch up."

Bo drew his brows together. "Why would he stay in the area?"

Beth Ann looked at Bo. "It's a long hike to get there, but we used to go and spend the day there. The rocks form a cave. He could hide there, kill anyone who approaches."

Bo was even more certain that the warrior did not intend to keep the babies alive. He was afraid Beth was right. It was a trap.

Wolf divided the group and pointed. "You men stay with Stinky and Duckman. Follow the trail. The rest of us will circle around in case Standing Horse changes directions and heads west."

It went against everything Bo believed in to watch the men and Dove ride out. He kept his arm around Beth Ann as much to keep himself anchored as to comfort her. The bleakness in her eyes and her sobs broke his heart. "They'll find them, Bethy. They'll find them." They had to.

306

Chapter Fifteen

Margaret lay in John Red Shirt's arms, staring up at the sky. They were on a blanket, the remains of lunch forgotten. Both were without a stitch of clothing and completely sated.

"I love you, John Red Shirt."

John pulled her on top of him. "As I love you, Margaret Yellow Woman." He pulled her against him so there was no space between them. "You belong to me."

Margaret lifted her head, stared into his warm brown eyes. She ran her fingers though his long, jet-black hair. "And you are mine."

They kissed, sealing their vows of love. Feeling him growing hard, she giggled. "Not again, John."

He bit her ear. "Going to stop me?"

Lifting her head, she smiled. "That wouldn't be nice of me, would it?"

"It would be cruel."

Eager to take him into her, she lifted her hips, then froze.

"No teasing, Margaret." John tried to pull her back down.

"Wait," she hissed, cocking her head. "I hear something."

About to make a pleading comment, he went still. She was serious.

He sat, and together, they listened. "Sounds like a baby crying."

Standing, John pulled on his clothing and helped Margaret with hers. "Wait here."

"Oh, no," Margaret said. "I'm done being ordered about. I'm not staying here alone."

"Then be very quiet." He took the lead.

Margaret followed, moving silently as John had taught her—keeping light of foot and placing her feet where he stepped. The crying grew louder. It sounded as though there were more than one baby crying.

Who was out here? Had one of the families come out for a picnic, like her and John? Was it a settler family? Her blood froze. What if it was another tribe of Indians? An enemy. Her heart raced as she remembered all the horror stories of white women being taken captive.

She didn't want to be captured. Now she wished she'd stayed behind.

When John held out a hand, she stopped and got low, imitating his every move. Peering under his arm, she saw an outcropping of rock. She recognized it. John had brought her out here for a day of being silly and climbing.

She grinned. First time she'd ever climbed rocks. And after. She touched her lips. He'd kissed her. Her first kiss. John had said the children weren't allowed out there any longer because many of the boulders had tumbled, closing off what had been a natural cave of sorts.

Slowly, inch by inch, they crept closer, circling around as most of the rock was in an area that was bare of trees. Once again, John stopped.

He swore, so soft Margaret barely heard him. Again, she peered past him, then had to cover her mouth to stop her own gasp of horror.

Standing Horse had Beth's babies. She could see them behind the warrior who was sharpening his knife. He also had a bow, a quiver of arrows, and a rifle.

A line of boulders kept the toddlers penned. She frowned as her gaze traveled up a rope that hung just over their heads. She followed it up, saw that it was wrapped around a huge boulder.

"Oh, God," she breathed. The rock was precariously balanced. She and John had climbed on the other side. He'd told her that side was not safe. Now she knew why. Several rocks looked as though a strong wind might bring them down.

To her horror, the wind whipped through, sending the rope flailing like a dancing snake.

John motioned her flat. "Stay here. Don't move." Again, his voice was a bare whisper.

"I've got to go get help, and I can go faster without you."

Scared senseless, Margaret nodded. She'd slow him or alert the warrior to their presence.

John faded away, silent as a shadow. Margaret rested her head on her hands, afraid to breath or even shift to avoid the rock digging into her ribs.

The sound of loud chattering above her head nearly tore a scream from her throat. A squirrel had climbed down the trunk and was staring at her. And chastising her for being too close to her tree.

Go away, Margaret yelled in her mind. She breathed a sigh of relief when the animal scampered back into the tree. With her heart pounding, she glanced through the brush and frowned. She saw the babies but not that warrior. His bow was still there but not the rifle.

Oh, no. Had he heard or seen John. Had he gone after him? She wasn't sure what to do. She wanted to run out and grab the babies, but she'd never get back on her own, especially if he was inside what remained of the cave.

A loud crack from behind stopped her heart.

****

"Bo, what are we going to do?" Beth Ann paced from one end of Jessie's cabin to the other. He stood by the open window.

"They'll find the twins, Beth." He fisted a hand, longing for something to hit to rid himself of the frustration of being unable to do anything constructive. He hated feeling helpless.

Matt and Henry sat near the fireplace. Sofia and Rook were trying to save the warrior's life in their cabin. The skunk had once again curled up to sleep on the blanket across Henry's lap.

The man looked miserable. In pain physically and worried sick about his great-grandchildren.

On the other side of the fireplace, Mattie nursed her newborn son. Reed and Tyler were patrolling outside in case Standing Horse returned for Beth.

"I'm so sorry." Mattie looked exhausted and miserable.

Beth Ann went to her. "It's not your fault." She turned and met Bo's gaze.

"I know, but—"

Bo joined the two women. He reached down and squeezed Mattie's shoulder. "If you and Annie hadn't alerted us, it would have been near dark before Beth realized the twins were gone. We have a chance to get them back."

Mattie sighed. "Beth Ann, you know how much I hate this."

Beth Ann gave her hand another squeeze. "I know. I can't imagine having the gift of sight, but as Bo said, we are grateful."

Bo loved Beth more in that moment as she included him in her comforting words to the blind woman. But that didn't help not knowing what was happening. He wished he'd insisted on going, yet when Beth leaned her head against him, he accepted that his place was with her, not tracking down the warrior who wanted to take everyone Beth loved from her.

Annie, not used to sharing her mother tried to climb onto her mother's lap. Her lower lip trembled when she found her baby brother cradled in her mother's arms. The little girl, just a few months older than the twins, had been quiet and subdued all afternoon.

Noticing the baby had fallen asleep, Bo stroked the soft head of black hair. "I'll take him, Mattie."

Mattie handed over the infant and pulled Annie into her arms. "Come on, Bo. Let's change him." Beth took the infant and with Bo watching, she made quick work of changing the wet diaper. Standing, she stared down at the content baby. "Where are they, Bo? Are they scared? Hurt?"

Bo drew her against him. "We'll get them back, Bethy. We'll get them back." In that moment, he knew he had to go. He couldn't sit here a moment longer. Before he could tell her, the door burst open.

John stuck his head in and called out, "Jessie, where's Wolf?"

Jessie came out of the kitchen. "With the search party out looking for the twins." She took a good look at John, then hurried to the door. "What's wrong? Why aren't you with the others?"

"Standing Horse has the babies."

"We know." Jessie frowned. "Why aren't you out with the others searching?"

"I wasn't here. Took Margaret out for a walk. Sofia packed us a lunch."

Bo scooped the baby up into his arms and hurried to the door with Beth at his side. "Where are they, John? You've seen them." It wasn't a question.

"Up at Stone Castle." He drew in a deep breath. "That's what Margaret called it the first time I took her there. We were in the area, heard crying and went to see where it was coming from and saw them with Standing Horse."

"Are they all right?" Beth Ann's voice quivered.

Bo put his arm around her. His heart pounded so loud in his ears he could barely hear.

John looked sick. "They were fine when I left but that bastard—sorry."

"You speak the truth. Go on," Jessie ordered.

"The bastard rigged one of the unstable stones to fall on them if anyone gets too close."

"We have to go to them," Beth cried.

Jessie glanced outside. "Where's Margaret?"

"She's still up there."

"You left her up there?" Jessie's voice rose in horror.

"I had to get here fast. And quietly. She's out of

sight."

"Go find Reed and Tyler," Jessie said.

Bo shook his head, planning his next steps. "No. They need to stay here. I'll go back with John." Bo turned to John. "I need you to take *me* there. When we get there, you find and stay with Margaret."

"I'm a good fighter," John said. "A good shot. I didn't have my rifle with me though."

"Get it." Bo strode through the room and handed the infant back to Mattie. "I've got to get mine." Everything inside him screamed for him to hurry. He couldn't bear for anything to happen to either twin, and not just because of the pain to Beth. In that moment, he knew he'd sacrifice his own life to save her children.

"I'll get it, Bo." Beth Ann ran outside.

Jessie had stepped outside and let loose with a shrill whistle. Tyler and Reed came running.

Bo explained what was going on. He decided to take Tyler with him and convinced Reed to stay in case the others returned. No one mentioned that Mattie needed him close.

He checked his weapons—his revolver, the long blade hanging from his belt, and another short knife stuck in his boot. He wasn't surprised when Jessie joined him, weapon in hands.

Beth joined him, holding out his rifle. Taking it, he frowned when he noticed that she had her bow and a quiver of arrows slung across her back.

"You are not going," he said firmly.

"Bo, you want to be part of this family, you best learn that the women do not stay home when their family is threatened. Let's go. I want my babies home before dark."

All signs of tears were gone. The blues of her eyes were cold and determined.

****

Beth Ann glanced at the sun, noted that it was beginning its descent in the sky when she and Bo, along with John, Tyler, and Jessie surveyed the scene before them. Not only had Standing Horse captured Margaret, he'd wrapped the rope dangling from the boulder around her neck.

Margaret sat in frozen silence. If she struggled or tried to run, she risked loosening the unstable rock.

Bo studied a second length of rope wrapped around her arms. Standing Horse held the other end around his hand, leaving little slack. "Can't risk shooting the bastard. If he goes down, he might pull Margaret over."

The twins were asleep at Margaret's feet.

Beth Ann looked at Bo. "What do we do?"

Without warning, Standing Horse came alert. He lifted his rifle and sent a shot into the air. "I want Beth Ann. Send her to me."

The twins woke screaming.

"What the hell? He can't know we're here." Bo's voice was low and harsh.

Jessie tipped her head. "It's too quiet. He's been here hours. Probably rode back the night he was banished. He'd know the rhythm of this place."

Beth Ann covered her mouth with her hand to muffle her cry of alarm. "I have to go." She started forward.

Bo snagged her arm. "No. I'll go. This is a fight between us. He wants you but hates me. I'll use it against him."

"Bo, no. He'll kill you." Tears streaked down her

314

face.

Jessie put her hand on Beth's arm. "If he can buy me time, I can sneak around, cut Margaret loose, and get Riker and Kimi out of there."

"How are you going to get him to fight you?" Tyler asked. "He may just unload that rifle in your chest."

"No. He wants a fight. I'll give it to him. Winner gets Beth Ann."

She sucked in her breath. Everyone stared at Bo as though he'd lost his mind.

Frowning, Bo shook his head. "Not for real. But he won't know that. Soon as the twins and Margaret are safe, he's a dead man." Fury deepened his voice to a primitive growl.

"He's a seasoned fighter, Bo. He'll kill you."

He held her face between his hands. "I'm not looking to be a hero, Cupcake, but I can keep him busy." He kissed her.

Tyler narrowed his eyes. "I'm going with Jessie. There's three needing rescuing down there. If he takes that rope off to fight you, I'll have a clear shot." He eyed Bo. "I get it, I'll take it."

Bo nodded. "Said I wasn't looking to be a hero." He turned back to Beth. "Stay here with John."

John shook his head. "He knows someone was with Margaret and that you'd never have found this place by yourself. I'll go with you." He set his rifle down and removed his hunting knife.

Drawing herself up, Beth Ann pulled an arrow from her quiver. "I'll find a good position with a clear shot. I won't let him kill you, Bo. Honor be damned. It's my fight as well."

Bo sucked in a breath and nodded. As soon as he

and John got to the edge of the forest, he stepped out. He'd left his rifle behind and his revolver.

Standing Horse raised his rifle. "Where's the woman. Bring her here, and you can have her children."

John took a step forward. "Beth Ann is not here. She is a woman. This is between you and Bo. That is the way of our people," John said in Lakota. Though dressed in the white man's clothing, there was no doubt he was a formidable warrior.

"She's mine. She was mine as soon as my brother died. That is the way of our people."

"You must earn the right." John folded his arms across his chest.

Bo stepped forward. "You coward. Fight for her." He stripped off his vest and shirt and shook his shoulders and arm muscles loose.

Standing Horse growled with fury. "You think you can fight me and win?" He stared into the forest. "I am not a fool, white man. I take off this rope, I'm dead. You have no honor." He pointed his rifle into the forest. "Where are the others?"

"The others are tracking you. Half following your trail, the others cutting off your escape. I stayed behind to protect Beth."

"Where's the old man." Standing Horse kept the rifle trained on Bo.

Bo let his hands dangle at his side. "Patching up the warrior you shot. He probably won't survive. We going to talk until it gets too dark to fight? I should warn you, the others will be here before dark."

Standing Horse hesitated, his gaze scanning the forest.

"Should've run for it, you bastard. When they get

here, you're a dead man."

"I want the woman, not her children. We fight for the right to claim her. This is the honorable way of our people." He glanced at John, made a loop with the rope, and slipped it over his head and shoulders, tightening it around his waist. He left enough slack for him to fight but not so much that he couldn't yank the slack out and kill his hostages if needed.

Standing Horse pointed a finger at John, then gave the rope a good yank. Margaret yelped. "You move, they die." He laughed a bit madly. "Either way I win. If I don't get the woman, she loses her children and her lover."

Bo flexed his fingers, then wrapped them around the hilt of his knife and moved closer. "There is only one person who dies today."

He crouched, shifted his weight to the balls of his feet and watched. His father's old foreman had taught him to fight. And the first thing Bo learned was to always watch the eyes. The eyes always gave away a man's intent.

He studied the rope and knew he'd have to be careful. If Standing Horse went down, Margaret and the twins were at risk.

Moving closer to Standing Horse, Bo circled. The warrior didn't have much room. They moved in a half circle, to the right, to the left, with Standing Horse keeping the forest and his captives in sight.

Bo caught the slight bunching of Standing Horse's thighs and the shifting of his eyes to Bo's left. Bo evaded the man's thrust and followed with a jab of his own. He felt a moment of pleasure when he saw a line of blood on the man's arm.

Furious, Standing Horse lunged, thrusting the knife toward Bo's gut in an upward slash meant to disembowel. Bo sucked in his stomach and danced on his toes, moving quickly out of harm's way even though he wanted nothing more than to beat the crap out of his enemy.

Unless he could kill him and keep him from tugging that rope, Bo had to keep him busy and allow Jessie and Tyler time to get to the hostages. So he played with the warrior, gave him openings, evaded, and sent out his own jabs, always careful not to cause the man to go down.

"Too bad you're tethered, you bastard. Not much of a fight. A bit of a cheat, really. Afraid to fight without restrictions?" He eyed the rope. When the time came, he'd slash the man's chest clean through and cut that damn rope off.

Laughing, Standing Horse shifted the knife from hand to hand. "Kill me, kill them. Or you can admit defeat and send the woman to me." He struck, his knife a blur.

Pain across his chest told Bo the man had scored. Sweat dripped into his eyes as he circled, lunged, and jumped out of the man's reach. He crouched and charged, then whirled away, trying to make himself a target to get the other man to shift his position.

Standing Horse made another short-stepped charge as Bo thrust his knife toward the man's chest. He felt the sting to his forearm. Though it hurt, Bo refused to back down. The sight of blood sent Standing Horse into a wild frenzy of slashing, thrusting, and charging forward. Each miss made him furious but not enough to take the rope off and come at Bo with everything he had.

"That rope will be your defeat," Bo called out. "You can't get to me."

Seeing an opening, he went in low after deflecting the knife and slashed a long cut on the man's thigh.

His breathing grew ragged. Even with the warrior being unable to come at him fully, the man was better than good, and Bo knew it would only take one hesitation on his part to lose this fight.

He wasn't just fighting to save Beth's babies. He was fighting for his life. He gritted his teeth when he felt another cut, this time on his thigh.

He got in more nicks and slices, but Beth was right. Standing Horse had more experience, and he was plain crazy besides. It was time to play to his strengths, not his enemy's, especially with the sun lowering. Time was running out.

Over Standing Horse's shoulder, Bo saw Jessie and Tyler creeping low to the ground. Acting more tired than he felt, he waited for Standing Horse to charge. Bo twisted his body out of the way and used his motion to land a good solid kick with his boot to the man's stomach.

Standing Horse bent over to catch his breath, the line going taut. Then the warrior charged, uncaring that Margaret was crying out as the rope pulled against her.

Bo forced the man back to ease the line. Over and over, they kicked out, slashed, and thrust, with Bo forcing the warrior to turn enough so that the man couldn't see what was happening behind him. He moved to the side, and then back, in a dance he'd seen boxers use to keep the man's attention on him. He planned his next move. The hell with honorable. What kind of man kidnaps babies and puts them in danger. He was not going to let the woman he loved down.

He loved Beth and she loved him. Nothing else mattered. And nothing else was going to come between them.

He needed to cut that damn rope.

He danced forward, taunted the man, trying to get him to come to him one last time.

****

Beth Ann stood poised at the edge of the forest, shielded by branches. She held her bow, arrow nocked, and watched. Everything had gone silent, even the wind rustling in the treetops. The only noise to reach her was the sound of the two men fighting. Even her babies were quiet, as though not wanting to distract Bo.

She closed off her emotions as her mother had taught her and focused completely on the fight. Her arrow tracked Standing Horse, her finger twitching with the need to let the arrow fly.

If she killed her enemy right now, Bo would catch him, keep him from falling and yanking Margaret from her perch.

No, that was emotion speaking. She would wait. And trust that Bo would not be hurt. Or worse. She kept her gaze on the man she loved with all her heart.

It'd been a while since she'd used her bow, but she knew she could still hit any target she chose. Her mother had taught her well, and she was that good.

She nearly gasped when Standing Horse sliced Bo's arm. The sight of Bo's blood reminded her that the warrior had already tried to kill the man she loved.

Watching the blood drip down Bo's elbow and splatter on the ground, she pulled back, her arm steady.

The blood drove Standing Horse into a frenzy of attacks. Fearing that Bo was tiring, she knew it was time to end this.

Higher, child. Remove the threat.

Startled, Beth Ann nearly dropped her bow and arrow. She glanced around but no one was with her.

I came to you long ago. Have you forgotten me? The voice was soft and calm.

She took her eyes off the men and scanned the branches above her head. She spotted the owl.

"You've come to me," she breathed.

I've always been with you. Be ready.

Once again, Beth Ann took aim. She remembered Owl's words. "Remove the threat," she whispered, her eyes going to the precariously perched boulder and the rope wrapped around Margaret's neck. She studied Standing Horse.

He was the threat to all she held dear.

Higher.

Once again, she studied the rope. *Remove the threat.* Movement drew her attention. Jessie and Tyler were almost to her babies and Margaret. Standing Horse stood with his back to them, and Bo was trying to keep the man's attention on him. She couldn't make out the words he flung at Standing Horse but knew he was taunting his enemy.

It was time to end this. She took aim. And let her arrow fly.

****

Bo heard the whistle of the arrow, saw it fly high above Standing Horse's head, slice through the rope, then arch downward.

Standing Horse whirled around, his hand on the

rope. He gave it a hard yank, but the end of the rope came flying back at him. Tyler had cut the other end from around Margaret. Once Standing Horse saw that the boulder no longer posed a threat and that he no longer had hostages, he screamed and ran full out at Bo with his knife high over his head.

Bo stuck out a foot and tripped the warrior who rolled and got back up.

John hurried to Margaret, as Reed, with his rifle pointed, took aim at Standing Horse.

"He's mine," Bo shouted, dodging his enemy. Now that there was no rope to hamper the movements of either man, Bo was eager to finish the fight. On his terms. "You will pay for what you did to Beth and her children. You are a coward."

"She's mine. She was mine before my brother stole her from me. You won't take her."

Bo crouched and circled. "She will never belong to you. If you kill me, she'll kill you. Maybe I should let her have you." Pride washed through him when he spotted Beth, standing with her bow drawn.

The warrior narrowed his eyes. "We fight for her. This is our way. It is honorable. You agreed."

"Kidnapping babies is not honorable," Bo said as he rushed the man. He took another shallow slash to his chest, but he now stood between the woman he loved and the man he was going to kill.

"Cupcake, he's mine," he said to Beth Ann.

"Then end it," she said softly. "I said I wanted my babies home before dark."

Despite his shortness of breath, the pain from multiple cuts, Bo grinned. "That's my Bethy," he told Standing Horse. "She's one hell of a woman and too good for the likes of you, you rat-bastard."

He went in low, kicked out one sharp toe and got the man in his dishonorable balls, then twisted safely out of the way as Standing Horse doubled over and fell, driving his own blade into his gut.

Chapter Sixteen

Beth Ann let out the breath she'd been holding and dropped her bow and the quiver of arrows.

"Bo!" She ran to him. Watching him fight Standing Horse had been hard enough, seeing all the cuts and blood and knowing he was fighting for her and for her children had nearly broken her heart.

She reached him. He was still bent over at the waist, breathing hard. "Are you all right. Let me see, Bo."

He slowly straightened, sheathed his knife, and pulled her against him. "It's over, Bethy," he said, his voice low. He tipped her chin and kissed her.

"I never want to see you fight again," she cried, her arms wrapped around his neck. Each time Standing Horse's knife made contact had been a slice to her own heart.

"Go to your babies, Bethy, and let's get out of here."

Shaking her head, Beth Ann slid her arm through his. "Our babies. We go together."

Bo nodded, but before they could move, Jessie and Tyler were there with the twins.

Beth Ann held out her arms for her children. The twins wrapped their arms around her neck, sobbing and hiccupping from crying. "*Ina's* here. Everything is all right," she soothed, both in English and Lakota, her tears mingling with theirs.

Bo wrapped them in his arms. Beth Ann leaned into Bo, unable to hug him with her arms so full.

"Hell, Bo, remind me never to piss you off." Tyler stared at Standing Horse who wasn't moving. He bent down to see if the man was still alive.

"Dead," he announced, standing. Tyler nudged the warrior over with his boot. He was staring up at the sky, his eyes blank.

"I'm glad you killed him, Bo." Beth Ann's voice shook with emotion.

Bo pulled her away from the ugliness of death. "A bit underhanded and not so honorable."

"He was not honorable." Beth Ann sniffed her disgust.

Shaking his head, Bo marveled over how brave his woman was. "No. He wasn't." He pulled her closer. "It's over, Cupcake." He eyed the sky, noting that the sun was setting.

"Thank you, Bo," she said. "You risked your life to save Riker and Kimi."

Bo glanced up and stared at the rope dangling from the boulder. "You're one hell of a shot, Bethy."

She shrugged. "Lucky. Good thing there wasn't any wind." She smiled. When they'd arrived, the wind had been blowing. Later, in private, she'd make an offering to Owl and the spirit of Owl Woman for her role in helping her make that shot. Had it been windy, she'd never have been able to do it.

A shout drew their attention. Warriors, along with Striking Thunder and Wolf were pouring out of the forest.

"Think the Calvary has arrived," Bo whispered.

"Good," Beth Ann said. "I want my children and my husband-to-be home. Before dark."

Bo bent and kissed her. "Whatever you say, Cupcake."

****

In Rook's cabin, Bo submitted to the man's ministrations. Several of his gashes were deep and required a stitch or two. He bore the pain as manly as he could. The shots of whiskey Rook gave him helped, as did the fact that Beth Ann refused to leave his side.

The fire burned bright and warm, and several lanterns were on the table, providing light. The air held the scent of food. With everyone back after dark, food was being served outside.

Watching the older man pull the edges of the worst gash together, he noticed the man looked tired. Worn. The warrior he and Sofia had tried to save had died.

"I'm sorry to add to your burden."

Rook's bushy brows shot up. "Boy, you saved that gal and her babies. You are not a burden." He grinned. "You're a hero to every woman here."

While Rook stitched, Beth Ann gently washed the shallow cuts and applied some sort of salve, then a dressing. Outside, the celebration was in full swing.

"There, that should take care of it," Rook said.

Stiff and sore, Bo stood, swayed a little, partly from the whiskey Rook insisted he down, mostly from exhaustion and pain. Beth Ann handed him his shirt, helped him button it up, and handed him his coat.

"I'm taking you back to my tipi," she said, leading him outside.

Cheers went up. The air was filled with the woodsy scent of burning fires and cooked meat. Sofia marched over to them. "Come eat, you two. I fixed your plates."

"Okay, then he needs to rest," Beth Ann said primly.

They slid onto the bench of the nearest table, and Sofia slipped two plates in front of them. She pointed to Bo. "You eat. Need to replace the blood you lost and regain your strength." She smiled proudly.

"Yes, ma'am," Bo said, realizing he was starved.

Dove and Jeremy joined them, each holding a child. "I don't think they'll wait until you're done, Beth Ann."

Kimi was struggling to reach her mother. "I can hold her," she said, pulling her daughter onto her lap. Riker Takota flailed his arms, also wanting his mother.

Bo held out his good arm. "Let me." He didn't expect that the child would accept him, but to his delight, the boy settled on his lap and began picking bits of food off his plate as though he belonged there. The boy surprised him some more by offering him a bite of bread.

Jeremy grinned. "Welcome to the family, Bo."

Those within hearing echoed the sentiment. Striking Thunder got up and came over. He leaned against the table. "Did you really bring him down with a well-placed kick?"

Bo groaned but nodded. "I fought dirty, not honorable—"

Striking Thunder slapped him on the back. "I'm glad." He whistled as he walked away.

"Tell us about the fight, Bo." George sat next to his hero. Bo grinned at the boy who was wearing his damaged hat. The boy refused to go anywhere without it.

Beth Ann let the conversation surround her. She was so happy and so lucky that everything had turned out for her. Across from her, her grandfather yawned.

Beside him, her parents were listening to Bo. He was telling them of her part.

Her mother reached across. "Taught her myself. My little warrior," she said with a smile.

Beth Ann smiled. She'd tell her parents about the spirit of the Owl Woman. And one day, perhaps she'd tell Bo and her grandfather the story of how Owl Woman had come to her when she'd been held captive.

But tonight, she just wanted to enjoy her family. And there was something else she needed to do. She cleared her throat.

Bo glanced down at her. "What's the matter, Bethy?"

"Nothing." She smiled. "Everything is wonderful." She took his hand in hers and glanced at her parents and grandfather.

"I have something I need to say." She felt both sadness and excitement. "Mattie said I had choices to make. She was right. And wrong. There is only one choice." She reached across to take her mother's hand. Dove had tears in her eyes as though she knew what Beth was going to say.

Beth Ann let go of her mother's hand and reached out for her grandfather's hand. "Grandfather, I am returning home with you and Bo."

Henry shook his head. "Your place is here, child. As much as I want you near me, I can't take you away from your family."

Tears rolling down her face, Beth Ann leaned close to Bo. "My place is with Bo. He is my husband or will be as soon as our chief marries us. And you are also my family."

"Beth." Bo's voice was soft and emotion-filled. He turned her. "Are you sure? Really sure?" His fingers gently wiped away her tears.

"I'm sure, Bo." She stood. "I'm taking my family home."

After several rounds of hugs, kisses, and well wishes, Beth got her family into her tipi. She handed Kimi to Bo then set about making a small pallet close to the one she shared with Bo. She glanced at the back wall, and saw that it had been mended.

Together, she and Bo lay with the twins, rubbing backs. Beth Ann hummed softly until the babies were asleep.

"Will they sleep here on their own?" Bo got up, went to the pit, and started a small fire to chase the chill out of the air.

Standing, Beth Ann went to Bo. "It's time for them to learn to sleep on their own." She wrinkled her nose. "They may crawl into our bed during the night."

"We'll deal with it," he said. "I don't mind."

She just smiled and led him to her bed. "Sit."

Gently, she removed his shirt, then knelt in front of him to remove his boots. On her knees, she checked each bandaged wound, her fingers trailing over his chest. She stood and held out her hand.

He took it, but when she went for his belt buckle, he closed his hand over hers. "Not sure I'm up to doing that, Cupcake."

"You are going to sleep." She removed his pants. Standing, she pulled her dress overhead and slipped into bed beside him, keeping a bit of distance between them. He needed to sleep.

"You're awfully far away, Bethy."

"I don't want to hurt you."

He reached out with his least injured arm and pulled her close. "Worth it," he murmured, kissing her gently then tucking her head beneath his chin.

Beth Ann sighed. "I was so afraid for you today."

"Not something I'd like to repeat, but I'll do whatever it takes to keep you and your babies safe. And happy."

Reaching up, she brushed her fingers along his jaw and smiled. "Our babies. Our family."

She felt him smile. "Yeah, my family." He rubbed the top of her head.

"I can't let you go, Bethy. I thought I could, but I was wrong. I'm glad you're coming back with us. But you should know that I wouldn't have left you. Whatever it takes, we belong together. You are mine, Cupcake, for better or worse."

"And you, Boo, are mine. But I meant it when I said I was going home with you."

"No regrets?"

"None."

"Bethy." Her name was a soft, happy sigh. Bo couldn't say more. He wanted her more than anything. She was his family, she and her children.

"What about your family?" He'd seen the tears in her mother's eyes and sadness in her father's.

"I'll miss them. But I can't live without you." Bo felt an overwhelming rush of love. He bent his head and kissed her, long and hard.

"Bo, you need rest," she said when his body made it clear he wanted more than kisses.

"You're better medicine than sleep. You made me the happiest man tonight." He skimmed his palms down over her breasts and splayed his hand over her belly, then threaded his fingers though her nest of pale curls.

Moaning, she tried to pull back. "But your arms and chest. You can't."

Chuckling, he agreed. "No, I'm not in the best of shape. But there's nothing wrong with you."

He eased to his back and held out one arm. "I'll lie here and take my medicine like a good boy."

Beth lifted herself up and let Bo guide her over him. She giggled. "You, Boo, are incorrigible."

He moaned as she slowly took him inside her. "And you, Cupcake, are irresistible."

Outside, fires died down and darkness crept over the land. The soft hoot of an owl called out into the night. A soft breath of air fluttered the owl's feathers. Together, Owl and Wind soared through the forest.

Epilogue

Beth Ann stood inside her nearly empty tipi. All that remained were some fur blankets. Everything else was loaded on horses. It felt strange knowing she was leaving behind the life she'd lived for so long to return to the one she'd been born into.

"Ready, Mrs. Quinn?" Bo stepped inside.

She nodded. "Yes." She smiled, admiring how his buckskin shirt molded his wide shoulders and narrow waist. He held out his arms, the fringe swaying gently. On his head, he wore a new hat. It wasn't the same as the one ruined by Standing Horse, but it had been the best she could get. Wolf had gone with the trappers and Jocelyn to the fort. She'd asked him to try to find Bo a new hat. She'd presented it to him at Christmas.

He held her for a moment, taking in her new dress. "You're going to put every woman within fifty miles of our ranch to shame. You are beautiful, Cupcake."

Beth Ann giggled. "Coralie and Eirica made me some dresses."

He pulled her close. "You're sure, Bethy." He glanced around. "I'll admit I'm going to miss your tipi and your way of life." Two months had turned into nearly four.

Beth Ann nodded. "I'm sure." And she was. She took his hand and stepped outside where Henry waited, along with everyone else. Tears threatened, but she smiled bravely.

Rook and Sofia, along with the trappers came forward. She hugged each of them and gave the skunk a final pet. Bo contented himself to just shaking hands. He owed the men more than he could repay for taking Jocelyn to the fort. He and Henry had also sent letters home, explaining their delay.

When Henry held out his hand to Stinky, a head popped out from beneath his jacket. Mother and baby skunk glanced at each other, then cuddled up with their human pets.

Beth and Bo chuckled.

Bo shook his head. "Don't know what Mildred's going to say, Henry."

"Hell," was all the proud man managed.

They went down the line of family members. They weren't the only ones leaving. The tribe was due to arrive any day to claim their children, and everyone else was heading out to return to their homes as well. When they got to Matt and Margaret, Bo pulled them in for a hug. None of them mentioned Jocelyn.

Dove and Jeremy came forward. Beth Ann couldn't hold back the tears. "I'm going to miss you," she sobbed, hugging each in return, then pulled back. "It won't be for long, but I'll still miss you."

Bo wrapped an arm around her. "We'll be back before you know it, Bethy."

"Just going to be gone long enough to sell the ranches and pack up," Henry added.

Beth glanced around at the cabins. "I can't believe Wolf and Jessie are selling all this."

"And so are my brother's," Jessie said, coming over to join them. She waved at James and Jordan and their families, all on horseback, waiting to ride out.

The family meeting, held right before their holiday celebration, had been short. Once Wolf announced that he and Jessie had decided to sell and were moving away, everyone else decided to join them. Family was too important. They would all meet back here mid-summer. Beth Ann didn't know where they were going, but it didn't matter. Wherever they settled, her family and, hopefully, most of her tribe would be together. As Henry had said, there were enough people here to start their own town.

Wolf and Striking Thunder strode over.

"Ready?" Wolf asked.

Bo nodded. "Waiting for George. Where is he?" He let out a shrill whistle.

From the barn, George, in his blue shirt and black Stetson came running. "Sorry," he yelled. "Took me a while to find her."

Bo went to the boy and took something from his arms. He turned to Beth. "I figure I owe you this for a very late birthday gift. She was a bit too young to present to you at Christmas." He placed a wiggly pup in her arms.

Beth Ann stared at the white pup. "Bo! She's beautiful. You remembered." She buried her nose in the soft, fluffy fur. Staring at the blue- and brown-eyed pup, she grinned. "She's one of Wolf's pups."

Wolf reached over. "She's special. Every once in a while, we get a throwback to the wolf I once owned."

Jessie grinned. "My dog, your wolf. And we still have their bloodline."

George rode up to them. Bo took the puppy and handed it to the boy who had a large leather cradle in front of him. He set the pup inside. "Don't worry, Beth Ann. I'll watch her good for you."

Beth Ann couldn't help but smile. George's uncle had passed away, and the boy had adopted Bo and was returning with them. Bo helped her mount, then handed Kimi to her. Then he mounted Samson, reached down to take Riker Tokota from Jeremy. He glanced at Beth as they rode to join the others. "No regrets?"

Beth shook her head. "None."

Not only was her family staying together, but she was making a new life with them and the man at her side. She wondered when she should tell him he would soon have a child of his own.

Mattie and Reed pulled up beside her. Mattie had baby David in a cradle on her back. She grinned. "Good choice, cousin. Now you need to choose a good, strong name for your son." She nodded to her husband and let him lead her away. They took their place in line with Renny and Tyler and their children.

Bo's head whipped around. "Son?"

Smiling, Beth Ann nodded.

He leaned over and kissed her. "And when were you going to tell me, Cupcake."

With her heart in her eyes, Beth Ann uttered one word. "Boo."

Susan Edwards

List of Heroes/Heroines by Book

White Dawn
Emily & John Cartier

White Dusk
Swift-Foot (White Cloud) & Small Bird

White Shadows
Winona & Clay

White Wind
Sarah & Golden Eagle

White Wolf
White Wolf & Jessie Jones

White Nights
James Jones & Eirica

White Flame
Striking Thunder & Emma O'Brien

White Dreams
Star Dreamer & Grady O'Brien

White Dove
White Dove & Jeremy Jones

White Deception
Mattie O'Brien & Reed Robertson

White Vengeance
Renny O'Brien & Tyler Thompkins Tilly

Books by Susan Edwards:

White Series
White Christmas
White Vengeance
White Deception
White Dove
White Dream
White Flame
White Nights
White Wolf
White Wind
White Shadows
White Dusk
White Dawn

SpiritWalker Series
Summer of the Eagle
Autumn Dreams
Winter's Heart (Coming in 2016)

About the Author

Susan Edwards is the author of fourteen Historical Native American/Western/Paranormal romance. She also writes erotic romance under the pen name Sydney St. Claire.

Susan resides in California. When not writing, she enjoys crafts of all sorts including quilting, sewing, cross-stitch, and knitting. She and her husband of thirty-plus years are avid gardeners. Camping, fishing, biking, and hiking are other outdoor pursuits she and her husband enjoy. She is, of course, an avid reader and hates cooking and housework.

Connect with Susan/Sydney on the web.
https://www.facebook.com/sydneystclaire
https://www.facebook.com/pages/Susan-Edwards/40226247104
https://twitter.com/Sydneystclaire
sydneystclaire@aol.com
or susan@susanedwards.com
http://sydneystclaire.wordpress.com
http://susanedwards.wordpress.com
http://www.goodreads.com/author/show/5051440.Susan_Edwards
http://sydneystclaire.com

To chat with Susan Edwards and other Wild Rose Press authors of erotic romance, join us at www.groups.yahoo.com/group/thewildrosepress